THE *gift* OF story

Marion Halligan is one of Australia's foremost writers and reviewers and the author of four collections of short stories. *The Living Hothouse,* her first collection published by UQP in 1988, won the Steele Rudd Award for the best book of short stories. Her *Collected Stories* was published by UQP in 1997. Marion Halligan has also published three nonfiction books, a picture book for children, and five novels, the latest being *The Golden Dress*, and has won a number of major awards including the *Age* Book of the Year for *Lovers' Knots* and the Geraldine Pascal Prize for critical writing. She was chair of the Literature Board from 1992 to 1995.

Rosanne Fitzgibbon is UQP's fiction editor and has edited many of the collections of short stories published by UQP over the last three decades, beginning with Michael Wilding's *Aspects of the Dying Process* in 1972. She has been responsible for UQP's fiction list since 1989. In 1992 she was awarded the inaugural Beatrice Davis Fellowship and spent three months working with US publishers in New York. She and Marion Halligan are sisters.

UQP

THE *gift* OF story

Three decades of UQP short stories

EDITED BY MARION HALLIGAN & ROSANNE FITZGIBBON

UNIVERSITY OF QUEENSLAND PRESS

First published 1998 by University of Queensland Press
Box 42, St Lucia, Queensland 4067 Australia

Typeset by University of Queensland Press
Printed in Australia by McPherson's Printing Group

Distributed in the USA and Canada by
International Specialized Book Services, Inc.,
5804 N.E. Hassalo Street, Portland, Oregon 97213–3640

This project has been assisted by the Commonwealth Government through the Australia Council, its arts funding and advisory body.

Sponsored by the Queensland Office of Arts and Cultural Development.

Cataloguing in Publication Data
National Library of Australia

The gift of story.

1. Short stories, Australian — 20th century. I. Halligan, Marion, 1940– . Fitzgibbon, Rosanne (Rosanne Eleanor).

A823.0108

ISBN 0 7022 3066 9 (cased)
ISBN 0 7022 3016 2 (paperback)

To Graham Halligan
husband and brother-in-law

CONTENTS

INTRODUCTION

Australians see themselves as having a special affinity with the short story. When you look at anthologies compiled over the last thirty years — with various intentions, theories or pretexts in mind — the one thing they all have in common is an assertion that somehow the short story expresses some quintessence of our national character, that it shoulders the burden of carrying our distinctive ethos.

This may be spelt out: as a kind of sternness belonging to the frontier mentality which gave us our being, plain and no nonsense, or as a laconic but sensitive expression of pain. It may be a small slice of the realism that is our daily fare. Or perhaps the busyness of an always hard life needs the short sharp bite of the story rather than the extended gentle grazing of the novel.

Different generations have found their own desires in the form. They have made various associations of gender and genre. Traditional preoccupations with fringe-dwellers and frontier experiences have been handled both metaphorically and literally. In the seventies Judah Waten and Stephen Murray Smith had few problems identifying what they saw as the classics of the Australian short story. At the same time

Tabloid Story helped to reinvigorate interest in the form by providing new outlets for more experimental works influenced by international trends. *The First UQP Story Book,* edited by Craig Munro in 1981, had only the male writers of the previous decade to draw upon, but by the end of the eighties Gillian Whitlock (in the introduction to her anthology *Eight Voices of the Eighties*, 1989) was describing society's surprised recognition that women had joined others marginalised or dispossessed — migrants and indigenous Australians — who found the short story a particularly suitable vehicle for their writing.

As editors of this anthology we have had no polemical intentions, no canon to identify or thesis to promulgate. No gender divide to arbitrate nor geographical territories to negotiate. We don't need to assert that the short story is alive and well and living in Australia, nor to claim that the three decades covered by this book provide a definitive account of the form. What we are offering here is a celebration, a gift — a gift of story.

The thirty-four stories are selected from more than fifty single-author volumes published by the University of Queensland Press, from Michael Wilding's *Aspects of the Dying Process* in 1972 to Cassandra Pybus's *Till Apples Grow on an Orange Tree* in 1998. As we read the collections it became apparent that Australians have long had a love affair with the short story. In all its forms and modes and styles. In prose that is dazzling or pared-down plain, simple or decorated, vernacular or poetic or didactic, comical or tragical, experimental or conventional but always artful, writers have pursued the story as they would pay court to the beloved.

Of course there are fashions, for little slices of life, for neat anecdotes with twists in the tale, for experiments with form, for making patterns on the page, for mythologising, for debunking and despair. Exploring new territories, different kinds of complexities. These offer the pleasures of variety; there is change and difference, not necessarily development or improvement.

The short story has a lot in common with poetry. It begins before it starts and finishes long after it ends. Much can be left out; its economy needs the readers' imagination. It asks a lot of them, and repays their attention. The short story needs to be lived in for a while. Like a love letter, it should be read several times, returned to, pondered over, savoured, enjoyed.

✧ ✧ ✧

The stories in this collection are arranged in order of publication, which makes for some interesting fellows. Some serendipitous collusions. Some curious collisions. They dance with and against one another. A surprisingly complete range of Australian writing is represented; there are few significant writers who haven't done a collection with UQP. Frank Moorhouse, who is a sad absence from this book, was nearly eligible, but the University of Queensland administration made it clear that the Press's future as a publisher of fiction would be jeopardised if *The Americans, Baby* was published at that time. Moorhouse is almost present in Wilding's story, as the absent Joe who is cruelly used in a betrayal that is literary rather than sexual.

When asked what his stories are about, Joe's girlfriend has no hesitation in replying "Joe, of course", and it is tempting to apply a similar assessment to many of these stories: they are about the person who is writing them. Some don't appear to be, some are mysterious products of a lateral imagination, but the form does seem to invite autobiographical examination, at various stages of remove from the actual life that inspires it. And the stories often involve children, borrowing the freshness and clarity of their perceptions to make sense of what adulthood has discovered. This sense of closeness to life gives immediacy to the form.

This is the place to look for the spin of the nineties. We live in a period which has become obsessed with fact, which has come to the curious conclusion that being told something actually occurred immediately validates it, which is in danger of forgetting that the real magic of fiction is to invent the truths that will illuminate. Instead, people expect a writer to tell them that this really happened, rather than make them believe that it's true.

Reflecting this trend, the most recent pieces are overtly autobiographical, but they still embody the power of story-telling. In the context of this diverse collection they offer just another way in which writers turn their lives into stories. It doesn't make them any more true than fabulous narratives like Peter Carey's "Conversations with Unicorns". When we realise that this story is about the gift of death, and that these animals, "without gods or enemies, will sink into despair", we can see current truths embodied in mythical beasts.

The gift of death... the gift of life... and a celebration of all the stages in between ... that is what story has to offer.

Marion Halligan
Rosanne Fitzgibbon
August 1998

Thea Astley

CUBBY

When he was twelve he fell in love, quite deeply, for the first time. A long time. He loved for eleven years. They were in the same class but sat on opposite sides of the room. Still, they lived on the same side of the beach town near the pine groves, and propinquity completed the ravishment that dark eyes and curls had begun. She was small, neat-boned as we imagine French women to be, and silly. He could see that now, but of course it didn't matter then in the long summer days of apricots and kisses. Both of these divinities they enjoyed in a private meeting-place, a tree-house they had built together in the tallest and certainly one of the thickest of all the pines that fringed the bay.

After it was complete they dragged up a rug and boxes and sat there eyrie-drunk watching the swell of green water that was tree and blue water that was ocean. Their scratched and browned legs dangled thirty feet above the turf as they giggled and shoved and munched, flinging apricot stones into the breakers of branch. In the current of the trades that blew up in spring they could have sworn they were afloat.

One month after he was fourteen they were sitting up there in the heart of summer, foot-paddling in the light of six o'clock, syrupy and golden, that melted over township and sea. The girl rustled in the wooden box they kept their fruit in and her hand closed on the last apricot of their store.

"Only one left," she said. "I'm lucky last!"

The boy was lying on his stomach, drowsy with day, but he opened his eyes and, reaching across with a grin, grabbed her hand.

"Leave go!" he said.

"No! It's mine!"

He struggled into a sitting position and their bodies lurched close with laughter and rage.

"Careful," he warned.

"Oh, Davey! Let go!"

"You'll make us fall. We'll be killed."

"Your fault. Serve you right!"

But he prised her fingers one by one from the bruised fruit as if he were lifting back the sepals of a flower and waved the apricot triumphantly above his head. Suddenly she was angry.

"Oh, you're mean! You're mean! I wanted it. I got it first. It's mine."

"Bargain?" he asked. She hesitated. "Bargain, Sukey?"

In the darkening air a mile away the town lights freckled roads. The purple sea rocked dangerously under violet sky. It was time they went home.

"I'm going," the girl said. She pushed her hair back from her small brown face. "You're mean and I'm going."

He relented at once. "Here, Jenny. You have it" — he paused and said softly — "for a kiss."

They stared at each other. He could hardly believe he'd said it. But it was out now and Jen didn't look cross at all. Pleased, somehow.

"Like yourself, don't you?" she said.

He held out the apricot and she snatched at it but he pulled it away quickly.

"Bargain," he said. They never broke bargains. Jenny leant forward, warm and smiling.

"That's easy. All right" — and her lips paused against his. Their faces moved apart, shy, startled, and neither spoke.

"Here's your ol' apricot," he said then. "Have it." But she stared past him at the sea.

"I don't want it, really."

"It was a bargain. You got to have it."

She shook her head and moving quickly and tremulously as a butterfly swung over the edge of the cubby down the ladder they had made. From the ground as she gazed back up she could see his curly head sticking over the platform.

"You ol' Davey!" she yelled, and raced away among the trees.

But it had happened. After that everything became easier.

Kiss for apricot. Apricot for kiss. And it was the season. It became a kind of game — their special one — that for every kiss an apricot stone was dropped back into the box. Not that the tally was accurate. They became so dangerously in love with kissing that apricots were forgotten and lip measured out ecstasy on lip long after the leaves fell from every fruit-tree in the town. Pine scent filled hair and hands and clothes. The boy carved initials all over the tree, being romantic, and they did nothing more than kiss, although it is true they were expert.

During the next spring Jenny's family moved a hundred miles away to a town on the far coast. They wept in each other's arms lying along the tree-house floor the afternoon before she went away, and after she had gone he used to go up there all through that next aching spring and summer and lie in anguish with the scent of the pines drowning him as he read over and over the stilted letters in her unformed scrawl.

At seventeen he followed her, took a job in the same town, and after tentative hand-claspings, they became lovers. He was not her first. Her expertness terrified, amazed and soon delighted him. She whipped him with the violence of his own passion so that he became silly as a dog, and rather like one with his big shambling body, his warmth, his mass of shaggy hair.

"Bark!" she almost said. And he barked.

"Kiss me," she ordered. And he did. "Not like that, silly. Like this." And he did.

"Marry me," he pleaded.

"Perhaps," Jenny said, "when you're rich."

He knew she had other lovers. His jealousy nearly killed him, but his infatuate sacrifices could have left only the most callous heart unmoved — and Jenny was not really callous. Finally she drew away from all others and for two years they met and made love, talked, danced, walked the lambing flats, nuzzled the earth on the hills outside the town. As months slipped away it was Jenny's turn to ask, "When?"

"When I can keep you as I want," he said. "Wait a bit. Give me another year. I'll move to the city and come back like a king."

So Davey went away. They parted in an agony again, though his was less than that first time, perhaps because, as with most men, physical fulfilment had blunted the edge of his need. They wrote. God, how they wrote! Long, passionate letters verging on the pornographic. "In a year," he would promise. But the year swelled, grew big with its own imaginings and melted away. He sought no one else and yet a tiny edge of ice bordered their letters until suddenly she wrote a final one. He dropped it trembling. And did not answer. She married within the fortnight a raw-faced, lank insipidity she had known for a year. But he promised reality, not dreams, and her neat brown hands, whose fingers curled as naturally as petals into the position of receiving, reached up to grasp her new husband with the merciless tenderness of a skilled taker.

Davey wept. He became solitary, avoiding women. The mere glimpse of an eager dark face was enough to cause a leaping of heart that was unbearable. And time was the slowest mender. This puzzled him, because he was, after twelve months, realist enough to begin looking about him once more with an opportunist's eye. What man would not, romantic or otherwise?

"It must have been the real thing," he used to assure a work crony over a drink. "It still hurts."

"Nuts," his friend would say. "You're nuts. Six weeks and another dame and that could be the real thing too."

"Ach!" he would grunt into his liquor. "You don't understand."

"A dame is a dame is a dame," his pal used to say brightly. And perhaps was right, for after an interval he loved again and married someone so different that in his coldest moments when self faced self and *tu* accused *te* he wondered if that action, too, were an attempt to obliterate. He became successful, popular, a party man, a ladies' man. He told elegant and amusing stories. He drank — but better still, was sought as a drinking companion. Surface appearances showed no trace of the introspective moroseness that had shadowed him for years. His wife adored him. But it was still there, tiny and perfect, a sense of loss, of whipped pride that caught up with him in the oddest places. Even at parties, at the peak of social success, he glimpsed out of one twinklingly benevolent eye the boy lying with grief across the tree-house floor, and tasted again his first and most vicious failure. His wife was beautiful. The attentions of other men repeatedly assured him of this. He had charm too. His occasional infidelity substantiated that. But he was not satisfied. There was something. Something.

He was thirty-six, perhaps a little more, when finally he caught a train back from the northern city where he worked. His birthplace was two hundred miles away, a matter of a few hours. For the fortnight since the thought of returning had visited him with the sweetness of the unexpected, he anticipated deliverance. Work did not take him back. No. It was an illicit return planned with all the jealous detail of calculated infidelity. He kissed his wife's calm and wonderful face goodbye with the impatience of the unfaithful, waving to her perplexity on the station in an excess of restlessness he could hardly conceal.

Stations and scenery revisited by his adult eye had him in a state of idiot nostalgia that was near to rapture, so that when, at last, crumpled but elate, he stepped onto the platform he had known as a child, he felt such an ocean-tide of misery and joy his plump face wrinkled into the seriousness of his boyhood and, for the first time for years, simplicity, that used to be the one wild light on his face, trembled all about him.

It was early afternoon. His impatience nudged him along the main street where for one minute, aching with tears, he stared across the one o'clock blue bay water, past the new stone monuments, the pavilions. The stone grove used to be at the southern end of the town. It was still there. Its dark green shadow, now so many years taller, thicker, filled him with the quivering, intolerable sickness of a sinner about to be shriven. No one noticed him, a portly, still-young man, full of assurance, walking briskly across the esplanade to the southern road. Yet he was conscious of his oddness, his out-of-place-ness among the pine caverns where paths were still so well-remembered, he whimpered aloud. And found unerringly the tree, thicker, more densely branched. He put one pudgy hand on the rough bark. It seemed hardly likely the tree-house would still be there. Could still be there. When he peered upwards the fronds were so thick it was as if he were trying to see through water deeps, but above him, miraculously, so unbelievably he cried out, one corner of the platform was visible.

He removed his coat and then in shirt and braces he swung up and began to climb. Plump, puffing, twenty years beyond the shy boy who had moved so lithely. He heard his trousers rip on a broken branch but he did not care. Grotesque though he knew himself to be, he laughed and panted and scrambled until he came to the branch immediately below the platform. For a moment he thought he would never make it. He rested his agony breast-high against the edge of the pine floor, then hideously, grunting, heaving, pulled himself over and sat there in his expensive tweed. Sat, looked across the breakers of green trees, smelt the pine everywhere and then rolled on his side in tears, weeping and shuddering. Twenty years squeezed out of his eyes in those five minutes, and after a while he sat up to stare puffily about him. The box was still there where their browned and freckled legs had shoved it during their last afternoon together, well over against the bole of the tree. He looked inside. Still there, dozens and dozens of apricot stones, rock hard and black. He picked a handful up and let them drop back in again, one by one — kiss after kiss. He thought he had grown beyond sentimentality. He prided himself on his sophistication. But he was soft as love. Quite soft. He sat there for a while, steeped in anguish — but he was shallow enough to enjoy it and deep enough to know it. And then, very deliberately, he removed the stones in handfuls, packing them onto his person in trouser pockets, vest, shirt, until the box was empty. Then he dropped that over the side, gently, carefully, thirty feet to the turf below.

Back in the township he put all the stones in the wooden box and careless of absurdity went to a store where he bought wrapping paper. Not everyone can box-up love like this. But Davey did. He boxed it and addressed it to Jenny. He knew where she lived, having often inquired with pretended indifference over the years. And then he took his parcel to the post office and sent it away to her — registered, because he was always a careful man.

Once that was done, peace came to Davey. He had printed Jenny's name on the paper without a tremor and, having watched it weighed, stamped and taken across the counter, it was as if he had sent to her the wretchedness that had lain at the back of his heart for years.

Oddly enough he never thought of her again.

DAVID CAMPBELL

I WOULDN'T MISS CHRISTMAS

Overhead in the still summer sky above the orange-tree, swallows were feeding their young on the wing, meeting and hanging breast-to-breast at the top of steep curves. Watching their windy flight over the creek and the yellow paddocks, Janet said:

"Wouldn't it be good to be grown up?"

She would dip, fly, over Bald Hill and the metal towns, mountains and pointed waves.

"But you'd miss Christmas," Billy said.

"They have Christmas, too."

"But they don't get much. A book or a pair of pliers."

"I wouldn't miss Christmas," Babs said.

"You'll miss it if you go on dragging your feet on Len's paths."

"You're doing it too."

Janet pointed her shoulders.

"I know," she said. "Let's play grown-ups. Let's dress up in their clothes."

For the children had the house and garden to themselves. Everyone else had gone to town to vote.

"That's a good idea," said Billy.

In the cool tall bedroom where they had been born, where their mother used to sit at night brushing her long hair while they said their prayers, where their earliest memories moved like sun and shade in the vine-filtered light, Janet began taking out silks and treasures, enchanted in the scents of rosemary. The dim colours ran through her hands like water.

"I think ..." she said, fair head on one side, lips together. "How does this suit me?"

"What about me?" Babs said. "Who am I going to be?"

"Oh, you're too small. Nothing would fit you."

"I want to be Mummy," Babs wailed.

"I'm Mummy. We can't have two, stupid."

"I don't care, I want to be ..."

"I know ..." Janet's voice was suddenly affected, honeying over her impatience. "Keep quiet, and I'll dress you up. There" — the corners of her eyes were merry and white — "you can be Miss Frost."

"But she smells," Babs wailed.

"You're Miss Frost," Janet said, "or you don't play. But you can wear Mummy's clothes. Billy, guess who Babs is."

"What's going on in here?"

Billy came thumping sternly out of their father's dressing-room in a pair of riding-boots that met his short pants above the knee. An old army tunic dwarfed him for a greatcoat, and their father's new city hat with the dents in it rocked on his ears. He had a boot-black moustache.

"What are you children up to now?"

Janet rolled among the silks, sprang up to adjust him.

"You almost frightened me," she said. "Just for a second. Here, I'll fix you. Say it again."

But Billy wrenched away, pacing stonily, struggling to retain his pose.

"Late as usual, Josephine."

But when he went to look at his watch, the sleeve of the tunic hung down and he ran laughing from the room. A moment later, he was back.

"I'm sick of waiting," he said. "I'm sitting in the car."

Janet laughed more than ever.

"I want to play Mummy," said Babs.

"You can't. You're Miss Frost."

"Come on," Janet said. "It'll be fun. You'll be funnier even than Daddy."

In two minds, Babs gazed at her small figure in the dim glass.

"I expect," she said, "I could tuck some socks down my smock."

"Oh, yes!"

"But hurry up," Billy said.

The girls were ages getting dressed. Billy paced and

fidgeted about the room, glancing at them, walking out and coming in again, no longer acting, while Janet smiled secretly, alone and bewitched in the feminine mirror-world of lace and powders.

"There," she said, dusting the rouge on her cheeks, "I really am quite like Mummy."

"Oh, come on," Billy said. "Don't be all day. Really, Janet, you spoil everything."

"If you hurry me any more," Janet said, "I won't play."

Her eyes, as she looked at him from the looking-glass, were wide and candid. Billy turned and walked to the door. He stood there for some time, rattling the china doorknob.

"You're always late," he said. "You spoil everything."

"Button me up," said Babs.

But at last they were ready. Janet swept across the floor, her small fair head tilted upwards, while Babs trailed behind, a tiny pouter-pigeon, tripping on her skirts. In the unfamiliar sitting-room they all paused, self-conscious of a sudden, at a loss.

"The flowers," Janet said in a strained little voice. "They're lovely this year."

She began adjusting a vase with her long fingers. She really did not feel like playing. Billy's impatience had upset her. For some reason she had the feeling that their governess, the overseer, the jackeroos, were all in the room. The men had risen and were looking at her.

Billy, hiding laughter, paced to the fireplace. Hands behind his back, swaying from heels to toes, he glanced about the room. He was enjoying himself, his irritability forgotten.

"Well, my dear. Children all right?"

"Oh, yes. Thank you."

"That's good. Garden looks well."

"Yes it does, doesn't it?"

Billy was really doing marvellously. He was glancing about, at ease, making the conversation, just like their father in his rare boisterous moods before dinner. But Janet still felt constrained, shut in, as if the room were full of strangers. Even Billy seemed different; he had spoiled the day.

The chintz curtains stirred, and, gazing out at the blond wavering paddocks, he had a good idea.

"The water," he said. "The pump has broken down. You'll have to go steady on the watering."

Immediately Babs broke into tears. Her eyes closed and her mouth opened.

"The flowers," she wailed. "They'll all die. What will Mummy say?"

Billy, standing at the fireplace in his big boots, looked at her in amazement. He thought he had been doing very well.

But Janet gave him a swift look and led Babs crying into the bedroom.

"There," she said, "it was only a game. There's still plenty of water."

"I must have been really good this time," Billy said from the door. "She thought it was real. I can do it when you don't laugh ... What's the matter, Jan? Aren't we going to play any more? Oh, come on!"

Janet was undressing Babs, folding the things away in the sweet-smelling drawers, doing everything the way their mother did.

"Come on, Jan. I don't understand."

He hovered about the room, annoyed, bewildered, feeling like crying himself, clumsy in his big clothes.

"We'd only just started. I don't understand," he kept saying.

"That's just the whole trouble," Janet said.

But suddenly she was sorry for him — for her father as well as her mother.

"Oh, well," she said. "You get changed and we'll all walk down the avenue and meet Mum and Dad at the first gate."

Outside the swallows were still swinging and feeding in the vast cloudless sky.

MICHAEL WILDING

JOE'S ABSENCE

Driving through the bush, past the level sweeps of still gums, motionless, silent on the bright windless day, Graham began to wonder why he didn't live permanently out here somewhere, away from drinking too much and writing too little and going to movies the only nights he didn't go to the pub or a party. Joe had stood in the pub five o'clock on Friday, his skin browned, his hair bleached light at the tips from the sun, announcing, as they were crushed into the corner between the cigarette machine and the wall, that he had written a dozen stories in the last two months. Graham was about to ask how many of these were rewrites, not having written a dozen in two years unless you counted the abortive novel as several, but Helen had started to giggle and nudge Pat seeing him and Joe wedged in and talking. She'd never really forgiven Joe for dropping her, or him for knocking her back after a party one night. So Joe pushed through the crowd to put his arms round Helen and Pat, and Graham moved along to where he could see some other girl's head, and pinch her bottom affectionately.

When the pub had thinned out a bit about a quarter to eight, he could see Joe again, in his jeans and ex-army bush shirt, shouted drinks by all the people he hadn't seen for so long, coming up so rarely now, leaning against the bar with the peace of a beachcomber.

"So why don't you come down?" he said. "You can stay there, there's two rooms."

"I might. So how many have you sold?"

"I'm not; I'm putting them into a collection. I'm not trying the magazines. I'm keeping them till I've got them all ready to publish at once."

"You write all day?"

"In the mornings; then in the afternoons I usually go to the beach and swim and read and lie in the sun; sometimes I write in the evening; it depends; sometimes I just make notes. Then there's Margot."

"Then there's Margot."

"She keeps me company."

The gums were high and never seemed to have any birds in them, no movement, no rustling; yet they must have done; perhaps if he stopped the car and got out and watched, he would notice some. But just looking as he drove past, he could see nothing moving at all, just that huge stretching silence, reaching over soil and rocks no one had ever stepped on. It was frightening when you thought of all that emptiness reaching right out into the centre, it was frightening like looking at the stars was frightening, the terror of those inconceivable distances. It was the terror that made you cluster in the cities, clinging like ants on a dead lizard's sore, sucking sustenance from the skin's small crack.

Yet Joe had been able to give it away. He rarely came to the pub now. But stabbed reams of white paper with neat black characters, sheet after sheet, and in the afternoons lay on the beach, casually trickling through his fingers the innumerable grains of sand, sleeping at night between the immense silence of the sea, and the mute stillness of the bush.

With Margot, of course.

Margot had come into the pub later and he'd hardly noticed her. She'd nestled round Joe and started to talk to him quietly.

"Meet Graham," Joe had said, and she smiled and said Hello Graham and carried on talking.

"Graham's coming down to stay with us," Joe had said.

She smiled again; good teeth; and carried on talking to Joe. She spoke too quietly for Graham to hear anything; Joe seemed to resent her doing that, being secretive, so spoke loudly.

"All right," he said, with the same volume he had used to introduce Graham. "I'm not stopping you; go on; go on and have dinner with your friend."

She smiled at him and went out, waving.

"We have a free relationship," Joe said. "She's gone off to screw some old friend." He ordered two more middies, and later intercepted Helen and Pat as they were leaving so that they all went for a meal together, and after the pub closed went on to a party.

A few houses clustered round the edge of the bay, with a shop that did duty as a post office. He drove past, following Joe's directions of turning up a track past the houses. Where the track stopped, was the house.

He left the car on the rough road, and walked to a gap in amongst clusters of lantana where a piece of broken board nailed to a post indicated the house. Joe's burnt poker work had marked it 75, as an urban affirmation. But the house was rough stone thrown together, like a cairn marking a food cache, or a body unburiable because of the rocky ground. It had a window and a door, and a corrugated iron shed roof on top of the blocks of stone. It was about big enough to hold a small car. All around was scrub.

The door was shut, locked, Graham looked through the window on to a bench with a typewriter, a sheet of paper in the carriage. He could not read what had been written because the typist had been facing the window.

He walked round the shack, seeing only bush stretching

in every direction, blue, grey, green, dusty, mile upon mile. A kookaburra called out, just once, and everything was quiet again after its mechanical harshness.

Stopped back at the beach he leant his elbows on the top of the open car door, and looked for Joe. He liked the look of the beach; all that sand, all that water; for an afternoon at least it would be pleasant, talking to Joe. Watching the occasional girl, perhaps. There was one in a yellow bikini, lying on her stomach, her legs spread apart, a book propped in front of her on a heap of scooped sand, her chin resting on her fists, one hand above the other. She might have been asleep or looking at the sea. He swept his eyes from her, like a withdrawing wave, and examined the few groups of people lying in the sun; a middle-aged mother with three children, two old men walking, a group of five or six teenagers.

"It's like Big Sur," Joe had said at the party.

His eyes drew over the girl again, an impersonal wave, but ready to settle. She must have felt him; she swivelled round on her belly, looked over her shoulder, her eyes engaging with his. Seeing her face he wondered if it was Margot. Even if not, to ask her would inaugurate a conversation. Having driven so far, the least he could do was have a conversation.

"I thought I'd seen you somewhere," she said. Her voice was

young, welcoming, unguarded. But as it was Margot he stopped evaluating the curve of her hips, the flow of her legs, and sat down on the sand.

"Have a towel," she said. "I've got two."

He sat on it, though the sand was dry.

"What are you doing?" she asked.

"I came down to see you."

"Me?" She cocked her head on one side and smiled at him, as if she were pleased.

"Well, Joe and you, yes."

"Oh, pity," she said. "I think he's in town."

"Christ, he told me he'd be here; he bloody well invited me down."

She shrugged her shoulders and turned the book face down. "He stayed in town last night. He had to see someone or something today. I thought he might have been seeing you."

"So did I."

She pulled a face. "He might come back on the ferry for lunch if he said he'd see you here," she said.

"When's that?"

"I don't know; I never carry a watch. I sort of like to forget time down here." She stretched her arms out, yawning from the comfortable sun, wriggling her wrists as she gave a final reaching stretch, and then lay on her stomach again. "Why don't you sunbathe?" she said.

She began reading her book. Graham took off his shirt and used it to lay his head on, and kicked off his thongs. He had no shorts with him, so lay in his jeans, too tight to roll up. He watched her, but dragged his mind away to Joe's last bird. He'd gone for Lydia. She'd been much more attractive than this one. It might be worth doing something about it now; he'd ask Joe her address. He'd only made a line for her once; that didn't count the first time he saw her at that conference he'd talked at. They'd all had several beers over lunch, and he'd stayed on for the afternoon paper, sitting next to Lydia, because Joe wanted to be in the front to attack the speaker. They'd grinned at each other every time either of them nearly fell asleep. It was the time after, when he and Joe had talked at some literary festival about new directions in literature, that he'd made the line. Funny how no one else had noticed it sounded like nude erections. They'd been given a bottle of grog each in lieu of payment; Joe got whisky and he got brandy, by moving quickly and not looking at the wine labels; at the party afterwards after the pub had shut he shared his brandy with Lydia, telling her she should relax more, be less frigid, more swinging. She kissed him to convince him she was. But either he or she or Joe had got wound up with somebody else and that was the end of the evening. And he'd not seen her since. This new one, Margot, didn't seem as frigid, as aloof. He couldn't decide how less attractive she was. Her breasts were fuller than he'd remembered. He liked full breasts and small bottoms. She had small feet that she curled, turning the toes over so that the soles of the feet moved, the skin wrinkling, tensing, relaxing, as if it were being gently tickled.

"It's a beaut place," she said. She had put her book down and was looking at Graham who lay watching her, wondering after all. "It's quiet and there's hardly anyone here except in the school holidays. Then they come down a bit. But not much. And you don't get the surfies; the bay breaks the waves, so they can't surf here. That land along there sweeps round as a sort of arm of the bay." She half raised herself to point towards the sea, her breasts lifted so that their tips just touched the sand. "Sometimes there isn't anyone here at all, just Joe and me. And around the corner" — and she sat up, resting on her left arm and with her back towards him, pointed out beyond where their view was blocked by the close, wooded rise at the bay's edge — "there's another bay that you hardly see anyone on at all. It's almost totally deserted" — and the tanned skin of her shoulders rippled. Having pointed she stretched herself again, the line of her back arching, her hair dropping back, hanging over but not touching her shoulders, as she bent her head right back. She rubbed her eyes, watery from yawning, and then lay down, sunning her stomach. She tipped her head on one side to look at him while she talked. "I've been so sort of healthy since I've been here, swimming and lying on the beach and walking, walking miles, along the beaches, stretching on and on, miles of gleaming sand. If you walk below the tideline you can see your foot tracks just one line, stretching right out of sight. It's quite eerie in a way. Just you and the sea and the sand." Her breasts rose when she breathed in deeply, breathing in fully and smiling, content. Her stomach was flat, downy, the downy hair glistening golden in the sun. Grains of sand clung to it in little patches. She scuffed hollows for her heels to settle in. "You'd think Joe would be the sort of person who'd hate it, but he's crazy about it. He's written a dozen stories, and he's got a stack of notes for others he keeps leafing through. They're much better than anything he did before. At least, I think they are. I didn't know him before, but I've looked at some of the things he wrote then. And they're not as good. Not as good as these he's writing now." She raised her bottom off the sand, her weight on her shoulders and feet, for no other reason than that in the sun she felt healthy, active. "That's the ferry," she said, rolling on to her stomach again, leaning her breasts on her folded arms and watching the small boat approach the landing jetty at the right of the bay, beneath the slight, sloping promontory. "Joe'll probably be on this if he's coming back for lunch."

He stopped looking at her and watched the arriving ferry, being impersonal, and asked, "What are Joe's stories about? The same themes?" Restraining a pejorative old.

"Joe, of course." She smiled at him.

One of the crew threw a rope from the ferry round the wharf post.

"What do you do?" she asked, conversationally.

He turned back from the sea to her. He wondered why Joe hadn't told her; or whether she'd not bothered to remember. He said, slowly, "I write; a bit; not so prolifically as Joe seems to be doing."

"He never has before, he says," she said, as if to touch his arm consolingly.

He watched the gangplank being thrust from the gap between the rail across on to the jetty.

"No," he said.

"What sort of things do you write?" she asked, probably as she'd first asked Joe. It was a good opening and he'd followed surely along it before. But he just looked at the passengers crossing the gangplank and the mini-bus backing to meet them. "Stories," he said, watching for Joe to arrive.

She borrowed five cents for the phone, and he watched her

walk to the road, the line of her bikini on her hips rising and dipping to alternate sides with each step, a yellow sun receding, alone distinguishable as the bra strap was only a narrow cord. Instead of returning directly, she walked diagonally across from the road to the water and swam, as if he had not been there at all. And when she swam underwater nothing remained to show she ever had been there, except her towel and book beside him. He wondered idly what the book was, but did not bother to reach for it. He lay prostrate, facing the sea, watching her head occasionally surface, and then her head and neck emerge, her breasts, her hips, her thighs, and soon she was running up the beach, bending over him to pick up her towel, water dripping from her hair on to his hot back, running in rivulets down her neck and throat, over her breasts in separate runnels that met between them, in trickles over her belly and thighs. She shook her head, her hair flung round scattering drops of water like a dog, drops dampening the white sand to brief disks of mud. He noticed how the elastic of her bikini ran taut across her hips but left two small gaps between the inside of her hips and the rise of her belly. He watched a trickle of water run towards and then away from the gap, and when she bent over to comb her hair it fell from her side to the sand and was lost among the hot grains.

"Joe's in town," she said, as she lay down again, flat on her stomach, ignoring the towel and lying in the hot sand. She lay down so that they faced each other and their bodies were in a straight line.

"Uh-huh."

"He's not coming down till tomorrow."

They looked at each other. He smiled ruefully for many reasons. She looked straight back at him.

"He must have got so pissed he didn't bother to remember, the bastard," he said. And even momentarily convinced himself he felt annoyance.

"It's a beaut day, anyway," she said; and, his chin resting on the sand, her breasts were directly ahead of him. "At least it won't be wasted."

"I could have been writing another short story," he said; "like Joe."

"Joe didn't seem to have had time to think of one."

He wriggled deeper into the sand. How much, after all, had he wanted to talk to Joe, and be competitive about acceptances and women? He thought it would be pleasanter alone with her.

Yet he found her strangely distant; though not consistently. She had swum as if he had not been there but, after they had eaten crisps and cashew nuts and chocolate which they bought at the shop, she suggested they should go to the other beach which was always deserted.

They walked between lines of shells, stopping to examine those with fine colours or rare shapes, or to touch twigs round and smoothed by the tides. No houses reached on to the beach, no roads passed it. The waves broke gently on the sand, the only sound. The bush stood still at the beach's edge.

It was not a physical distance. They walked along together leaving an irregular, merging, quadruped track, sometimes bumping against each other when one of them stopped or crossed in front of the other for a shell or fragment of coral; and she would halt him by touching his lower arm when in front of them a single claw probed through a sand hole into the air, probed slowly and at their slightest movement dropped out of sight. But there was another distance, a sort of obliqueness that disturbed him. Alone on this stretch of beach he felt naked with her, unwatched, unhampered, unprotected by the smallest of societies. The emptiness menaced him, left him without covering or support, and without people to crush against him, their solitary closeness on the empty beach seemed like an immense distance. Yet it should have been a closeness. Though asteroids collide despite the infinite spaces, brushing together on that huge strand could not be casual. On the beach when footsteps scuffed into each other's, there must have been some contrivance; which must have implied more than a physical closeness.

But in the emptiness her laughter bounced off the bright sand as if it could never, would never, penetrate. Her laughing, her flinging her hair, her brushing his arm with her breast, her skipping, all the incidents fondling him, stroking his cheeks, relaxing his set eyes, might just have been handstands and cartwheels on firm surfaces.

And Joe?

And Joe, after the coolness and poise of Lydia, might have gone for girlishness; which was distant too, like Lydia.

If it was sexy too.

Space's infinity turns back on itself. Revolves through its first, its perpetual, question. How could he tell if she was sexy?

He laughed to himself; how could he tell if she was sexy! He looked at her, whose inventory he could recite from memory after looking for so long, at her catalogue of movements.

"What are you looking at?" she asked.

"You."

"When Joe looks like that I know there's going to be trouble."

"Like he's going to rape you?"

"Not me," she said. "That wouldn't be a trouble."

"Oh, he's all right," he said; but not restraining a taint of scarcely concealed doubt from lapsing over his voice.

"He's sexy, too," she said. And then she said, "I'll race you to that fallen gum."

Before he could refuse, she had begun running, so he padded after her, the gap between them widening at every gasp.

Joe had said it was just like Big Sur.

He dropped the towel from his neck and her book and comb from his pocket and then flopped down, sweating.

"You should stay here," she said, "get healthy."

He grunted, making slow flailing motions in the sand like a turtle, struggling to pull off his shirt.

"I'm going to have a swim. Why don't you come in?" she said.

He brushed the hair from his forehead for coolness.

"You don't need any trunks here," she said.

"Sure?" he said, not hastening, not rushing, not sure of her still.

"Sure," she said. "I'm going to take off my bikini anyway; it's more sort of, I don't know; I like the feel of the water against me."

And the waves lapped round them both, fondling them in a joint embrace, while they swam or floated, and when she floated on her back her breasts just rose above the surface, her nipples pink in the silvered blue water.

It was when he lay on the towel, drying in the sun and the wind that was blowing up, that his penis grew stiff and tumescent, joining the heat of his sunburn with a spreading heat of his own. He watched her lying there, her breasts firm, her nipples taut, her stomach flowing in gentle curves to the triangle of her pubic hair, to her open legs. She turned her head on one side and looked at him, and when they both smiled, he reached over a hand and grabbed hers. They competed in the pressure of their grips.

The wind that had blown up brought spots of rain.

"We could do a Lady Chatterley in the storm," she said, "or go back to the shack."

"The shack might be better," he said. "Besides, I haven't got any flowers handy."

Besides, he felt the need to think. And walking along the beach, returning parallel with their double line of footprints, and walking up the bush track that was a short cut, he tried to think, as he bumped against her, or put his arm round her when she seemed likely to make the slightest stumble, the tips of his fingers pressing on her warm body.

How could he be sure Joe wouldn't be back, anyway, or

come back on a later ferry, or in a drunken car? But that wasn't it, not the detection. It was screwing her in the first place. Why did Joe always get such attractive birds? He pondered his loyalties to Joe, which needed only to be few. He had Joe's comment that it was a free relationship; and Joe's absence as support. Why wait till Joe dumped her? Why not move in now? What difference was there, except in wasting time?

Though it was Joe, after all; who hadn't two-timed him ever; as far as he knew; and whom he'd never two-timed yet; except perhaps by speaking for twenty minutes at that conference when he'd agreed on ten minutes, and Joe had only ten minutes prepared. And rubbishing his stories privately; but Joe probably reciprocated that.

He watched her hips move, following behind her on the last narrow stretch of the track. A kookaburra called out, and another picked up its cry. They flew off into the bush, still cackling. The rain began to fall heavily so they ran the last stretch to the car.

They stood close to each other as she took the key from under a stone and opened the door. Inside, they held against each other, pressing their bodies into each other. He put his hand against her back, slipping it down to run over her buttocks beneath her bikini. He kissed her and would have steered her to the bed, hoping by haste to forestall thought. But she took one arm away from him and pressed its index finger just beneath his shoulder bone.

"What," she said, gently pressing for emphasis with each word, "what about Joe?"

"Since you mention it," he said, "I'd been wondering."

"It's not me as much as you: I know he's going to dump me sometime like he always does; but you're both good friends."

"We're just good friends," he said, licking the salt around her ear.

"But seriously," she said, like a little girl: "I don't specially want to betray him; but I think he'd be more hurt if you did."

"Betraying's a bit melodramatic, isn't it?"

"And sexy too."

He let her go, fondling her stomach when she turned round.

"Why don't we eat first?" she said.

"Could do," he said, casually, adding, "I'll be surer then."

"Surer which way?"

"One way."

"You're not sure now, are you, at all?"

He replied "No," but it hadn't been a question; nor something he had wanted to remember.

"I know, I could tell. That's why," she began; and then gave him a kiss full on the mouth, as if to show she didn't hold it against him; and to stop him from answering.

"I'll make an orgiastic meal," she said.

"Why, aren't you sure?"

She looked at him: "I'm always sure," she said, "but I'm also hungry." And she might have been.

She put on jeans and a sweater and lent him a sweater of Joe's as, now it was raining, it was cold inside. She lit an oil lamp. The walls were bare stone, the floor concrete on which they had thrown rush mats. A hardboard partition served to create two rooms, a bedroom one side, a combined kitchen, eating room, and spare bedroom the other. She cooked on stored gas in one corner. An old mattress lay on the floor for seating and visitors. She brought a flagon of red wine and a couple of glasses from the bedroom, and sat down on the mattress beside him, snuggling against him.

"What's the masterpiece?" he asked, pointing to the typewriter with its sheet of quarto.

"Why don't you have a look?" she said; but it was warm against her and she might relent, before eating.

He drank some of the wine and shrugged his shoulders. And added, "I don't like anyone looking at what I'm working on. I don't even like them reading it in typescript when it's finished. It's a sort of intrusion. It makes me feel exposed and vulnerable."

She pressed her hand close into his side. "Joe's the same," she said. "That's why I don't know what it is."

"But you tell me to look at it," he said, putting his arm round her.

She grinned at him. "You're not me."

And as he pulled her closely against him, she said, "You can have caviar, Polish duck, Hungarian goulash, Mexican chicken, pickled onions, pilchards, sardines, pickled herrings, smoked oysters" — she got up and looked in the cupboard — "Indian mango chutney, hot curry, sweet curry, peaches. I don't think there's any Christmas pudding left, any sort of soup" — she turned round to face him, crouching at the cupboard by the oven — "and there're probably other things, if you like. I can't see very well, it's a bit untidy. We've got no money so we have to get everything on Joe's account, and they only sell things in cans; or bottles. And since it caters for the bourgeoisie, it only sells exotic foods; but I think they're nice — don't you? The possums come up to the dump outside and rummage around in the cans; they seem to like it."

They began with caviar and biscuits, flavoured with sesame seed.

✧ ✧ ✧

"So you don't know what he's been writing about?"

"Yes, I told you: Joe. I sneak a look now and then when they're finished — when he's out or something, you know."

She came over from the cupboard and poured herself some more wine. The light cast a golden sheen over furrows in her sweater, over her cheeks, so that she looked warm, soft, glowing.

"I wish you wouldn't look like that," he said.

"Like what?" The sheen rippled as she moved to put the flagon down, and he grabbed her hand and pulled her down to the mattress again.

He said. "It just wouldn't be a brilliant idea; it's not even that it would upset Joe —"

"Thanks."

"No, but on principle he probably wouldn't let it. But it would be a betrayal even if it didn't, wouldn't it? Even if he never knew."

"Sometimes," she said, "I wonder if anything could upset Joe, if anything could affect him or get through to him at all. He's almost anaesthetised. He goes from disaster to disaster and just carries on doing the same things. And writes about them. And then goes and does them again. It's as if as long as he can make a story out of it, he doesn't care: it just doesn't affect him, doesn't hurt him or anything. He cares more about his stories than about anyone — even himself.

You know, sometimes I think if I could find a way of getting through to him, of hurting him so he'd have to feel something, I'd do it; just to hurt him so he'd feel it. But I can't think of anything."

She filled up both glasses again.

"Even if I did go to bed with you," she said, "I don't think he'd care. He'd just sort of, you know, sort of laugh, and —"

"And write another story."

"He would. So, I don't know, sometimes I just feel so helpless, so frustrated, you know."

"So there's no point in sleeping with me?" He said it in a tone of agreement, like a statement that had already been agreed on.

"No," she said.

"Thanks"; his turn this time.

"Sorry," she said, "but you know what I mean."

She put her glass down and kissed him again, and they lay on the mattress together.

"Look," she said, "look, honestly, mostly I don't want to sleep with anyone else anyway. You probably can't understand it but I love him; I just don't want anyone else."

She pulled him very close while she spoke.

"It's just, oh Graham, it's just so hopeless. I couldn't 'betray' him because I don't think there's anything he cares about; I can't do anything; he's not involved with me, all he's involved with is his stories."

He grinned, sympathetically, for all of them. "I've just got fewer stories," he said, "but I know what he feels."

And she hugged on to him. While the more he thought about Joe, the more Margot said, the more he wondered why he should care at all about betraying him, why he should even use so absurd a word. That concern on the return from the beach had been merely a terror of Margot, a terror of getting into some absurd relationship with her and Joe. The strength of the recoil from the idea of "betraying" Joe was a measure, perhaps, of how much he wanted to, how much he should, perhaps, betray him. But having thought about it all again, and considered the difficulties and objections, even if to reject them, raised his doubts. And though he lay beside her kissing her, and her hands stroked all over him, his mind hovered separately, doubtingly.

"But it would be nice," she said, holding him, pressing him.

"Let's eat first," he reminded her.

So she stood up sadly. And he was afraid he had now made her annoyed.

She stirred the soup and looked at him — sitting on the

mattress and looking at the rough walls, the typewriter on the table, the darkness through the window.

"If you don't want to read the one he's working on, what about the others; the ones he's just finished?"

"Won't he mind?"

"He won't know."

Outside there was just the darkness, and the rain drumming on the corrugated iron roof, the shafts of rain beating against it and sluicing down the furrows. He stood up to join her to let his hands stroke over her breasts but she wriggled free.

"Don't," she said, shortly, "because you're not going to do anything so don't just mess around. It only makes me irritable."

So he went across to Joe's desk.

Before he took out those unsmutched white sheets from their manila folders, before his fingers probed the collection, fumbling along the edges of the pages, easing off paper clips, he knew that Joe would mind. Each story had its own folder, which he spread open, gently bending and pressing it to stay flat, as bees force open the petals of flowers. Sometimes a clip he had not noticed would spring off as he bent back the covers, snapping like a cord breaking. He unclothed the stories, taking them from their covers as if he were prising open oysters. He glanced at their titles and then softly flicked through their pages, flicking at the sheets, unopened since they'd been corrected, flicking sometimes five or six times before catching at an edge that would open for him. He looked through them for their titles and their settings, rapidly yet carefully, his sight washing over words softly, silently, like a quiet sea over shells. His fingers turned the pages gently. He was not rough. They were the same fingers that had stroked Margot's buttocks, that had held off from fondling her nipples. But they did not hold off here. He lay on the mattress, wriggling his hips into a comfortable position, the stories beside him. He was glad, when she called soup, to delay a reading of them. But after the hot soup he lay down and, taking the topmost of the stories, holding it by its edges as film is held, rested it on the mattress before him.

He read slowly at first to evaluate Joe's development, to establish whether there was any development. He read to see if Joe was on to anything new, in case a new richness had thickened or there had been a blaze of metaphorical efflorescence. The display of Joe's emotional life was only a subsidiary interest. He did not have Margot's investment in that. She asked him if he'd got to the story about Lydia: he wasn't sure as except for the finely marked face and the small breasts, he knew nothing about Lydia. Why need he care, as Margot did, about Joe's past life, his past loves, his past betrayals, his current infidelities? "That bitch in that story, the one he goes over the mountains with," she called, from the oven: but it wasn't that bitch that interested him, but Joe's lyrical treatment of the mountain trip and the swim in the cool clear sea, their early morning bathing in the sharp translucence. That, and the ending, and the framework he had set the story in that so enhanced it. "Oh yes," he agreed when she told him it was Helen, "she is a bitch." But it was Joe's new control that he was cursing, the bitch of assurance that was in Joe. "But don't you think it's a waste of a good story on her?" He hadn't thought of it at all. He didn't see that she had anything to do with the story, but was like one of the drops of clear water beading on her breasts, or the striped pebbles at the sea's edge. That any of them had any existence other than in the story or any gratitude to, let alone claim on Joe, he had never considered. "Don't you think she's a rat to him at the end?" she said. He wondered how Joe had achieved that ending, with its fine balance, the irresolvable ambivalence of attitude between the two figures, the complexities of involvement and repudiation, the final frozen tableau that represented the whole action and like a pedestal supported and sustained it.

But the old flatness was still there. He could find traces of it, of the old over-explicitness, the clumsiness: gold amongst the dross, the silt, the rubble. It gave him a sense of comfortable familiarity, an ease. He registered the redundancies, the spelled out endings, the unrealised and untransmuted autobiography, and said nothing. And he said nothing about the new control that Joe's bush exile must have given him; he imagined it was the exile, and not just Margot. Though at the thought he took another drink and looked across at her, licking her fingers with relish for the Polish duck.

"Have you read the one about the abortion?" she said. "I don't know who it is. Joe won't say. And you can't tell with his crummy stories, you can't ever identify people from them." She poured out most of the remainder of the flagon. "I only guessed it was Pat from what he'd told me about her once; when he was pissed of course." She joined him on the mattress and flicked through the manuscripts for the abortion. Her fingers left grease stains, but she just pulled a face. "Too bad," she said, "he'll just have to type those pages out again; or give up being anal about them." "I read that one," he said. "Did you read the gang bang one?" she asked; and when they'd read that, as well as he could with her interjections and with eating the last of the meal and drinking the wine, she ruffled through the sheets again to find the day his wife walked out. "And I don't blame her," she said.

He lay there, sated with duck and soup and caviar, his eyes

tired from reading in the poor light, his back burning from the sun. He felt tired now from having spent so long in the sun, in the open air. He rested his head against her breasts and she stroked his hair affectionately. She got up to go and open a tin of camembert that she'd left warming in the oven. She opened a bottle of wine because they had finished the last of the flagon.

He turned on his back and lay looking at the iron roof and the beams supporting it. His head was muzzy with wine and the reading and the sun-swimming, waves breaking and stirring up the sand, muddying it again each time it settled, ceaselessly shifting the particles and blurring their gritty identity to a cloudy suspension. He nibbled at the cheese but he had eaten too much already, sipped at the wine with no great enthusiasm, no great need. He stood up for comfort, for change, to stretch his legs and clear his head. There was no room in which to pace around, so he leant over the typewriter table and leafed through the few pages of the story Joe had begun. He brought them over to the mattress and read through them and handed them to Margot, who spilt wine on them, a spreading red stain, when he bumped against her as he stood up again to get the last unfinished page. It ripped as he pulled it out of the typewriter because he had not released the carriage. There wasn't anyway enough of the story there to tell how it was going to develop or whether its features were successful; he started to read the notes for it on the table, but couldn't be bothered to finish them. Between them they completed the rape of the stories.

He lay down on the mattress again, looking dully at the roof and yawning.

"I'll come back to town with you," she said. "I don't like staying here alone." And she shuffled the stories roughly together and stacked the plates on the oven. The cork for the wine had got lost so they left it uncorked as they didn't feel like finishing it. The camembert was thrown outside for the possums.

They didn't have much to say on the drive back. There was nothing to see except the rain that obscured even the stars. He was so tired from the sea air, the sunburn, the wine, the reading, that it was a strain enough to keep his eyes on the road.

He dropped her off in town at a friend of hers and refused coffee. When he got back to his own place, he went straight to bed and flaked.

PETER CAREY

CONVERSATIONS WITH UNICORNS

1.

The unicorns do not understand.

We have had long conversations but it is difficult for them. They insist that I have come to collect the body of one of their number, but at the same time they point out that there is no body, that it was collected by another man before I arrived. They continue to insist on these points, laughing that I have come for something that is not there.

I have asked them why they think that I could only have come for one reason, and they have replied that this is the way it has always been; that the men come, like vultures, when there has been a death, to take care of the body.

I have suggested to them that men are cruel, but they have denied this, saying that men perform their God-given tasks efficiently. The men, they say, cannot be held responsible for the death of unicorns.

I mention guns. But they have no knowledge of guns, or, it turns out, of weapons of any sort. So I describe for them the deep trench that runs across the top of the ridge. I describe the parking lot behind the trench and the cars that arrive, filled with men and guns. They have no idea of the nature of cars or of their purpose — this is a red herring and I do not answer their questions about the nature of cars. I explain instead that the head of a unicorn is greatly prized by men who pay three thousand pounds for the privilege of shooting one. I explain how the men climb into the trench and wait for the unicorns to run across the moor.

When I return to the subject of guns the unicorns laugh, tossing their heads high and falling about the cave. And their leader, Moorav, smilingly warns me against blasphemy, saying that only God has the power to take life.

He tells me then how in the early days the unicorns lived forever, being revered by both men and animals, and having no natural enemies. He says, however, that this was in pagan times, before God came into the world. God, he informs me, bestowed upon the unicorns (and I use his exact words) "the gift of death".

There is an old tale, he relates, which tells how the unicorns were brought across the water from a hot and strange land to this moor which is now their home. It was here that God gave them his promise regarding death and here, also, that He decreed that the males should live together in the caves on the North Knoll and the females in the caves on the South Knoll. These laws are still strictly observed to this day.

I ask if perhaps the God in the story had the appearance

of a man. And Moorav replies that he does not think so, and that God, should he have any appearance at all, would be most likely to have the appearance of a unicorn, although he was no expert in these matters, and thought it better I ask one of the priests for confirmation of this.

I point out that it is only in the stretch between the males' cave and the females' cave — some two miles of open moorland — that the unicorns are killed, and Moorav says this is only natural, because they go nowhere else. He doesn't think it surprising that unicorns should never die in their caves — this, after all, has always been the case.

The unicorns are beginning to appear stupid to me, but this only increases my desire to protect them from the wealthy industrialists who come to hunt them.

I insist that they should guard themselves against the men who come to kill them, pointing out that God does not fire guns. They become more serious with this point, and I think perhaps I have made some progress. Moorav leaves the circle and goes to confer with others deeper in the cave.

To those remaining with me I say that if there is a God he certainly doesn't use a gun. I begin to explain the nature of the gun, its mechanism. I take as my model the Lee Enfield .303 with which I have had some little experience. I draw it in the dust of the cave floor. I explain the nature of men's wars and allude to weapons more complex and more cruel than the one I have outlined to them. I give them details of man's cruelties to man and to animals. I give, as examples, the slaughter of seals, the systematic murder of sheep and cattle, the subjection of horses, the killing of lions, the establishment of zoos and circuses.

Most of these animals, however, are unknown to them, although the lion is described in one of their legends.

I ask them what they eat. Mistaking this for a request, they bring me a meal: wild honey, brown bread, and milk. I ask them if they eat meat. They do not understand this. I explain that meat is the flesh of animals. This also is taken for a request (although I stated, explicitly, that this was not the case), and they become troubled, talking to each other in whispers.

I continue my dissertation on the crimes of men but am interrupted by Moorav who has returned with two of his fellows. He begs me to stop my talk. I reply that I am only concerned for their safety. He introduces his two friends, one of whom is a priest, wise in the ways and laws of God. The priest is old and has a white beard, something I have not observed in the others. I explain again, for his benefit, the nature of man, his need to kill other creatures, his consumption of their flesh.

At this point I find myself pinned on two sides by young unicorns, their huge flanks almost crushing my rib cage.

The priest is saying something about blasphemy.

I say, I have only come here to save you from death. I did not come to discuss theology, only facts. I ask them if the death of a unicorn is not always accompanied by a loud bang.

The priest says that this is so, but that there are also many bangs which do not signal a death.

I revert once more to a discussion of guns, ammunition, ballistics.

The priest asks me how it is that the unicorns have never seen these instruments. I describe, once more, the deep trench that runs across the top of the ridge, and explain, again, that the men can kill from far away. I describe the way in which the unicorn's head is removed and how it is mounted on the walls of the homes of rich men. I am becoming angry. They continue to whisper among themselves, not wishing to listen. Their accents, at first pleasant, seem to have become more rustic and so more stupid.

They also, it would appear, have become disenchanted with me. My clothes are ripped from behind. They force me, somehow, to a kneeling position and make me run on all fours, coming at me from all angles with their horns. They are calling me a blasphemer. There are tears in my eyes, but not caused by pain. A large unicorn sits suddenly on me, pushing my face into the dirt. My ribs have surely broken.

There is a searing pain in my side and a dull blow to my head. That is all I can remember on that occasion.

2.

The hunters found me on the moor and, unaware of my missionary activities, treated me kindly, taking me to a nearby hospital where I was well looked after.

Upon my release, my right leg in plaster and my ribs securely taped, I returned to the moor, taking with me a rifle I had purchased. I would demonstrate to the unicorns the nature of the gun, and, with luck, arrange for them to make an exodus from the area to some more remote part of the moor where they might never be found.

I bore them no ill-will for the attack. It was the product of ignorance and I could expect no more.

3.

Moorav was surprised to see me. However neither he nor his followers were unkind to me. They fed me well and the priest came over and ate bread beside me, asking if I had recovered. He referred to my behaviour as "your trouble" and asked me if I was better.

I said I had brought an instrument that would prove me either right or wrong. The priest smiled and said he hoped I wasn't about to start all over again. I indicated the gun and gave it its name. He looked at it and asked some questions which I answered simply enough. They related more to the materials of manufacture than to the function.

After the meal I persuaded them to come with me to the door of the cave. Moorav was nervous, but I was insistent. With the unicorns standing in a semi-circle behind me I raised the gun to my shoulder and fired across the moor.

Strangely, they were not at all impressed. The bang, they said, was in no way like the bang of death, and for proof they pointed out that no one had, in fact, died. And they began, once more, to laugh at me. I, for my part, became angry and desperate that I should prove my point.

Eventually Moorav stepped forward and suggested that we should only settle the matter if I pointed the weapon at him. I said no, for it would kill him. He laughed once more and said I was frightened of failing. (I had noticed, on this second visit, that they treated me as a mad man, perhaps having decided that I was ignorant but not dangerous. The charge of blasphemy was not raised again.)

Sadly, I asked Moorav if he was prepared to die for the sake of his people.

He said, it was only the unicorns in pagan times who did not die, I am not frightened of dying.

I engaged in no calculations for I knew that, should I do so, I would never prove my point. I raised the rifle and pointed it at his head. For an instant I hesitated, but then, with the unicorns behind me still laughing, I pulled the trigger. Moorav moaned and staggered. Blood rushed from the wound in his head and he sank slowly to the ground, his eyes rolling.

There was silence behind me. No one spoke.

4.

I myself buried Moorav in a shallow grave. It was a slow process as the unicorns possess no digging tools, and they still expected that a man would come to remove Moorav, a man other than myself.

5.

The cave has been quiet all day. Unicorns lie in groups but do not talk. Finally the priest approaches me and indicates that he wishes a word. He says I have done his people a grave disservice, that I had removed the gift of death from them. He says that his people will now surely move to another part of the moor, as I had wished. There will be a return to the old times and no one will die. The unicorns, without gods or enemies, will slowly sink into deep despair and spend their hours in search of sleep, where, perhaps, they will dream of dying. They will forget, eventually, that dying was ever possible.

The priest now reveals that he has attempted to persuade the unicorns to remain where they are, but they are frightened and, should he put his authority to the test, they would not obey him. He asks me only one thing, that I should use my instrument on him. He would regard it as a great favour.

I load the rifle, sadly. Inside the cave the unicorns lie quietly, unaware that they will live forever.

MURRAY BAIL

PORTRAIT OF ELECTRICITY

There were three guides. One did all the talking, the others nodded in agreement. They wore plain maroon jackets. The tall one with short hair had extraordinary blue eyes, but that is probably irrelevant. We were given special shoes to wear, like cotton slippers, and the older women were giggling — it was like dressing up. Inside, it was a museum like any other. The rooms strangely impersonal, exhibits arranged in cabinets against the wall, special objects located towards the centre.

We crowded around the guide.

"Before we proceed, I must ask you to refrain from smoking. What you see here are his possessions, and you will not find a single, solitary ashtray. He was living proof, you might say, against the anthropological argument that tobacco is an instinct fundamental to Man. Some people" — here, a note of disapproval altered his voice — "out of malice, or to test him, would give him expensive ashtrays as gifts. We have a small room full of them."

"Goodness!"

"The other thing, of course, is that smoke has a corrosive effect on permanent exhibits. This is well-known."

"Like the cave-paintings in Lascaux, France."

"Exactly. Now —"

"What about drink?" a man asked, interrupting.

"He took the occasional small glass, in private. Now" — turning to the first exhibit — "here we have his chair. This he sat on during his last twenty-five years, received visitors in it, and so on. Note the flattened contour of the seat. Caused by his body weight."

The chair was immediately surrounded. Last year, the museum attracted 142,870 visitors from all corners — tourists, family people, and even businessmen. There were two New Zealanders down the front wearing nylon haversacks. They had the best positions.

The chair, a soft brown one, had ordinary curved sides, and a blurred stain where his head must have been. Although it was encased completely in glass they'd put a piece of rope across the arms as double protection, like a man who wears a belt as well as suspenders. It was easy to imagine him sitting there, hunched slightly forward, his body weight exerting pressure downwards.

Someone asked, "Was he such a heavy man?"

"I can tell you," the guide replied. "The pictures you've seen tend to suggest a large man. Last recorded, his weight was actually 113 lbs (51 kilos). He had an abhorrence of figures, by the way — as you probably know. Preferred pronouncements, slogans, instructions, counter-proposals, manifestos, modifications to previous judgments. That sort of thing."

"I haven't seen any photographs," said a number of people, fairly loudly.

The guide who had moved off waited patiently at the next exhibit. Some Americans and others were quickly taking photographs of the empty chair. They rejoined, wearing that peculiar breathless expression of photographers, as our guide was reminiscing.

"I remember the day we met. He was speaking and looked at me. I listened. It was as though guns were thundering ... he had that effect. My experience of his magnetism, but purely personal. Then he died at seventy, almost seventy-one. I remember the day as if it were yesterday."

An austere Englishman murmured, "Three score and ten ..."

"To some of us," the guide went on, "it seemed impossible that he would die. His sheer presence was something ..."

His voice (or his memory) trailed off.

Everyone waited, then followed his hand as it tapped the top of the cabinet.

Horizontal, neatly labelled, was a piece of blue carpet, raised to waist level where it could be studied closely.

"This was taken from under his desk," the guide explained. "He had the habit of clearing his throat, and at the same time, shuffling his feet. Those worn patches you see were made by his shoes — size eights. In effect, he has *scratched evidence of his existence on earth*, materially speaking, although to us onlookers now, we can conjure up all kinds of thoughts. What was he thinking as his feet shifted and scraped? Was he frowning?"

Having asked these questions the guide himself peered at the carpet.

"We were anxious to include one of his shoes, but could only obtain the sock you see on the left. Black. For all his boldness he was basically conservative."

Our surprise must have shown, for he smiled.

"Conservative, yes, in dress."

The worn carpet was strangely compelling. Then the sock. It was dirty and needed mending.

We moved on to another room, following the guides. With each step we seemed to draw closer to him, acquiring greater knowledge, like a fan spreading outwards.

And there in the next room stood a tall empty rectangle, of wood, painted cream. It too was roped off so nobody could "use" it.

"Gallows?" a man said, aloud.

In every pack there's a joker. This one was middle-aged

with a rectangular face, holding a girlfriend in her twenties. She was the one who laughed.

The guide cleared his throat.

"This is important. If you could look at this. His *body* travelled through what you see before you, sometimes several times a day. If he paused in this doorway, as I'm sure he did, his shape would have been framed: and since no full-length portrait exists, this is the nearest we have. All that is required," he said, staring at the joker, "is a little imagination."

He stepped back and the doorway was quickly surrounded. Women put on the expression they use when choosing wallpaper. One of them touched the guide's sleeve. "The photographs. Where can we see his photograph?"

"Ah, the postcard counter had some, but I think they've sold out."

"Oh, that's too bad."

"They've all sold out?"

Then the Englishman spoke up. Like several others, he was taking notes.

"How tall was he?"

The guide knew exactly.

"Neatly palindromic! 1.81 metres. If you prefer it, 5 foot 10. He had — let's see — a foot to spare in the doorway.

Nevertheless, he instinctively stooped. This gave the impression, to some, that he was a man of *humility*."

Everyone laughed. How could anyone think such a thing?

Smiling, the guide said, "Let me ask you a question. Is humour more important than history?"

Now obviously this was directed at the joker. A murmur spread as the question was repeated. The Englishman tapped his nose with a silver propelling pencil. Humour more important than history? One of the young ones, a student wearing sandshoes, replied by asking a question:

"Did he laugh? Was he that sort of type?"

"Yes," a woman added; she had hairs above her lip. "Was he *happy*?"

The student turned to her.

"You're confusing the issue. I said, Did he laugh — not whether he was happy or not."

"I'm sorry! I don't see the difference."

She turned to the rest of us. I thought she was going to cry.

The guide smiled at the floor.

"Happiness," he said, "is notoriously difficult to describe."

People began nodding.

"The most rudimentary textbook tells us it takes seventeen facial muscles to laugh, yet only three to frown. So! His most obvious quality was not so much happiness *per se*, but the ability to attract loyalty. People looked up to him. He became an inspiration ... a comparison. Would that occur if he was patently happy? I think that is the question we should be asking."

Mmmmm.

Lips were pursed. Most, I think, took the point. No one added to it; and the guide moved slightly away to the side wall.

A woman whispered to her husband, "Arnold, my legs are sore."

"Not yet. Listen to what the man is saying."

The guide was pointing at marks on the wall.

"A similar exhibit to the doorway. He came here one morning and happened to sit down. We think he was trying to remember something. Anyway, it was right here. And this is the shape his shadow made."

The lines on the wall suddenly made sense, like a country on a map, unvisited, but quite familiar. Helpful arrows pointed to features which might otherwise have gone unnoticed: NOSE FROM SIDE, CHIN (WHILE NOT SPEAKING), ELBOW, SITE OF HANDS, PELVIS, etc.

"Apart from knowing that he sat right *here*," said the guide quietly, "it does provide some idea of his body *mass*, although what you see is one-dimensional. He grew from something small into this shape. All the graduations, his history of growth, are contained therein, but invisible. It doesn't quite show his thinness, but the stoop of his shoulders is evident."

So we were standing a yard or two from where he had sat! It produced powerful sensations: curiosity, silence. Then people could be heard trying to work out the position of the limbs, filling in the outline.

A woman complained: "Well, I like to know the colour of a man's eyes."

"Grey," someone told her.

"Weren't they blue? I thought I saw a picture once."

While they argued others went on with the guide, trailing as you do in museums, searching ahead for things not yet seen.

We entered a small room which had a simple coffee table, glass-topped, placed in the centre. The guides exchanged smiles as we crowded around, trying to work this one out. A coffee table. Was that all? The student noticed a little arrow on the glass. It encouraged discussion, speculation. The young man was quite eager now: "I think I see something else too."

Then the guide stepped in.

"Very good. We almost missed this one ourselves. I am referring, of course, to the fingernail trapped under the glass. He must have been trimming, and it snicked out, to lodge down between the sides."

A woman pulled a face.

"Is that worth preserving?"

"It's part of him," the guide reminded her.

Clearly, some of the womenfolk thought it pointless.

"A small example," the guide argued, "of the growth of his extremities."

If only the fingernail was easier to see; I think perhaps that was the trouble. It could then be examined closely and carefully. A raised platform and special lighting would do the trick.

"So much is unknown about great men," said the guide, moving towards a showcase opposite, "that every scrap of evidence plays its part … piecing together the whole."

Here, he showed us a cup and plate, still dirty, mounted on velvet.

The joker elbowed his girlfriend: "The Last Supper."

The guide didn't seem to hear.

"Undoubtedly, the plate is the most important. Traces of his last meal are visible: lamb chops, mashed potatoes, carrot with peas. On the edge there you can see traces of ketchup."

Too many people were trying to see. Flashlights began sparking. Those New Zealanders had the best positions again. There was some ill-natured shoving.

"Some of you come around near me," the guide demanded, before continuing. The other guides pushed the timid ones inwards.

"You perhaps know about his appetite. It was so healthy it made certain people upset. Somehow they assumed all famous men would have perfect table manners! But he sat down to eat, nothing else, and to get it over with as soon as possible."

"I had no idea!" declared a lady; and she spoke for others.

"Surely," said the New Zealanders, both turning, "it's a sign of honesty."

The joker laughed.

The guides nodded however.

"If ever a man deserved food it was he. Who was it said: we must eat in order to think?"

"I know!" shouted the student. Heads turned in his direction. He pulled faces and went on clicking his fingers.

"God, now I've forgotten ..."

The cup and plate put us in a subdued, reflective mood. It forced us to see him from an ordinary unexpected angle: bent, inserting food into his mouth. Quite opposite to the established picture. Yet, instead of reducing our interest it seemed to bring him closer.

A few yards away a much smaller cabinet.

"I think this one can be passed over quickly," the guide said, scratching his neck. "We are still in the throes of deciphering it. One of his habits was to slip out unnoticed and mingle with ordinary people. He liked to keep in touch. This is a bus ticket he used one afternoon. One of us found it, still crumpled. You will appreciate that to keep it in its original state — screwed into a ball by one of his hands — means the number cannot be read. His destination on that day remains unknown. But that's our problem. And we're working on it. Now, if you could step along here ..."

The woman with aching legs held him by the sleeve. He turned, frowning. "Bob, show this lady to the toilets."

The rest including her husband went on; but two or three, led by the young man, crawled underneath the cabinet, squinting up at the bus ticket, perhaps hoping for the edge of a number, or something not noticed by the museum staff. They returned dusting themselves, wearing thoughtful expressions.

By then our group found itself divided by a strange barricade. It jutted out from a wall, V-shaped. Thus it ingeniously prevented each onlooker "using" the exhibit — a mirror fixed fairly high on the wall. Naturally people tried. A woman (with rubbery lips) had one hand poised for automatic hair-adjustment; and unable to stop the process took out a hand-mirror.

Our guide waited for quiet. I noticed he perspired slightly.

"His mirror: its importance must be apparent to everyone.

For at least twelve years" — he paused to let it sink in — "it registered his image several times a day. What is perhaps important: it has been established he was the last person to use it. His face, which was drawing to a close, was the last to be registered. And," he added, bowing his head, "we intend to keep it that way."

Nobody spoke.

An old member of the group, but wearing a floral shirt, said, "He used it for shaving, for instance."

The guide nodded.

"Odd thing was, you all know what he looks like — the bushy hair sticking out — [I think he said bushy hair sticking out] — well, he found as he grew older he had to shave *more.* I say odd, because that's against the physiological trend."

The floral shirt nodded.

"I only use the razor every two days now." He turned to us. "It's not a nice feeling, I can tell you."

"Three score and ten," murmured the Englishman again.

"Oh, don't let's bring any gloom into this."

Feet shuffled. We were strangers, but a vague unpleasantness spread.

"His shaving gear is in that cabinet there. But for some reason it doesn't attract as much interest as other exhibits."

So we missed that one and, after seeing his pillow and a photograph of the sky taken from his window, assembled around what looked like a stamp-dealer's cabinet. Out of the corner of my eye I noticed the guides shepherding back a middle-aged couple; they must have wandered off.

Ours gave a sudden smile.

"Who here takes an interest in graphology?"

A man who hadn't spoken before, shrugged, "We all do. It's extremely difficult to avoid."

The guide laughed. He was one of those men who say "*touché*".

Four specimens of handwriting were laid out in rows: character was bound to be revealed. The pushing and shoving increased as everybody tried to see, some using their elbows; but the lucky ones down the front suddenly lifted their heads.

"This is no damned good. It's nothing."

I think many of us felt disappointed then.

"It's upside down."

"Yes, yes," conceded our guide, "these sheets were taken from his desk. He had one of those blotters with leather corners."

"What's the point then?"

"It's one stage removed," admitted our guide. "But! Why should you expect everything to be clearly revealed? Let us admit it: he was not easy to understand. We were with him! We know! He could be quite nasty sometimes. Vain. Often moody. Some days childish almost. But a genius. A man of his calibre cannot be 'read' head-on. As it is, you are privileged to be standing as close as you are now."

"But —"

"Excuse me, the blotter denotes his former presence, the weight of his body. His elbow must have rested on the edges. He used a blotter because he was born in the nineteen-tens. His thoughts were 'dried' by the blotter. So far as his actual hand is concerned it was small with long descendencies. The signature was rapid though, with appropriate flourishes." He smiled again. People were nodding. "After signing a letter he'd sit back and say, 'There now!' "

"I wrote to him once," said a man sadly. "He never answered."

"Ah, there were many demands on his time. And you could have been a crack-pot. All sorts wrote to him with strange requests, heart-rending ones even. You can imagine. He had to be ruthless."

And so people looked again; and it wasn't long before they were pointing and exclaiming, identifying the occasional word. The guide finally had to clap his hands, and quite loudly a second time, although not in an annoyed way, before anyone moved; and then a man and his wife remained, intent on reading the "hand-writing".

We saw a smooth piece of yellow soap (thought to be

his), tweezers for removing unwanted hairs, and the old belt that held up his trousers for thirteen years. We saw his shirt size (15), hot water bottle, the tennis shade he used when reading. Some of us were tired. Naturally. How far had we walked? Then across a room we saw a wall covered in what appeared to be advertisement posters.

These were tradesmen's calendars, twenty or thirty years arranged chronologically, the days crossed off with various pens and pencils, a pretty quilted effect. It illustrated the span of his life, the abruptness of death.

Words were unnecessary.

Several made sad, clicking sounds with their tongues.

"He must have had," said someone admiringly, "a strictly methodical mind to mark his days like that. I'm surprised."

This brought a simple answer.

"It's out of fashion these days," a man said. "People tend to use mechanical self-advancing calendars."

The group nodded. There was wisdom in that.

Then I think it was the Englishman spoke.

"One knows he was methodical, even fastidious. There are those stories too about his tightness with money. It's all connected. But what was he really like? One only knows *about* him."

At this the guide became angry.

"You say he was fastidious. Alright. But I would have

thought the way to study a man is not by trivia and gossip, but by his influence. This museum — created with some difficulty, I might add — concentrates on showing the *force* of his existence. He had weaknesses, of course. Great men are invariably selfish, intolerant. He disliked drunks, advertising, talk of the weather, women's perfumes, cigarette ash, indecision, coathangers and fools."

He waited as some of us found scraps of paper, the backs of envelopes, to take this down.

"He was uncomfortable with the opposite sex. He disliked oranges, and anyone touching him. Never married. Towards the end of his life he'd smile at the heads of small children. His pyjamas were striped flannel. He was always hungry, although he never exceeded 113 lbs. He was suspicious of photography, but later grew to respect it. Any questions? No. Then we'll carry on."

But there was a general reluctance to move, so absorbed were we in the list he'd given us, adding it to what we already knew. A clearer picture was beginning to emerge, and with it, a kind of spreading elation. We felt we were standing close to him, on the very edge of important, intimate knowledge. To move would break the flow. The guides however began clapping and pushing, whistling like drovers, and so we became confused. One of our number shouted, "Quit this shoving. We're moving, we're moving."

So we entered, or were herded into, the adjoining room, probably the last, for we could hear the turnstiles clicking behind a wall. Our bad-temper could have also been due to museum-fatigue. It had taken a steady toll. Some stood one-legged like African birds, linoleum tiles on concrete not exactly helping.

The guide was all smiles. He must have noticed our annoyance. He pointed to the now-typical glass cabinet.

Almost immediately those in front drew back, the women especially: they could not disguise their disgust. All I could see was a shallow metal tray.

The guide cleared his throat.

"Not everyone's cup of tea, this one. I should explain: we were in two minds whether to include it or not. But to be squeamish would be to miss the point. Bodily functions are at once both fundamental and intensely personal. Remember too the banal fact that nothing succeeds in levelling a man than the sight, or the concept of, his ordure."

"You mean 'shit'," said a figure down the front, one of the New Zealanders. Turning to us, he grinned. "There's a turd on the tray here."

"Dejecta. Coprological data," corrected the guide.

I wondered how they'd got it.

The joker put a handkerchief up to his nose.

"*Please*," said a woman with a pained expression. "You're not funny."

The guide quickly went on. "Interesting to realise the obvious: that this was inside him, and rejected by him. Let me say that again. This was *part* of him, part of — for want of a better word — his life-force. Hence its undoubted importance."

Hearing this, people returned to the cabinet, and some began making rapid sketches. This encouraged others. A flashbulb went off. Those towards the back soon found it difficult to glimpse a corner of the tray, let alone appraise the substance inside. The fascination may well have been primordial. That would explain the persistent but blank expressions people assumed as they pushed forward, anxious to improve their positions. Again, noticeably less interested were the womenfolk. One had elbowed her way out, saying, "The last thing I want to see is that."

She was ignored.

The guides stood together, hands in their pockets, surveying the scene. Ten or fifteen minutes passed before our man spoke up.

"Please," he said in a loud voice. "This way, please. Thankyou. One final item is here." Adding, over his shoulder, "A recent, major acquisition."

This is the small room by the exit door. A cabinet was lit

by a single spotlight. Under glass lay the handpiece (only) of a black telephone. Attached was a foot or so of dusty cord: ripped from a wall.

"And through these wires," the guide was saying, "through the electrical copper, springs, the black *bakelite* you see, he spoke, propelled his thoughts."

The two guides were looking over our shoulders. They were breathing reverently.

We could see dandruff caked on the earpiece.

"His breath travelled along these wires, his personality travelled along these wires."

The words fell on the discarded telephone. The rest of the room lay in darkness. Someone coughed. "Any questions?" asked the guide.

Then a woman asked, "What was his voice like?"

I think that was one of the things we all wanted to know.

The guide, clearing his throat, smiled. "Let me attempt an imitation."

Gerard Lee

PIECES FOR A GLASS PIANO

Pianos used to be quite popular in the home. By manipulation of the piano machinery (red and green felts, nifty hammers, wooden levers, wires and brass pedals) one could produce music. During the early sixties this was overlooked and pianos suffered.

Elderly women enjoyed the traditional and familiar sound of the piano. You can win their hearts by playing the old tunes. They might sing along. You can become popular by playing for them, and make their lives happier for a few moments.

It's possible to learn a tune a day if you don't need to pass exams. A brick room is ideal for the inhibited beginner.

In 1968, pianos were cheap. Their price has steadily increased over the years making the instrument a good investment as well as a dignified piece of furniture.

Pianos were the first machines to be mass produced. Elderly ladies probably don't know that.

A Concise History of the Pianoforte:

The sketchbooks of Da Vinci show that white birds first imagined pianos. Elsewhere on the same parchment a note, "apples are the essence of silence", and, at the bottom, a scratching in black ink concerning the uses of apple juice. Rumour has it that Da Vinci built a huge wooden apple and fitted it with a keyboard.

For centuries, folk had confused smooth stream stones and creamy milk with a faint notion of harpsichord, but once Da Vinci's discoveries were accepted throughout the halls of Europe, progress began toward a clearer foundation of harpsichord and this was to lead on to pianoforte. But even then, the decadent French courts related the piano's ancestors to rich multi-tiered cakes, to garish gold-leafed trimmings, to lace and snuff boxes. However, the notion of piano survived.

Moonlight passed across the keys.

Our own century has seen many variations of the piano:

(a) The white star-spangled pianos of vaudeville quick-buck shows, packed with tinsel to go on the road, their tongues hanging out like brash alcoholic jokes

(b) The blues piano shining like a light (containing ivory and white birds) in a ghetto of black writhing and sad bodies

(c) The honky tonk, danced on by a wailing siren in fishnet stockings

(d) The baby grand at the Cream Bun Bistro that cops a gobful of bra and garter every night. And loves it

(e) The piano on whose wood sleazy women singers roll voluptuous curves of flesh

(f) The eisteddfod piano backing a choir of prepared-carnation children

(g) The padded grand that's insinuated into the Martini Bar, playing a semi-classical Musak

(h) The Uncle Sam piano sweating out a Dixieland rhythm

(i) The pianos of the sixties which remained silent under the axes of guitar-crazed youths breaking with tradition

(j) The piano in which Yoko Ono (wrapped in a hessian bag) did her thing

(k) That surrealist piece, the baby grand, stuffed with a mutilated donkey

(l) The Beale, which they say is the FJ, the Holden of pianos

Rules for Piano Keepers:

1. Always sit at the piano with a straight back, making sure the hands are washed and manicured. (Strong but tender fingers are required.)
2. Reserve the piano top for special photographs (weddings, etc.), never vases of flowers.
3. Provide the piano with the correct stool, it gives the piece a clean finish.
4. Mice which eat the intricate felt pieces inside the piano

should be treated kindly. Entice them out with a portion of bread dipped in vanilla essence.

5. Never take off all the wooden panels at once.
6. Do not open the top of the piano more than once or twice per year, or something will happen.
7. Small wooden boxes of child things, hidden inside the piano, enhance its magic.
8. Elegant curtains hanging near a piano add to its stillness.
9. Illuminate with candlelight or firelight in the evenings, or by the dusky light of the late afternoons. Never open the piano in the mornings except on rare occasions.
10. Never take a piano to a funeral, particularly as a coffin.
11. Dilapidated pianos, wrapped in green felt, should be carried by hand into the forest, there becoming homes for mushrooms and luminous fungi.

Rules for Glass Piano Keepers:

12. Peel off skin immediately after delivery.
13. Remove all the apples carefully, gently picking them off the finer glass strings.
14. Perspex piano stools tend to scratch.
15. Glass pianos have very sensitive felts. Do not confuse glass pianos with hospitals, the equipment used in laboratories and old people's homes, or make any other

pharmaceutical connection as it may seriously injure the felts.

16. For best performance, glass pianos should be situated in spacious rooms with high arched windows showing only the sky.
17. Sit at the piano after dark and under bluish light.
18. If the moon should suddenly appear at the windows, do not turn to look at it directly.
19. Never use a glass piano as a means of frivolous entertainment. Or something will happen.

Practise This Easy Piece:

A bag of silent apples is hidden among the roots of a large tree. A nearby stone looks like a moss-covered planet. In fact, there is a planet, one million times the size of the stone, wandering in a distant galaxy. Everything about the stone and the planet are exactly the same — except for size.

A shaft of glass limelight breaking through the treetops catches the stone and illuminates a pianist, sitting magnificently at a glass grand. The piano machinery is made from insect limbs. The strings, distilled from apple juice, move out of the piano and merge with the burning racing sap streaming through a tall tree. The pianist is contemplating the symphony of a distant mossy planet. He knows a bag of apples has been hidden in a forest there and his fingers now play the silence of those apples.

Trevor Shearston

COWRIES

He was in the Melanesian section of the museum in Sydney, sitting in a straightbacked chair beside a display case of lime spatulae and body decorations from the outer islands. There were two exquisite shell bracelets I wanted to see again. I nodded to him and bent over the glass.

"You like shells?"

I resented the interruption. I think I just grunted and looked back into the case. He was silent for a moment but I could feel him watching me. Then he cleared his throat.

"You ever seen any like these?"

I thought he was referring to the shells in the case. I replied "yes" without looking up.

"No, not them ones. These."

I turned my head and saw that he was holding a necklace out away from his shirt collar with his thumb. It was evidently quite long for it hung loose from his thumb and looped back into a fuzz of ginger hair at his throat. I took a step closer and examined the necklace with curiosity, then disbelief. It was a string of small black cowries speckled yellow and lipped crimson. My astonishment must have been obvious for he smiled grimly.

"You know something about cowries then," he said.

"Yes. I collected over thirty of the specimens in this museum."

"But you never collected any like these, did you."

I shook my head.

"Where did you get that?"

"I was eighteen years on Mitan Island."

"Are the cowries from there?"

He shrugged.

"Who knows? If they are I don't think you would find them."

I straightened up and studied him. He was about my age or a bit younger, in a suit that was worn but clean, and a white shirt. My glance paused at his feet for he had on a pair of pink thongs. He noticed and lifted his foot and slapped the rubber.

"I've gone barefoot all my life. You got to wear something in a city and these things are all I can stand now."

I looked back at the necklace.

"I've heard of your island but I've never been there. Is it volcanic, or an atoll?"

"I don't know."

"Well, origin can usually be guessed from appearance. Are there sharp peaks rising from the sea, or is it flat and sandy?"

"I can't tell you."

"I'm sorry, I've misunderstood. I thought you said you lived there for eighteen years."

"Yes."

He must have seen the same thought flit across other faces for his voice when he spoke was patient and tired together.

"No, mister, I'm not gone in the head. I owned a plantation there eighteen years and I can't tell you much more about the place and the people except they existed. You say you haven't been there?"

"Never."

"Then you're no use to me, are you."

He smiled.

"You don't look as blank as most. I've had a few call the curator. I come here most days and wait. I don't speak to everyone. Just the odd bloke like yourself who looks like he might have poked around a few places. There's a story of course. I suppose I owe it to you if you're interested."

"You don't really expect me to say I'm not."

"Mister, I gave up expecting the obvious years ago."

He stood up.

"You don't mind if we walk around while I talk, do you? I'm sick of sitting."

So while we walked slowly past the masks and spears and old carved gods, he told me his story, and even as I write this I can feel what it awoke in me — an echo of the wedding guest:

"My name is Joe Cook. I was years in the islands before I went to Mitan, on boats first, then plantations. See the backs of my hands? That's what a life in the sun up there does for you. So, I should have known better than to cross the old bugger.

"I'd been assistant on a place on New Britain for five years, near Talasea if the name means anything to you. Our boat came in and the mate told me that Stroess's guts had finally packed up with the rum and that he was selling his place on Mitan and going south. He'd let it slip the last few years, and he had to get to a doctor quick, so he wasn't asking much. I had enough in the bank to get a loan so I went across and bought the place cash. Put the cheque in his hand the morning he left.

"They were good *kanakas* on Mitan. It's funny — I can remember things about them, even though I can't remember them. Same with the island itself.

"They wouldn't have any foreign labour on the island. By foreign I mean *kanakas* from other parts of the country, especially mainlanders. They'd worked wages for Stroess and he'd always done right by them, so they were happy enough to work for another white. There was no chief, but there was an old bloke who ran things. I once knew his name as well as I know my own. And his face. He was a sorcerer — you know, making things happen and fixing the others when they got crook.

"At Talasea I'd been living with a Gasmata woman, so I brought her with me. Lesi her name was — I can remember that — in fact I can remember her and Talasea and every other place I've ever been in clear as day except Mitan. The afternoon she arrived the old man told me if I wanted a woman it had to be one of theirs. It was that, or no labour. Well the answer was simple enough. There'd been no kids, so I gave Lesi two hundred and sent her back home. I did without a woman in the house for two years. Went into town when I wanted one. I heard Stroess gave them up altogether and settled for a bottle, but that wasn't me in those days. After two years I got tired of waiting for boats, so I told the old man I was ready for one of theirs. So he brought one. She was untouched when I got her. That's all I can remember about her. After three years we'd produced no kids. They always blame the woman. The old man took her away and brought her sister. The first one married another man. I have a feeling I should remember his name too. We used to go fishing a lot or something. Anyway, within a year they'd had a kid, a boy it was. I think. So it had to be me. The old man said if I wanted live seed he could cure me. I could see no beauty in being half a man so I said yes. He took me somewhere. Near the sea. He gave me a juice to drink. I went out like a light. When I woke up there was green leaves and muck all over my balls. I wasn't allowed to touch the woman for a week. He made sure of it. Every night he was in a tree near the house. A big brown eagle with a white head. I remember him as the eagle because I saw him again years later, on the morning I left.

"A year after that she had a boy. Then, two years after him, a girl. I think I was happy there with them for a long time.

"Then I got restless, like all the other times before. It was a long stretch that one. My longest. Eighteen years. But I wanted to come home, to my own kind. So I told them I was going finish. The old man said, all right, you can take the boy and leave the girl with the woman. The boy was eleven then, the girl nine. I said, no, I'll sign the plantation and everything on it over to the woman and the kids. It's theirs. I'm leaving with nothing but my money, my rifles, and the clothes I'm standing in. The old man wouldn't have it. He said, the man takes the boy to teach him to be a man. I said, you teach him, you know more about your ways than I do. You don't understand, he said. I want you to take him to your place, teach him to be like a white, then when he is grown and you no longer love him, send him back to us. When I heard that I made up my mind so that nothing could change it.

"The night before I left I called the old man in to give him the papers. He looked at my bag and then he looked at me. You haven't much cargo, he said. I haven't much I want to take, I said, only memories of you all, and the island. He nodded and said, I wasn't sure that you valued memories as we do. To us they are all a man really owns.

"In the morning they were on the beach, the whole village. I can't remember them, just that they were there. The workboat sent a skiff ashore for me. I said goodbye to the woman and the boy and girl and waded out to the skiff. The old man came with me. When I got in he turned me towards the open sea. Then he said, I have a parting gift for you. He placed the shells round my neck. As he did so he pulled my ears gently, then kissed me on each eye. Don't look back till you reach the ship, he said.

"I kept my eyes on the workboat until I'd boarded her. Then I looked back towards the beach. And it wasn't there. The whole island wasn't there. We hadn't even left the bay and I couldn't see the shore. Just a rolling mist. I shut my eyes and looked away to sea. It was still the same, and the channel in the reef. But when I looked back again to the island it was just mist, and already then I couldn't remember the faces of any of the people I had just embraced on the beach, or the words they had spoken, or the music of the song that had been following me in the skiff out over the water.

"I kept my eyes on the mist until we cleared the channel but it broke only once, high up where there was nothing but sky, and the big brown and white eagle came out and hung against the grey.

"I thought it would all come back to me in time — the island, and the faces and the language. But that was ten years ago now, and it never has. Sometimes, like a moment ago, I think I'm about to remember the old man clearly, just for an instant. But he beats me."

"You know the name of the island and where it is," I said. "Why don't you go back?"

He stopped walking and stepped in front of me.

"My money is gone. I'm on the pension. But suppose you gave me a thousand dollars tomorrow, and I went back. And one of the crew — the mate say — touched me on the arm and said, there's the island sir ... What if I looked and could see nothing but rolling mist with an eagle floating against it? What then?"

John Emery

PINE GAP

"All right," the clerk said. "Then what's your occupation?"

"Ship-wright."

He began to write it, then he looked up. Ted's face was blank.

"Ship-wright?"

"Yeah, you know, ship's carpenter."

"Are you having me on? Do you know where you are?"

"Port Augusta, isn't it? They told me to turn right at Port Pirie. They didn't say anything about the rough road, though."

"All right," the clerk said. "Very amusing. Do you really want some kind of a job?"

"We want our trade jobs."

"And if you can't get them, I suppose you'll apply for benefits?"

"That's right, isn't it?"

"You're in bloody Alice Springs, and it's a thousand miles to the nearest water. OK? Now, I can give you a job as a carpenter, if you want it. And if you don't want it, you can work as a labourer, and if that doesn't suit you, you can push off."

"Not much of a sense of humour," Ted said as they went out.

"Carpenters, eh?" Barry scratched his head. "Have we got the right tools?"

"All we need's a saw and a hammer. They'll put us on form-work for sure."

"Collins Radio Company?" Barry read his slip of paper. "What kind of show is that? Pine Gap? Where the hell's that?"

"Out of town, on a creek somewhere. Come on, let's have a game of pool."

COLLINS RADIO COMPANY. ALICE SPRINGS. AUSTRALIA. JOINT SPACE DEFENCE RESEARCH ESTABLISHMENT. PROJECT MATCH, USAF. THIS END UP.

"Holy fuck," said Ted. "What is it?"

It was a shack, built from broken up packing cases. It looked like a set from a Wild West movie. A couple of carpenters were putting the finishing touches on the walls.

"Good-day," said Barry. "We're looking for the foreman."

"He'll be along soon," said one of the carpenters. "He's just over licking the site manager's boots."

"Huh?" said Barry.

"We're the new chippies," Ted explained. "Hey, what's the shack for?"

"Ah, the bloody Septic Tanks. They want a special shack for visiting engineers. There wasn't one in the plans, so there wasn't any spare building material, so we had to make it out of crates."

"Those crates come from the States?" Ted asked.

"That's right. They don't use anything local … except the sheilas."

"Yeah? Those crates passed quarantine, then?"

"What do you mean?"

"Quarantine. Foreign vegetable matter has to be fumigated or destroyed before it lands on our shores."

"You're having me on?"

"No way, mate. Look, what do you want us to do? Form-work?"

"No, everyone's on form-work. Can you put up a ceiling?"

"Ahh … yeah. Yeah, why not?"

"Well, put the ceilings up in Fred's Place."

"Fred?"

"He's the supervisor, a Septic Tank. One room's started."

"Ted?"

"Uh huh."

"How the fuck do you build a ceiling?"

"Hang on, mate. There's one in this room. All we gotta do is copy it."

Then it was smoke-oh time. The site was on an area of spinifex between a low range of hills and a creek. Like all creeks, it had no water in it. A couple of miles past the creek was a saw-toothed mountain range. On the site were two air-conditioned caravans, a mess hut, and Fred's Place. Then there were the graders levelling for foundations, carpenters doing form-work, and steelies tying wire for the concrete. As yet, nothing had risen above ground level.

The queue wandered through the mess hut door. It filed past two urns. In one urn was a mixture of water and old tea-leaves. The other held mostly water. Everyone picked up a mug from the bench by the urns. They all looked closely at the mugs, searching for the special insignias they had engraved to claim ownership.

On the tables were jugs of powdered milk. The powder had not dissolved. On one bench a young man was asleep.

"Who's he?" Ted asked a steelie.

"That's Johnnie, the canteen manager. Don't disturb him, he's had a heavy night."

While they were sitting there, a steelie came in late. His pupils were pin-pricks and he had a dopey smile. He undid a Bex powder and poured it down his throat.

"This is a stop-work meeting," he said.

"Ahh, shit," someone muttered.

"They won't negotiate any more, and they won't pay travelling time both ways. We've got no option but to strike."

"Ahh, fuck that," said a carpenter.

"Watch it, mate." An old steelie leaned towards the carpenter.

"Come on," the delegate said. "You've got nothing to lose. They don't want to shut the job down. They don't want to sack you and have to fly another bunch up here. We've got legitimate grievances. We're only on award rates and everyone else in town gets over-award."

"Yeah, but everyone else is on casual rates. We're permanent. We get return air-fares paid when we've been here twelve months."

"Bullshit! You watch them put you off."

The foreman looked into the shed. "Time's up," he said.

"This is a stop-work meeting," the delegate said.

The foreman looked to the carpenter who had complained.

"Ahh, to hell with it," he said. "It's too hot out there. Let's have a stop-work."

They broke the strike in the following manner. They imported WOWIC huts from Adelaide, dragged them up on trucks, and then set them up. They suggested everyone now live on the site, thus eliminating the controversy over travelling time.

Some blokes went to live in the huts, mostly carpenters — who are always the first to go back. The carpenters then found there was no way they could get into town, because they had all been flown up and had no cars. So, they shifted back to town.

They then brought in a mess. It was a magnificent mess. It was air-conditioned. It had water-coolers. It had a place to wash your hands, and a mirror in which to inspect your face and check your singlet was tucked in. It had a menu longer than Menzies' Hotel's. Then they proposed a meeting at the mess, to discuss the strike.

We had been eating at Commonwealth Hostels. Every Sunday everyone came down with the gastric — sometimes from the pork, sometimes from the fish, sometimes from the steak, sometimes from the ice-cream. A dozen years later, Prince Charles ate there and the same thing happened to him, too.

They took us into the mess. They had a chef in a white hat. They had soup, crumbed cutlets, T-bone (real T-bone, not fucken buffalo), lamb chops, pork chops, sixteen vegetables, apple pie, ice-cream, cream, custard, real coffee. We all stared at it. We fell on it.

Afterwards, they proposed that we end the strike and continue eating at their mess. A carpenter took around the forms to sign back on.

We came back and the first thing we did was burn Fred's Place. The health inspector had checked up on the quarantine regulations.

The steelie who was the delegate got the sack. He applied at CES for another job and they told him to piss off out of town. The other members of the negotiating committee were promoted to leading-hands and given nothing to do. Then they were sacked.

Every now and again a plane-load of Septic Tanks would arrive. They were all (except Fred, who was built like a bull-frog, and Clyde, who was built like the Mafia) seven feet tall and wearing sneakers and short-sleeved white shirts. The first thing they would do was look at the waterbags. They'd scratch their heads and gently poke the bag. They'd watch it swing a moment. Then they'd unhook the spout and run some water into the mug. They'd drink it cautiously.

"Goddamn," they'd say. "Hey, have a goddamned taste. It's goddamned cold."

✧ ✧ ✧

"Hey, Johnnie!" Clyde yelled to the canteen manager who'd lost his job when the mess was brought in, and got onto the steel gang because he and the foreman like Johnny Cash. "Hey, Johnnie! Go get some goddamned gas for the goddamned welder!"

Johnnie found the oxy-welder and unhooked the gas cylinders, flagged down a passing truck, and went and exchanged them. He brought them back. Clyde stared at him.

"Got the gas, Clyde."

"I said goddamned gas for the goddamned welder! You goddamned little mother-fucker, what you got there?"

He pointed at the arc welder. It needed petrol. He looked at Johnnie a while longer then walked away, shaking his head.

"Goddamned Aussies. I used to think goddamned nigras was dumb."

Johnnie shrugged and went looking for his pal Bob, the randy Pom. He wanted to borrow a book from him.

Bob was hired as a labourer and had evolved a scheme where he wandered around the site pushing a wheelbarrow half-full of sand, with a shovel sticking out of it. He never did anything else, except read, and at smoke-oh urge the blokes on.

"Listen!" he'd say. "You're not going to let a bunch of Yanks tell you what to do, are you? You're not going to let them walk all over you. Now, you get back out there and you bludge! I don't want to see anyone working, OK? I don't want to see any pick-axes, any hammers, or nothing. I just want to see you all down the bottom of the six-foot trenches, or under the radome, OK? Now, you had a reasonable bludge in the first half, but you've got to go all out now, this is the Big One!"

Bob was fronting a waitress at the Oasis. The secret service was staying at the Oasis. It wore a Hawaiian shirt and black, lace-up shoes. It had a crew-cut. After it had talked to him, the manager button-holed Linda (the waitress).

"Listen, that bloke you're going with, Bob?"

"What about him?"

"He's no good. He's a communist."

"A what? What do you mean?"

"It's for real. He's a communist."

"Come on, Willy. Someone's getting at you."

"Look, I'll prove he's a communist."

"OK."

"He's intelligent, isn't he?"

"Yes."

"Well, there you are. What's he doing here? He's got a lot of books in his hut, hasn't he?"

"How do you know, Willy? Have you been in it?"

"Well, hasn't he?"

"Yes, I guess so."

"Well, there you are. He's not going to be here long. The secret service is watching him. When he's done his stuff, he's going to disappear into the desert, and a Russian sub will pick him up. There's one lying off Exmouth now, waiting for his signal."

"What's this job for, any rate?" Ted asked Fred.

"It's a goddamned job, my boy. A goddamned job. That's all it is. Don't you worry about it."

"Yeah, but what does 'Space Defence Research' mean?"

"It's just a name. They've got to have a name so the accountants back in Dallas can cost it. Don't you worry, son."

Fred chewed tobacco. He was about fifty and wrinkled up. He wore a ten gallon hat while all the other Septic Tanks wore sixty-four gallon hats. He offered Ted a chew. Ted declined.

"You know," he said, "I went for a flight out there." He indicated the saw-toothed mountains. "Goddamn it, it scared me. There's nothing out there. Nothing. I used to think Texas was empty, but … nothing." He looked at Ted. Ted nodded.

Bob turned in the job to go to Darwin. He bought a ticket on the bus. All the way up he was conscious of a man in a Hawaiian shirt and sunglasses, sitting across the aisle from him.

In Darwin he hung around a while on the beach. He kept his ear to the ground and finally got a berth on a trimaran that was going to Fiji.

An RAAF Hercules followed the trimaran all the way to the Solomons.

Clyde held the land-speed record. Fifteen minutes from the site to town. Johnnie, the ex-canteen manager, ex-steelie (after he'd incorrectly slung a load of roofing materials and it fell off the hook and onto the roof of the caravan where Clyde had, finally, got his hand up the girl in the office), was now on deliveries. He couldn't match Clyde; though they both had the same automatic Valiants.

He had an injury in the back the day he was chasing Clyde. Some labourer had shot himself with a Ram-set gun.

The water-truck had just been through. He lost it on a bend. The road was sunk below the level of the mulga. The car kept hitting the bank, bouncing back, sliding to the other side, bouncing back, and so on. The injury kept moaning: "Let me out. Let me out. I don't want to die. Let me out."

He got it back under control, came over the next hill, and found Clyde's Valiant upside down. Clyde was leaning on the door. His face was white and his cigar was out.

"Hit a mother-fucken rock," he said.

"That's the second car you've written off," Johnnie said. "Do you reckon they'll give you another?"

"What the fuck," said Clyde. "They're insured. Jesus, man, your car stinks!"

Johnnie sniffed. He looked in the mirror. The injury had pissed himself.

Barry got a letter from his best mate, saying his fiancee was having it off all over town. He got the next plane home.

Ted and Johnnie decided to stick together and go to Darwin. Ted got his ute overhauled. They stole a month's groceries, and headed off. The garage still has the bill.

Johnnie asked around Darwin for Bob and found he'd gone to Fiji.

All the carpenters were laid off after eleven months and three weeks on the job.

When all the construction work was finished, they got rid of everyone. They brought in their own computer operators. No Aussie was allowed near the place. As a public-relations exercise they ran a boat in the annual Henley-on-Todd regatta. By that time Ted was back at sea, experimenting with LSD on watch. Barry and his wife were into B & D. Bob couldn't get a visa for the US and stayed in Fiji. Johnnie went to Perth, tried out for a job, didn't like the accommodation, and returned to Adelaide.

A couple of years later he applied for a job in Canberra. He had all the qualifications, but they knocked him back. The job would have taken him close to Orroral Valley and Tidbinbilla Tracking Stations. He was a security risk.

NICHOLAS JOSE

BEER AND WINE

They were given to experiment in those days. If anything was learnt it was forgotten soon enough.

Jon picked Brett up from his parents' place by the beach. A new crowded Burger King stand defaced the poetic sea.

"Nuh. Stobie poles and hamburger joints are as beautiful as everything else," said Jon. "As ugly too."

Their chat was embarrassed as they drove towards the hills. In the few months since school they'd developed in rather separate directions. Jon disagreed with Brett's scathing remarks about the music on the radio. He steered the car exultantly along the hills highway, leaning hard against the door.

"Can we stop at a pub?" said Brett. "Get some beer?"

"Yeah, but wine?"

"You get wine. I want beer."

"We can't afford both."

But they wouldn't compromise. They stopped at the Crafers pub and Jon gave Brett his note reluctantly. While Brett was inside trying to act the legal age, Jon heard a song on the radio which made him glad. *It Don't Matter To Me*, not because of the lyrics particularly, though he agreed that nothing could matter enough to worry about; but just because. Brett returned with six cans in a carton under one arm and a flagon of red under the other.

The cottage they were to sleep in was a little place down a hill. Brett had the use of it for a few days. Inside there were all sorts of posters and artworks. Brett chose the armchair by the empty fireplace and set himself up with his beers and his tape-recorder around him.

"We can hear something really good now. Bessie Smith."

"Superb," said Jon.

Brett said you could trace the development through from her to Joplin.

"Yeah, she's really great." Jon had the flagon open between his legs. He sloshed the claret into a peanut butter glass. Red wine made him feel sensual even if he wasn't.

They had discussed, in fearfully detached terms, the heated curiosities of their schoolyears together, and did so out of habit tonight. The room was dim. Jon's flagon was emptying and Brett was getting drunk too. You could see him watching Jon, making sure his friend had more than he did. Brett started to talk about his admirers. "You know, a lot of people say I look like Mick Jagger."

Christ, thought Jon, admitting that a resemblance was conceivable. Brett had an aggressive, desirable way of holding himself. He was working, temporarily, as a brickie. But although the conversation had taken its customary sexual course, Jon wanted to tell Brett about his philosophy.

"It's a gas. Life is a gas. Really. That's what I think. Good and bad, ugly and beautiful, black and white. They really don't matter if you look from high enough."

Brett sneered at his friend's silliness. "You miss a lot if you think like that," he ventured. "What about love?"

"Love makes you happy. That's how you decide."

"Bullshit."

"It's up to you."

Brett began again with precision, first settling his hair back behind his ears to achieve his finest logicality. "If you're *sincere* in seeking to fulfil your emotions, then you *can* direct your morality that way."

Jon had broken a cork in half and was juggling the bits. "I think moral judgments are crap," he pronounced and emptied his glass.

Brett drank up too. "I quite agree. Conventional morality."

Jon was chewing half the cork. "Can we have something to eat?" he mumbled.

"What?"

"Toast. Vegemite."

"Okay." They went out to the kitchen, which showed the familiar signs, and sawed up a stale loaf haphazardly. While it was under the griller they both stood silent, respecting a sudden communion in the heart of the house.

Brett rushed the browned toast from the oven to the plate, cradling it in his hands, and Jon spread on butter and vegemite. They bit and smiled. A line of butter dribbled down Jon's chin.

Afterwards Jon went into the garden. Under the pines it was misty and shadowy. He walked through the damp grass into a grove of hydrangeas and pissed there. It was a gentle place.

Back inside they took up their seats again, opposite each other, and raised their drinks while the last of Bessie Smith played.

"Have you done anything with anyone?" asked Jon. He was curious about Brett's body.

"I nearly made it with Jane. You know the girl from the bus. She's only fifteen. Incredible for that age. She's coming back this weekend." He threw his hair back.

"Hope it goes well."

"I've also got hold of a book by Genet. *Our Lady of the Flowers*. It's banned. It's stunningly beautiful. Our Lady is a teenage boy and everyone wants to make love to him. Shall I read you a bit?"

Brett would have read all night, adoring his imaginings, but they were tired and, paradoxically, restless, wide awake.

Jon was kept from relaxing by a pulse of energy testing his blood. He lay back in his chair with his legs apart and looked at Brett reading. Each was anticipating a move.

"Do you think sex is mind or body?" asked Jon.

"I don't understand."

"I think true love, even with sex, is spiritual. For want of a better word. But sex can exist on its own. Pure physical delight."

It was a persuasion to fit the drunken mood. Brett ran his hand over his chest.

Jon said noncommittally, "I feel lustful."

"So do I. But if we did anything we'd be using each other."

"Can't you see it all doesn't matter? If you want to or not, I don't care." Jon spoke against the undercurrent he felt, hobbling across the ambiguities and hesitance of desire. He stood up suddenly, grabbing the flagon, and said, "I'm going to bed. See you tomorrow."

Brett packed up the tape-recorder disconsolately and stripped for bed. He was drunker than he'd realised but his drunkenness hadn't achieved anything. He stumbled through to the kitchen for a glass of water. The door of the room where Jon was sleeping was shut. He couldn't bear to make the decision so, half-oblivious, he fell against the door and pushed it open, slumping himself against the doorpost, framed against the light.

Jon was awake and looked at Brett's thin shoulders and hips, and the undeveloped muscles beneath the skin. He got up slowly and walked across. Brett stayed still obediently while Jon put a shepherding hand on him and brought him over to the bed. They lay on their backs, watching the ceiling, smoothing each other's bodies. Here was wonder. Then Brett pulled up the sheet to cover them and, rolling onto Jon, tried to relax and enjoy. At last they were romping happily in the different textures of their bodies.

It was when a climax was imminent that Brett exclaimed. "No! Christ! I'm sorry, but Jesus, we might as well masturbate. I've gotta go."

"It doesn't matter … does it?"

"But you understand?"

"Go by all means."

"You think I'm a bastard."

"Go if you're going. I really don't care. We might as well get some sleep."

Brett left Jon gazing out the window. The fields were pale blue, as if enchanted. He thought of Peter Pan never growing up.

In his own room Brett was pulling himself hard, the image

of his ideal love before him. He came and filled his navel hair with the spunk he'd worked up on Jon.

When Jon woke he didn't realise where he was. Brett called "Good morning" from the kitchen where he was cooking sausages and brought Jon a towel. The bathroom was concrete and reminded him of his grandparents' farm. Brett called out to him under the shower. "Do you want tea or coffee?"

"Tea. What are you having?"

"Coffee. I'll make you a tea-bag."

Jon was gazing out the window again as he dried himself. The grass was bright with dew and the morning was wonderful. God's in his heaven, he thought.

At breakfast Brett said, "I really apologise about last night."

"Don't worry."

They were tired and had to leave by eight. Jon put his overnight bag and the near-empty flagon in the back of the car. Brett locked the cottage. The sun already had the full warmth that comes at the beginning of a scorcher.

Jon drove Brett to his worksite and thanked him for having him. Brett said it had been good to see him and hoped he didn't mind …

But Jon had slammed the car door, turned the radio up and pushed down on the accelerator. He began to sing vigorously, until he noticed a fruity smell. The flagon had tipped over and the wine was running everywhere. But Jon didn't much care. The smell was faintly intoxicating and he kept on singing.

ANGELO LOUKAKIS

DANCING

"But it's a fuckin' wog dance, mate!"

"Yeah, so?"

"Who wants to go to a fuckin' wog dance?"

"Plenty of pussy there, Jimbo. That's why I wanna go."

"Yeah, that's what you think! You try to put it up 'em and their old man'll put it up you. How'd you like that? Funny ay, Nicko? Ay mate?"

"Yeah, funny."

In Petersham we're discussing the night. At my old man's Milk Bar things are on the boil. Old Spiro reckons he's gonna take us to the Greek Ball tonight. All of us. Even the old cheese. You can imagine what it's gonna be like. But never mind what I'm sayin' to Jimbo, I'm tryin' to get out of it.

I keep tellin' my old man I'm too old, it's kid stuff. And poofy. Anyway I'm not a Greek, I tell him.

"You are my son. I am a Greek. Therefore you are a Greek," he tells me.

"And you're all fuckin' philosophers too, you old bastard," I tell him. Under my breath.

My old lady's got the blue number on. *The* blue number.

She's got the earrings and the hair and the paint. She's a Christmas tree.

"I don't like Greek dancin', Ma!"

"It's beautiful, very beautiful," she tells me. "I danced the Sousta beautiful when I was young girl."

"What about modern stuff?"

"What modern stuff? Rubbish that's what."

"Disco, y'know, Travolta and Bee Gees and that. That's what I like."

"Disco is Greek word," she tells me.

"Ah Christ," I say and grab Jimbo.

We go out the front where it's cool.

"Jimbo, they think this is the village."

Jimbo's shakin' up a tin of Pepsi. The local Iti's are on the prowl in a black Fiat 850. Typical wog act. He's gonna give 'em a spray job next time around, he reckons.

"Is your father gonna wear his suit?"

"He sure is, mate. My mother's been sewin' it up all afternoon. I even saw him trimmin' his moustache this afternoon."

"Sounds like he's gonna do the full greaser trip."

"Yep."

"Are you still gonna go?"

"I got no choice."

It wouldn't be so bad goin' if we didn't have to go in the

flamin' Valiant. I can't stand the cushions and the pom poms in the back window. He's even got a dog there noddin' its head up and down. I ask him sometimes why he's got all that junk and he says, "What's wrong with it? I like it." You can't argue with him when he's defendin' the pom poms.

So I keep my head down on the way to Paddington Town Hall. That way I can't see the people calling us names as they drive past in Monaros and that.

Once a year we come to this bloody dump — it must have been an aircraft hangar once. Because the Kiloan Brotherhood puts on a do. And we're Kiloans, they keep tryin' to tell me. Me, I'm from the moon.

One look at the deal and I'm off for the loo. It's cooler there.

When I get there who should I meet up with but a couple of me mates from school. It's Bill and Con. Bill's real name is Vasilli and we're all in sixth form together so that we can go to uni and be doctors and lawyers. We'd be lucky to get enough marks between the three of us to pass one subject.

"Hello, boys," I say. "What's happenin'?"

"What d'you mean 'what's happenin'?' We're here aren't we?"

"Got any ideas?" I ask.

"Plenty. But they'd kill us if they caught us."

"Yeah?"

"Saw this beautiful chick. Doesn't look too Greek either, y'know?"

"She's for me," I say.

"That's what you think."

"Where is she?"

"She's hangin' around the Ladies with her mates, just like we're doin'."

"Let's go," I say.

So the three of us head for the Ladies loo to check out the scene. You never know your luck, Con reckons.

We cross the floor. There's tables and chairs all around the walls and the centre of the hall is for dancing.

The whole thing'd make you laugh if it wasn't so sad. There's this band of pensioners playin' fiddles and mandolins and bouzoukia and wailin' and screechin', and all the Kiloans are jumpin' around holdin' hands. And they call it dancin'. Meanwhile the sweat's pourin' off the lot of 'em.

As we're crossin' over my old man sees me before I can get away.

"Why you don't dance, *more*?" he says, like he's gonna kill me if I don't.

"I got a sore foot," I say. "Maybe later."

I manage to get away from him to join the others. They're

so hot to trot they've already cornered the chick with her mates. She's a beauty, no doubt about it.

Just as I get there they turn around and start walkin' towards me.

I can hear one of the chicks sayin', "And you can all get nicked". She sure didn't look as rough as she sounded.

"What did they say?" I ask Bill.

"Ah, stupid here put the hard word on 'em too early," he says, pointing at Con.

Con's hangin' his head as if he knows he's wrecked it.

"Doesn't matter," I say, "doesn't matter. They sound like real teasers to me."

"Greek chicks are all the same," says Con, tryin' to get back in the good books.

"What'll we do now?" asks Bill.

"Let's rack off for a while," I say.

"Where to?" asks Bill.

"I dunno ... pub maybe."

"There's a Milk Bar down the road," says Con. "Got machines and stuff."

"Ah, I don't know," I say.

"Come on. It's better than this dunny," says Bill.

So here we are. It seems like I can't escape these flamin' joints. Milk Bars forever, ay!!

Still, it's more fun than the Kiloan Ball at Paddington Town Hall.

"You want some music, Nicko?" Bill asks me.

"Yeah, gimme music."

"Got a coin?"

"Yeah, ya bludger."

He puts twenty cents into the juke box and presses the buttons. Pretty soon the music is blastin' out . . .

You make me feel like dancin' — gonna dance the night away!
You make me feel like dancin' — gonna dance the night away!

Olga Masters

A YOUNG MAN'S FANCY

He woke and saw the empty place in the bed and knew at once he should worry about it. He turned over away from the sight and thought through his half sleep what she might be doing.

After a while he could bear it no longer and got up and went to the back of the house. He dodged past chairs in the living room pulled to odd angles. There were toys on the floor, a cup half full of coffee near the leg of the television, a half-knitted garment near a pile of tangled wool.

In the kitchen he saw the toaster showing a line of scarlet and there was a smell of hot metal. He snapped the power off and let himself out of the house, standing in the bleak cold with the yard emerging from the morning fog equally bleak.

There was the clothes hoist and under it a hole dug in the clay. Nearby was a battered doll's pram and a cardboard carton on its side sheltering a few pieces of dolls' furniture. Everything looked colder and more neglected for its film of dew.

He felt eyes. He jumped and so did Mrs Lake next door, who had pulled aside a branch of a cassia bush on her side to look at him there shivering in his pyjamas. She dropped the branch, pretending to look into the shrub.

He wanted to say, "Have you seen my wife?" but couldn't bring himself to.

He heard her steps going back onto her porch. She stopped abruptly and into the silence called out: "Your wife's on the road there, Mr Benson."

He was as startled to hear her speak as to hear himself addressed that way. Hardly anyone called him Mister.

"Thank you," he said, his voice coming out in a croak, and went back inside. It was time for him to shower for work.

He couldn't see any clean shirts so he wore the one from yesterday, pushing his tie up under the collar hoping to disguise the dark line from his neck.

He heard some tinkling and knew his wife was in the kitchen.

The door of the little girls' bedroom was shut and he felt relief that they were still asleep. Should he waken and feed and dress them, he said to the growing fear in his eyes reflected in the mirror. He laid down the hairbrush and went and gently opened their door.

They were there, thank God! At first he thought the little one's cot was empty. But she was curled in a bottom corner with a large rag doll across her rump. He worried that the older one lying half on top of the bedclothes might be cold but he resisted the temptation to cover her and closed the door almost without a sound.

His wife passed him then in her old skimpy dress and cardigan. Her thongs slap-slapped into the bedroom and she shut the door. He felt over himself and yes he had his wallet. But no car keys.

He tapped the door gently with a knuckle and almost at once there was the noise of a lumpy body flung against it and the key turned in the lock.

I'll go on the bus, he thought, staring at the little girls' door and willing them to safety behind it.

He went out the back again feeling that he should be carrying something but it was months since she had packed him a lunch.

Over the fence now clearly seen, Mrs Lake was bringing her milk in. Her face was more yellow in the reflected light from the cassia bush, and her strange hair had patches of custard yellow showing through the grey.

"I'm locked out," Chris said. "My wife's in the shower and can't hear. I don't want to wake the girls." He was pleased with himself for lying so well.

Mrs Lake saw him skinny and fair in his trousers flared out from the knees covering most of his strange shoes round as tennis balls in front.

"Come in and ring up," she said. "She might hear that."

"Thank you," he said, only glad because of something to do.

But her phone rang as she entered her front room.

"Excuse me," she said, trying not to look important.

With the receiver to her ear she motioned him on to the kitchen. There was a pan on the stove with some grease in it and some brown fragments from fried eggs. A pot on the stove bore the homely marks of dribbled coffee. Every home in the world is sane but mine, he thought.

Mrs Lake came in. "It was my daughter. She got a bedspread off layby and wants me to go across and see it on the bed this morning." She simpered a little with embarrassment giving him such details. But her yellowy face was full of pride while her eyes avoided his. He thought she might be making a secret and satisfactory comparison between her daughter and his wife.

"Would you like to ring?" she said, bustling about clearing the table as if a trifle ashamed she was not further advanced in her day's work.

She put her hands around the coffee pot. "I'll pour you out a cup," she said.

He didn't move and thought about not going to work but sitting down and asking her for help. The hot coffee made his eyes water.

"Those little girls," she said with her back to him wiping down the sink. "The little one. She doesn't say anything but when she sees me she points her finger. Just points her finger." Holding the dishcloth, Mrs Lake pointed her finger the way the child did.

"That's Heather," he said, although Mrs Lake would have known because when they first came to live next door she and his wife talked to each other.

"What's the other one's name?" Mrs Lake said. He got the impression she didn't like the older girl so much.

"Trudy," he said.

He longed for her to say into the silence that she would take them with her to her daughter's who lived on the other side of the reserve. The little one would point her finger at interesting objects in the bush, like a horse that strayed there and half-tame magpies. He pictured the peaceful scene of Mrs Lake and the little girls bobbing along the bush track and smiled as he set down his cup.

"Thank you. I'll go and get the bus," he said and screwed his wrist to look at the time but hadn't put his watch on.

"You'll get it," Mrs Lake said, bustling ahead of him to the front having noticed his wrists blue with cold and that he was without a jacket.

"My car keys are inside unfortunately," he said to her back.

"The bus'll do, only the damn thing doesn't always come," Mrs Lake said. "But it'll be here this morning."

It was as if she couldn't believe his bad luck could extend that far.

"Thanks, Mrs Lake," he said running down the steps.

"Goodbye, son," she called after him.

On the bus he dreamed he took the little girls in to her every day. He imagined her scooping them up in her arms, loving them equally. He pictured them at the table with her bustling about talking to them while they ate. He moved himself and the girls into the Lakes' house. Mr Lake died, he thought, with no callous intent as he believed him to be more than sixty. The bus bumped on and the woman next to him, glancing at his bony wrists on his knees, pulled her mouth down when he sniffed deeply. I hope there is no drip, he thought, because he had no handkerchief. He put a hand to his nose and felt there was. The woman got up and took another seat.

It allowed him a window seat. He would leave the suburb (too far out) and he and Mrs Lake and the little girls would live in one of the houses flying past the bus. That one, he thought, getting a good view of it because it was close by the last bus stop before the railway station. It had a yard at the side sloping down to a little creek. There was a low thick tree halfway up the slope blobbed with ripe oranges. Perfect, he thought, looking back when the bus moved on.

In the bustle of everyone getting out and the hiss of the train pulling in he was able to sniff deeply without detection and waggle his nose dry on his sleeve.

Passing through to his office he swooped an arm over a glass partition and plucked up some tissues from someone's box, grateful for the feel of them on his nostrils.

A clerk named Gail was at his cabinet looking for a file, a paper cup of coffee in one hand and the fingers of the other splayed out holding a cigarette.

"Hi there," she said. "Tim Thomas wants to cancel and I think Jack wants you to go and see him and see if you can change his mind." She shut the cabinet with a twist of her hip. "The best of British."

"I should ring home first," he said. But he only stared at the phone.

Gail stood looking at him, her face and slightly prominent teeth pushed forwards between the peaks of her heavy hair.

"Oh God, I forgot!" he said.

"What?" she said, very interested.

"I came in the train. I've got no car today. I couldn't — I mean it wouldn't —"

"You can take mine," she said, taking keys from a deep skirt pocket and laying them on his blotter.

"Oh thanks," he said, putting his hand over the keys as if they were her hand. "Love," he said inside his throat, not sure if she should hear.

She turned and went out with lowered lashes, carrying her coffee with care.

He watched her back and thought of her moving in with him and the girls. He stripped her of her black jumper with the high collar touching her ears and put her in a flowered apron. He saw her putting the living room in order, clearing the floor of toys with the little girls swooped on top of her.

She was laughing and trying to get free. The dinner table was set with table napkins at jaunty angles on bread and butter plates and silver winking and every now and again there was a gentle spit from meat roasting in the oven.

He saw them together putting the girls to bed and smelled the girls' clean hair and clean sheets. Later he closed the bedroom door on Gail and himself. Watching her while she tossed her hair back and sat down to work, his eyes pulled her jumper down over her naked shoulders. His thighs strained inside his pants. Oh my God, my God, he said inside him.

We would keep the two cars, he thought, driving hers towards Tim Thomas, New and Used Vehicles. No, we would sell one and have no debts. He steered his mind from the bills piled under and around the clock on the kitchen shelf.

Tim Thomas left him standing holding his plastic folder (there was nothing in it relating to this visit but he usually carried it) while he finished a conversation with another caller. He took his time staring at the tips of his shoes, waggling his hands inside his pockets and looking past the boy's cheek at the car posters on the wall.

Chris looked at the stairs going up to a flat over the premises. The door had a brass knocker and he pictured Gail again in her apron with a finger covered by a rag polishing away at the knocker. The little girls were pressed against her legs watching. Tim Thomas had given them the flat rent-free in return for a little bit of caretaking at the weekend. The girls went to a nearby nursery school.

He and Gail took turns at delivering and collecting them. They kept both cars, he decided now. Of course. The sale of the house at a very good price took care of all his outstanding debts.

Tim Thomas was ready for him.

"I told them I cancelled for this week. I got nothing new to advertise. I told 'em." He fiddled with papers on his desk and twisted about.

"I know," Chris said, his eyes travelling up and down the stairs before returning to Thomas's putty-coloured chin.

"It's OK, Mr Thomas," Chris said, his voice gentle as a girl's. "I just called to see if we could help in any way at all."

"Well —" Thomas was unable to look into the boy's blue eyes. Suddenly he threw a pencil across his desk. "Damn it! I don't want to lose the space —"

Chris moved to go, his eyes back on the brass knocker.

"I'll tell 'em. Thanks, Mr Thomas." He slipped out, aware that Thomas was watching his back with dissatisfied eyes.

Back in his office he looked about wildly for telephone messages. There was nothing. But the phone looked as if its creamy ear could hold some dark and terrible secret.

It rang. He took it up, listened a while, said it was OK and laid it down.

Gail came in then and saw his large swimming eyes.

"That was Thomas," he said. "He told me down there he was taking the ad then rang to say he wouldn't."

"What a bastard!" Gail said, putting a file back in his cabinet.

"Gail!" he said, and her hair swung round followed by her face.

He looked at her without speaking, straining his eyes against the tears. A slow red ran into her face.

"Oh, the keys," she said, picking them up from his blotter and going slowly out.

"Don't look now," she said to Karen, the girl at the next desk. "But I just got the come on."

Karen did look. She was currently without a boyfriend.

"Not for me," Gail said. "A fruitcake for a wife and two kids!"

But when the red dye left her face her eyes were brighter.

He caught the train at five o'clock and then the bus which dropped him at a corner store three blocks from home. He went in and picked a pack of sausages from a refrigerator and laid them with a carton of eggs on the counter.

A door behind the counter opened into the rear of the shop where the owners lived. They were a man and wife named Franks. There was no light on but flames from a fire licked at a black grate. A fat ginger cat sat on an easy chair which sat on a hand-hooked rug on linoleum. There was a table covered with an old-fashioned green fringed cloth.

He saw the little girls kneeling by the chair, each with a hand on the cat, their tangled hair smooth with brush and comb.

He saw Gail come in (in the apron) with a basin of steaming soup and the girls leave the floor and stand by her peering into the basin.

He removed Mr Franks to hospital with a terminal illness. Mrs Franks unable to run the shop alone sold out cheaply and gratefully.

Gail was busy and happy all day. He saw the four of them while the shop was closed on a Sunday afternoon walking on the reserve, linked by their outstretched arms.

He turned, surprised to see the dying Mr Franks, looking quite robust, come through the front door stamping wet leaves from his feet. At the same time Mrs Franks came through the living-room shadows up to the counter.

"I thought you'd be back," she said with irritation.

"I chased the siren down Cook Road and around into Regent Street …"

Regent Street. That was the boy's street. He laid his hand on the eggs and held them.

"Well, was it police, fire brigade, ambulance or what?" Still testy she dropped the boy's money in the till with a little clatter.

"It got away from me," said Mr Franks, and he went with head down to stir some oranges in a wire basket and straighten the sign that said they were locally grown and cheap, and moved from there to fuss with the magazine stand.

Chris took up his things and ran. She had burned the house down, he thought. My little girls are dead. He saw them outlined in flames beating at a window.

He pulled up panting at his gate and they were at the window. He saw their ecstasy when they saw him. The little one threw back her head and laughed and pointed. The older one's smile made her turned-up nose turn up more. They jigged about as if they wanted to break through the glass to reach him.

They raced into the kitchen to meet him there, wrapping their arms around his trouser legs while he peeled the wrapping from the sausages and turned on the stove.

"The stove's a clock!" The little one screamed with laughter when the element began to tick.

He gave them a nurse on each hip, moving to the doorway to steal a look into the living room. His wife was on the couch under a rug, her eyes on the television screen. Her heavy body was hidden and her hair spread on a cushion, golden in the half light. Her face was turned from his but he saw her cheek fair and smooth as butter.

Moving back to the stove he set the girls gently down.

They brought her to the table while he served the eggs and sausages onto their plates.

They chewed in silence and he moved his eyes over her once or twice then back to his food.

He stripped her of the excess flesh and the old cardigan half-falling off her shoulders. He put her into a white blouse he always liked with a frill that brushed the points of her ears when she moved her neck. He smoothed her hair and swept it into a knot on top of her head, the way she always used to wear it.

He saw the backyard through the window not gloomy

and barren but filled with flowerbeds and little waterfalls and stepping stones the way she planned to do it. He saw a hose playing gently and a light shining through hanging ferns.

It was the water that did it. He had to excuse himself and leave the table to go and look for a handkerchief.

VICTOR KELLEHER

THE ROAD

We never did have a son. I used to tell myself it was just bad luck, one of those things you have no control over. My wife, when she considers the matter at all, still regards it in that way. But more and more in recent years, I've come to see it as a kind of judgment. It is almost as if the child has been taken away from me. Thinking of him, now, I find it hard to realise he has never existed. I can visualise him perfectly, not as a vague shadow, longed and waited for, but as a real person, a silent young man, lost somewhere in the past. It's that idea, the irresistible sense of loss, which is hardest to come to terms with. Increasingly, when I'm alone, I find myself searching back through old memories, especially through the years spent in Africa, as though I expected to find him there, to rescue him from some half-forgotten event. The whole exercise, of course, is pointless — it is irrational and, inevitably, reveals nothing. Not a trace of him. For always, no matter how carefully I sift the past, I am drawn back to the same futile recollection: a picture not of him, but of myself, at the age of eighteen, standing late one afternoon at the side of a dirt road in Central Africa.

That picture, at least, is not imaginary. The road was real enough: dusty and badly corrugated, it lay to the east of the main north-south highway, close to the Lake, in what is now called Malawi. And I did once stand beside it, waiting for a lift. At the time I was hitchhiking home to Lusaka, after three months of aimless wandering in East Africa. I had been dropped on that particular section of the road by a police patrol, shortly after midday. Much later that afternoon I was still stranded there: for five hours there had been no south-bound traffic. It is that late part of the day, almost the evening, which I recall most vividly, which keeps recurring whenever I think of the child — like the answer to some other question, one I have never asked — the time and the place so clear in my mind that I can still feel what it was like to be there.

The heat of the day had passed and I had left the shelter of the bush and was standing on the dusty verge of the highway. I can remember how still it was, how deserted. In the tired yellow light, the shadows of the trees lay sprawled across the dust at my feet. The bush, everywhere, was quiet and unmoving. Behind me, back from the road, raised slightly above the beaten earth clearing, was an Indian trading store built of plastered mud brick, with a tin roof and a covered front veranda. The setting sun was shining directly on to the veranda, picking out the few larger items displayed there — the black tin trunks, the multicoloured pressed cardboard suitcases, an old bicycle tied to one of the supporting roof pillars by a piece of white sisal string.

I too was facing into the sun, beginning by then to feel anxious about where I should spend the night. A hundred yards back along the road was a huge sandstone boulder, much higher than any of the surrounding trees. I walked over to it, left my light rucksack and canvas water bottle in the long grass, and scrambled to the top. Over to the east were the vast reaches of Lake Malawi: from the shoreline, less than half a mile from where I sat, it stretched out into the evening, its waters shining black, untouched by wind. Much closer, between me and the Lake, was a cluster of African huts. To the north, I could see at least three miles along the road. But there was no sign of a car, no tell-tale coils of dust; just the unbroken thread of brown dirt, streaked with shadow, curving away through the darkening green of the bush. I waited there, perched on the top of that rock, feeling lonely and isolated, until the sun had fallen to a point just above the horizon; then I slithered down and, for the first time that day, approached the store.

That in itself was not an easy thing to do. In those days a young white man born and educated in Africa was not supposed to ask a non-European for help, and as I climbed the five mud steps which led up to the open veranda I felt distinctly uncomfortable — not so much vain or proud as unsure of myself. Below me, the ground was already in darkness, but inside the store it was neither wholly night nor day, the last rays of the sun, entering through the door and windows, cutting narrow corridors of light across the shadows. I was met by the usual smell of paraffin and stale bread; a treadle sewing machine stood beside the door; on either side the walls were lined with shelves filled with cheap cotton cloth and tinned food. A short fat Indian, middle-aged, with a pock-marked face, stepped into the light.

"Is there anywhere around here I can spend the night?" I asked.

He shrugged his shoulders and I saw immediately that there was nothing of the unctuous Asian shopkeeper about him.

"We have no place here," he said. He looked and sounded completely unconcerned.

"No police station? No farms nearby?" I asked.

"There is nothing," he said, spreading both palms on the wooden counter as though to emphasise the finality of the answer.

"And your house ..." I began. But it was too embarrassing even in that rapidly failing light.

He shrugged once again, not even bothering to answer.

"Here then," I said more firmly, indicating the shadowy room in which we stood.

"The law forbids it," he said. "Nobody can sleep in a store where food is kept." He paused. "It is the British law," he said meaningfully.

There was no mistaking either the tone or the significance of that last remark and I turned towards the door. The world had grown visibly darker: only the top edge of the sun was still showing through the trees. But to my surprise he called me back.

"There is the compound, near the Lake," he said.

I didn't understand at first.

"The African compound," he repeated, "down near the Lake."

His tone, as before, was flat and non-committal, but I knew precisely what he meant. He wasn't making a serious suggestion; he was taunting me. And for the first time in two or three hours I ceased to feel either anxious or embarrassed.

In recent years I must have re-enacted a hundred times or more what followed, though the bare events in themselves are ordinary enough. It's hard to say what keeps drawing me back to them. Partly, perhaps, the notion of an unborn child, the persistent belief in my own lost fatherhood. But also a desire for reassurance. It is peculiarly comforting to find that I can recapture completely the last fading moments of that day. Later that night and the following morning everything becomes increasingly blurred, but those moments at least are clear. Now, years later, when I think of that Indian storekeeper's attitude, I can still feel the upsurge of indignation hardening immediately into resolution — a resolution so unexpected, so divorced from my limited background and experience, that it continues to amaze me.

Walking back to the counter I said, "Why didn't you tell me that at first?"

He did not answer and by then it was impossible to see his face clearly: but I like to think that the way he suddenly leaned away from the counter was an indication of surprise.

"Do you sell spirits?" I asked.

"I have no licence," he said.

"Yes, but do you sell them?" I persisted.

He reached into one of the shelves behind him and produced a large bottle of gin. "Sometimes I make gifts," he said tentatively.

"To the Africans in the compound down there?"

"Yes."

"And how much are your gifts?"

Again he shrugged. "I am not a rich man," he said.

Quickly, before he could change his mind, I paid him more than the bottle was worth and left the store.

Outside the dusk had deepened almost into night, leaving

barely enough light to locate the path behind the store. I found it at last, after stumbling around in the bush for several minutes, and followed it as it wound between the shadowy shapes of trees. I was still too angry to think clearly about what I was doing and before I could collect my thoughts I had reached the village. As I stepped between the first two mud huts the dogs scented me. I caught a glimpse of a fire surrounded by a small group of people and then I was too busy swinging my rucksack, trying to keep the dogs from my heels, to notice anything else. They backed off only when an African ran over, swearing and brandishing a stick.

As soon as the barking had stopped he stepped back several paces, respectfully, waiting for me to speak. He was a short, slight man, of indeterminate age in the near darkness.

"Who is the chief here?" I asked.

"He is there, *Bwana*," he said, pointing to the group by the fire. I went over to them. There were twenty or more people in the clearing between the huts, but only four men seated or crouched by the fire, all of them elderly, one of them very old. He alone remained seated, wrapped in a blanket, grey-haired, his eyes disfigured with cataracts. There were murmurs of greeting. The man who had beaten off the dogs came forward. I could see now that he was young, not more than twenty-five, with a round very black face. He was indescribably ragged, dressed in cast-off baggy trousers and a short-sleeved shirt, both of them many sizes too large.

"They don't speak English, *Bwana*," he said quietly. "I worked for the government, three years."

I looked at the row of old faces.

"Ask them ..." I said, and hesitated.

"Is the *Bwana*'s car broken?" he asked, trying to be helpful.

"I have no car," I said, and at the same time took the gin from my rucksack and placed it on the warm earth beside the fire.

I expected them to talk among themselves for some time, but almost immediately the very old man rose slowly and, bending towards me, beat the fingers of one hand gently in the palm of the other in a gesture of thanks. Then he signed to the young man who disappeared into the shadows for a few minutes, reappearing with a collection of tin mugs and chipped enamel bowls. The gin was divided equally into six portions and, one after the other, each of us drank his share. The old chief began the ritual. Raising his bowl carefully, he drained it in two or three heavy gulps. The strong liquor made him wrinkle up his whole face, but after the first shock he nodded contentedly to himself several times. While the others drank, he produced a dirty old rag from somewhere in the folds of the blanket and carefully wiped each of his rheumy, reddened eyes.

Afterwards, they talked quietly for a few minutes. I couldn't understand them, but it was obvious they were discussing me. When they stopped, the young man again went into the shadows. I had squatted down on my rucksack and now I moved up closer to the fire, not for the heat, but to get some protection from the mosquitoes. We sat there together, silently. Occasionally, the old chief looked across at me, pointed to the empty bottle, and nodded with satisfaction. At the end of about an hour, they all stood up, again made the gesture of thanks, beating the fingers of one hand into the palm of the other, and filed off towards the shadowy outline of the huts.

Apart from a few thin dogs, curled up just outside the circle of the fire, I was alone. The only sound was the usual night clatter of insects. Silent, in the huts all around me, the whole village slept. A light breeze had sprung up and I could smell the Lake nearby — a kind of damp earth smell, slightly musty. When I listened very hard, I thought I could hear the light slap of water, of small waves washing in among the reeds. I settled myself more comfortably, wedging the rucksack behind my back for support. There was enough wood to keep the fire going for several hours yet and I took it that I had been left there for the night. The prospect didn't really bother me. I was hungry, but I understood the reluctance of the old men to spoil the slight effect of the alcohol with food. Lying back, looking up at the stark outline of Orion pinioned somewhere in the blackness of space, I thought of the huge sandstone rock where I had sat watching the road, and of the Indian store, empty now and in complete darkness, its two front windows staring sightlessly out onto the deserted clearing. He had said tauntingly, "There is the compound, near the Lake," knowing that for people like me that was no alternative. And suddenly, unexpectedly, for the first time that evening, I felt happy about what I had done. Not just content: positively happy — sitting there alone, yet ringed around with all those warm and silent sleepers.

It was then that the ragged young African came back.

"Please for the *Bwana* to come," he said.

I gathered up my things and followed him into the darkness. One of the dogs, lying nearby, lurched to its feet, round-backed, almost skeletally thin, and hurried across our path. He walked to the edge of the village and stopped, out of sight of the fire, in front of a small round hut, made of packed mud and with an untidy, overhanging thatched roof. He pulled aside what I later discovered was a rusty length of corrugated iron and revealed a low doorway.

"For the *Bwana*," he said simply.

I had to bend low to enter the hut. As soon as I was inside, he replaced the makeshift door and I heard his footsteps as he walked away. I never saw him again after that.

It was pitch black in there. I had expected it to smell stale and dirty, but it was merely warm and airless. Crouching down, I groped blindly forward and touched someone's foot. Oddly enough, I don't think I was very surprised: I must have realised almost immediately that for the old man the question of hospitality went beyond the idea of mere shelter, and that the person in the hut with me was a woman. I felt the ground around her and found she was lying on a woven reed mat, little more than three feet wide. There seemed to be no other floor-covering in there, just the bare stamped earth all around. Crawling forward, I lay down beside her, using my rucksack as a pillow. She had not moved or made a sound, but I could hear her quick shallow breathing and knew she was awake. Lying so close to her, I could detect the faint wood-smoke smell of her skin. I reached toward her, brushing her arm with my hand, and touched the warm soft cotton of her dress. Slowly, I slid my hand up towards her breast and then down to the curve of her stomach and onto her thigh. She still did not move, her whole body strangely passive.

"Did the old chief make you come here?" I said. But she did not understand.

"*Bwana*?" she said questioningly, her voice little more than a murmur in the stillness of the hut.

For some reason the intervening years have eroded the

actual sound of that voice, made it peculiarly indistinct. Whenever I try to listen to it, to picture the person behind it, I automatically imagine a fully mature, even motherly, woman lying there in the darkness beside me. Yet at the time it seemed so different: what I heard or thought I heard was the voice of a very young girl, virtually a child, unsure of herself, too frightened even to protest. She said nothing else, just that one word: but it was enough. I withdrew my hand and turned away, rolling over to the very edge of the rush mat, as far from her as I could get.

For some time after that I too lay quite still, listening and waiting. Only when her breathing became deep and regular did I allow myself to relax. But even then I did not change my position; and I was still clutching the edge of the thin rush mat when I eventually fell asleep.

I like to think that is important — my being turned away from her at the moment of sleep. It shows that although I may have been impulsive or unrealistic, I was not hypocritical. Consciously, at least, I acted in good faith, with no other guide in all that darkness but her young voice. Regardless of whatever else happened in the course of the night, nothing can alter that fact.

What did happen is that I awoke, minutes or perhaps hours later. The time doesn't really matter. The main thing is that it was too late, because at the actual moment of waking

I was already leaning over her, touching her, and by then there was no going back. I neither have nor had any recollection of moving towards her or of pulling up the loose-fitting cotton dress. All I can remember clearly is the wood-smoke smell of her skin, pungent now, seeming to fill the hut, and the quick wakeful rush of her breath against my face — nothing else until I was lying beside her once again, listening to the rustle of the mat as she pulled her dress down.

It was probably then that I really began to wonder what she looked like. I spoke to her again, asking her whether she was all right, but she did not answer. Outside, the wind had risen, sweeping in from the Lake, stirring the thatch above our heads and rattling the makeshift door. Somewhere, in one of the nearby huts, a baby began to cry, quietly at first, and then more loudly, the sound going on and on, the same wretched wail repeated endlessly. Nobody else seemed to hear it or to be bothered by it; it was as though everyone had stolen away from the village in the night, leaving me alone with the child. I cupped both hands over my ears, blocking out the sound, and eventually, after what felt like hours, I managed to go back to sleep.

When I awoke again the sun had risen and she had gone: light was spilling through the open doorway on to the mat where she had slept. I crawled across the dirt floor and looked out, half expecting to see her, but the village was almost deserted, the women already in the fields, the men probably fishing on the Lake. I shouldered my rucksack and water bottle and walked between the rows of huts to the spot where the fire had been the night before.

The old man was sitting there alone, crouched on a low wooden stool in the morning sun. As soon as he saw me he brought both hands up to his forehead in greeting and then called to someone behind him. A tall, large-boned African woman, no longer very young, came out of one of the huts carrying a round black pot. She neither spoke nor looked at me. Kneeling beside the ring of stones she began preparing a fire to heat the food she had brought. As she brushed aside the cold ash, revealing the still live coals beneath, liberating the warm smell of wood-smoke, it suddenly occurred to me, with a sense of shock, that this could be her, the girl in the hut, this large gaunt woman, so passive and silent, obeying without protest the orders of the old man. I had no positive proof that the girl had been young — only the one word and my own impression to judge by; and I could have been mistaken about the voice, misled by the darkness.

The woman was breaking small sticks and placing them carefully on the hot coals. I crouched down beside her and said sharply, "What are you doing?"

She looked up, startled. "*Bwana*?" she said nervously.

It was the same word, the same tone of voice. But there,

in the bright morning light, it was impossible to match the two sounds, the one made by the visible ageing face, the other spoken out of the darkness.

I stood up. The old man was sitting with his eyes closed, dozing in the early warmth. Without disturbing him, I made my way over to the eastern edge of the village, to where several paths curved away through the undergrowth in the direction of the Lake. The one I followed led me down to a small sandy bay, flanked on either side by heavy floating weed. There was still a breeze blowing, scuffing the tops of the low waves, making them sparkle as they flowed in towards the shore. Further out, the deep water looked shiny black against the flat-bottomed clouds which lined the horizon.

I had not washed or changed for the last twenty-four hours and I undressed and waded out through the small waves. The water felt cold at that time of the morning, but not unpleasant. When it reached almost to my armpits, I ducked right under, sinking down until I was sitting on the sandy floor, with fragments of mouldering leaf and half-rotted weed, kicked up by my feet, whirling past my face in the cloudy water. As I came up, a single egret, very white and clear-winged, glided down over my head and landed on the grassy bank above the bay. To the left of the bird, on the path I had just taken, a small group of African children, dressed in ragged shorts and old cotton singlets, was watching me silently.

They ran away when I swam back to the shore. Left to myself I sat down for a few minutes on the warm sandy beach. But I was in a hurry now; I did not want to spend another night near the village. As soon as I was reasonably dry, I took from my rucksack the one change of clothes I carried with me, dressed quickly, and climbed up toward the huts.

The woman had gone and the old man was alone once again. He smiled, showing a row of worn even teeth, and indicated the pot resting in the warm ashes of the fire. Inside there was a ball of *nshima* — boiled maize meal, cooked stiff and dry, almost like crumbly white bread — and two small fishes, deep-bodied talapia taken from the Lake. I had had no food since the previous lunchtime, but I ate only enough to take the edge off my hunger. Then I thanked the old man, using the triple handshake he was familiar with, and hurried away toward the road.

The Indian was standing on the open veranda, but as soon as he saw me he turned and re-entered the store. I, too, did not want to be watched and so I walked a short way along the road and waited in the shade of a tall overhanging tree. Within half an hour an old Bedford truck came down the road and stopped beside me in a swirl of powdery dust. There were three African labourers crouched on the back and another one in the cab, on the passenger side. I heard the driver, a European in his late thirties, say to him, "Get out and let the *Bwana* get in." The African opened the door and swung himself on to the back, grinning affably at me as he did so. I climbed in and sat down in his place, the seat still warm from his body.

"Where're you making for?" the driver asked.

"For Lusaka."

"Hell," he said. "I'm pushing through to Blantyre. Best I can do is drop you off on the Fort Jameson road."

He put the truck in gear and pulled away. Above the road noise and the roar of the engine he half-shouted, "How'd you get here at this time of the morning?"

I glanced over my shoulder, through the back window, at the Africans crouched behind the cab, trying to keep out of the wind. One of them had tied a dirty piece of cotton cloth around his face as a protection against the billowing dust.

"I slept out," I lied. "In the bush."

"Well you chose the right time of year for it," he said. "Just the same, it's a bit risky. There're still leopard around here, you know; not a lot, but still some."

I nodded. The truck rattled on over the uneven surface.

"Mind you," he went on, "leopards aren't the only problem." He jerked his thumb over his shoulder at the four men on the back. "If the truth be told, they're probably your biggest risk."

They were huddled together behind us, placid and unmoving, their faces expressionless in the rush of air.

"Oh, you can't judge them by the way they look now," he said. "They seem peaceful enough. But think about the way they treat their dogs and their cattle — or their women come to that, especially when they've had a drink. They're like animals then; you really see them as they are."

"All of them?" I said.

It was at that moment, I think, that the feeling of bitterness and impatience began to well up.

"Enough of them."

"Enough for what?"

He laughed. "Enough to make it risky sleeping out alone in the bush miles from anywhere," he said, and laughed again.

There was nothing new or startling in what he said. Most of the farmers and policemen and government officials who had given me lifts over the previous three months had expressed similar ideas. But on that particular morning I didn't want to listen any longer to their faded arguments. It wasn't simply a case of objecting to a racist attitude; that would have been relatively straightforward. No, there were other more personal and involved reasons for that sudden upsurge of bitter impatience; a whole series of them, starting with the painful realisation that I had only gone to the village in the first place because I had felt outraged, insulted by an Indian storekeeper, and ending with a group of children standing by the lakeside, silent and fearful. It becomes increasingly difficult to be more explicit than that; because I don't pretend to understand the situation completely, not any more. Yet at the time the whole thing seemed clear enough — so clear that it was impossible to go on sitting there, beside the man, in the comparative comfort of the truck, for a hundred miles or more.

"Would you drop me off here?" I said loudly.

"What was that?" he asked, surprised.

"Would you stop? I want to get out."

He glanced across at me, puzzled. "Is it something I said?" he asked.

"Not really. I just want to get out."

"Look, I'm sorry …" he began, but I had already reached over, switched off the ignition, and pulled out the key.

"What the hell are you doing!" he shouted.

He braked sharply and the old truck slithered across the road and came to an abrupt stop. One of the Africans in the back let out a short, almost childlike, cry of alarm. I jumped out of the cab, tossed the key on to the seat, and slammed the door. He shouted something else, but I wasn't really listening. I had already decided what had to be done, and even before the truck had started up again I was hurrying back along the road.

It was a long walk, three miles or more through the bright, increasingly hot morning. I saw nobody on the way. The wind from the Lake had died completely and the bush was as quiet as the woman in the hut, the umbrella tops of the thorn trees poised in the still air, the tall yellow grass already fallen sideways in the early summer heat. The store, when I finally reached it, looked like a derelict citadel, with its grimy plaster walls and corroded tin roof. I crossed the clearing, going first to the tap at the side of the building to fill my water bottle for what lay ahead; then I climbed the five mud steps for the second time.

The bicycle, an old black Rudge, was still there, tied to the pillar with the sisal string. I didn't want to go inside the store again, so I called from the veranda, "How much do you want for the bicycle?"

He came to the door, as reserved and apparently unconcerned as he had been on the previous evening.

"Four pounds," he said.

I took out four of the six pounds I had left and gave them to him. He folded them neatly and slid them into the top pocket of his shirt.

"Another gift?" he asked drily, with just a trace of sarcasm.

But his attitude didn't bother me any more; whatever anger I may have felt was no longer directed at him.

"No, not a gift," I said, purposely misunderstanding. "I gave them my gift last night. This is more of a debt."

As I spoke, a small Indian child, dressed only in a light smock, crept out of the store and stood behind him, peering round at me with large dark eyes.

"They are simple people," he said seriously. "The other gift was enough, without this."

"The bicycle is for myself," I said.

He frowned, not understanding.

"But there is no town near here, nowhere to cycle to; Lilongwe is over a hundred miles away."

The child encircled one of his legs with both bare arms — the smooth young skin, with its slight sheen, a soft diluted brown against the white of the cloth.

"Yes, I know," I said.

It took me only a few minutes to prepare for the journey. I lifted the bicycle off the veranda and tied my rucksack firmly to the carrier with the piece of sisal string. The water bottle I slung across my back. He picked the child up as I set off. I rode slowly out of the shade, into the sun, bumping across the bare clearing. At the road I turned southwards, pedalling laboriously, trying to avoid the worst ruts, forcing those thick old-fashioned tyres through the deep clinging dust of the little-used road.

I can picture the scene with perfect clarity: the fierce, late morning sunlight; the surrounding bush, sunk in drought, almost watchful in its stillness; the glaring white furrow of the road, walled in on either side by tufted grasses. I can even recapture my own physical sensations: the strain of pushing the pedals down, one after the other; the prickle of sweat across my back; the cool patch on my side, where the water bottle had slid round. But that is all. The rest, what I was thinking and feeling, what it was that ultimately drove me to make that pointless gesture, is largely lost, buried in the darkness of the village — for it is there that the most personal memories first begin to fade and blur. And all that remains is a jumble of unconnected ideas: remorse, anger, determination, bitterness, disappointment, futility — mere words.

To some extent it's like watching another person ride away, unsure of where he's going and why; no longer myself that I picture. I'm often tempted to think of him in that way, as somebody else, young, fair-haired, idealistic, silly in many respects; somebody I was once close to but have grown away from now. I still know a lot about him, plenty of facts. He could be impulsive, venturing into areas of life he hadn't yet learned to cope with; he could be careless, emptying his seed thoughtlessly into the body of an unknown woman, with what results I shall never know; and he was peculiarly prone to regret. But all of that is observed from the outside, as it were: the person himself has become a kind of stranger.

Which, as always and for a variety of reasons, brings me back to the point at which I began: to my son — unborn, unknown, lost; the thwarted memory a kind of judgment.

KATE GRENVILLE

REFRACTIONS

Once a year, for a week, the Harbour is surprised by a deep red stain throughout its waters. For a week, the tides that jostle the hairy pilings move sullenly as if conscious of some shame, and the seagulls shift from one foot to the other and inspect their underwings at length, waiting out this time when the water is dark and opaque and fishing is impossible.

One drop at a time, the dark red water is as clear as ever. The spray that flies off the tips of Louise's oars and lands on the seat of the dinghy dries without a stain, and the oars themselves, bone-white from the years, do not emerge dripping red. From time to time, as she pulls slowly around the headland, Louise feels a jellyfish cling to the oar for a moment before falling back sluggishly into the water. No matter how many loads of sticky jelly she tosses up onto her ragged lawn, no matter what masses of flies gather and crawl over the melting heap, and no matter how many black trails of ants lead away from it into the bushes, it is impossible to get rid of all these flaccid domes from the Harbour during its season of red water. She slices down hard with the oars and can imagine jelly severed by the blade and translucent shreds of flesh floating in the wake. The jellyfish have arrived with the red stain and will disappear with it, but for this week they drift through the Harbour, the lace-like frill around their edges undulating as they move slowly along the currents.

In the small park at the entrance of the bay, children scramble up and down the sea-wall, dislodging periwinkles and squealing at the sliminess of a captured jellyfish. On a still afternoon such as this, when each oar cuts through a palpable film on the water, the children and their dogs sound the same at a distance. Dogs nose at the lovers lying under the trees, and utter short boasting cries as they leap to fetch a stick thrown into the water. Men alone sit on benches, with ample room beside them for three or four companions, and watch closely as the lovers stand up and the woman plucks her damp dress from the back of her thighs. The children hurl their slimy handfuls at each other and shriek. When a jellyfish lands wetly on the ground, blades of grass and leaves cling to its surface and after a short time the first exploratory ant begins to investigate the frill.

Feeling the oar bite deeply into the water, Louise swings the boat sharply to enter the long narrow bay. On the bank a wet dog with streaming stringy hair runs along the edge of the sea-wall, pursuing the boat, barking and scrabbling at the edge of the rocks as if looking for a path across the water.

It follows her as far as the fence where the park ends and a shapeless patch of scrubby waste ground has resisted civilisation. There the dog cocks its leg at the palings and delivers itself of a brief glittering stream. Louise can remember when the whole headland was covered with this dull scrub. In those days she rowed to the point and went ashore to explore with a water-bottle hanging from her belt and a long whippy stick for the snakes. Now, years later, there are no longer any snakes, but once or twice every summer, a child will scream suddenly from the bushes and limp home crying, one hand on the shoulder of a supporting friend and the other holding the curved shard of dark beer-glass.

The man rises from the bushes as smoothly and silently as a periscope and stands half-hidden behind branches. She sees his head turn slowly as his attention is drawn towards the park, where two children, their sex indeterminate at this distance, are trying to prevent the dog from rolling on its back near the fence. They tug at its collar and thin shrieks carry across the water, but Louise sees the dog's paws in the air as it writhes in ecstasy on something beside the fence. As Louise rests on her oars she sees the children swing themselves around the end of the fence where it drops off at the edge of the sea-wall, and crouch on the other side of it, waiting for the dog to have had enough and wonder where they have gone. They crouch behind the fence and Louise remembers how it feels to be panting and giggling and trying not to make a sound, squatting, feeling a dry grass stem tickling the back of a bare leg and an ant running across a foot, peering through a crack in the fence.

A little way along from where they take turns at pressing their noses to the crack, Louise sees a glint as the man raises his hand to the front of his shirt and his shiny watchband catches the sunlight. His head swivels on his neck so that he is now staring straight at Louise across the short distance of water that separates them. As he undoes the last button of the shirt, he glances again towards where the children crouch, and hesitates before pulling the shirt off and dropping it beside him. Something gold on his chest glitters as he runs his hands over the muscles.

The dog is shaking itself vigorously. Louise sees debris fly off its body like dust off a mop twirled from a window, and sees the children shift in anticipation behind the fence, one now crowding on top of the other so they can both look through the crack at once. The dog noses along the ground in a loose circle, raises its head to sniff, and lollops to the fence to stand against it, tail waving like a ragged banner, so that it must be eyeball-to-eyeball with the children. Louise hears excited shrilling as they back away from the fence and begin to pick their way through the bushes to hide where the dog cannot see them. Louise remembers the brittle grey quality of the sunlight in the mazes of the scrubby bushes, the sandy soil underfoot full of twigs and small hard knuckles of driftwood, and the way the spines of the bushes catch at hair and brush along an arm like a long-nailed hand. She knows how it's possible to find oneself trapped in a cul-de-sac in the dry bushes, in some spot where a barrage of wood and flotsam was jammed between branches during the last spring tide, and how it is necessary to double back and try another path through the scrub. The progress of the two children is erratic, but they are moving steadily closer to the man, whose body is completely still in the sunlight except for his hands, invisible behind the bushes but busy as if with a stiff belt buckle.

Many small rooms surrounded the huge central space in which lengths of rusty chain swayed slowly from the ceiling far above, and the old warehouse reeked of the forbidden, of all those warnings from Mum. The chains could have been swaying from the habit of earlier days, when they hung weighted with loads and moved at the shouts of muscular men, or it might have been just a trick of the blood rushing to the head as Louise tilted her head back to look up dizzily at the rafters, almost invisible in the dusty gloom overhead. Through holes in the roof, sunlight slanted down, heavy with dust and warming small patches of the greasy floorboards so that a strong smell of hot oil rose from each patch of sunlight. The silence here throbbed in Louise's ears and she held her breath and stared at Kevin.

—Just a dirty old place, she said and glanced around, surprised at the loud wavering quality of her voice.

—You're scared, Kevin said, and turned as if to go. Having established that Louise was frightened, it seemed that he could now go back to the clean sun outside, and games in air that moved and breathed instead of hanging thick with dust and the smell of dead machines.

—We've got to get a souvenir, Louise said, trying to speak more softly so that this time her voice would not shake the hushed air, and finding that instead her voice was a breathy whisper.

—A what?

Kevin was also whispering and he glanced around as if checking that the broken window they'd come in by was still there.

—A souvenir. You know, proof.

There was nothing on the rotting wooden work-benches but a thick layer of dust which formed a greasy ball when Louise ran a finger through it.

—Nothing here, said Kevin. Nothing here. Let's go.

Louise saw how he stood in the very middle of the space, as far as possible from any shadowed corner where things might be crouching and watching. She spoke loudly as if to warn any lurking creature to retreat:

—You go then, scaredy-cat. Wait outside then.

Feeling him follow her, but at a distance, she walked out of the well-lit centre of the warehouse into the shadows where doors opened reluctantly into small rooms like cells. In these rooms the smell of oil and rotten wood was overlaid by a rich organic scent of animal decay, and the silence sang in Louise's ears like the noise inside a shell. In the second room, Kevin stepped into a coil of turd which crumbled under his sandal, and he gasped as if bitten. The windows in these rooms were heavily boarded and the thin bands of sun that penetrated between the planks lit up stiff clumps of rag and brown-smeared newspapers, and made a green bottle gleam like an eye. The six brass nails, new but without heads, which they found on the bench in this room seemed enough of a souvenir, and, feeling them grow warm in her hand, Louise made her way quickly back into the open space where the chains seemed to be swaying faster now, as if to throw themselves in a long weighty arc over the children beneath. Lit up by a single crisp bar of sunlight, a loop of metal sat on the floor like a snake and above it on the wall Louise read a daubed word.

—F-L-I-C-K, she spelled out. What's that mean, FLICK?

Kevin stared at it and she watched his lips moving as they

always did when he read. As he mouthed the last letter she saw him understand.

—What's it mean, Kevin? Why'd they write FLICK?

He glanced at her and pursed his lips the way the teachers did when they wanted you to guess.

—You're so smart, he said. Work it out for yourself.

He ran across to the broken window and for a moment Louise felt alone in the middle of this silent space. She watched the soles of his sandals as Kevin crawled out, and waited until they were both standing outside before she put the brass nails ostentatiously into her own pocket, without offering to share them. She found herself shouting into the air outside, here where cicadas shrilled from trees and grasshoppers leapt out of the dry grass with a crackling like fire. She felt the breeze blow in her face and was aware of every hair on her body standing erect.

—Come on, tell me, come on. Louise shouted at Kevin's silent face, and it was some moments before she turned and saw the old man behind her.

In the shadow under the brim of the dark hat, one eye was completely closed and Louise watched a fly crawl towards the other eye, which was pale as if boiled and leaked shining tears. One large hand was waving towards her as if trying to locate her by touch. *Come on closer come on.* Louise saw his tongue, pink in the darkness of his mouth. *Closer where I can see you, closer.* Louise backed step by step against the wall of the warehouse and felt the heat it threw out into her back, and its splinters in her palms. *Don't be scared come closer come on.* The wall had stored up a whole summer's heat and smelled of creosote and ants. *Where are you be nice to a poor old man now.* His clothes were dark and dense and as he reached towards her again she smelt sweaty hot serge and felt splinters in her back. His other hand came out of a pocket and thrust close to her face. *Look, nice lollies have a nice lolly put your hand in go on.* His trousers close to her face were hot and huge and the small paper bag was greying along its creases. The enormous hand moved and she saw the bag fall to the ground and two shiny red lollies bounced and came to rest. She felt the hand take hold of her shoulder, covering it with immediate damp heat, and felt his breath on her cheek and could see the shiny white of his eye in the shadow of his hat. *Yes yes closer yes.* She felt her shoulder cool as the hand left it and brushed down to where her shorts ended. The hand slid up and down her leg and she felt the heat in her back as she squirmed away from the puffs of breath on her face and the hoarse voice rasping *yes yes here we go yes.* The thumb slid up under the cloth of her shorts and she felt it jabbing and probing into her, harder and harder between her legs until the man grunted and the thumb was abruptly withdrawn. She turned her cheek against the splinters and smelled the creosote as she drew in a long quivering breath.

When she opened her eyes again she saw the man turning in a crouch towards Kevin who was standing shocked and still, with a hand up to his mouth. The man reached out with both groping hands, whispering urgently, *the boy, come on sonnie where are you now.* Louise felt the splinters catch at her shirt as she straightened against the wall and saw the dark hat with its darker band of sweat hovering over Kevin's wide eyes and the huge exploring hand fumbling down towards the front of his shorts. The man took a clumsy shuffling step closer to Kevin and Louise saw the red lolly crushed into shiny chips under his heel.

The boat wallows and staggers in the water as Louise digs down hard with an oar and the slithering weight of the jellyfish on the floorboards slips to one side. Now that she is rowing towards him, she can no longer watch the man, but takes a glimpse over her shoulder after every few strokes and tries to keep her course straight towards him. She sees him bend behind the bushes and pull as if at a trouser-leg and along the sea-wall the children are darting between the bushes, always looking behind them at where the dog whines and claws at the fence, never looking ahead to where the man is standing now with his hands at his waist behind the bushes. Louise takes only a glance before bending to the oars again and wonders how close she will have to be before she can call out to the children.

The jellyfish in the bottom of the boat are shedding their first layers of slime so that the water that slops over her feet is full of long slippery strands. Her palms against the leather grips of the oars are sticky with dried jelly and a floury damp smell rises from the floor. At her next twisted glance over her shoulder she is close enough to see the man's dark eye-sockets, shadowed by the sun, and sees his watchband glint again as he raises his arm as if in farewell to the children, who have turned without ever catching sight of him, and are making their way back towards the fence. They throw dried seaweed at each other as they run along the sea-wall and Louise hears the splash as a clump lands in the water and one of the children begins to shriek.

Along the waterline on the sea-wall, bright green weed floats like hair and at each deep insuck of the swell, fleshy brown kelp washes into view for a moment seething and coiling. The man no longer even glances in the direction of the children's cries, but stares at Louise intently as if trying telepathy. As she sits holding the oars blankly, he beckons her with imperious gestures that make his watchband wink in rapid semaphore, and begins to move towards her through the bushes. Holding branches carefully away from his body, he advances steadily towards her as if planning to march straight across the water to where she now struggles to get the heavy boat moving. As he bends back the last branch that hides him from her, his stare opens into a grin that exposes every tooth and the shining pink end of a wet tongue. He continues to stare directly into her eyes and she has to stare back as she propels herself away from him with convulsive jerks on the oars, feeling her palms slip on the leather grips and long fibrous threads squeezing between her toes.

Janette Turner Hospital

MORGAN MORGAN

My grandfather, Morgan Morgan, was a yodeller and a breeder of dahlias. On Collins Street and Bourke Street, I could tug at his hand and plead "Please, Grandpa, please!" and he would throw back his head and do something mysterious in his throat and his yodel would unfurl itself like a silk ribbon. All the trams in Melbourne would come to a standstill, entangled. Bewitched pedestrians stopped and stared. But this was nothing compared with former powers: when he was a young man on the goldfields, handsome and down on his luck, the girls for miles around would come running. Yodel-o-o-o, my grandfather would sing, snaring them, winding them in. The girls would sigh and sway like cobras in the strands of his voice. He was a charmer.

"Get along with you, Morg. You're bad for business," Mrs Blackburn would say. Flowers bloomed by the bucketful around her. She would lean across roses and carnations, she would catch at his sleeve. "Here's a daisy for the Nipper," and she'd tuck it behind my ear. She didn't want him to move on at all, even I knew that. "Your grandpa," she had said to me often enough, "is a fine figure of a man, they don't make men like him anymore." She'd pull one of her carnations from a bucket and swing the stem in her fingers. "A gentleman is a gentleman," she'd sigh. "Even if he is poor as a church mouse and never found a thimbleful of gold."

It was not entirely true, Grandpa told me, that he'd never struck it rich on the goldfields — the *Kalgoorlie* goldfields, he'd say, with a loving hesitation on the *o*'s and *l*'s, a rallentando which intimated that music had gone from the language since The Rush petered out.

In those exotic and demented times, men were obsessed with the calibration of luck. Not Morgan Morgan. While other men mapped out their fevers with calipers, measuring the likely run of a seam from existing strikes, Grandpa Morgan simply watched for the aura. Wherever the aura settled, he panned or dug.

"Crazy as a bandicoot," the publican told him. "You've got to have a *system*, mate!"

But Morgan Morgan knew that gold was a gift, it never came to men of system, never had. "King David danced before the Lord," he pointed out, "which goes to show; and his goldmines were the richest in the world, I read it somewhere, some archaeologist bloke has proved it." Grandpa had his own methods of fossicking; in scripture or creek bed, it was all the same to him. He found what he wanted, or at any rate learned to want what he found.

He laboured at strings of waterholes that were known to be panned out. He was after the Morgan Nugget. This was how it appeared to him in a vision: as big as a man's fist, blackened, gnarled like a prune, cobwebby with the roots of creek ferns. He expected its presence to be announced by an echo of Welsh choirs in the tea-tree and eucalypt scrub. And it was, it was. One day, with the strains of *Cwm Rhondda* all around him, he scratched at a piece of rock with a broken fingernail and the sun caught the gash and almost blinded him.

"Solid gold," he told me. "And big as a man's fist." Not for the first time, he knew himself to be a man of destiny.

"What did you do with it, Grandpa?" I was full of awe. When he spoke of the past, I heard the surf of the delectable world of turbulence that raged beyond our garden wall. We were still at the old place in Ringwood then, across from the railway station. If I buried my face in the box-hedge of golden privet, I could hear the rush of Grandpa's life, the trains careering past to Mitcham and Box Hill and Richmond. He would listen too, leaning into the sound, and I would see eyes travel on beyond Richmond, beyond Footscray even, out towards the unfenceable Nullarbor Plain and Kalgoorlie.

"What did you do with it, Grandpa?"

"With what?" he would ask from far away.

"With the Morgan Nugget?"

"I put it down again," he said, "right back down where I found it, inside the vision. It's still waiting just where I put it. Listen," he said, "if you put your ear to the Morgan Dahlia, you can hear it waiting."

I buried my ear in those soft salmon ruchings of petals and heard the deep hush of the past. And then *pop, pop*: he pinched the calyx with his fingers. "That's the sound of the Morgan Nugget," he said, "when it gets impatient. It's waiting for one of us to find it again."

"Dad!" Grandma Morgan, with a basket of eggs on her arm, came down the path from the hen house. "Don't confuse the child with your nonsense." She lifted her eyebrows at me. "Always could talk the leg off an iron pot, your Grandpa."

"Pot calling the kettle black, I'd say," he grumbled. He hated to be listened in on; I hated it too. I didn't like the way the Morgan history drooped at the edges when other people were around.

Grandma Morgan was picking mint and tossing the sprigs into her basket. The leaves lay green and vivid against the eggs. "Came to tell you the pension cheques have arrived," she said.

"Well, praise be," said Grandpa, mollified. "Praise be. There's corn in Egypt yet. And on top of that," he whispered, as she moved off towards the house, "the Morgan Nugget's still waiting."

"Dad! No more nonsense. That child is never going to know the difference between truth and lies, you mark my words."

"Got eyes in the back of her head," Grandpa grumbled. "And ears in the wind. No flies on her, no siree."

It was one of his favourite sayings: *No flies on so-and-so, no siree*. To me it implied an opposite state, an unsavoury kind of person, stupid, sticky, smelling overly sweet in the manner of plums left on the ground beneath our tree for too long. I imagined this person — the person on whom there *were* flies — to be pale and bloated, and to have bad breath and unwashed socks.

There was a man who delivered bonemeal for the dahlia garden on whom I thought there might be flies — if only one could see him at an unguarded moment. His clothes gave off a rich rancid smell. When he laughed it was like looking into the squishy dark mush of fruit I had to collect from the lawn before a mowing. Those few teeth which the bonemeal man still had — they announced themselves like unvanquished sentinels on a crumbling rampart — were given over to a delicate vegetation. I recognised it: it was the same silky green fur that coated the fallen plums over which floated little black parasols of flies.

Yet one day, when I came out to the dahlia garden just as the bonemeal man was leaving, Grandpa Morgan was tossing his fine head of hair in the wind and laughing his fine Welsh laugh. The bonemeal man was laughing too, trundling his barrow down our path, doubled up with mirth between its shafts, his green teeth waving about like banners.

"Grandpa, what is it, what is it? Why are you laughing, Grandpa?"

"Oh," Grandpa gasped, patting me on the head in the way that meant a subject was not for discussing. "No flies on *him*, no siree."

This was the best thing: I could always count on Grandpa Morgan to be outrageous. That was the word people used: the neighbours, my grandmother, my mother, my uncles. "He's *outrageous*," they would say, shaking their heads and throwing up their hands and smiling.

If I asked him to, he would yodel in the schoolyard when he came to fetch me, and abracadabra, we two were the hub of a circle of awed envy. When I passed the Teachers' Room at morning tea time, I'd hear the older ones whisper and smile: "That's Morgie's granddaughter."

On our walks he would stop and talk to everyone we met, "to *anyone*, anyone at all," Uncle Cyril would groan. He spoke to the butcher, the baker, the lady in the cake shop, to men who did shady undiscussable things, even men who smelled of horses and *took bets*, whatever that was.

"What can you be thinking of?" Grandma would say, "with the child hearing every word? A man *known* to be mixed up with off-course betting."

I knew bets to be deeply evil. I imagined them to be huge and ravenous and almost hidden behind fearful masks. Once upon a time, in Kalgoorlie, Grandpa himself had made bets, but that was before the Lord saved him and showed him the light. Now, he said, he only bet on the Day of Judgment. Still, he couldn't see any harm in talking to people who "knew horses". He would introduce me. "This is Paddy," he would say. "A man who knows horses if ever anyone did." I myself had no interest in knowing horses on account of their large and alarming teeth, but I rather liked those brave horse-knowing men.

Sometimes Grandma, shocked, would call out: "Dad! I want to have a word with you, Dad." From the front window, she would have watched us coming over the bridge from the Ringwood Station. The most *interesting* people came off the trains and walked over that bridge. Grandma would have seen us stop and talk to some gentleman who wore string, perhaps, for suspenders, and whose shoes were stuffed in an intricate way with newspapers, and who gave off the rank smell of the pubs. "Dad!" she would say. "What are you *thinking* of, to introduce the child to such strangers?"

"Strangers?" Grandpa would raise his eyebrows in surprise. "That wasn't a stranger. That was Bluey McTavish from back of Geelong. We don't know any strangers."

This was certainly true, though we'd only just met Mr Bluey McTavish of Geelong, whose life history we would discuss over the sorting of dahlia bulbs. I don't know what it was about Grandpa Morgan, but people told him a great deal about themselves very quickly. "There aren't any such people as strangers," he told me. "Or if there are, I've never met them."

"I don't know what's going to come of that child," Grandma Morgan said, throwing up her hands and trying not to smile. "But one thing's certain: she'll never know the difference between truth and lies."

Grandpa said with ruffled dignity: "One thing she'll know about is dahlias."

The dahlias, the dahlias. They stretched to the edge of the world. When I stood between the rows, I saw nothing but jungle, with great suns of flowers above me, so heavy they nodded on their stalks and shone down through the forests of their own leaves. Such a rainbow of suns: from creamy white to a purple that was almost black. The dahlias believed in excess: they could never have too many petals. The dahlia which could crowd the most pleatings of pure light about its centre won a blue ribbon at the Melbourne Show. It was an article of faith with us that some year the Morgan Dahlia would win that ribbon.

Grandpa Morgan did things to the bulbs and the soil. He married broad-petalled pinks to pintucked yellows; he introduced sassy purples to smocked whites with puffed sleeves and lacy hems. He watched over his nurslings, he crooned to them, he prayed. To birds and snails he issued strong Welsh warnings (the Lord having taken away a certain range of Australian vocabulary). As his flowerlings grew, he murmured endearments; and they gathered themselves up into a delirium of pleats, rank upon rank of petals, tier upon tier, frilled prima donnas. The colour of the Morgan dahlia was a salmon that could make judges weep, the salmon of a baby's cheek, the colour of a lover's whisper. And it did win yellow ribbons, and red, at the Melbourne Show, but never the coveted blue.

"Is it waiting till we find the Morgan Nugget again?" I asked.

"Very likely," Grandpa said. "Very likely."

The day Grandma came out with the news of Uncle Charlie, we were deep in dahlias.

"Dad," she said. "Charlie's gone."

Grandpa paused in mid-weeding. A clump of clover and crabgrass dangled from between his fingers. He sank down on the ground between the dahlias and rested his head in his hands. "Well," he said, sadly and slowly. "Charlie. So Charlie went first."

"Where's he gone?" I wanted to know.

"Uncle Charlie's gone to heaven," Grandma told me, and Grandpa said: "He's dead." He pushed his trowel into the soil and lifted up a handful of earth. It was alive with ants and worms, we watched it move in the palm of his hand. "I'm next," he sighed, and he smelled the earth and held it for me to smell, and he rubbed it against his cheek as though it were a kitten. "I'm next, I suppose."

"Next for what?"

"Next for dying," he said.

"What happens when you die, Grandpa?"

"They put you in a box and they bury you under the ground with the dahlia bulbs."

I stared at him in horror. "Uncle Charlie should run away and hide."

"You can't run away when you're dead," he said.

"Grandpa," I whispered, beginning to shiver, "will they do it to you?"

"Yes," he said.

"And to me?"

I crept between his earth-covered arms and he held me tightly and rocked me back and forth between the dahlias. "Yes," he sighed, "one day, yes. That's the way it is. But then we'll be with the Lord."

I didn't want to be with the Lord. I had a brilliant idea. "Grandpa," I said, "we'll run away *before* we die. I know a very good place in the woodshed; they'd never find us."

"Dad!" Grandma's voice steamed over with exasperation. "Now just what have you been telling her this time? How will that child ever know the difference between truth and a lie? Uncle Charlie," she said to me, "has gone straight to heaven, and that is the simple truth."

Mr Peabody knew the truth. Every Sunday it spoke in his bones, it shook him from head to foot.

There must have been some obscure and ancient rule at church. It must have been this rule which forced Mr Peabody, week after week, to sit directly in front of Grandpa Morgan. Mr Peabody was a tiny man, elderly, and seemingly frail as a sparrow, though he must have had enormous reserves of stamina on which to draw.

Behind him, sheltering in the leeside of the Spirit of the Lord as it blustered and rushed through Grandpa, my little brother and I kept score. When the spirit moved, Grandpa shouted *hallelujah* in his fine Welsh voice. The shock waves hit Mr Peabody sharply in the nape of his neck and travelled down his spine with such force that he would rise an inch or two from the pew. Most of his body would go rigid, but his head and his hands would quiver for seconds at a time. *Glory, glory,* he would murmur in a terror-stricken prayerful voice.

These seismic interludes infused Sundays with extraordinary interest. And there was also this: from monitoring the passions of Mr Peabody, my brother and I learned self-control, the ability to tamp down an explosion of mirth and turn it into a mere telegraphed signal of gleaming eyes and a coded numerology of fingers.

But then came the day that a shaft of sunlight fell from a high amberglass window in the church and placed a crown of gold on Mr Peabody's head. "Oh!" I gasped aloud. "*Look!*" And Grandpa shouted *Hallelujah!* and Mr Peabody rose up into his corona like a skyrocket and I saw a million golden doves and the gilded petals of all the dahlias in the world rising up into the pointed arch above in which God lived.

"It was the Holy Spirit you saw," the pastor told me. "The Holy Spirit descending as a dove."

"Going *up*," I corrected. "Lots and lots of them, and dahlias too."

"The Holy Spirit," he said again, less certainly. "In the form of a dove."

"I'm not so sure," my Sunday School teacher said. "She makes things up."

"Out of the mouths of babes," the pastor reminded her.

"She makes things up," my Sunday School teacher insisted. "She handles the truth very carelessly. She believes her own lies."

"Grandpa," I asked, "how can you tell the difference between truth and a lie?"

He was working bonemeal into the soil around his dahlias; over us nodded those heavy salmon suns. He went on kneading the rich black loam, intent on his labour.

Apprehensively I persisted: "Is the Morgan Nugget true?"

He went on sifting the soil.

I thought hopefully: perhaps he made up death.

"The truth," he said at last, "shall make you free. John, chapter 8, verse 32."

"Grandpa," I said, "there were doves with gold wings, and dahlias too. Mr Peabody made them fly. I saw them."

"I know you did."

I leaned towards him. "And the Morgan Nugget?" I breathed.

"Is true," he said. "Is true."

PETER SKRZYNECKI

THE BIGGEST BONFIRE OF ALL

The land is cleared and the creek dredged, although paperbarks have been left growing along its crumbling edges. The deep flow of water has been reduced to a stream with small pools in the clayish recesses. A green scum floats in patches and grasses straggle in pockets of soil. The bulrushes and blackberries have disappeared altogether. The council has often planted eucalypts in the open paddock, but they seem to die out as soon as they're planted. The brown weeds are tall and bothersome when you wade through them. Burrs will attach themselves to your clothes. There are no blue-tongue lizards or kingfishers or cranes. Turtledoves and peewits have survived, though their numbers are small.

Beyond the last rows of houses there are the factories of industries that have sprung up like the stone and steel walls of an alien city. These follow the creek as it continues out of sight and into other suburbs. Miles away, it joins the Parramatta River. Engineering works. Paint factory. Waxed paper mill. Smash repair workshops. They all fire their waste into the sky or it runs into the creek ... Between them and the backyard of the house I stand in is *the* paddock: my childhood playground, my Adventureland and Frontierland; where I learnt about nature, sex, Australia and its customs; where I caught tadpoles and made bows and arrows; where I was once a member of a "gang" of children and, for a brief time, earned the reputation as the builder of the biggest bonfire of all.

"Hooray! Hooray!"

The words are thrown like a multitude of hats into the sky by the whole school as Sister Dymphna announces that tomorrow will be a holiday to celebrate Empire Day.

Although we stand to attention in the autumn sun and listen to an Irish nun's voice over a loudspeaker tell us about the might of Great Britain, its colonies and what all the pink countries on the map of the world belong to, our minds are in a bushland, two miles away, standing back and admiring the towers we have built out of branches and leaves. Our minds ignite each spire with a single match and see the night sky blaze with flames and sparks that swirl up to the moon and stars. Fireworks explode in the bush and neighbouring streets. The air quickly becomes filled with smoke and the smell of gunpowder. Dogs bark over fences. Voices call out. Adults. Children. It is an excitement that comes only once a year. Who cares about tomorrow or the afternoon's lessons as we march into the classroom? Our holiday has already started.

It was always "Bonfire Night" or "Cracker Night" and we were "Balts", the children of parents that had emigrated to Australia from Baltic countries after World War II. But despite our differences, we enjoyed ourselves as a group, Australians and Balts alike; and there was a fierce competitiveness about Cracker Night, when we all tried to outdo each other by building the biggest bonfire. There was no first prize, no ribbon or medal, just the knowledge that there was one that was better than the rest. Our youthful egos basked in the glory, boasted of our skill and later, at the culmination of Cracker Night, watched our efforts reduced to a heap of ashes.

The actual preparation for Cracker Night would be at least a week before the announcement of our holiday — and then, when we did rush home for the day, it was spent mainly in putting the finishing touches to work in its penultimate stages of completion. By that time, most of the wood — twigs, branches, whole trees even — had dried out, though enough of it was still green to create smoke. If it became too dry it would burn too quickly. Your own bonfire had to be the biggest and burn the longest.

The trick was to fill the centre with materials that would take a long time to burn; in this regard, old car tyres were the best. They were prized, sought after and hidden when discovered (stolen, even, from the backyards of homes when they could not be found at the dump), especially when the twenty-fourth of May drew near.

At first I was very impressed by the bonfires the Australian children made; but as I watched them burning and noticed how hollow the insides were, I decided I could easily build a taller and wider one by making the frames higher, lowering their bases so they would form a wider circle and then filling the centres with as much material as I could find — tyres, crates, boxes, plastics, anything that would burn. When this tepee-like structure was completed, I built it up with brackens on the outside from base to apex. All the other bonfires resembled giant tents; mine was more of a haystack. Heavy. A giant rectangular prism. Up on its end. The top slightly peaked. Like a mountain.

That year my bonfire burned longer and brighter than the other five or six in that wilderness. As double-bungers and jumping-jacks exploded, sky rockets trailed and whistled into the smoking black sky and sparklers showered their harmless fires over hands and warm clothing, I stood back like a king, like the inventor of an ingenious machine that would somehow contribute to the progress of the world. Everyone else marvelled at this fire.

"Gee, isn't it great?"

"Good on yer, mate."

"How'd yer do it?"

"Crikey!"

And even next morning, as we sifted among the ashes and searched among weeds for "fizzers" — those fireworks that didn't go off — I beamed with pride and satisfaction as my playmates congratulated me all over again. But I knew that next year they would try and beat me. The competition would start again. I just knew I could build an even bigger bonfire.

Sluggo Johnson was the toughest boy in our neighbourhood — not a bully, just an expert with his fists when it came to settling disputes or laying claim to something that did not belong to him and he may have wanted. Not very tall, he was a walking brickwall, with legs and arms that resembled logs. Also, he was not very fast on his feet. Most of us could beat him in races; but as athletics were of little interest to children who admired brawn and muscle, the gift of speed was considered to be of no value — except when you had to get away from Sluggo. But he was patient, with an animal's cunning, and would study your routines if he wanted to lie in ambush. It only took one punch to find out that he hated being offended.

He came from a poor family. His mother spoke with a

defect and his father limped. Both parents drank heavily. There were rumours that his parents had once been acrobats in a circus. There was always an old rust-bucket of a car parked in their driveway. The backyard of their fibro Housing Commission cottage was knee-deep with weeds, and engine parts lay overgrown like war trophies.

Sluggo did not like school. He believed in truanting and would encourage us to go down to Duck Creek with him for the day, bringing money with us so that we could buy cigarettes. He was always promising to teach us how to blow rings with cigarette smoke and how to smoke properly without getting sick. He laughed when he told us about getting caned for "wagging". The cane was a joke, he sniggered; it didn't hurt and the teachers were all "sissies".

He hardly spoke of his parents and rarely invited any of the migrant children to his home. If he met us on the way to school he would greet us with "Wat'cha got for lunch today?" He never refused the food we offered; and we never felt intimidated by his approach in this respect, even though we knew how skilful he was with his fists. Perhaps we felt sorry for him because of his home situation. However, if we did, we did not know it.

Ronny O'Toole was the only boy in a family of seven or eight girls. They were part-Aboriginal and lived a block away from Sluggo. Ronny was slight, weedy. He walked as though his backbone was collapsing. His mop of black hair was always combed back boldly into a wave, as if to keep his head afloat. He wore lairy clothes, often a yellow shirt and red or brown trousers. He giggled a lot. He trotted after Sluggo like a calf after its mother.

Yet it seemed that Sluggo never sought his attention or went out of his way to be seen in his company. He never called him "mate" and would contemptuously refer to him as "Slimy" whenever Ronny came up in conversation. At best, Sluggo seemed to tolerate the hanger-on who boasted of the money he could steal from his mother's purse or the goods from any shop Sluggo nominated: cigarettes from the papershop, fruit from the greengrocer and even jewellery from the local chemist.

The time of year that I had my confrontation with the pair coincided with Cracker Night and my attempt at building the biggest bonfire for the second year in succession. Various ideas had hatched in my head over the preceding twelve months and I believed I had hit upon a way of making my "haystack" even higher.

The key to success in a bonfire's stability was its frame; the stronger it was, the more weight it could take. If I secured this, then I could heap a lot more wood and branches on it and be reasonably sure it would not collapse.

There was no defined time or period when the building

started, but like cicadas we knew when our season had arrived. Armed with tomahawks and axes we would invade the paperbark forest, forget it had been our playground for the past year, and select the trees we wanted. There was an unwritten law that you did not steal anyone else's tree once it had been chosen, nor did you interfere with the building of the bonfire. If you wanted to, you helped. We were social insects assigned by nature to complete a specific task. Our instincts guided us. In our spare time, after school and on weekends, we worked. We worked without rest.

A week before Cracker Night I finished — and, yes, once again I had built the biggest bonfire. My frames held because I worked the base of each post into the ground. I also used a tall centre pole which I stabilised only after I started to stack the exterior with branches; this had been done when no one else was around and I prided myself on having thought of it alone. The pole was first placed through several tyres and then pushed into the centre. The space between wood and rubber was stuffed with debris and I even squeezed bricks in to make it more steady. They would not burn but they had weight and would help to prevent the pole from shifting sideways.

Empire Day itself, as a holiday, was an anti-climax for me. The bonfire was finished and I had nothing to do. Some of my fireworks had already been let off and I wanted to save the rest for the night.

For an autumn day the weather was warm, the day bright though overcast. I stood on the back steps of my home and saw the peaks of the bonfires that our gang had built — green cones of foliage rising among the treetops. Who cared or understood what we were celebrating? The night would be unique. Not even New Year's Eve could match it. From a child's point of view, the only other day that surpassed it in expectation and joy was Christmas morning and the opening of presents.

My mother let me sleep in that morning until ten o'clock. My breakfast was Weet-Bix and two boiled eggs which she wrapped in a towel to keep warm and left on the kitchen table. My father went to work at six o'clock. Both parents would return between half past four and five. The day was my own. I chose to ignore clocks and breakfast routines. Tonight was Cracker Night and all my thoughts and energies were geared in that direction.

But none of our group was around the bonfires. I called and searched around their homes. Where were they? I continued to wander along the fences of their homes. Then it occurred to me that they may have gone at the last minute down to the dump to search for more junk and tyres to burn. I decided to run down and see if I could find them. I was angry for not having been woken earlier; but most of all I became hostile and impatient at the thought that I might be missing out on a new adventure or some kind of excitement.

All of a sudden the day became an urgency — a burning desire to complete a task that somehow I had been neglectful in accomplishing.

Time. The weather. Birds. The creek. Bushes. Trees. The elements.

Everything seemed to summon me through the paperbarks and gumtrees, along tracks made by children's feet, over paths we could virtually follow with our eyes closed, knowing where they joined up or ran into dead ends.

But when I arrived at the creek, I realised that in my haste I had blundered. My intention had been to follow the tracks through the bush as far as possible, then cross the creek at the last point. Now I had to cross earlier, following the far bank along the high paling fence that enclosed the local playingfield and park. It made the whole trip a little longer. Never mind, I knew the way.

Crossing the creek on one of our makeshift bridges — planks or a tree trunk laid flat at a point where the banks of the creek were narrowest — I scuttled up the side and heaved myself on to the track that skirted the oval's fence. The grass was tall and thick. The going was slow.

In several places the palings had been broken away by

children and adults (it made entry to the park easier and one could view a game of football or basketball for free). As I stamped through the grass, pushed aside bushes and hoped I would find my friends at the end of all this, I glanced into these openings without expecting to find anyone or anything. At the fourth or fifth intrusion, suddenly, my blood froze! I dared not move.

With both hands on either side of the opening, as if about to climb through, I was confronted by two bodies — Sluggo and Ronny. Both had their trousers pulled down around their ankles. Ronny was lying face-down in the grass. Sluggo was lying on top of him and moving his body in an up-and-down motion. What were they doing? I was intrigued. Both had their faces turned the other way. Both were grunting. Or puffing.

Then Sluggo turned his head upwards and I spun around as if hit by a truck.

"Get that bloody kid!"

Fear impaled my heart. I was terrified out of my head. Dumbfounded by the unknown. I did not know why I had to run, but I knew I had to run faster than I'd ever run in my life. Run and hide myself behind a locked door. Sluggo sounded mean and I knew he would make mince meat out of me with those fists if he or Ronny caught up with me.

When I reached the creek I did not bother with the

bridge. One. Two. Three. I jumped through water, bulrushes, mud. I felt a sharp jab in my leg and knew that I was cut, probably by glass or a piece of tin. As I ran towards the back fence I heard their voices behind me.

"Wait'll we get yer, yer bloody little bastard!"

"Bloody little bastard!" Ronny echoed.

When I saw the fence I knew that I was safe. Leaping and reaching for the top, I pulled myself up and over — dropping hard to the ground and on to my knees, not cat-like as I usually did. My knees hurt. I was stunned. Even my jaws shuddered from the impact. But there was the house. The back door. Only a few more seconds. I gasped as I ran.

Once inside I flopped down on the mat in the kitchen. My left leg was cut on the inside and bled freely. A small cut, but deep. In the past I had had wounds like this and knew how to staunch them quickly.

Hopping up on to the sink I put my leg under the tap and let the water run over it. As the skin became cleaner I saw how the skin had been turned inwards. Squeezing it with an upwards pressure, I held a dishcloth against it hard and left it there. By now my breath was returning to normal and I began to take stock of my situation.

Both my knees throbbed and were very red. They felt hot. There was an inner soreness which would probably come out as bruising. With my free hand I brought water up to my mouth, gulping it and splashing my face to cool down while checking my cut at the same time.

When the flow of blood had almost stopped, I slid down from the sink and limped to the bathroom cabinet; there I got out a bottle of iodine and prepared for the worst part of my experience, for the bite and sting of that dark liquid that would sterilise the wound. I placed the mouth of the open bottle against the cut and quickly turned it over.

Long needles of pain jabbed through my leg, through the left side of my body and into my head. I could feel myself perspiring. I gritted my teeth, locked them. In a few moments it would be over. Finally, putting away the bottle, I reapplied the bloodied dishcloth and brought several band-aids and a roll of bandages out with me to the kitchen.

As I entered the kitchen that overlooked the backyard, a huge column of black smoke and flames was visible through the window above the sink.

My bonfire!

Set alight and blazing in full daylight! All my work — the hours spent collecting trees and tyres!

Who had done it?

No sooner did the question enter my head than I answered it myself. Instantly.

Sluggo and Ronny!

This was their revenge!

"Stop it! Stop it! Put it out!"

I dropped everything that I was carrying and tore across the backyard to the fence.

Cut leg. Iodine. Dishcloth. Bandaids. Bandages.

Everything else was forgotten.

Fifty feet away my bonfire roared: a stack of green and brown that flames shot through and smoke curled out of; heat could be felt as I peered over the top of the fence, and the ash could be seen floating in the air.

But no sooner had I started to heave myself over the top when a hail of stones showered against the fence and over my head. One hit me on the hand. I cried out and fell back.

"That'll teach yer, yer rat!"

"C'mon, come and get yer head knocked off!" Sluggo was enjoying it, like a hound that could smell blood.

And Ronny chimed in, true to his slavish nature.

I crouched behind the fence and peered through the palings at the conflagration on the other side — at the raw, hungry appetite of fire that was gorging itself on my tower. I also noticed that my leg had started to bleed again, but I didn't care in the slightest ... even if it fell off. What I wanted to save was burning up, and there was nothing I could do to stop it. As this realisation struck me, I heard a crash and saw that the centre pole had collapsed. My bonfire was no longer the biggest and I began to sob and cry, so hard I thought that Sluggo and Ronny would hear me. Turning around I ran back into the house and locked the door behind me.

There was still blood on the stainless steel sink. I stood over it and cried. The smoke was dense and black now, tyres and plastics burning. In the background, Sluggo and Ronny were retreating, closer to the creek. I could not stand it any longer and I shut myself in the bedroom, howling like a wounded animal.

That evening I ventured outdoors again. My father returned home and found me asleep. I lied about the chase across the creek and explained that I cut myself by falling over in the bush; but I could not disguise the crying and tears and I told my parents that Sluggo and Ronny had burnt down my bonfire.

Why, they asked.

I said that I did not know ... and that, as far as I was concerned, was the truth.

What had I done? What were they doing?

Nothing more was asked about the incident, though I sensed I had stumbled on to a secret for which Sluggo and Ronny wanted to punish me. There was a strange awakening of a sense of power for which I had no explanation.

My parents offered their consolations. So did my friends.

They had been down at the rubbish tip collecting materials for burning, and although they ran when they saw the smoke above the bushes, they arrived too late. Sluggo and Ronny were gone.

Cracker Night lost its glory and importance for me that year. I exploded my bungers, fired my skyrockets and drew pictures in the night air with a box of sparklers, but it was at the side of someone else's bonfire, where I was a visitor and where, I could not help feeling, I was invited out of pity.

Several mornings later I met Sluggo on the way to school. He knocked my school case out of my hand, threateningly.

"If yer smart, you'll keep yer gob shut. Or next time we'll burn yer house down." With that he clouted me over the head and walked off, chuckling, flexing his muscles for extra effect.

As I walked to school along the track beside the railway line, I kicked at dust and pebbles with the joy of a new discovery, even though my ear burnt from the whack of Sluggo's hand. My bonfire had been destroyed and my pride wounded, yet I knew that tough Sluggo had a weakness and I knew he did not want it revealed. I was ignorant of the nature of the knowledge that had come into my possession, but I knew it was terrible and Sluggo was vulnerable in that respect. I had lost my status as a builder of the biggest bonfire, but something else was gained — a knowledge of something primitive and elemental, as urgent as the desire of children to compete with one another in the building of bonfires that were reduced to a heap of dry ashes. As I continued walking with Sluggo's threat in my head, I failed to comprehend.

Today the bush playground is gone. The creek is dredged regularly by the council. I bring my own children to the oval and try to explain what was once there. I hark back to a description of summer days, swallows skimming above the creek and blue wrens at play in the blackberry bushes, pointing out how the creek once curved out of sight, hidden by bulrushes, past the factories.

Bonfires are built no longer. I can't say what happened to Sluggo, though it was rumoured he moved to Queensland. About Ronny, I know nothing.

The old paling fence was torn down and replaced by one of cyclone wire-netting with barbed-wire on top — to keep out intruders, especially children.

MATTHEW CONDON

MUD AND IVORY ELEPHANTS

I saw my mother's body one Sunday on the front page of a newspaper. I hadn't heard from her for five days because we had an argument over a pair of socks and there she was, just her calves and feet showing, half buried in river mud, in the newspaper. She only had one shoe on in the picture.

I had been to the pubs the night before with the boys from the garage where I worked. I got drunk and ended up sleeping on the beach down near the gymnasium. When I got home to my room at the boarding house the landlord was waiting for me with the newspaper and told me the police had been looking for me. He gave me a cup of coffee and I read about the woman found in the river.

Children had discovered her washed up on a bend, her body covered in silt. She still had a handbag over her shoulder, the newspaper said. And she wore an old ivory necklace of little carved roses and elephants. A policeman was quoted as saying she had not been positively identified, but I knew from the description of the necklace that it was my mother.

I still have the front page of the newspaper. It is frayed

along the folds. I took it with me to Australia because I thought it was important that my sister see it. I didn't know some of her friends had already sent it to her home at Sandgate. After a while it was not a sad story to read because it was not about our mother, but the body of a woman, written in clipped newspaper sentences. A woman without a name, in the cold river.

It was a silly argument, about the socks. Elaine was making a pair for me and so was my mother. Elaine was a quick knitter and she finished them in a couple of days. I was wearing them by the time my mother had finished the toe parts of her socks. Looking back I think my mother was in constant competition with Elaine, but she couldn't keep up. They argued, until I could not bring them together at all.

My mother kept telling me I was all she had after my sister left and married a pearl diver in Australia. She said Elaine was trying to steal me away from her. I told her that was a load of codswallop.

My mother had bad eyesight. They tried to tell me later that my mother just walked into the river. A doctor signed a paper that stated my mother was almost blind with cataracts. She could still knit though, I told them. She never had the lights on in the house much, and often she sat in the front room holding a handkerchief in the dark.

The newspaper said that there were no suspicious circumstances. I know that is their cute name for suicide. They never say "suicide" to save the family embarrassment and the strange looks from neighbours and shopkeepers. I didn't believe an argument over a pair of socks had caused it. It sounds bloody ridiculous but even now, whenever I put on a pair of socks, I think of my mother's death.

I have read lots of newspaper stories since then, about ordinary men who kill someone over a woman, or a car, or money in old people's pockets, and I think what a fine line it is between being alive and dead.

The last time I saw Elaine was when I went to the river on that Sunday. She watched me from the bridge as I walked along the water's edge. I remember I looked up and she was there, leaning on the railing with her arms apart, watching me with my trousers rolled up to the knees. I wanted her to sod off. I was looking for my mother's missing shoe. I felt that the river had stolen it from her. I know now it was a strange thing to do.

I went further around the bend and she moved along the bridge. The last I saw of her she was leaning out, holding onto the street lamp at the far end as I went out of view. I went into the reeds and found a path that children had made up into the village. I imagined she waited for me to come back from the river, muddied and damp.

I stayed in the gymnasium for a couple of days before I

left to catch the ship. My friend, Dave, came with me. I'm not sure if Elaine followed us to the docks near the city. We stood on the ship's deck with hundreds of others. People down below threw streamers at us and long lines of stockings, the toes and waists tied together. The streamers tangled, and people cried on the ship and on the shore. I thought I saw Elaine with confetti in her hair.

I grabbed a red streamer and tried to find the stranger at the other end, but it disappeared into the crowd. The paper stretched and then flicked upwards as it broke, and down. Dave waved. As the ship moved away from the pier, men in small boats waited with sticks, ready to pluck the hundreds of broken streamers from the water.

The ivory necklace curled in the plastic bag next to the bundle of his mother's clothes and a moist shoe. The bag, a foggy sack. The identical cream flowers on the dress rotting, the mud still soft in cotton.

The bag was tied tightly at the top with a piece of twine. A tag was attached, the ink of her name smudged. George picked up the bag. A triangle of water formed in the corner, the mud thin and wispy like the long brown hair of a girl, diving.

He stood facing the counter in the police station, holding the bag up to the light. Drops streaked across plastic. The necklace was tangled. Tiny elephants dripped river water. The ivory rose petals between tails and trunks were clotted with mud. The stench from the dress took him momentarily back to the river. Into the bag of air and ivory. The necklace he bought his mother with his first pay packet.

He had seen the newspaper report about the drowned woman and rang his mother. When there was no answer he called the police and they asked him to come to the hospital. They said the woman had not been identified because she had been in the water for days. He thought of baths, white curves and swaying green water. It was his mother. He knew when he saw the necklace.

George gathered her clothes under his arm and held the plastic bag in his right hand. Elaine was there, her eyes red, swollen, sitting beneath the unshaven faces of wanted men on a noticeboard. He walked to his mother's empty house, blindly, as if he was swimming in the muddy river with his eyes open.

When George was young he swam with other boys in the river. They met at a secret clearing, not far from the bridge. The bank there was worn from wet feet with the finger-bones of roots on its surface. In summer the boys stripped off their shirts and shorts, dropped the clothes in bundles or flung them onto the knife-points of reeds, and swam in their white undershorts. George preferred the excitement of the river to the local baths. He enjoyed the currents that buffeted his body, branches that brushed his legs in the murkiness and the dusk patterns of seeds and leaves on the surface. Later, at home, his mother would pick the seeds from his hair.

It was next to the river, squatting in a circle in a wet nest of reeds, that George and his friends learned about women. Magazines were smuggled into the circle. They peered at creamy limbs and silk as the evening cold came up through the mud. A mother's call from a kitchen window would send the boys skittering home, crushing reeds as they ran, the magazines left open. Naked women facing the sky.

In winter the boys lit small fires, fuelling them with exercise book pages and pencils. George loved the blue smoke and the warmth of the fire, so close to the river.

Years later he worked as a mechanic at Whitey's Garage and took his girlfriend Elaine down to the river bank for lunch. They sat in the park on the other side of the bridge. He looked through its stone arches to the patch of needle reeds and thought of strong liquor and the cigarettes he used to light from the fires. Elaine brought sandwiches for him and she ate fruit. He knew the conversation would lead to his mother.

"Is it going to be like this when we get married?" she said.

"Who the hell said we're getting married?" He rested on his left elbow on the grass and watched the pieces of straw and wood in the river ease past.

"Everyone expects us to," Elaine said.

"You mean your girlfriends at the gas company."

"Not just them, everyone."

"Everyone will have to wait," George said.

"Yes, until your mother is ready, I suppose."

They had the same argument many times. George looked across to the trees, their corded roots clawing onto the bank. The roots emerging from the mud on the river bed.

"Maybe if your sister had stayed you wouldn't feel so guilty," Elaine said.

"I'm not guilty for anything," he said. "I'm her bloody son, for Christ's sake. Stop pushing it."

They walked back to the centre of the village. She worked next to the jewellers and stopped there most times before going back to the office. George stood with her in front of the shop window and the dark reflection of his overalls was filled with arcing pearl necklaces, watches, velvet cases and gold claws gripping diamonds.

On Fridays he went to his mother's house for dinner. It was winter, cold and dark early. He rode under the balloon haze of streetlights to her house at the hill end of the village. She always turned on the downstairs light on Fridays and he coasted his motorcycle into the garage.

He took off his jacket and leather cap and walked up the back stairs in his steel-capped boots, the vibration from his weight deep in the house's foundations. He remembered the same shudder from when he was a boy. The clink of a tea cup, or an ornament, and the arrival of his father.

"Hello, Mother."

She stood at the sink in the stark kitchen light, scrubbing a stain from the white china. She couldn't remove the shape of the flame where the cold water dripped onto the back of the sink. It wasn't as dark after her scrubbing, but it was still there.

"Have a nice day at work?" she said. "I can't get this stain off."

She kissed him on the cheek and he sat at his place at the table. Elbows on the tablecloth, pressing against a flight of food-specked geese. She went back to the scrubbing.

"You wouldn't think water could stain so bad," she said.

She went to the stove and stirred soup with a wooden spoon. George watched her concentrate on pouring the soup into a bowl, the steam across her powdered cheeks. The smell of tomato and talcum. For an instant, he saw the young woman in her face.

"What did the doctor say about your eyes?" he said.

"Not too good," she said. "They're getting worse. They don't seem any worse to me."

She poured a bowl of soup for herself and sat opposite George. She spilled some drops onto the tablecloth as she ate. Onto small wings.

She put her glasses on and took the fish from the oven.

"I'll get you some new glasses," he said.

"Don't want to waste your money. You've got to save now."

"What for?"

"For when you get married," she said.

"What has Elaine been saying to you?"

The smell of fish went right through the kitchen, its headless body arcing in the baking dish. The tail dry and stiff above simmering juice.

"I heard it down at the markets," she said. "I thought you might have told me."

He saw the stars in a black sky outside the window. As he rode home after dinner he could still hear in his head the peck of cutlery on his mother's crazed china plate.

George's mother threw the socks into the fire. They burned quickly, the bone needles still embedded in the wool. It took a while for the bone to burn. He left after the argument and later imagined the needles, frail, with beads of ash at their ends, resting on the logs.

She knitted slowly because of her eyes, carefully locking the black fibre. Thick work socks for winter. Elaine made George a pair in a couple of nights. He wore them to dinner at his mother's house. They argued and he told her she was a silly old woman. It was the first fight they had had since his sister went to live on the other side of the world.

His mother threw her unfinished socks into the fire and he said he wouldn't come back until she made more sense. He stomped down the back stairs and rode away.

The boy told the police he saw a woman walk into the river. She was wearing a dress with flowers on it and carrying a handbag. Just walked into the river, as if it wasn't there. He didn't tell anyone for a couple of days because he was smoking cigarettes down in the reeds, and he was scared he'd get into trouble.

Police and volunteers went to the river and searched through the reeds on both banks. In the late afternoon, when the river rose slightly, people watching on the bridge could hear the sucking noises of men's boots being pulled from the mud. The searchers used torches, the blue beams cutting through the reeds. Thousands of strands, swelling at the waterline.

Someone yelled and there was a splash. The men rushed to the bend and pointed their torches at the woman's body. A statue in the silt. Blue light reflected off the mud. One of the men took a photograph and the flash turned everything white for a second. Then it was blue again.

George ran his thumb along the knobs of ivory, the smooth elephant shapes. Jagged rose petals. He felt the necklace through the plastic bag. He stood in his mother's kitchen, the tablecloth clean, the soup stains gone. He put the damp clothes and necklace on the table and went into the front room.

The sofa and chairs were just bulky shapes in the dark. Photographs on the wall stains in heavy wooden frames.

He went to her room, sat on the edge of the bed and switched on the bedside lamp. There, on the quilt, he saw a baby's pink cardigan. It smelled of mothballs. Its wool flat and dull, with knitted animals on each small pocket. The cardigan was neatly spread out, the arms outstretched as if in surprise. The buttons were so old they were cracked.

The tin gypsy wagon was next to the cardigan. George's childhood toy, with the smooth roof and square windows, painted red with gold lettering. The wheels loose, leaning inward.

He turned off the light and saw a glow from the village

through the curtains. Spinning a wheel of the wagon, he thought he heard a young voice tangled in the squeak of tin.

Liam Davison

THE SHIPWRECK PARTY

Captain Youl was a man in control of his ship. He stood with his hand firmly on the brass lever at his side, looking out to sea. When he pushed it forward a message was sent through the wire which ran like a nerve through the body of the ship. It went through the two crowded upper decks, through the mezzanine to the bar where drinks were being served, down through the four-inch steel plates of the bulkheads and along the 310-foot length of the ship. At the engine room a little bell was rung. Men responded to the bell. They opened furnace doors, adjusted valves, sweated, and the 1,410 tons of steel moved a fraction faster through the water.

To John Bannister, who watched from the balcony of the Grand Hotel, the change in speed was barely noticeable. Later, he would say that things seemed to be running as normal, but then he wasn't an expert on ships. He'd watched the *Hydra* make three round trips to the point on the opposite side of the bay, not so much out of interest but because he enjoyed the sun. From the balcony, he looked out over a calm sea. Even along the shore it had given up throwing itself at the sand and lay there, flat and exhausted, waiting for the day to end. Children wet their feet without interest. Men and women sat talking on the lawns in front of the hotel or else walked slowly along the esplanade in pairs or out to the end of the pier for something to do. In the rotunda, a little way round to the right, musicians were packing away their instruments. All afternoon, music had floated up through the heat to the balcony and out across the bay.

Beyond all this, the *Hydra* created only a small disturbance in the water. John Bannister took little notice of its moving back and forth. Each time he looked out to sea and caught it in the periphery of his vision, it seemed to be in exactly the same spot as the time before, so it might not have been moving at all. That's why at first he couldn't quite tell what had happened. There was no noise, no obvious sign of disturbance, but something, something important had changed.

Eventually he noticed that the *Hydra* had stopped. It tilted slightly to one side like a picture that had slipped on its nail. Everything else was the same but the sight of the crooked ship disconcerted him. He looked back to the straight pier, the people on the esplanade, the musicians in the rotunda, trying to avoid it. But, as usual, the one blemish on the scene, small as it was, kept catching at his eye. The *Hydra* was sinking.

By late afternoon it was listing badly and a flotilla of small craft had converged on the ship. Men who would normally never have taken to the sea took off their coats, rolled up their sleeves and rowed out to look for themselves. The children, happy that something had finally happened, ran round to the point for a closer look. Even the ladies craned their necks from the end of the pier.

The passengers were removed safely from the ship. Ladders were lowered over the sides to the small boats waiting below and, as each one was filled, it made its way slowly to the end of the pier. Some of the ladies wet their feet and one, unsettled at being part of a shipwreck, dropped her parasol into the water. It floated for a while like a cotton jellyfish then sank slowly to the bottom.

As more boats came in, word came back to the hotel that Captain Youl was firmly in control. His name was passed from person to person, each time with some new reference to the way he was handling things: Captain Youl continued giving orders from the bridge, Captain Youl had saved a man from drowning, Captain Youl was the last to leave the ship. So by the time John Bannister heard his name it had already established a reputation.

It was with this reputation that the captain himself finally arrived at the Grand Hotel. He seemed unperturbed by the day's events, happy even with the interest he'd created in the town. A cable had been sent to Melbourne informing the company directors of what had happened. Questions were asked about how a ship could simply run aground like that. People spoke of an inquiry. Negligence was mentioned more than once. Captain Youl made light of the situation, speaking of far worse calamities he'd seen at sea.

"There's not much can come of a shipwreck the likes of this," he said. "Hardly a shipwreck at all when you think of things."

From the hotel the *Hydra* looked as though she was sinking further into the sea as the tide came in. Her great wheel was little more than a hump in the water at her side, and her twin funnels pointed obliquely like guns at the sky. Others commented too on the nature of the sinking. "There should be more to a shipwreck than this," they said, "more noise and confusion." Shipwrecks, they knew, shouldn't be tidy affairs.

Captain Youl glanced only occasionally at the sea and seemed unperturbed at the prospect of an inquiry. Even ashore he was in control of things. People turned to him to see what would happen next or else they spread rumours about his colourful past so his reputation grew beyond belief. When he announced the party it was as if that was what people had been waiting for. Even the least adventurous were excited by the idea of a party on board a sinking ship.

There was talk of irresponsibility of course, and questions of safety. Some argued about the likelihood of the ship taking more water and tilting further on its side or the possibility of it turning completely over, but all of this only attracted more interest to the idea of the party. John Bannister watched with reservations as the preparations were made.

Crates of Pimms and glasses were carried to the end of the pier and loaded into the same small boats which had, only hours before, brought passengers ashore. The captain himself directed the loading. He wore full uniform with his cap sitting straight on his head as if he knew it might soon be gone. Four crates of poultry, a pheasant under glass, boxes of fruit and two round cheeses all found their way from the hotel kitchens into the waiting boats. A case of wine was brought for the captain's table along with a dozen crayfish all pink and whistling with steam. One by one the hotel's kitchen staff filed into the boats to be rowed precariously out to the ship. "There's nothing to worry about," the captain reassured. "Nothing to worry about at all." Finally the musicians from the rotunda were crowded into a boat. They huddled over their instruments, anxious about the water, and a gold tuba sprouted like a funnel from the back of the boat.

John Bannister was one of the last to leave for the ship, except for those who weren't invited or were too afraid to go. Strings of lights had been roped between the funnels and around the decks so it looked like a floating palace. The musicians had already started playing their music and it floated out across the still, black water. On board, everything was tilted to one side. The guests gripped tightly to railings to stop them from slipping into the water which they were surprised to find beside them instead of beneath their feet. It was as if they were already drunk even before they'd had enough to drink. Women fell willingly into men's arms. The musicians felt their stools slipping away beneath them and wondered whether the ship was moving. The decks, awash with spilt drinks, sloped dangerously away.

The captain welcomed John Bannister aboard, his strong arms lifting him up the last few steps of the ladder and his face smiling out from beneath the cap. "Welcome aboard the *Hydra*," he said. "We thought the last had arrived."

John Bannister felt the ship slipping away beneath his feet. "I hadn't planned to come," he said, "but then ..."

"You don't like ships, Mr Bannister? Or parties?"

"I don't mind either," he said, "but perhaps not the two together. I don't like sinking ships."

"The *Hydra* is quite safe as she is. She's grounded on rock," said the captain. "Can I get you a drink, or introduce you to someone perhaps?"

"I was wondering, Captain Youl, with a vessel the size of

the *Hydra*," he looked along her polished deck and up to the crowded promenade, "how can a ship just sink like this?"

"You're not experienced with the sea, Mr Bannister?"

"I watch it from the shore," he said. "It seemed harmless enough today."

"Things aren't always what they seem, Mr Bannister, especially not the sea. You'll learn that if you stay by it long enough."

"But there must be charts? Navigational aids? It doesn't change that much."

"The sea has many variables, Mr Bannister. And I have many guests. If you'll excuse me, you'll find drinks being served in the bar."

The captain returned to the foredeck where a group of ladies waited patiently for his return. They stood close by him, attracted by the uniform and hanging on every word he spoke. Some of the younger men, anxious to make themselves known, stood back waiting for an introduction. John Bannister made his unsteady way towards the mid-deck doorways. Some of the guests had started a game, seeing who could walk the length of the ship without slipping or clutching for support. They filed past him, arms out like tightrope walkers, laughing and calling to him to join their fun. Inside, the crowd leaned against each other marvelling at the idea of the party on board the ship.

John Bannister stood by the open doors watching as they grew louder and more excited trying to serve themselves food from the sloping table. A woman, making for the doorway, careered into him, spilling her drink onto her shoes and laughing at her poor coordination. She trailed another man behind her as a sort of balancing device.

"Are you a friend of the captain's?" she asked.

John Bannister guessed she was talking to him. "I've only met him the once. In fact …"

"Then you're staying at the hotel," she said. "Yes, you look like you'd be staying at the hotel. Then you must let me show you the ship." She let go of the other man and leaned heavily against John Bannister's arm.

"I'm sorry …"

"What Miss Martin means, Sir," said the other man, "is that everyone staying at the hotel was invited aboard."

"You must let me show you. We're going below the decks."

"Below the decks?"

"There's a group of us. We're going to open the hatches. It will be fun don't you think?"

John Bannister looked to the other man for an answer. "It can't do any harm," he said. "A few drinks. The damage is already done."

"But the captain."

"You don't know the captain, Mr ...?"

"Bannister. No, I don't know him, but surely he wouldn't approve."

"The captain is a man who believes in taking risks. That's how we come to be where we are." He took a cigarette from his pocket and lit it. "Have you any idea how much the captain lost today?"

He felt Miss Martin's body leaning close to his own.

"On the crossing, Mr Bannister. You're not a gambling man? There's not much excitement in Sunday excursions for a man like Captain Youl. So, a little money changes hands. The *Hydra* is a fast ship for its size. People are prepared to bet on it."

"What sort of people?"

"Business people, Mr Bannister. Syndicates. Their names might come out in the inquiry. But then again ... It had to happen, of course, given time. You can only get so close to the reef on a lowish tide, even with Youl at the helm."

Outside, the band was starting another tune and people were trying to dance on the sloping boards. Miss Martin still held John Bannister's arm. She called out across the room something about opening the hatches and spilt more of her drink on the floor.

"But why give a party?"

"The captain's a man of style, Mr Bannister. I mean,

you've only got to look at him to see. Even when he's losing he does it right and, when it's all said and done, there's no real harm resulted. No one's been hurt. People are enjoying themselves. That's the function of a party."

Miss Martin drew him away towards the hatches, her arm linked through his. "No one will know," she said. "There's only a few of us. We've found some lights."

At the rear of the ship, two metal hatches were set tight in the decking. A man, already clumsy with drink, was trying unsuccessfully to prise one of them open while two women and another man stood watching, offering advice and giggling with anticipation. "Get your fingers underneath it and it should lift straight up," the man said. "There's nothing to stop it."

John Bannister looked back towards the rest of the party. Miss Martin drew him on. "They say there's passages," she whispered, "leading right through to the front of the ship, and they won't all be filled with water. Imagine," she said, "if we all came up from nowhere through that hatch at the front of the ship. Wouldn't that be a surprise? Wouldn't that just stop the party?" The others nodded and laughed their approval. John Bannister stood looking down at the hatches.

"Do you think it's really wise?"

"Of course it's not wise," Miss Martin laughed. "It's fun. Where's your sense of adventure?"

The man giving advice thrust a light into John Bannister's hand and bent down to open the hatch himself. It lifted heavily outwards revealing a dark square hole in the deck. The sound of lapping water came out of it and strange echoes from deep inside the ship. There was an iron ladder disappearing into it.

"Shine the light inside."

John Bannister did as he was told. The light showed the hole opening into the hold of the ship. Water dripped from the metal beams and lay in great dark puddles on the lower side of the ship. Miss Martin undid the straps of her shoes and set them neatly by the hatch.

"I'll go first," she said. "I'll lead the expedition."

"Perhaps someone with a light should lead the way," said the other man. They looked at John Bannister.

"It should be a man," said one of the other women. "It should be a man with a light."

John Bannister removed his shoes and placed them beside Miss Martin's. "I'll wait at the bottom then to give some light," he said. "I really don't know about going further."

Inside the ship, the light reflected strangely off the water, throwing distorted illuminations up onto the steel walls. All around he could hear the dripping of water and the hollow booms of things nudging against each other further inside the ship. There was a passage leading forward from the hold.

Miss Martin edged him towards it. "That will lead to the cabins," she said. "You go first."

They moved warily along the passage, leaning against the lower wall and moving their feet through water. The ship creaked and strained, and every now and then they heard a louder bang like something heavy falling far away as one of the steel plates shifted or buckled under the weight of water. There was a machine noise too, a regular humming of the generators used to light the decks, and further on they could see that some of the passageways were lit irregularly with weak yellow lights.

They moved past great chambers opening off the passageways, steel compartments half-filled with water. Further inside, the water rose almost to their knees and was filled with floating things, bits of wood and personal belongings. John Bannister felt them brushing past his legs as he moved deeper into the ship.

"The crew's quarters will be further forward," said Miss Martin. "Then there should be stairways leading up."

They passed metal ladders leading further down into the body of the ship, into the engine rooms where dark shapes rose out of the water, and somewhere beneath it all, the steel plates had been rent apart exposing the black rock of the reef. Above them, they could hear the muffled sounds of the party, the music coming down through a maze of openings and corridors and mingling with the ever-present sound of water. John Bannister imagined he could hear the captain's voice. The passage they were in turned sharply to the left, towards the list of the ship so the water rose even higher up their legs.

"I think perhaps we might have come far enough," John Bannister said. He could hear Miss Martin's breathing close behind him and the sounds of the others pushing through water. "We'll have to go back."

"We can't go back," she said. "We're almost there. Listen, you can hear them." The others laughed and splashed behind them, showing no intention of turning back.

The passage turned again towards the bow of the ship and was filled with moving light which reflected off the water up onto the walls and ceiling. They passed a number of doors, all shut tight with water, with the names of crew members stencilled onto them. John Bannister shone his light through the round window in each of them and saw mattresses, broken chairs, bits of paper, all floating in the murky water. In the last window his light shone into a small chamber with the body of a man floating face-down inside it. Its swollen arms bumped against the bottom of the window and John Bannister could see other things floating beside it — a small chest, two books and the back of a chair — but his eyes came back to the body. Floating like that inside the steel room, it hardly seemed human at all, more like some strange creature glimpsed from outside a dark aquarium. The name on the door was Hughes.

The others followed John Bannister along the passage, unknowingly past Mr Hughes's quiet door, and into the stairwells which took them up, out of the water, back towards the surface. Miss Martin and her friends giggled with excitement as they appeared, dripping with water, from the body of the ship. She stumbled away, screeching with delight as she went. "You'll never believe," she squealed. "Such an adventure. The whole length of the ship."

John Bannister let them go, feeling conscious of his wet trousers and the party going on around him. Few people noticed their arrival.

On the foredeck he found the captain. He looked remarkably at ease on the sloping deck, unaware of what floated at the heart of his ship. Even his cap sat straight on his head. John Bannister caught his eye.

"Captain Youl," he said. "If you'll excuse me for a moment? There's something I think you should know about your ship."

MARIAN ELDRIDGE

THE WOMAN AT THE WINDOW

Sharon takes out another cigarette and reaches for the lighter. Today, before she catches sight of Mickey again, she is letting herself use the lighter; after that it's matches. It's one of her good luck things. She's standing by the kitchen window but she can't take anything in yet because she's still shaking. Thank God people in the other flats wouldn't have heard, they'd have left for work. When Mickey nags it's not a soft mosquito's whine like little Trace but a piercing shriek, as though she's belting the life out of him when she's never so much as laid a finger!

"*Stop* it, Mickey!" she hisses as the sound goes on echoing in her head. She touches her shin. It's going to come up like one of those purple and green eggfruits where the little devil's heel caught her. She grabbed his arms and pushed them into his jacket, the one he ripped but it's got his name and address pinned on to it, then she dragged him, roaring and flailing, out to the landing and gave him a push towards the stairs. "Get lost, Mickey!"

She jabs out her cigarette in a dirty cup. It's matches now — she can see Mickey's bobbing blond head. He's fine, he's just fine. Arms spread like wings, he's scattering dozens of magpies as he runs across the grassed area between the flats and the church centre. His sneakers will be soaked again. There's a perfectly good path but he never remembers. Sometimes a man comes on a toy tractor and mows the grass. Squawk park, Sharon calls it, because of all the magpies flapping and clamouring and poking their beaks down one another's throats. Now Mickey's stalking one of the parent birds. Walking just ahead of him, the magpie keeps one eye on him and one on the grass. A young bird flies clumsily towards it, overshooting the spot and landing yards away. You often see them dead on the ring-road. Mickey watches the parent run to feed the squawking baby, then himself continues to run, arms outspread towards the flats.

The magpies nest in the trees overhanging the flats and some of the residents feed them. It stops them swooping, the woman in the adjacent flat tells Sharon. She corners Sharon one morning on the landing, just as Sharon is about to close her door on Mickey and the woman is coming out of hers, all rugged up against the sharp August morning and clutching a plastic bag full of something soft and oozing. Chopped up rump, she tells Sharon. I feed them every morning on my way to work, she says. Sharon ducks her head; the memory of her voice is as sharp as a beak. They don't like mince, the woman says, even though Sharon's door is three-quarters shut by this time and Sharon is staring over her head at a patch of blue sky through the landing window. I told the butcher, I said That says something about the quality of mincemeat, doesn't it, when the magpies refuse to eat it!

Maybe if they swooped a bit more the ranger would come and shoot a few! Sharon says, or thinks about saying. After that morning she's careful never to open her door at the time the woman will be leaving for work, not even if Mickey's teasing baby Tracey or demanding more Cocopops or screaming till Sharon's head bursts.

I could ring the ranger myself, Sharon thinks, hurrying from the kitchen to the living room where the window looks onto the ring-road. There's a phone box below her, next to the pedestrian crossing. She sees herself going down the landing stairs and around the corner, pushing the phone box door inwards so that it folds up on itself like a trick door and dropping in the coin and then the ranger coming with his gun bang! bang! He's wearing his smart ranger uniform and Mickey's off playing somewhere — standing by the pedestrian crossing actually, with his hand on the button. In the palm of her own hand Sharon feels the button beating like a slow loud heartbeat. *This time, this time, this time.* The baby's still asleep in Sharon's bed — no, Mickey's cot, it would have to be Mickey's cot — and she says I have always admired that uniform would you care for a sherry ... only she drank the last of it yesterday, the empty bottle is lying in the middle of the living room. Would you care for cocoa? — cocoa because she's run out of tea and coffee, milk too she remembers, Mickey had that on his Weetbix. Sure would! says the ranger. I have always admired —

But, Sharon interrupts herself, how can I make that call, is it still twenty cents or has that box been changed over to thirty? Is it twenty or thirty? And she twists her hands in her nightdress until it tears a bit more at the shoulder.

Mickey is still standing by the crossing. He's swinging his foot at a dead baby magpie squashed on the ring-road. Every time a car rushes past, its feathery wings blow as though it is trying to fly. Traffic is heavy at this time of day. A stream of cars is pouring into the car park. The signal on the crossing changes from red to green, then back to flashing red. As people from the flats hurry across towards the shops and offices of the city centre, Sharon feels a surge of excitement. The drunks on the seat under the elms at the corner have been shopping already. This time the big man is carrying the paper bag. He places it carefully between his feet, opens a bottle, drinks and passes it to the next man. One of them starts to laugh, bending over then flinging back against the seat until the others join in, rocking backwards and forwards and slapping one another's shoulders. The big man grabs the bottle and, putting it to his mouth, holds it high like a trumpet.

Stragglers on the crossing scurry as the light turns red. Mickey isn't with them. He is pushing between the road edge and the low hedge in front of the flats. Sharon can see his bright curly head through gaps where the hedge has died. His hair curls on to his shoulders. It's like Rob's, soft and fair, whereas Tracey's is straight and dark like Peter's. It was Peter who helped her get this flat. You're in luck, he said. Most people have to wait months. Peter doesn't know about Tracey. He's working in Sydney now.

Sydney, Sharon says, and feels a wave of nostalgia, bitter as morning sickness. Sydney is sand and tanning oil, and your thoughts melting like ice-cream. Sydney is your sisters chatting up that lifesaver with the gold crucifix while you whined Come on, Mum'll get mad! Sydney is voices creeping out from broken tiles, Come on Shar, come and have fun!

That's how she met Rob.

It was at a party. There was this guy down from Canberra. He kept looking at Sharon. His eyes felt like hands on all the secret parts of her body. Sharon's friend shouted Who wants a ride on Rob's Harley Davidson? When it was Sharon's turn she heard herself saying Why don't we keep going till we get to Canberra? and that made Rob laugh. You'd like Canberra, he said. Sharon pictured a big white

Parliament House surrounded by enormous houses with curving drives and huge green lawns where no one had to fight over whose turn it was in the bathroom. They arranged to meet the next day. It was Rob's last day in Sydney. She rode on the back of the Harley to a quiet beach where Rob had to see some people. Sharon thought she would go mad if Rob didn't keep touching her. She thought Rob's friends looked at her funny; didn't talk much in front of her. Try this, Rob said, passing her a thin, damp cigarette. They lolled around on the sand while the sun soared over them like gigantic surf.

When she returned home her mother, who thought she had gone into town for the day to look for a job, took one look at her and screamed "Don't start telling me a pack of lies, I don't want to hear it!" The next morning, while her parents were still sleeping, she stuffed what clothes she could into her old school haversack, stole her mother's collection of Charles and Di fifty-cents and climbed out the bedroom window. She could have walked out the front door but the window seemed right. At Central Station she bought a ticket to Canberra and she hasn't been back home since, not once, nor written, nor telephoned.

"God, this place!" Sharon exclaims, turning her back to the window. There's a new stain on the sofa, and Mickey must have been at the horsehair again; it looks like a little animal trying to hide. Panic washes into Sharon's throat like a scummy tide. There are dirty cups on the TV and the floor and the window ledge; how long is it since she washed up? She seizes the empty sherry bottle; rushes cups, plates, baby's bottles and cutlery into the sink and pours cold water on to them; snatches up all the clothes she can find on the floor, over chairs, under the bed, never mind if they're dirty or not, she doesn't waste time looking — out, out they go, into the laundry basket. If they all go in, she thinks, if they all go in and nothing falls on the floor, *it will mean good luck*. Sometimes she starts off the day like that: if a bird flies past the window ... if Mickey wakes up before Tracey ... or it might be the other way round, if Tracey wakes up before Mickey. The last thing, Mickey's bottom sheet that he's wet again, catches over the edge of the basket and hangs there, touching the floor but not falling either. Sharon's hands are shaking. She needs another cigarette. She's using the lighter again; that's allowed now.

She's down to her last cigarette. There are plenty in the shops of course, milk too, cigarettes and milk and the other things she has run out of. The shops are on the other side of the car park and the car park is on the other side of the ring-road and the ring-road is on the other side of the window.

She has to look away quickly.

She looks away to the seat under the elms where the drunks sit all day, even on days as nippy as this. She has a little fantasy that Rob is one of the men on the seat. Any minute now he'll look up and wave and she'll lock the kids in the flat and go down and they'll share the bottle or maybe a joint. It couldn't be any colder under the elms than it was in midwinter in the garage where she lived with him when she first came to Canberra.

Canberra was ace! Rob took her to parties and gigs or they stayed in the garage smoking hash or cuddled inside two sleeping bags zipped together, or they went over to the house where people were always coming and going. She never got to like the people in the house as much as Rob did; they talked to him more than they talked to her, and they'd bang hard on the bathroom door when she was daydreaming under the shower. Also they never cleaned up the kitchen, no one did except herself. Annie, the other girl who lived there, said "I don't know why you do it." But then Annie ate out; she could afford to, she had a job. She was a very bossy sort of girl, *woman* she insisted on, she hated *girl*. Sharon took to going over to the house only when Rob did, even if she was bursting, or she'd hang on till night time and squat behind the fig tree.

At first she thought it was just her body playing a trick. Rob said "Shit! You'd better do something, Shar!" and gave her six brand-new fifty-dollar notes but she kept on putting it off, she got scared, she kept hoping her mother would write or just turn up on the doorstep.

And after a while it was too late.

Rob left Canberra soon after that. He said it was what they'd been talking about all winter, him and her zipping north on the Harley. He's back again now; he does the lighting for a new theatre group just up the road at Gilmore House. He stopped her one day when she was taking the two kids for a walk. "Sharon! How's things?" He's even been around once with a huge Mickey Mouse for Mickey, but when Sharon said "What about some regular maintenance, Rob?" he laughed. He said "You must be joking, Shar. I'm on the dole."

It was Annie who put her up to saying that to Rob. Annie's at Gilmore House, too — she's part of a women's video group — and she drops in at the flat sometimes for coffee. She drinks dandelion coffee so she brings her own. When Annie's talking, Sharon nods and says Yes Annie, yes, I should do that. Get your name on the waiting list for a three-bedroom house, Annie tells her. You're eligible, Sharon. When Rob cleared out, Annie persuaded her to move into a group house with Annie and two other women. They brought Sharon cups of herbal tea to stop the retching. They massaged her temples. They showed her articles about the effects of smoking on the developing foetus. They said You'll have no trouble getting family day care, Sharon, that's one of the good things about Canberra. They wanted her to have the baby in the house, with everyone helping. They began to talk about "our baby". One afternoon, while someone was practising on the drum kit in the living room, Sharon got dressed, climbed out her bedroom window and caught a bus into the city. In the city she did two things; she booked herself in at the hospital, and put her name down for a government flat.

The baby Tracey totters into the living room. She is crying, slow tears washing down her face like July rain. She's wearing an old pyjama coat of Mickey's, so shrunken her arms stick out to the elbows. Her napkin and plastic pants have fallen around her knees. Sharon pulls the napkin right off, then, sliding down to the floor, takes Tracey on to her lap and puts her to her breast. Tracey is going on two but if Sharon tries to wean her she cries, not a full-blooded roar like Mickey but *NnnnNnnn* like an insect trapped against glass.

When Mickey was starting to walk Sharon tried to get a job, a cash-paying job so as not to lose her pension. Cleaning, she thought. Annie wrote her a reference. Every Saturday she bought the paper and went through the Sit. Vac. The first lady she cleaned for asked her not to bring Mickey again, "little sticky fingers", so Sharon left him locked in the flat until one of the neighbours said that he cried and Sharon got scared of losing her lease. The second lady worked during the day so there were no worries there about taking Mickey. Sharon had the run of the house, she could dream out the windows, gaze all she wanted to at the pool and the green lawns, the mountains so sharply blue they made her throat wobbly, the fledgling new Parliament House with its seven cranes bending down to it. Two days after starting work for this lady she received a letter: "Dear Sharon, Here is the money I owe you. I shall not be requiring you again. I wonder my dear if you have ever cleaned a house before? . . ." Sharon cried. She thought Tracey wasn't showing yet but the third lady said, "You wouldn't be able to continue for long, would you, dear? I'm very sorry but I really want somebody permanent."

"It isn't fair!" exclaims Sharon, putting Tracey aside and jumping to her feet. "It's all right for you!" she declares, staring at someone invisible across the room. Tracey tugs at her nightdress. Sharon snatches her up and thrusts her back at the breast, but the baby twists her head away. "Go down on the floor then, Tracey," Sharon sighs. She can't get over how different girls are from boys, even kids this age; when

Mickey's inside he's at her all the time for Weetbix, fizzy drinks, biscuits. "What *is* it? Stop it, Trace. You want more titty? Trace?" She bends to lift her once again, but the child slips out of her grasp and, going into the centre of the room, falls to the floor and cries, *NnnnNnnn. NnnnNnnn.*

Sharon goes into the bedroom and closes the door. Stumbling over Mickey's broken tip-truck she discovers her purse on the floor, so she sits on her bed and empties it into her lap. She puts the five-dollar notes on one side of her, the twos on the other; with the coins she makes a little tower that keeps falling over. After a while she peeps into the living room. Tracey has fallen asleep on the floor. Sharon picks her up and puts her into Mickey's unmade cot and pulls the side up. Heaving at it, she feels sick again, and remembers that she hasn't eaten anything since yesterday lunchtime when she finished off Tracey's tin of chicken dinner.

At the back of the refrigerator she finds a slice of bread in its plastic wrap. As she eats it at the kitchen window she watches the magpies in squawk park. The parent birds jab at wriggling things underground, run to the nearest begging baby, run run run on legs like twigs to find more food. The baby birds never stop pestering. Sometimes one of the parents gets really bossy, standing over a young one until it shuts up and pretends dead. Suddenly they all fly up into the trees. Two women and two children are coming along the path. One of the women is much older than the others; she is the mother, Sharon decides. The other woman is younger than herself, a girl really. She is swinging a man's purse by its wrist strap, and she isn't wearing a parka and beanie and scarf like the others, but a coat patterned with great zigzags of colour, red, green, purple, gold.

The mother and the girl in the coat stop to study a map. Visitors to Canberra, Sharon thinks, just as she once was. A tiny bubble of excitement surfaces. The visitors disappear around the corner of the flats and she runs to the living room window to see them reappear by the road. While they are waiting for the green light she tiptoes into the bedroom and pulls on her Indian cotton dress and the thick woollen cardigan that Annie gave her. She stuffs her money into her purse and hurries back to the living room window. There they are; the light has turned green but they are not crossing. *They are waiting for her.*

Mickey is still there between the hedge and the road, jumping on the spot as the cars fly past. Maybe he's said something cheeky to the family because as Sharon watches, the mother pushes past the hedge and speaks to him. He's not listening to her at all, jump jump jump. Sharon can feel those little pounding feet in the back of her head. She'll give him such a belting if he's been swearing again! The mother edges back to the others and speaks to the younger woman, the girl. The two kids giggle. The girl looks up at the flats, shrugs, then, although the light is angry red, turns her back on her mother and stalks across the road. Sharon feels a hot wave of excitement. When the light is green again the others cross too. Now the mother and the girl seem to be having a row. They stand under a pine tree in the car park, the woman pointing back at the flats and waving her arm and the girl staring down at the ground, sulky, Sharon decides, a bad girl, a runaway. Finally the woman and the two kids return to the lights and cross back towards the flats, but whether the girl follows Sharon doesn't wait to see. She didn't want the family to fight. She goes into the kitchen and puts the kettle on. There's a used teabag on the sink. Maybe she can squeeze another cup out of that.

The doorbell rings. That little shit Mickey! She's told him once this morning that there aren't any biscuits. He must have found a chair somewhere to stand on to reach the bell, must have dragged it all the way up the stairs. RRRing! RRRing! If she doesn't answer, if she holds her breath and pretends he's not there, he'll give up and go away again. She hears him ring the bell of the flat next door. The cheek of him! Pity the magpie woman's not home to give him what for.

She lights her last cigarette and goes back to the living room window. The family is still there, all four of them.

They're standing by the phone box with their heads together. The mother goes into the box and after a moment comes out. The girl fiddles about in her purse and hands her something, a coin, Sharon supposes, then moves off a short distance, not quite part of the family and not separate either. The mother goes back into the box, leaving the door open. The two kids poke their heads in and listen.

Mickey's down there with them. He's holding on to his doodle and if she's told him not to do that she's told him a dozen times. Before she has time to think she hurries downstairs and around the corner.

"Get upstairs, Mickey."

The mother is out of the phone box by now, the two kids at her elbows.

"Excuse me," says the mother. "Is this your little boy?"

The girl in the bright coat comes a bit closer at this.

It takes Sharon a few moments to register that the woman is speaking to her. "Yes?" she says, abrupt and questioning at the same time. The girl and the mother exchange glances. The two kids are staring. Sharon pulls Annie's cardigan closer.

"He was standing — jumping — right on the edge of the road," the mother begins, as though she wants someone, the girl, Sharon, to take over.

"Yes?" Sharon repeats.

"The traffic's pretty heavy," the girl tosses in, then stares over everyone's heads as though it's all nothing to do with her.

"And that pretty fair hair," the mother adds eagerly, so that Sharon thinks Bet you wish yours was still the same! "He's so pretty," the mother is saying. "I mean I didn't realise he *was* a boy until I saw his name pinned on his jacket."

"And his address," puts in one of the kids importantly. "That's how we knew ..."

Sharon says slowly, "Well what business is it of mine?"

Their faces crumble with doubt. "But he *is* your little boy?" the girl asks, while the mother echoes, "This is your mummy, darling?"

"Of course he is!" Sharon snaps. She adds, "He knows about going out on the road. I've told him. He knows."

"But playing right on the edge —!" says the girl, while the mother cries, "Such a pretty child! Someone might snatch him away!"

"Then it'll be his own fault, won't it?" retorts Sharon. "If he goes out on the road it'll be his own fault. He knows!" cries Sharon. "I've told him! You get along upstairs, Mickey!"

On the stairs she keeps saying "Hurry up, hurry *up*, Mickey!" She adds, "You heard what those two said — if you're not a good boy someone will try to steal you!"

"*They* did!" wails Mickey. "That old lady tried to steal me!

She telled the other one she would give me to a policeman. She said, Come on, Mickey, you come with me. And the other one said —"

But what the runaway girl said Sharon doesn't hear, because at that moment the door bell rings again. This time, since it can't be Mickey, she opens it at once. On her doorstep, sharp as a mountain peak in his trim blue uniform, stands a policeman.

He says to Sharon, "Good morning, madam. Madam, we have just had a phone call ..."

Sharon stands at the window. Through a dead patch in the hedge she can see Mickey clearly. As his mouth opens she stuffs her fingers in her ears but she can't shut out the bellow. Her hand is still smarting. As though he can't bear to stand still Mickey jumps up and down, up and down, jump jump jump jump, he jumps out into the road and as a car whizzes by he jumps back against the hedge, out and back, out and back —

This time! shrieks a voice in Sharon's head. *This time, Mickey, this time, this time!*

Rosie Scott

SENSELESS VIOLETS

It happens like this. A tall, robot-faced punk wearing a tartan tam-o'-shanter stabs a man in the street. The man staggers, grunting in a way which makes my senses leap. It's as if he had been waiting for this knife for a long time. The blade is driven right up to the hilt in his slight chest. The wicker basket he is carrying falls, scattering groceries and a pair of leather gloves, the brown fingers curling grotesquely on the pavement. The man drops heavily against some stone steps and lies like a huge twisted bird, startlingly dead. Later on in my dream I can see the body motionless under a ragged blanket, one shoe poking out with ghastly coyness. Someone has picked up the basket and repacked the contents — it waits beside its owner like a dog.

As soon as I wake I know it's Angel and his seedy diary. I shouldn't have read it, sure, but it was still lucky I did because it was even more psychotic than I had ever suspected. The dream hits me again when I'm sitting at the table eating peaches out of a tin for breakfast. It gives me a thump of anxiety in the chest. It's as if some repressed forbidden longing has activated a switch and the reels have begun to turn silently, projecting troubling figures on a tiny screen in my brain.

In my sea-green studio with its morning shadows, the radio murmuring in the corner, my cigarette smoke hanging in the air, Angel's presence has suddenly become electric. I know for sure I have to get rid of him today, he is like an evil black bird circling over me. I hadn't ever thought consciously that I was in any danger. I've tolerated him for so long because in lots of ways we do suit each other, we're like Siamese twins.

For instance, he is the only visitor I've had for years who let me know that I was a freak the minute he set eyes on me. I am so tired of sycophantic people from the art world coming and murmuring at me. They murmur, their eyes averted reverentially as if I were some living icon. And here I am like a huge pale subaquatic monster sitting at the bottom of a greeny-dark pond, snuffling for the few particles of light slowly filtering down to me.

(Miss Rathbone, I was wondering how you see to paint?)

Visitors just ignore the whole bizarre set-up and pretend we're sitting in a drawing-room and that I'm a trim, bright-eyed matron. They all say such nice things and keep their faces so wonderfully smooth and untroubled and delighted with everything. I still remember the day Angel came — his startling orange hair close against his skull, making him appear deformed. We looked at each other in instant, amused recognition. I liked that. He instinctively knew me. He could see all the grotesque desires which still drive my old bones. With one glance that inhuman adolescent could see that I am an old person in whom the natural ageing of the impulse, the dignity of resignation, is completely absent.

Later on as I got to know him well, it was always amusing to watch his struggle between utter contempt and an almost hysterical desire to be my disciple, my friend, manage me, slime in on my creative energy, muscle in on my fame and somehow, anyhow, go down with me to posterity. His presence brought a strong meaty whiff of the streets into my closed-in old world, there was something dangerous about him which was at least alive. Like a hunting beast, with his rodent face and deformed skull. He needed me for other purposes as well. I had been feeling that strongly recently — that was why I finally read his diary which he left in his desk.

It's as if he has started to feed off my flesh. I can almost feel his pointed little teeth. He's so small and pale and reptilian with his orange death's-head skull and flat insect eyes. The only genuine carnality about Angel is the dab of crusted spittle on his lips. Once recently he touched me by mistake and I suddenly imagined us in bed together. It was horrific. My huge wrinkled body, elderly smell, and Angel, small and sinister, grotesquely excited, burrowing in my flesh like a maggot.

The worst of it is that he seems to guess my fantasies, which he mostly finds contemptible. He somehow meshes in with them, feeds them. Here I am, a gross old baggage, lying in bed at night feeling a hollowness because I haven't got a man in bed with me. At my age. Me, imagining the young body and soft curls on my mouth, the clean musky smell. Even I know there is only a thin line between Angel and me and the pit. I probably didn't even need to read the diary to know that.

And then of course, straight after I met him we worked together on what proved to be my most famous series. Angel even named it — "Senseless Violets". My dream is actually a replica of some of those paintings. It caught the selfsame quality I had been trying to express in the series — that graceless, clumsy, almost sensual way men move in their slow-motion dance of violence. The sensuousness as they close in for the kill. I've probably carried those muddy images round for years, long before I met Angel, but it was his unwholesome adolescent presence which triggered them off. I see now of course that it would have been better to ignore the urge. Six months of working like a dog, sleepless nights — feeling blank and stressed and twitchy all the time. Of course Angel helped in every way he could.

The paintings, I see in hindsight, must have been meat and drink to his disordered soul.

I'm too sheltered now, that's the problem. That's why Angel's crudity was such a breath of fresh air. I've been living here for so long in this house that I'm like a foetus pickled in formalin. Immersed in my environment, peering wistfully out. It's possible Angel is the only breath of reality I've had for years. Once, quite recently, a clutch of Polynesian kids came to my door by mistake. I could see they were quite terrified of me when I opened the door. They could even smell me. They stood there, poised like little gazelles, their nostrils delicate, sniffing the wind. They were lovely. I savagely wanted them to stay, just for a while. I told them their friend didn't live here and asked them if they wanted something to eat. It was dumb, but I actually had some dates in my hands at the time — they looked in absolute horror at the blackish mass I offered. I really wanted them to stay, I even called out to Angel to bring them something to eat, but they made a bolt for it, right in front of my eyes. They were silly with terror. They ran down the path past my funny garden with the old iron sculpture. It was banging and scraping desolately as it does when there's a southerly. Angel came to the door, looking petulant for some reason.

It was such a wounding insight into how I really looked to some people. I did one of the first self-portraits I have done for fifteen years as a result of that — of an enormous woman blocking out a doorway, looking down on some children, a mound of dates like worms in her hands. The painting was slanted down to the children's perspective. There was a brown spiky nettle at the corner of the house. I liked it very much, but a lot of my friends were horrified. They thought it was a grim view of myself. They said I must have bad dreams. Angel thought it was a bit overboard; he said I was grotesque, sure, but not quite so unwholesome as the picture suggested. He has that ludicrous cool way of speaking which almost makes me laugh in his face sometimes. He takes himself so seriously, always calculating the most advantageous response to anything. Sometimes he calls me Dorry and it always sounds like a threat.

But this morning I'm not exactly frightened. I know he's due to come in soon and I want to finish it all in one chop, I've had enough of this bizarre game we've played for so long. Going through my morning routine — cleaning up, getting the canvas ready, dawdling around smoking roll-your-owns — I feel sharp as a fox, I've got all my wits about me. I know instinctively how to deal with him — it's almost like dealing with myself.

When he does come in, it's an anticlimax, my head has been buzzing so much. It's as if I have conjured him up out of my imagination. He walks so softly in his white sandshoes, my creation. I see how super-ambitious he is under his studied manner, all that nonsensical chic.

"Hello, Angel," I say, leaping straight into the breach. "I'm going to paint you this morning. I had a dream about you. You were murdering someone."

He is quite quiet and I sit there watching him attentively, my cigarette smoke wreathing around my head as he stands poised. I feel all-powerful, huge, absolutely still.

"What do you mean?" he whispers.

"You know, Angel." I'm not afraid of him. It's as if our whole association, the great festering swamp the two of us have been dabbling in for a year is to be drained with one brutal cut. We've looked at a few things together, Angel and me, and now I'm itching to tell him to go.

He says softly, he is recovered almost instantly, "Have you been reading my diary? I thought I'd left it here. Were you reading about the performance art? Snuff movies, you name it. Hacking grotesque old women to death. Body art maybe. They video it, you know."

He knows all is lost, I can tell he is wishing he could say something else to me, his partner in crime, his real mother. Such courageous bravado nearly makes me lose my head.

"Sure I have. The trouble with you, Angel, is that you're quite ordinary. You're straight out of *The Professionals*. You know, the wizened little psychotic who's been doing all the killings. He's nearly always caught in the last frame. Before the credits start coming up. You're on nearly every week."

Of course I'm going too far but he's really irritating me, it's good to be drawing blood, piercing his sour skin.

He says, "I've never liked you much, that's true. Why do you think I hang round you all the time?"

For the first time in our association I hear a whine in his voice. He sounds quite young and pathetic.

"Don't be dramatic. Come on, we've leeched on each other quite long enough. You're not coming here again."

I guess I knew how it would go, right from the minute I woke up.

"I hope you have more bad dreams, Dorry," he says, so softly I have to learn forward. I don't want to miss anything he says. His face is soft in the dusk and sea-green room. The cats are watching us steadily with their wicked eyes. I can see he is still rigid with the desire to somehow win me back and keep his power, even though he knows deep down he's lost it. He's still not ready to go out into the wide wide world, poor Angel.

"Body art," I say insultingly, smiling a bit. It's just to help him out.

He laughs, suddenly, giving up. He is quite genuinely amused, I'll give him that.

"Alright, alright. I'm going. But I'm coming back."

It's only a friendly admonition. Angel, the murderous dream, my huge black bird, moves out of my sight.

Settling in with my paintbrushes and the cordial smell of canvas in my nostrils, I feel relaxed, uplifted, easy. I even talk to the cats, who shift unhappily at my voice. It's still hours till my first cup of tea.

Beverley Farmer

BLACK GENOA
In Memoriam: Marjorie Barnard

She had moved to the south coast in autumn to live in the house she had bought, an old weatherboard with long windows and old trees growing against them into the sun. One room in particular, the one behind the apple tree next door, glowed all day as if there were a lamp on inside as the sunlight moved over one wooden wall after another. The walls smelled of incense and quivered in the light wind; on every sunny day a banner with large characters on thin gold silk went wavering in the wind on one wall or another with every flicker in the branches at the window. The characters changed in size and shape and so, no doubt, in meaning. She put her bed in here, and hung a dark blue paper blind with white gulls stencilled on it over the window, though as often as not, and without fail when there was a moon, she would roll it up again once her bedlamp was out. Day by day more apple leaves fell until, with all but the last few stained leaves gone, the whole beach showed at this window when she woke, opaque and still on some mornings, glittering on others, or turbulent, white and dark blue.

She wrote a poem about the window and on impulse sent it in a note to an old friend, Joanna, who lived in the city but had grown up on this coast. *There's a spare bed if you'd like to come down and stay,* she added. *All these clear cold beaches — that's if you can get away, of course.* (Joanna had three children still at school.)

WINDOW

Branches at this pane
turn it into gold lead light
in the winter sun,
they spread a large butterfly
on each wooden wall in turn,

who comes in early,
settling where she's supposed to,
poising each black-veined
wing at the right slant, only
twitching in a wind, or when

birds happen to perch
on a vein — all are black birds,
turned wingpatches. Black,
all the new buds. She'll be blocked
in, blocked out, when the leaves grow.

On full moon nights, two slabs of white marble stretched under her two bare front windows; and the bedroom window was white marble, watered with shadows. So quiet was the wash of the sea that she heard the engines of boats in the Rip. Sometimes in the middle of the night a loud rattling made her sit up and switch the bedlamp on. It was one of the mirrors quivering on the wooden wall, and as she watched the other mirror began and the double sound shuddered in the hollow space between that wall and the wall of the next room, then in the spaces of the rooms themselves until the whole house was throbbing aloud for as long as it took for the ship to edge through the passage.

She slept lightly in the house and had more dreams than usual. In one, her friend Joanna wrote back that she had cancer. Soon afterwards they met by chance and stood talking, so weighed down with intense sorrow that Joanna had to lie down in the grass. She was impossible to lift; trying only made the bones come away out of her like a baked fish's, leaving the flesh, a soft mess of pink and pearly white. Seeds, she thought, but they had a black speck and began to move. *Maggots*, she spoke aloud. Joanna said nothing more. Dumbfounded, she woke and was herself lying stretched out, but in the gold box that was her room on a bright morning.

In one of the half-read borrowed books that she was always

leaving lying round she read an extract of a letter from Marina Tsvetaeva to Boris Pasternak, written in November 1922, an autumn letter, and copied it into her notebook:

> *My favourite form of communication is in the beyond: in dreams. To dream of someone. The second choice is correspondence. Letters are a form of communicating in the beyond, less perfect than dreams, but subject to the same laws.*

Joanna rang in answer to her letter to say she would love to come down to the coast, but her father's cancer, which he had fought for months, had invaded his whole body. They had stopped the treatment and sent him home but now he was back in; now even he had to admit it was the end. She had promised to be with him while he died.

Every day she sat on the beach sketching ink edges around the pallor of it — a still scoop of water as thin as cold air, as if the bay were an empty shell, an earshell, pearl-pale and dotted inside with a line of rocks. When she was cold she walked on the sand. A wet spaniel's head she found one day at high tide in the hairline of the marram grass turned out to be a drowned penguin, its dense wings folded under and hanging out like earlobes. Between them were hunched feathers and there, poking out of them on a fine chain of bones, waggled a small skull black-beaked, formed of fretty translucent folds like bloodstained paper. Carefully she snapped the chain and carried the skull home wrapped in a sheet from her sketchbook to dry in the sun. Every day there was sun, though a wad of fog materialised over the dunes and the sea in the afternoons and often was still there until late next morning. Her house was not far from the lighthouse on the point; the horn's relentless hooting haunted her sleep. Waking, she read in the lamplight or wrote on scraps of paper.

He slips on a muddy embankment. Beside him something emits a foul sweetish stink: a corpse swelling against its buttoned jacket. It has the head of a pig, blue-tinged, dark red on the cheeks and snout. Dark red means that it is decomposing, he reasons, proud that he is still capable of reason. Everyone is starving. This is a terrain of war, covered with the dead and the dying. What did he last eat? The jacket of his uniform has a blue and dark red hand stuck in it. He climbs the embankment to a railway platform. He is busking, juggling balls, reciting a patter. He is waiting, as is his audience, to jump in front of a train when one finally comes. Meanwhile he juggles. A train hoots, hoots on a double note. It is out of sight, very far away still. The audience exclaims. A ball falls on to the gravel. Squatting to grope for it he sees in horror a thick brown pipe of flesh come out of him and prod the gravel. It disgorges a shiny brown mass. He sticks his finger in it to confirm what it is. He groans. His death has begun. He will miss the train.

After school on a dark afternoon. I am walking home from the railway station along the middle of the street between gutters full of puddles shining grey, rain-spattered, with silvery fish flickering to their surfaces. No cars come and none of the neighbours in front gardens has anything to say to me. The streetlamps blink on. I go to my room, collecting on the way clothes that my father has taken off and left on the floor. I hold his warm shirt and singlet to my face to breathe in the smell of him. My bed looks too small with him in it. There is sunlight in the flowers of the broom bush at the window; the rain has made them large and glossy as buttercups. His pyjamas are in a tangle on the floor. Scolding him, I pick them up. He turns his sleepy grey head towards my voice, his eyes still closed, waiting for a kiss. He has a grey fuzz all over his body except his knees and elbows, wherever the nap has worn off.

Joanna rang early one morning to say that her father had died quietly a few hours ago, as day broke. "When I woke he must have just gone," she said. "That could have been what woke me, I suppose." She had sat nine days and nights holding his hand. She thought she might come to the coast for a day or two, now it was over. The funeral was in four days.

Misty rain would cover the cemetery. Joanna would wear black. Old soldiers would hang around chatting, and old railwaymen, waiting for the priest to turn up; eventually a flustered substitute would arrive to mutter the words of the service while rain trickled from grey trees and a crowd of umbrellas. The box of darkness into which the coffin under its flowers would slip with a clunk was lined with creased, satiny clay.

Joanna came at nightfall and sat unable to eat, drinking wine, crying, smoking with a tremulous hand that made her strands of smoke ripple; folding, unfolding her hands between cigarettes. When the lighthouse uttered a blast she yelled. Startled awake, a dog howled in the distance. Again it blasted; again the dog howled. They opened the window a crack and fog came wisping in. No question of sleep now. They pulled on boots to walk to the lighthouse, which was invisible but for the twisting lantern until they were on the last steps; then like a rocket on the launching-pad it showed thick white. The shed that held the foghorn pumped out flurries of mist as bellow on bellow slammed through the cement platform, through their bodies. Just under the lantern, red tide-lamps burned. The tide was out of sight. From over the bay an echo came in thunderclaps.

They walked under blurred white lamps along the leggy

pier, its piles gnawed black at the ankles, above black rocks and the sandy sea floor, a thong here and there of black kelp winding in a net of ripples. The lighthouse flared, boomed, flared, boomed. Under the last lamp they were met by a huge groan. The lighthouse spoke, and the echo. The whole wide shell of the bay, seafloor and lip of cliff, reverberated. They leaned on a wet rail as with a groan, a roar, a groan, a cluster of lights came into sight, slid past the end of the pier and disappeared. Chord on slow chord sounded over the water. Their two shadows stretched along the seabed as far as the whirlpool of light where the ship had been.

The metal staircase up the cliff face from the beach spilled rain with a jingling at each step. The moon was a high bright smudge. A secretive soft dripping of water from the black trees seemed to fall silent whenever they halted; frogs were creaking. They came back in after midnight with their lips salty and their hair dank and strung with bright drops, having taken the rhythmic booms so far into themselves that they were no longer hearing them, they were no more bother now than breath, than heartbeat and eyeblink. They were soaked with fog, booming. Once or more than once in the night they woke to the deep music of a ship passing the lighthouse. Loud crows in the pines woke them when it was well into the white midmorning, and still the horn was sounding.

They flung up their sleepy white arms and stretched and

yawned and drank strong tea in the kitchen. "Waking up in this house is like waking up on board ship," Joanna said.

> *The lighthouse horn hooted all night on two notes* [she wrote in her notebook], *while I dreamed of a wrecked ship sunk into a pit so deep no light could wake it. Now in the sun the fog is lifting. The pines creak, heavy with crows.*
>
> *I opened the book by my bed and found this in a letter from Boris Pasternak to Marina Tsvetaeva in July 1926; a summer letter. "The groan is the loudest note in the universe. I am inclined to believe that outer space is filled with* this *sound rather than with the music of the spheres ..."*

At lunchtime Joanna leaned forward into a hood of sunlight, offering a damp paper bag in her hands, which though large and strong always looked helpless; and they still had their slight tremor. The bag was full of large bruise-purple figs, with a red crack in each one, a glow of seeds.

"The last of them and look, I've squashed them. I put them in the fridge and forgot all about them," Joanna said.

"They're only a bit squashed." She kissed Joanna's cheek in thanks and washed them in a bowl under the tap, watching seeds move on the surface. "I associate you with figs, you know, ripe figs, for some reason," it occurred to her to say.

"Fat and seedy. That's me."

"Opulent. Purple. Abundant, syrupy and gritty, bursting —"

"They called me the Purple Lady in at the hospital, did I tell you? I was a fixture. Everyone knew me. Here she is, they'd say. Hullo, Purple Lady."

"You wore all purple clothes?"

"I wore this *one dress.* I've had it on day and night for the last two weeks. Do I stink? No? I didn't have the time to change. No, it wasn't even that — in my tiredness I just couldn't think what else to put on. Last night I could hardly walk. How did I get through it?"

"You'd put your mind to it."

"The family are all against me. Anyone'd think all of us weren't Ray's kids too, only you were — that's what they're saying."

"It's the strain."

"You might as well go home, they said. It's not as if he can see or hear you, he doesn't even know you're there. But I promised Ray I'd be with him."

"Yes. And you were."

"He never came out of the coma."

"Whether he knew or not, you had to stay. But I think he knew."

"I'd lie in the armchair holding one hand then the other. I'd fall asleep and wake up holding a hand, listening to him breathe. Sometimes I dressed his wound. It was black and it stank. They stopped giving him water, did I tell you? For ten days we were wrenching his jaws apart and dabbing inside with swabs. He had a leather strap for a tongue."

"He wouldn't have been in pain." She tore a fig open and licked and bit flesh from its dark lining, pushing the bowl forward. Joanna grinned and shook her head, her eyes blurring again. "Like a ripe fig, am I? I feel as dead as Ray inside."

They went down the stairs and sat on the strip of sand in the sun while the tide washed in and the shadow of the cliff flowed down to meet it. Rocks raised their brown backs, scaled or furry, and dived under; weeds strayed in and out of channels. Joanna puffed at a cigarette. "I keep thinking I have to get back," she said. "To the hospital."

"I know."

"I was worried every minute I wasn't in the ward. I *would* have to be asleep when he finally went, wouldn't I?"

"Don't you always have a feeling who's with you when you're asleep, though? In a coma, mightn't it be the same?"

"I keep feeling that the death happened to someone else, Ray's still in there waiting? There was always someone dying. I got to know them all, the visitors too, everyone talked in there. All of us smoking our heads off nonstop. Funny, isn't it?" She sighed smoke. "I'm stopping when this is over."

"Is the funeral still on Wednesday?"

"Wednesday. Yes, Wednesday at ten. Oh God. You do still want to come, then?"

"Of course."

"Thanks. You never even got to meet him. I used to wish — oh."

"No." She poured more tea. "I had a weird dream the other night. I keep having these dreams — horror dreams, some of them, and wish dreams. I try to note them down, if I wake up in time. There was this old man in a railway uniform —"

"That'd be Ray. I have frightful dreams all the time. I'm scared to go to sleep."

When she had seen Joanna off she put the skull of the penguin, which smelled like salted cod now, on a sheet of paper beside a shell she had found and taken at first for another small empty-socketed skull, so many birds there were now washed up on the sand. A hole in the dome of it opened the shadowy ribbed chambers and the white column inside. Carefully with a fine pen she drew the skull and the shell and washed over them, blurring lines to make a watery shadow. I am an empty shell, she thought, not bothering with a signature; while my friend is brimful of feelings which spill out of her, words and tears, hour after hour.

Later, in the flickering room, beside a glass of daisies that had curled up like dead yellow spiders, she scrawled on the back of the sketch.

Dear Joanna,

I wish I could take on some of your pain. You would have taken your father's on, if pain could be shared. There you are overflowing with suffering, while I sit on the beach, empty, an empty shell.

My own father died fourteen years ago. We hadn't been close since I was small. We were shy and uncomfortable alone together.

I remember as a very small child waiting in the bathroom one winter afternoon so dark that we had the lights on waiting for him to come home from work and punish me for some misdeed that had angered my mother. I heard the front door and their cheerful voices suddenly lowered. When he stepped wearily into the bathroom I was cowering under the basin out of the greasy lamplight. He unhooked the razor strop from behind the door. I have no memory of the thrashing (of which we were never to speak), nor of the pain. I cried, I suppose. What I remember is disbelief: each of us staring at the other afterwards in a consternation of disbelief. He was never to thrash me again and that might have been in his face as well.

My father had a heart attack one winter afternoon twenty-five years later. He died suddenly, alone in the house.

The page was full. She wrote her initial, and sent it to her friend, whose white hands, folded, quivering, filled her mind. The day of the funeral she drove into the rain and back. Yellow day lilies opened and closed in the garden, a curled blue iris here and there, and daisies. In a low fork of the bare prunus tree she found a twig cup with nothing inside but dead leaves and broken shells, snail shells. Brown leaves lay all over the grass. Wandering into a garden shop one day — by then it was July, midwinter — she saw among plum and apple and apricot saplings a grafted stick with loose roots and no branches, as slender and dry as cane or dark bamboo. The label fluttered, a printed butterfly: a picture of figs, and a name a woman might have, she thought, in a book about the deep South: *Black Genoa*. She bought it and planted it where it would screen the sun at the kitchen window, digging a hole with four glistening brown walls, packing the roots in hard. As night fell the fog fell also; the lighthouse hooted. In the fuzz round the porch light, wet and cold, the skin of Black Genoa shone. Green hands would reach out of it one day, loose on spread arms; and a thousand pouches, purpling, oozing, burst apart.

Lily Brett

WHAT GOD WANTS

Every second Sunday Moishe and Esmeralda Zimmerman visited Bluma Zimmerman at the Springvale Cemetery. Moishe always wore a suit and Esmeralda wore her dark green hat and matching jacket. They cleared the stray leaves and odd bits of stone and earth from Bluma's tombstone. Even though Springvale Cemetery was well maintained, the graves always needed extra cleaning. Moishe paid Mr Arbat, who looked after a lot of people's tombstones, thirty dollars a week to make sure that Bluma's grave was neat and tidy, but Mr Arbat, Moishe decided, had too many clients to give the graves the attention they deserved.

Every second Sunday Esmeralda would polish the marble headstone and remove the dead heads from the azalea, which was growing vigorously in its concrete pot. Then Esmeralda would go for a walk while Moishe talked to his wife.

Moishe no longer felt Bluma's absence so painfully. For the first two years after her death he had felt as though he had a large hole in his chest. He could feel himself leaking from this hole. Every day he had woken up surprised that there was still some of him left.

Moishe wasn't sure when this had changed, but one day

he had caught himself talking to Bluma. He was telling her about Sofia Ritman's attempt to seduce him with her almond biscuits. And Moishe had realised that he had Bluma back. She was there, inside him, intact, and he could again share the details of his daily life with her.

Moishe told Bluma everything. He told her about his boss, Harry King, and how the business was going. He told her what the takings from the shop were each week, and which fabrics were currently most popular. He told her about Ruthie. Ruthie had looked after him very well since Bluma's death. She rang him every morning, and again every night. He knew that Bluma would have been proud of her daughter.

When he had decided to marry Esmeralda, the first person he told was Bluma. He knew that Bluma would have been surprised by the news. Neither of them would have expected that Moishe would marry again, but then neither of them had expected that Bluma, who had been eight years younger than Moishe, would have died before him.

Since Bluma was taken away from him so unexpectedly he had become wiser, and knew more about the surprises of life. And he knew that Bluma, in her death, would have learnt things that were difficult to learn in life. Moishe now knew that it didn't matter if people were Jewish or not Jewish. He knew that Bluma would now know that too.

He knew that there had been a lot of gossip about him and Esmeralda. Not many Jews in Melbourne had Filipino wives who were almost half their age. Moishe didn't mind what people said. As long as Bluma understood, he was happy. And he had explained enough to Bluma for her to understand that Esmeralda was as much of a refugee as any Jew. She had suffered hunger, persecution, war. And as for her age, in terms of what she had experienced, Esmeralda was as old as any of them.

Esmeralda hadn't taken over Bluma's house. She had quietly found a few spare spaces, and squeezed herself in. Bluma's presence was everywhere in the house. Bluma's creams and lotions were still in the bathroom. Her clothes were in the cupboards, and the bedroom drawers were still filled with her bras and girdles. Two of her clean, unironed blouses were in the laundry.

The Bluma who was present was not the sick Bluma who had wasted away with cancer. Esmeralda had put away all the medications, all the vitamins, the tubes and clamps and pumps, the disposable syringes, the special cushions and all the other accoutrements of illness.

The Bluma who was there was the healthy Bluma. The Bluma before the cancer. Photographs of her and Moishe at bar mitzvahs and engagements and weddings were on the sideboard in the lounge room. On the television there was a photograph of her at the beach with Ruthie when Ruthie was small. And in the bedroom, in the middle of the dressing table, framed in an ornate silver frame, was a photograph of Bluma when she was sixteen. It was Moishe's favourite photograph. You could see Bluma's quiet exuberance. It was a characteristic Ruthie had inherited, thought Moishe. Neither Bluma nor Ruthie had found it easy to express outright joy. And Moishe could understand why. They were Jews. And Jews knew that no matter how happy they were, a disaster could come and hit them at any moment. Esmeralda knew that too. If the phone rang late at night, she jumped. If there was an unexpected knock at the front door, she retreated.

When Moishe stood next to Bluma's grave, he felt very close to her. As he talked to her, he could almost smell her. He could almost touch her. Often Esmeralda interrupted Moishe to remind him of something that she felt Bluma should know. This morning she had come up to him twice. "Did you tell Bluma that Ruthie got an honour in Contract Law?" she had asked.

"No, I forgot," he had answered. "I'll tell Bluma straight away."

"And tell her how pretty Ruthie is looking," said Esmeralda. "Tell her that Ruthie looks more pretty every day."

Five minutes later Esmeralda came back. "I want you to mention to Bluma that I keep the house very clean for her."

"I think Bluma knows this," Moishe said.

"I want to make sure," said Esmeralda.

Once they had driven all the way back to the cemetery when Esmeralda had discovered that Moishe hadn't told Bluma that they had found Brownie, Bluma's old cocker spaniel, who had gone missing for four weeks. "Bluma will be very happy," was the first thing Esmeralda had said when Brownie had reappeared.

On Sundays, when Moishe finished talking to Bluma, he and Esmeralda usually went for a walk around the cemetery. Every fortnight there were new graves. The cemetery was almost full. Moishe could remember when it was opened. He could remember Morry Glatt's builders finishing off the red brick fence that circled the cemetery. Now there were very few empty plots left.

The cemetery was like a village. The gold and black lettering on the headstones looked like calling cards. Announcements of each particular resident, and their place in the universe.

"Look, Esmeralda," said Moishe. "There's Sarah Green's grave. Poor Sarah, she wasn't even cold yet when someone was trying to get her husband. Minnie Brot told me that at the minyan there were three widows with such low-cut dresses that nearly everything was falling out."

Most Sundays there was a funeral taking place. Today the

rabbi had just finished the prayers and the mourners were shovelling spadefuls of earth over the coffin. Moishe explained to Esmeralda that this custom was partly to guard against the ghost of the departed one returning to harm an old enemy. Thinking about some of the people who were buried there, Moishe felt that it was a good custom to continue.

Moishe and Esmeralda saw Sofia Ritman.

"I wish you a long life," said Esmeralda.

"I wish you a long life," said Sofia Ritman.

"I wish you a long life," said Moishe.

"You see, she is already a Jew," said Sofia Ritman to the woman standing next to her. "First she took a Jewish husband, and now she is taking on the Jewish religion. She knows the right thing to say on every occasion. At Pesach she wished me 'Shana Tova'. And somebody told me that she can play a good gin rummy. It is shocking."

"Which part is shocking?" the woman asked.

"All of it," Sofia Ritman replied.

Springvale Cemetery was a place where, sooner or later, you met most of the Jews in Melbourne. The community was made up largely of postwar migrants who were now being buried by their children and their grandchildren. Death was indiscriminate. The rich were dying and the poor were dying. And here at Springvale they lay one next to the other. Tied to each other, in the end, not by their donations to Israel or their mansions in Toorak or their positions on the board, but by their faith. Even the ones with no faith claimed their Jewishness in death.

Moishe and Esmeralda walked past Herschel Bodsky's grave. "It's a shame that you didn't know Herschel," said Moishe. "He was a simple man. He didn't make big money, but he would have given me and Bluma the shirt from his back. Whenever Bluma and I were in trouble we rang Herschel. He was like a father to us, which is a funny thing because he was only a few years older than me. He had a heart of gold."

"I wish I had known Herschel. I'll bring some flowers for him next time," said Esmeralda.

"Next to Herschel is Mr Schneider," said Moishe. "He is a big shot. Well, he's not a big shot any more, he is dead, but he used to be such a big shot. He owned nine factories. He came to Australia before the war. I worked for him for a few months. He paid me half the wages he should have. He did that to all the Jews he employed. He was such a stingy man. He shouldn't be buried next to Herschel. Herschel is too good a man to be a neighbour of Sol Schneider."

They had reached the section of the cemetery where only Cohens were buried. "Cohens are supposed to be the highest order of Jews," said Moishe. "They are supposed to be responsible for religious teaching. They can't even go to a funeral unless it is the funeral of one of their family. If they want to go to a funeral they have to stand far away from where it is being conducted. You should see some of the Cohens. If they are higher people then God must know something that the rest of us don't know. There is Shimek Steinberg. He was a Cohen. He was a shmuck. He cheated everybody, even his poor wife. Some higher person he was! Henry Baume, who killed himself, was a Cohen, but he can't be buried there. People who have committed suicide have to be buried far away on the edge of the cemetery. They have to be at least six feet away from any other dead Jew. People said that Henry Baume lost the will to live after his wife died, and now he is not even buried next to his wife."

"That's terrible," said Esmeralda.

"That's what God wants," said Moishe. "It's a funny business, this business of what God wants. It would be better if the things that God wanted were a bit closer to the things that we all want."

"Maybe there would be more things wrong if God listened to all of us," said Esmeralda.

Ruthie knew that something was wrong when Moishe arrived at her place at lunchtime on Wednesday. He still worked five and a half days a week, and never took a day off work.

She watched him walk up her driveway. He looked pale. She had a terrible sinking feeling in her stomach. She ran downstairs and opened the front door.

"Hello, Dad," she said. "What's wrong?"

"You can see straight away that something is wrong?" he said.

"You don't look well. Come inside and sit down."

Moishe sat down in the middle of the cream leather sofa. He sank into the overstuffed sofa and nearly disappeared. Suddenly he looked small.

"Ruthie, I don't know how to tell you this," he said. "To tell you the truth, it is not something that I ever dreamed I would have to tell you."

"What is it, Dad?"

"I don't know how to tell you, darling," he said. He looked down at the floor, and when he looked up again his eyes were full of tears. Ruthie looked at her father and started crying.

"Dad, please tell me," she said. She put her arms around him.

"Ruthie," he said, "Esmeralda is pregnant."

Ruthie felt herself go limp with relief. "Oh, Dad," she

said, "I thought you were dying, or someone was dying. I'm so relieved."

"Ruthie, darling, I feel ashamed of myself. I feel ashamed that Esmeralda is pregnant. Esmeralda thought that she was sterile, that she couldn't have any children. Ruthie, it is not that that part of our lives is a very big part, but we are two normal people and every now and then we did what normal people do, and now Esmeralda is pregnant. And now I feel like I'm going to bring shame on Mum's name, and people will talk even more than they are already talking. Ruthie, I am seventy-six."

"How does Esmeralda feel?" asked Ruthie.

"She was very shocked when the doctor told her. She was sure he had made a mistake. She went to him because her stomach was swollen. She thought it was constipation."

"Her stomach is already swollen?"

"The doctor told her she is six months pregnant."

"Six months and she didn't suspect anything?"

"Well I think that's because she has never been pregnant, so how could she know what it feels like?" said Moishe.

"And how does she feel now?" said Ruthie.

"I think that really she is very excited," said Moishe. "Except that she knows that I am feeling very mixed up and she is such a good person that she doesn't want to look too excited in front of such a mixed-up person."

Ruthie felt stunned. She didn't know how she felt. "Dad, I'm so glad there's nothing wrong with you," she said.

"Nothing wrong with me?" Moishe said. "I am seventy-six and my forty-four-year-old wife is having a baby. What else should be wrong with me to have something wrong?"

"I don't think it is such a disaster," said Eddie when he came home. "We can be grandparents while we're very young, without most of the hassle."

"Eddie," said Ruthie, "we won't be grandparents. This child will be my brother or sister, and your brother or sister-in-law."

"I don't think it's going to be a calamity," said Eddie. "Esmeralda is pretty calm. I think she'll manage well."

"It was a pretty strange feeling to have my father confessing to a pregnancy," said Ruthie. "My dad had tears in his eyes. I remember when I was young, the worst thing in the world that my girlfriends and I could imagine happening to us was having to tell our parents that we were pregnant. The abortion didn't seem to be the insurmountable problem. It was telling your parents. I was one of the few girls who never ended up having an abortion. Remember how I wanted to have an abortion when I was pregnant with Jonathan? And you insisted that I have the baby. I remember feeling so miserable about leaving uni. I've never really told you, but I'm very glad that you didn't let me have an abortion."

"I knew it. I didn't need a formal acknowledgment," said Eddie.

"This afternoon," said Ruthie, "when I was talking to my father, I had the oddest feeling of roles being reversed. It felt very topsy-turvy."

"Ruthie," said Eddie, "let's buy a beautiful nursery for this baby. We'll buy a cot and a pram and a bassinet and some toys and whatever else it is that babies need."

"You really are unbelievable," said Ruthie. "You support me and the boys. You looked after my mother and father, and you still look after my father. He has no idea how much you paid for his new car. And now you're going to look after the new baby."

"We've only got one family, haven't we, Ruthie?"

"Moishe Zimmerman is a pig," said Sofia Ritman to Minnie Brot. "At his age to shtoop so that that shikse gets pregnant."

"For a start, she isn't 'that shikse', she is his wife. And secondly, pardon me if I'm ignorant about this, and I could be because I myself haven't shtooped with anybody for a long time, but isn't it the same if you shtoop to get pregnant or not to get pregnant?" said Minnie. "And after Bluma Zimmerman died, weren't you yourself hoping to be the next Mrs Zimmerman, if I remember correctly? I may have forgotten about shtooping, but I still remember how much you were trying to impress Moishe Zimmerman."

"Yes," said Sofia Ritman, "but with Moishe and me, shtooping would have been like holding hands, not like what he did with the shikse."

"I wish you wouldn't call her the shikse. Her name is Esmeralda," said Minnie.

"Well, to tell you the truth, Minnie," said Sofia, "I noticed at the cemetery that this Mrs Esmeralda Zimmerman was looking a bit fat. I thought to myself, thank God it is not just the Jewish wives who become fatties. So, your daughter-in-law, Ruthie, is going to have a brother or sister over forty years younger than her?"

"It's not the worst thing in the world that could happen, Sofia," said Minnie.

"Nothing escapes Sofia Ritman," Minnie said to Ruthie. "None of us noticed anything at all, and she had already noticed that Esmeralda had gained weight."

"Sofia knew more than Esmeralda did," said Ruthie.

"How do you feel about the baby?" Minnie asked Ruthie.

"Well, it gave me a terrific shock," said Ruthie. "And, actually, the thought of Dad and Esmeralda making love made me feel a bit uncomfortable. I know it's naive to think that they wouldn't have been making love, but somehow I imagined that they were with each other for comfort."

"And you think that sex isn't part of comfort?"

"I guess it is. I've been thinking about babies myself lately. For the first time since I had my tubes tied, I've been feeling clucky. It's probably part of getting older and seeing my childbearing years coming to an end. I don't want any more children, I just don't like the thought of not being able to have any. I think this will be a good time for me to be a grandmother to Esmeralda's baby."

"You'll be the best-looking grandmother in Melbourne," said Minnie.

Ruthie rang her father. "Dad," she said, "I just want you to know that I am very happy for Esmeralda that she is pregnant. It was a shock at first, but now I've got used to it. Every woman should have a child. And Esmeralda's got no family except for us. So now we'll all have a bit more family. Dad, I want you to know that I'll always be here for Esmeralda and the baby. Eddie and I and the boys. We are your family and her family."

"Darling, you have made me more happy than you could know," said Moishe.

"Can I speak to Esmeralda?" said Ruthie. "I just want to say the same to her."

"I'll get her," said Moishe.

On 17 December, after a two-hour labour, Esmeralda Zimmerman gave birth to an eight-pound baby boy. Ruthie took the birth announcements to the *Jewish News*. She gave the woman in the office her announcement. It said:

> We wish to announce, with great joy, the safe arrival of Adam Zimmerman. Brother, brother-in-law, and uncle of Ruthie, Eddie, Jonathan and Jason Brot.

Moishe had written his own notice. It read:

> Moishe Zimmerman, widower of the late Bluma Zimmerman, and his wife Esmeralda Zimmerman, stepmother of Ruthie and Eddie Brot, and grandparents of Jonathan and Jason Brot, wish to announce the birth of Adam Zimmerman. Son, brother, brother-in-law and uncle.

Suzanne Edgar

VIOLET AND ROSE

The scent of certain flowers, the taste of blackberries, ornaments once worn by another — these things revive the past. For some, lavender among old linen calls up the loving grandmother who embroidered those edges.

As I was sewing today, working on a luxurious fur-trimmed stole, its touch stirred memories of a friend, and things learned long ago. I even imagined I smelt that slightly cloying "April Violets" perfume she used to wear.

My fingers are red with chilblains; pressing the lithe fur under the machine, I think of Violet and me in the war before the boys came back. If only I knew where she's got to.

In winter, as the plane trees in the street lose their leaves and the sky is bleached of colour, ladies, like squirrels in their rich furs, call with fashion magazines. Arranging their suits and spring dresses raises their spirits.

"What about this, Rose? Would it suit me?" They chatter away forgetting that I, on my knees with a mouth full of pins, cannot answer. They're hoarding the velvet and silks to nourish their gaiety during the depressing winter; Violet taught me that.

At the ironing board, I look out across red tiled roofs, remembering myself thirty years ago, a lonely woman of twenty-eight. "I'll have to go if Japan comes into the war," Roy always said. After he left I moved to the city.

At Holdfast Bay a Mrs Violet Gee had rooms to let near Bay Road; there was just a bed, stove and a meat safe. In the back yard under the almond trees was a fowl run, and along one edge, a garage. Inside, great bins of wheat and pollard lined the shadowy walls. I could see a flash Dodge motor car gleaming in the half light.

"I never drive now," Mrs Gee said. "My nerves play up if I even start the engine, so I had it put up on blocks. It's my husband Charlie's car, but since he went I don't know what to do with the thing. It'll spoil sitting here with no one driving it. The battery's flat already."

"I couldn't help there," I said. "Fancy a little thing like you driving such a big car."

Violet Gee was on her own, her parents disapproved of the marriage. When she spoke of her husband, she cried.

"I had to let the rooms, for company. Well, I could do with the money, too," she laughed, in a way that gave me courage.

"Would you mind if I used the front room for dressmaking and put a notice in the window, just something discreet?"

"Course not, love," she said. "I can send some customers your way to get you started. I'll lend you a table for cutting out, too, if you like."

Violet had style — olive skin and soft, dark eyes — a bit exotic. Younger than me, she wore her black hair swept up at the back and done in soft rolls over the ears. She dressed so smartly that I felt dowdy, the country mouse, but a dressmaker gets used to that.

Customers began coming; enough to pay the rent. I watched my pennies and put aside what Roy sent for furniture. I remember the lorry bringing my second-hand wardrobe, and how I enjoyed scrubbing it down. Hanging up frocks and folding underwear into the drawers, I felt at last I was making progress. Violet laughed at the mosquito-netting curtains I made.

"Tough enough to keep more than mozzies away," she reckoned.

I used to listen to her. In the morning she'd call her cat, and I'd hear the rusty lavatory chain; then the crockery rattling in the dresser. At eight she put on the wireless for the news. I always waited for the front door to slam again if she'd been out. Violet played gramophone records at night;

I heard her singing, before the last pull of the chain warned me it was nearly time to put away the sewing.

In her spare time she grew flowers out the front and vegies in the back yard. Thursdays, to go shopping, she'd slip through the back hedge to a lane leading to Bay Road. Her crouched back looked like Alice, disappearing into a tunnel to hunt for the white rabbit. On Sundays old Mr Gee, her husband's father, came to Violet for lunch; and in the afternoon they visited relatives.

The war news got worse and we were gloomy about getting the boys home. Violet took the paper; when she'd finished with it she'd call, "Yoo hoo! paper, Rose!" and leave it on the veranda for me.

Roy and I used a code to cheat the censor. "He can't say much, but he writes every week. It's the only thing keeps me going," I told her.

"Not Charlie. Won't put pen to paper if he can get out of it. He was pianist in a dance band before the war, The Virginians, can play any tune you hum, by ear. But he hates writing letters."

I noticed a change in Violet's routine. She shopped more often and dressed elaborately before setting off. I guessed she was meeting friends.

One Friday I browsed further up Bay Road than usual, past Ryan's Emporium where the goods are pricier. I went into a tea shop, The Primula, and eating scones at a window table, I saw Violet drift along the footpath on the other side of the street. Outside Tooveys' Fine Furs, she lingered near the front window where wax models displayed fur coats. She went in and spoke to young Mr Toovey behind the counter. I never found out why that young man didn't go to the war. At the Women's Auxiliary they said he had back trouble.

"A blind man'd be glad to see it," was my view. "It doesn't stop him being on his feet all day. You can hardly call selling furs essential work." A bachelor, he was a bit of a gadabout.

Next Friday I was at The Primula again and along comes Violet, all dolled up. She hesitated before going in to natter with that suave young fellow. I felt uncomfortable spying on her, I couldn't imagine what those two would have in common.

Violet had a way with men. In summer the ice man sometimes stopped to gossip after lowering the dripping block into her ice chest. If the grocer had time, they'd smoke a cigarette on the veranda and discuss her plantings. In spring she put in poppies, marigolds and pansies in a border round the front lawn. Under her bedroom window in the shade was a bed of violets.

"All the colours of the rainbow," she said to me, "to go with my name." And I heard her tell the grocer, too, with a little laugh. Romantic, that was Violet.

The baker was different. Jack Phillips stood up tall and dark at the back of his cart, whip upraised; he only climbed down to get out the bread. No trundling into kitchens for Jack; at his whistle, we women and the kids ran out in the road to queue up. Violet wasn't shy. She'd look him in the eye as she reached up for the warm loaf, as though he was handing down some priceless gift.

"Thanks, Jack," she'd murmur, low and husky.

Her visits to Tooveys' went on. One Friday I had a cold and couldn't go shopping. I heard Violet wash her lunch things and go singing into the bathroom. She appeared on the front veranda nursing the cat and drying her hair in the sun. Later on, out she came with her hair up and dressed to kill in an amethyst woollen suit. She picked some violets and pinned them to her lapel with a diamante dagger. It looked like a trap was being set; surely not for that oily little furrier?

Violet coo-eed. "Rose, honey, would you feed the fowls if I'm later than five?"

"Right-oh." She made me feel drab at the best, but that day my nose was red, my hair in a mess; her skin, glowing in the afternoon light, made me envious and cross.

"Ta. Here's the garage key." She clicked down the path in her high heels and green beret as though the King was waiting.

I worried about her all afternoon for of course she was

late. You heard terrible stories those days, of women with husbands at the war running off with some stay-at-home, or the Yanks on leave. I couldn't bear to think of Violet as promiscuous.

At half-past five the house was quiet, accusing. When I went to get the fowls' feed from the garage, there was something odd there too. Charlie's Dodge had gone. I couldn't believe my eyes, but there was nothing left of it but the patch of darkening oil on the stone floor where it had stood. I fed the fowls and went in to fry a chop, listening for the front door.

At six there's a knock and in comes Violet, wearing — a fur coat. I drew back as she pirouetted round my room, like some kitten, in that light brown, knee-length coat smelling of skins and money.

"Touch it, touch it, Rose! Isn't it soft?" I had to admit it was. Suited her colouring too. The two of us stood there like a pair of ninnies, me in my apron and slippers, Violet in the coat that rippled under the light. I stroked the thick fur and it was like nothing I'd ever sewn on a costume for trimming, though it was only lapin. Violet kept jitter-bugging about.

"Don't you love it? I'll lend it to you for special occasions."

"Old lumpy legs in a number like that? No thanks. I'll

stick to my gabardine. However much did it cost? And where did you get the money?"

She perched on the table. "I wrote to Charlie, and he agreed to sell the Dodge and split the proceeds — when he finally got around to answering. The day I got his letter the coat was reduced at Tooveys' sale. Joe Bradley took the car last Sunday when you were at church."

The rest I knew: her indecision; the fatal attraction; and the giving in to temptation. She'd blown fifty pounds in one fell swoop. I thought of the furniture I would have bought with that money.

For Violet, buying the coat was an act of faith. "You see," she argued, "to me this means the war is going to end soon, Rose. Charlie'll come home and our old life will start again. He likes to see me looking good, for the races and dances. The coat will give him a wonderful surprise." She snuggled into it, at home in its warm embrace.

Barbara Hanrahan

SLEEPING BEAUTIES

I had black hair as a baby and my eyes slanted up, so my father called me his little Chinese doll. He'd take me into the bar of the pub and show me off to the Mile End Boys, and then he got T.B. and had to go to hospital. My mother could go in the room with him, but I had to stay outside. My grandmother used to hold me up so he could see me through the window.

My father died the day after my first birthday. He was twenty-six. Then they found my mother had a shadow on her lung and she had to keep away from me and go to bed and rest, so I was looked after by my grandmother. My mother went to the chest clinic to have gold injections. They gave her bottles of Milk Emulsion, and told her to have egg flips and stout and cream cakes and everything to make her fat. She stayed thin for years, though the shadow went away and she got better and could cuddle and kiss me again.

One day my mother found my feet were icy cold and my head was burning hot, so she bundled me up with shawls and put me in the wicker pusher and took me down to the doctor at Torrensville. I started having convulsions and she had to stick a thing in my mouth to stop me from biting my tongue. I went all stiff and my face was a purple colour and the doctor rushed us to the hospital in his car.

The first thing they did was to give me a bath, though my mother tried to stop them. I had pneumonia, and it seemed I was going to die like my father, but the crisis passed and I stood up in my cot. My mother and my grandmother weren't allowed to go in to me, they had to watch me through glass: my curls were wet with sweat and I was smiling, but then I cried as bananas and jelly went past for someone else.

When I came home my mother and I slept in the sleepout because we needed lots of fresh air. We were hidden away by the back veranda in our room with windows round two walls. The wind blew on us and sometimes birds walked on our flat iron roof, sometimes cats. When it rained there were leaks, and we'd catch them with buckets and saucepans.

I grew into a girl who was always reading: I asked so many questions my grandmother said I'd want to know the ins and outs of a duck's behind. I was a crepe paper flower at the Baptist Sunday School concert, and I took nerve medicine and had habits: I scratched my head and chewed my hair and counted the pickets of fences and liked to stuff things. I was scared of moths, and my mother had to make sure there weren't any under the bed-clothes. Some nights she'd wake up and find I was trying to get out the sleepout door with my pillow under my arm, and I was still asleep.

We are four Sleeping Beauties, shut away behind the crinkly green glass panels of the front door and the cyclone fence that's hedged with roses.

My mother is a princess who smells of Blue Grass scent: her hair has a kiss-curl in front, she rubs on night cream, she smokes a cigarette in the dark before we go to sleep. We are bodies curled up together, and in the morning I kick her awake to tell me a story. We lie in bed and she sings "Cruising Down the River" and "Red Sails in the Sunset". She is the best dressed person in the street and I watch her put on mascara, rouge, lipstick: Elizabeth Arden, Helena Rubinstein. She tells me you must use the right colour lipstick, wear the right colour shoes: and it's common to wear socks with high heels. I wait for her at the tram-stop to come home from work, and sometimes she brings Violet Crumbles or Caramello chocolate or the *Women's Weekly*. She is a commercial artist and has a naked dummy that wears the clothes she draws for the newspapers. They used her legs in the stocking ad, and when she makes a dress she sews in the little Vogue label that comes with the paper pattern. She is as good as Scarlett O'Hara, or the Duchess of Kent. She was matron-of-honour at a wedding and she loves Laurence Olivier and she went on the Gulf Trip.

Every night before I go to bed my mother takes me to the lavatory at the bottom of the yard. I sit over the hole in the wooden seat and my mother sits on the ledge beside me. The black night's all round us and I tell my mother confessions, and make her tell me about my father. She pulls the chain and we go back up the path to the house. The wireless is on and my grandmother crochets squares for a rug; her sister, Reece, knits and knits or winds skeins of wool into balls.

My grandmother's fingers are wrinkly from washday and she can't play "The Merry Widow Waltz" on the piano any more. She goes out in the garden and prunes the roses and when she comes in her arms are torn and bleeding from where they pricked her, but she doesn't care. She hates doing housework; she just wants to be out with the roses, the violets, the sweet peas, the soldier boys by the path. In summer she wears a sun hat and she's got her clippers in her hand, and she's always planting flowers and pinching cuttings from other people's gardens at night.

She brings home damp newspaper bundles from the market: snapdragon, pansy, Iceland poppy ... Our fingers touch as we go on planting into the darkness and sometimes she still wears her going-to-town clothes. The black pintucks of her zebra dress stripe her body, and the marcasite elephants are on the collar of her astrakhan coat. Her big body is held in by corsets, and I like to watch her put them on; I like her white body spread out in the bath, Palmolive soap, her green silk nightgown sewn with pink roses.

My mother said I was born in a rose ... roses on the sleepout wallpaper; roses on the feather eiderdown. I put my head under the bed-clothes and am lost in blackness. I can't imagine dying. But I know I will find my father — he is with me, watching all I do. I feel he gave me his life. I save up bits of his childhood in a cutlery box lined with blue silk. A picture of the Madonna, little Catholic books, scout tabs, purple Catholic bands.

Other girls feel sorry for me because I have a dead father. In the wedding photo he looks like a film-star: Irish face with a dimple. And in the schoolboy photo it's my face, yet his, that looks out over Aunty Kathleen's shoulder. I want to live the life he didn't have, be part of an adventure. I stare at his photo eyes; I hold out my arms and he comes into them — or does he hold out his arms to me? I get into the photographs, too. He went to the Catholic school and I feel it makes him holy.

Tinker is my dog; he's like my brother. He's a black cocker spaniel with white on his chest and paws, and he has a pedigree. When I cry he cries, and his wet nose nudges me to stop. I wrap him in a shawl and wipe his sad eyes with his ears. When he first came I was afraid — he was so small and soft. His paws made a clicking noise on the veranda and he cried for his mother. Tinker isn't like other dogs — he doesn't go out in the street, and he doesn't cock his leg when he piddles.

I sit up in bed reading a book, and Reece brings me bread spread with apricot jam and cream. Reece is kind, she loves me. She is my great-aunt, but she stays a child and all her dolls are called Peggy. Her soft hands pat me, her soft mouth kisses me. The nuns couldn't teach her when she went to school and she can't read or write. Her tongue trips over my name and I have to move when she wants to sweep the floor or set the table. She is dressed like a little lady in a grey pleated skirt and a twin-set; her stumpy lisle-stockinged legs end in childish strap shoes. She has a hanky up her sleeve and begs pardon when her stomach rattles. She watches me through the picket fence of the school and waits out the front for me to come home. I am jealous of her because I think my grandmother loves her best.

Every Sunday my mother washes my grandmother's hair and Reece's hair and my hair, and then she combs in lavender setting lotion, and sets our hair in bobby-pinned snail-curls and rows of butterfly waves; and then we sit out in the sun to dry our hair, while my mother looks in the bathroom mirror and sets her own hair.

Some people have white roses or yellow roses or red roses, but all our roses are pink; and the rose nursery people go round everywhere there are nice roses and ask for the cuttings, and they always ask us. Lorraine Lee rose with a summery smell, and our house in Rose Street is covered with pebbledash and roses, and a rose smell gets into everything.

I pull off the rose-buds and pretend they're lipsticks, and we have a Royal Rose teapot and satin-stitch roses on the tablecloth for afternoon tea. Once I dressed up as a bride in the net curtain and Reece threw rose petals out of a paper bag.

My grandmother sewed pink ribbon carnations on a red felt table-runner, but that was when she was someone else: a girl in trailing black charmeuse powdered with jet sequins, and her hair dressed in love-curls, and she rubbed her hair with jasmine hair cream and she married a policeman, but he died, and then she married a man from Outer Harbour and when he ran away with a girl to Murray Bridge she slit the seams of all the clothes he'd left behind in the wardrobe. And she turned into my grandmother with silvery-blue hair, but her eyebrows stayed black (ladies on the tram said it was disgusting how some women dyed their eyebrows). The butcher says my grandmother is like a beautiful rose, just fading.

My grandmother cuts my sandwiches for school, and some lunch-times in winter she's waiting at the school gate in the cold with a paper cone of hot chips, or an egg-and-bacon sandwich. She makes us roast beef dinners, milk puddings sprinkled with nutmeg, butterfly cakes and rock buns; and some Sunday tea-times it's like a party with jelly and Woodroofe's lemonade, and the lemonade bubbles get up my nose. Reece is my grandmother's shadow trailing her round the side past the sword-leaved plant that comes out in a white bell flower every seven years. My mother's ambition is to walk down Bond Street, London. And my father is with Jesus: gentle Jesus with sausage curls and a lamb. Angels hover, they guard me from the sky. My body hides under my clothes and if I squint at the hairs on my arms they make a miniature wheat field. There is a well by the sleepout — a girl lives down it and I look into her face and call out to her.

Nick Earls

PLAZA

There was a Woolies on the site originally. Or perhaps a newsagent and a hairdresser and an empty bank building, with a Woolies across the road. This is of vague historical interest only, for when they built the plaza, they planned for expansion and soon enough it jumped the road, a fat foot of a department store on a spindly travelator of a leg. And each time the plaza became bigger, it became twice as big again.

It ate up them all, the newsagent, the hairdresser, the empty bank building, the Woolies, a boutique, another newsagent, two video stores, a turn-of-the-century post office, the service stations on two corners. It swung a broad limb over the railway station, adding eight cinemas, forty-six specialty outlets and the Second Largest Department Store in the Southern Hemisphere. It consumed the adjacent parkland, preserving its heritage-listed ANZAC memorial by encasing it in the foundation concrete of the Third Largest Building in the World. At the far end of the park, the next railway station too was surrounded, built over, engulfed.

And in the centre, at the hub of this marvellous era of marble and gold, the plaza itself began to swell. It towered easily above the workers' cottages and soon above the office buildings. It cast shadows the length of the river flood plain and then over the mountains beyond, until dawn was coming minutes later to the farms to the west. The photos of its opening, still, in the grand scale of time, in the very recent past, were subtly faded by a team of expert degradationists, from bright contemporary colours to an impressive archival sepia. Najee suits were retouched to be plus-fours, gaiters were added to Jag jeans and pork-pie hats appeared in ever increasing numbers. They toyed with the idea of painting in Captain Cook to cut the ribbon at the opening but, after consideration, settled for a late middle-aged Henry Parkes, accompanied by copies of the Tenterfield Oration and other documents relating to Federation. The plaza, then, had a history and had a place in history, so that people could watch it grow and be glad that it was growing, because every millimetre that made it a Bigger, Better Place made the country a Bigger, Better Place too.

The day the plaza reached Tenterfield would be a special one, a homecoming, the ultimate legitimiser. The specialty outlets had reached there already but, really, it would only be historic when the town, or at least the site of the town, was under the great dome of the plaza itself, joining forty-two other Historic Sites that were preserved, again in the fashion of the times, by encasing them in foundation concrete and placing a small exhibition of photographs, agricultural and kitchen implements and so on, on the new ground floor level. Such acknowledgments of our challenging pioneering past met with great public appreciation and were usually opened by a significant local figure, such as the premier of the state. Occasionally, exhibitions were, out of necessity, opened by two premiers, as state boundaries had become a little difficult to define, for however carefully they and their landmarks were preserved by the concrete, the surface all bore a challenging homogeneousness.

Unfortunately, though well loved by all, the plaza had struck a few teething troubles. Not that the problems were with the plaza itself, far from it. They were really, in essence, People Problems. The best way to look at this is to examine it from the point of view of one of the people in particular, one of the people and, for example, the travelators.

The person in question is about seventeen when she enters the plaza. She and her friends have set the day aside for shopping, for they are on holidays from school. They live close to one of the outlying precincts of the plaza and, of course, visit that part regularly, but today they have decided to head for the dome itself.

On the third level they connect with an arterial travelator. Here, the territory becomes less familiar. They were probably last here during the previous school holidays. They travel for about an hour, stopping three times to browse briefly in boutiques, and then decide to have coffee. As it's the holidays, they share a chocolate croissant, nonchalantly pulling pieces from it to eat, as unfamiliar boys watch. They laugh with their heads back, cross their legs, lick their fingers seductively when they've finished. When they are back on the travelator one of them points out that it's a shame they didn't have cigarettes. The others agree.

They're not sure when they expected to reach the dome, but they still haven't two hours later. They stop to confirm that they are heading in the right direction and lunch on toasted sandwiches in the second cafe they come across. The first looked nicer but the proprietor refused to sell them cigarettes. In the second they ask only for toasted sandwiches and milkshakes.

There are no boys to seduce with their lunch technique and the adjacent specialty outlets are uninspiring, so they are soon moving again.

In another hour, they join a much larger travelator, six lanes wide, and they know they must be nearly there. This is all new territory to them — labyrinthine arcades winding away to the sides at twenty, and now perhaps thirty levels, hanging gardens, fountains, enormous cinema complexes, a record shop on eight floors. Two more travelators sweep in beside them and soon another. They wonder how people leave the travelators when they have eight to the right and six to the left. But it means the dome must be close.

At home, night will fall soon. They talk about the prospect quietly among themselves, so as not to seem like adolescents with curfews. They decide to go on.

The ceiling is lifting. They notice that with each minute that passes it is higher above them, that the arcades have more floors and, just when the heights reach dizzying dimensions, the shops end, and they are under the dome. They step from the travelator and on to the tiled floor.

The roof is like a pink sky above them, a pink sky reaching far out across the plaza, sinking down eventually to the pink-tiled horizon.

They are briefly overawed by this. They watch the towering arcades of shops recede to their right and left and wonder where to begin.

The seventeen-year-old girl of particular interest to us heads for a nearby bank of price reference terminals, agreeing to meet the others in an hour. She finds an available terminal and keys in the appropriate codes for Levi 501 jeans. The computer tells her the best price is to be found in a department store on the other side of the plaza, confirms her size is in stock and puts a pair on hold. It prints out directions, which seem straightforward enough, and she folds the sheet of paper and puts it in her pocket.

She takes a lift to the eighty-second floor, and then a travelator leading north-east, high out above the centre of the plaza. She wonders how much of her day she will be on travelators. She should probably have told her parents she would be late home or, better still, that she planned to spend the night at the house of one of the friends. It is the holidays after all.

She is briefly concerned when, after twenty minutes, she has left the home end of the plaza back over the horizon and has yet to see the side with the bargain jeans. She tells herself people ride the travelators every day, pick up jeans, take them home. Such people are all around her even now. There is no cause for concern.

She doesn't look over the edge at the floor far down below. Heights have never been her best thing. She thinks about her friends. She'll be a few minutes late, but they won't mind.

Someone tells her that just last year the travelator ended about here, but since then the plaza has expanded rapidly, so it's still a way to go. The girl wonders how long, but no one can put a figure to it. Someone else says that about forty minutes from this point, on the same journey a week ago, he first heard the work party up ahead extending the travelator, and that the plaza came into sight five minutes later. That was the sign the girl would wait for, the noise of the work party.

It crosses her mind that the deadline is long gone, that she should head back, but she can do nothing. There is nothing around except the travelator on which she is moving at an ever increasing speed, but, without a reference point, she is not even aware of the acceleration.

Time passes, and eventually the batteries in her watch flatten. It has been daytime in the plaza throughout, but her watch has gone through numerous days and nights. In her conversations with her fellow travellers, she has talked about the passage of time and its inherent inevitability, but within the first month they agree only on the futility of such discussions and consensus is reached never to raise the matter again.

Gradually the influence of time is seen on a wide range of subjects and one by one it is agreed that these will not be talked about.

Approximately every twelve hours, five minutes is spent in silence, listening for the sounds of a work party. Eventually, a short man with a large nose admits that he has long ago lost any idea of what a work party might sound like. Someone tries to be helpful by mentioning electric drills and arc welders but, when pressed for the sounds that might be expected from them, says that it has been enough of a struggle to remember the names of the equipment. He says he believes that the drill will be olive green, but the others know he's faking it.

The girl meets a man and they eventually get on so well that they have two children, one of each.

It is when the boy is about twelve that something happens. It isn't olive green — the man, after all, was faking it — but it is happening, and it's up ahead.

The travelator begins to decelerate. Everybody knows something is supposed to happen next, but no one can remember what. The sight, far ahead, of a shopping arcade eight hundred storeys high, is therefore quite a surprise.

The girl, who is now a middle-aged woman, remembers her Levi 501s. She hugs her children close to her. The boy is unimpressed by this and wonders why his mother is behaving this way.

She watches the arcade grow bigger and bigger and, with everyone else who is old enough to remember, starts talking excitedly about shopping and movies and ice-cream. She checks the money in her purse and wonders if she can afford something special for the children.

Ahead, they see a crowd at the end of the travelator. There is shouting, perhaps cheering.

But the clothes are different, the faces unexpected. The woman steps from the travelator and hears laughter. But it is the laughter not of joy, but of mockery. She looks around her, looks in the shop windows, looks at herself.

Everything she is wearing is hopelessly out of date, her currency, her hard-earned money from the checkouts of Coles New World, is worth nothing. And noise, noise is everywhere and her children try to hide. But the crowd is after them, chasing them through the arcade, shouting unfamiliar abuse.

The woman takes her daughter's hand and her son runs beside her. But the crowds are used to this. They are catching them.

The woman dodges around corners, through department stores, tipping displays over behind her. But the laughter is louder, and the anger. Her pursuers are yelping like dogs.

Her boy is tiring and she reaches for his hand, but he is tackled from behind and lost to the crowd. A few screams and she hears no more.

Ahead there is a travelator. She runs harder, despite the cramp in her side. Her daughter's feet drag along the ground, but she's still there, still crying. A wiry looking man moves to bar their path.

From her handbag, the woman pulls the scissors her mother made her carry in case of attack, and she drives the point between two of the man's ribs and into his heart.

The crowd had not expected this, and holds back momentarily. She jumps on to the travelator, drops her daughter at her feet. Now, there is no pursuit.

In a matter of hours the arcade is behind them, and they are heading back the way they came. For a long time they say nothing, comforted by the silence.

Eventually the woman tells her daughter what life is like back at the far end of the travelator, where she had spent her early years. She explains to her daughter about trees and birds and school holidays.

She doesn't know it, but far ahead, war is raging. The world she describes is being reduced to wasteland. But the dome expands, now at exactly the same rate that the travelator accelerates, and year after year it will outrun them, growing ever bigger and then twice as big again.

VENERO ARMANNO

NOW THAT THE WALL IS GONE

Now that the wall is gone, anyone who ever had a half-day visitor's pass into East Berlin has a personal story about the divided city.

This story, however, takes place in Switzerland and begins not with the Wall or with Checkpoint Charlie or with the guard posts set behind barbed wire, but with the hands of Katherine Spiegler. I remember that they were long and faultless hands; full of grace we Catholics might have said. Well preserved, her doctor or gigolo might have thought.

It was my friend Helmut who first introduced me to Katherine Spiegler. Helmut and I were travelling together through Europe in late 1986, and when we ran out of money we ran to his distant relatives in Lausanne. We were in time for a family wedding, and at the reception I found myself seated next to an elegant old lady in white — the embodiment of Mary spending her winter years with St John in the Anatolian city of Ephesus.

Helmut had liked to tell me about his Aunt Katherine and her associate, Werner — fortyish, correct, dead-eyed — and about her photographs, which in those years you could have found in almost any glossy European magazine, and her escape from East Berlin in 1969. Through the Wall, as they say, where Captain Spiegler was killed, dying a defector against the border patrol's gunfire while a younger Frau Spiegler was dragged on into the West. Helmut had warned me not to bring these things up with her — as if I would have.

The reception took place in a lounge overlooking the dark waters of Lake Geneva. Helmut's family are German-Swiss so most of the conversations took place in their language. But his Aunt Katherine was happy to speak English with me, which she did throughout the bombastic speeches. Of course it was her hands that I first noticed, then her delicate frame all long and slender in the white lace dress. I was surprised when she invited me to visit the next day.

"Please be punctual at midday," she had said. "Werner likes to serve our drinks exactly at twelve on Sunday."

So the next day I made certain to be on time. Katherine Spiegler greeted me under the broad arch of her drawing room's entrance as a tall dark clock in the corridor echoed midday throughout the great house. My eyes went to her perfect hands, which I could have pressed to my lips. Instead we shook hands in the firm German tradition Helmut's family had long since made me used to.

Werner was punctual too.

He presented us with a champagne cocktail each, not

exactly what I'd been expecting for Sunday's midday drinks. They came on a silver tray with ornate edges and though I'd met Werner at the wedding, he didn't speak to me. A curt bow under the mahogany arch of the huge room was his exit line.

The cocktails sat politely before us on a low table as I listened to Katherine Spiegler talk about her work.

"But there is a certain image that is more difficult to deal with. The immediately recognisable, so to speak, but with the many levels evident. Such as the icons we use for our modern culture. The Christ figure, the hammer and sickle, the black baby at a puckered nipple. These are simple images but they perfectly convey their complexity, their many layers. Yes? And to find new images as these" — she shrugged, looking down to her flute glass as if that might have presented yet another lost image — "is the challenge. I detest the obscure. Equally well I detest the simple-minded, what you would call the clear definition of black and white. The difference I believe is there, the difference between nice photography and great images."

"I understand," I said to be polite, and she nodded at me with satisfaction. It was only in the silence that followed that I realised she was waiting for me to continue. "The Christ figure is interesting," I went on, searching a little desperately, "the many images that invokes in people's minds whether they're the faithful or not. Similarly other things. The pyramids, the peace sign from the sixties." I felt panicky at how quickly I was running out of ideas. But there was the obvious one after all and before I could stop myself the words came out. "The Berlin Wall."

A quiet smile came to Katherine's lips and as I watched her I saw that the skin of her face and neck was as flawless as that of her hands. Was she in her seventies? During the wedding reception the previous evening Katherine Spiegler in white had resembled an icon herself — the Mother of Christ.

The sun seemed to have lowered even though it wasn't much past midday. A yellow light shone against our profiles. And I'd mentioned the Wall. There was quiet as she continued to smile. Neither of us touched our drinks.

As if he had been listening at the door for the appropriate time to enter, Werner appeared under the arch again. This time he was carrying a tripod and a camera. At his feet was a large rectangular metal box that must have held other photographic equipment. It seemed he was ready to prepare Katherine Spiegler for work. He gently put the tripod and camera down then held a light meter up in front of his eyes, checking readings here and there.

"Not now, Werner," she said sharply. "Upstairs, take it upstairs, won't you?" The English was for my benefit and I saw the muscle in Werner's jaw become a knot. He abruptly dropped the light meter and it swung from his neck like an ugly necklace. "And bring us our coats." Katherine rose to her feet in a manner that made me think the visit was over. Instead she said, "You have only been in Lausanne a week?"

"A couple of days actually. Next week, after we've hitched to Vevey and Montreux, we'll take the night train over to Barcelona."

"You must make an effort to see more of Lausanne before you go. Do not let the weather deter you. In our terms, this is the mildest of winters. Still, you will need your coat and scarf." She turned then, and in the yellow light that filtered through the windows she lost twenty, thirty years. "If you will take an afternoon stroll with me?"

And Werner was back, waiting beneath the wooden arch with my coat and scarf over one arm, another set draped over the other. The light meter was still around his neck. I must admit I felt a moment of disappointment that he was to walk with us, but after Werner had us ready for the mild Swiss winter he walked off. His heels clickety-clacked as he disappeared and the memory of his wet-lipped smile was all that remained.

As we left I thought I saw the blue split-second light of a camera's flash coming from somewhere deeper in the house.

"Is he taking photos?"

Katherine Spiegler's smile could have meant anything.

Outside the great house she shared with Werner — "We all bet he's her lover, but nobody will ask her!" — it was as cold as anything I'd ever experienced. It was somewhere below five degrees but the weather didn't seem to bother her. We walked through a back garden that was in desperate need of care, then through a rusted gate in a wire fence. The house, like the lounge where the wedding reception was held, overlooked the great lake and soon we were arm in arm, nestled against each other like the oldest of friends, strolling along the clean esplanade that follows the Lausanne reaches of Lake Geneva.

"It is your art that allows you the time to travel so?" she asked as if I was some kind of wealthy painter. There was of course a hint of humour in her voice.

"And the restaurant work. I'm lucky that the past few Christmas breaks I've had the time to come to Europe. And pay for it the rest of the year, I'm afraid."

"But it is your art that funds you."

It was easy to laugh when she was so obviously teasing me, and with her arm so warm in mine I couldn't help but wonder at the twenty or thirty year age difference between her and Werner.

"I paint landscapes in water colour. It's hardly what you would call art."

But she was already changing the subject; my water colours were as dull to her as they were to me.

"You have been to Germany? Berlin?" The sound of her voice was different again, an old woman's voice, and the lake seemed overcome with winter cold. I remembered her in the drawing room with the low sunlight against her profile and I thought, — *Yes, this had to come.*

"The year before last. Just a few days."

"West Berlin. And the crossing to the East? It is very easy for a tourist, yes?" Katherine drew my arm closely to her as if I'd shown some sign of the cold. There was sharp colour around her high cheekbones. "Did you hate East Berlin?"

"Well . . ." but I was unsure what to say. "It was only an afternoon, not even a whole day. The place I guess is pretty easy to — dislike. But it's fascinating in its own way."

"Please. Do not feel you must be guarded. It has been so long since I was there. Twenty years and more, but things change only slightly. West Berlin thrives with its industry and wealth, a special kind of ugliness. I have photographed whole streets where the cars are Porsche, Mercedes Benz, BMW, over and over, end to end. And East Berlin dies in its industry — perfect ugliness. Fallen buildings, dirt and crude oil in the gutters. And the Wall as you so correctly spoke, the perfect image of our century."

I didn't look at Katherine Spiegler, I didn't want to see the edges of some old madness in her green eyes. Helmut had warned me of this. I watched instead the surface of the lake, the ducks skittering across the mist, the few boats moored and those further out, returning from the horizon.

"Did you feel it a pitiless place?"

"Well, no —"

"But art and thoughts and ideas, driven by none other than the State."

I remembered something from that afternoon spent wandering around East Berlin, something that I thought would appease her. "I saw soldiers goosestepping in a line. It was at a changing of the guard of some museum. The way they marched with their stiff arms and legs going up and down in unison, it was as if there had never been a war."

She stopped a moment, kissed my cheek with lips that seemed unnaturally warm, took my arm so that we again walked as one, our pace faster now. "Good, good, yes. Marching as if there had never been a war. It is just so." Katherine Spiegler smiled at me in a way that made me feel a sudden inspiration had come over her. "Let us return to the house. It is too cold this afternoon." And in a moment we were striding back the way we had come and she was saying, "Yes, I see why you are Helmut's good friend. Let me look at your eyes, yes, they are good eyes. Yes."

Helmut, can you believe that I almost thought I was falling in love with your poor crazy aunt?

We walked back to the house and hung our coats and scarves on wall hooks in the vestibule. I thought that Werner would have appeared but he must have been otherwise occupied.

"Would you mind," Katherine Spiegler asked me, "would you mind posing as a subject for me? Your friendship with my nephew Helmut is important. I would like to capture this, and your eyes, of course."

"When?" I hesitantly asked.

"Now! Now of course — you will come upstairs?"

I didn't know what to say or what to expect. "I must go soon," I said a little too quickly. "Helmut's meeting me."

"Good! That is perfect."

And I was already following her up the staircase to the second floor, where the house was darker. There were few windows and the long quiet corridor gave on to many rooms whose doors were shut. A musty odour was in the air. My companion moved briskly, with authority. As I've said, it seemed that some inspiration had come to her.

Katherine opened a door to reveal a huge room stuffed with furniture and all kinds of paraphernalia. In the middle of the room Werner was struggling with his camera tripod and lights. Katherine spoke to him in German. In answer, he smiled his wet-lipped smile at me.

I walked amongst the cupboards and chests of the room. The dark walls were covered with framed photographs and heavy purple curtains covered the windows, but what drew my attention were the many costumes hanging in the open closets.

"Yes, look at them, that is right. We once had a magic shop in Lausanne, but there was more business in providing costumes for children's parties. Now I sometimes use them for this," she said, indicating the expensive camera. Looming in a corner was a huge stuffed bear. "Look at him, his name is Hans. The children loved him!"

I looked from the bear to Werner, who was putting silver reflective shades up to the dismountable lights. How had he known Katherine Spiegler wanted to photograph me?

But she was running her wonderful hands over the shoulders of the hanging garments. "Take off your coat and try this one, perhaps it will suit you." She moved a mirror-stand for me so that as I slipped on a band-leader's gold and red braided jacket I could see myself better. "And this," she laughed, crowning me with a top hat which was also gold and red but which was much too large. In the mirror I saw my dark eyes staring out from under the brim. I remember thinking then how unsettled I looked.

Katherine Spiegler turned for something else and I saw another pair of dark eyes, from a framed photograph on the wall. The photograph was of an army officer with a stern face and moustache. It was centred amongst all the others and was a great deal larger. While I stood in my outfit the serious young officer looked on; I quickly took off the ridiculous jacket and hat.

Werner was straightening from setting up the lights and now rubbed his hands together briskly. He was smiling.

"Find the Pentax, I will take a few snaps with that to start," Katherine said in English, then from a deep drawer took a brown parcel tied with string. She placed it on top of a glass display case. Her slender fingers struggled with the knots.

"Can I help?"

"Please do not touch."

From out of the brown paper she unwrapped a clean grey coat, an army jacket of sorts. There were no braids or symbols, no markings of rank, only plain stitched seams and black buttons which spoke of war as plainly as the gunfire of a distant battle. Katherine held it out for me. Her face was intent and her lips were parted. I slipped on the jacket, standing again before the mirror.

"Do up the buttons," she said, and as I did my fingers were

drawn to three neatly resewn holes in the left side, beneath the ribs. In the strangeness of the room Katherine Spiegler's smile seemed anything but happy. "Yes, I believe here is the image."

Werner returned to the room. He was fitting a flash into the Pentax when he saw me wearing the jacket. An expression of sadness came to his face. The strength seemed to go from him.

"Oh Katherina, *nein*."

She ignored him, taking the Pentax from his weak hands. "You will allow me to photograph you like this? Here we could have very strong magic, do you not think, Werner — if we wished it so?"

Werner didn't say a word.

And Katherine Spiegler herself seemed to hesitate. It was as if she was torn between the desire to take the photos and the desire to touch the jacket again. Finally it was too much; she passed the camera back to Werner. The palms of her soft hands reached out to press against the resewn holes of the jacket. From the wall, Captain Spiegler's dark eyes watched us.

I could feel her palms as they pressed warmly to my ribs. Her face was so close I could have kissed her.

She hates the obscure, I told myself, the black and white. Here she has found the magic — Katherine Spiegler's new interpretation of the Berlin Wall. But this, her own depiction of the many layers, was somehow too perfect; through the jacket I could feel her graceful hands trembling.

I remember that we stayed in the strange room of the great house the whole afternoon. Now of course there is no need to establish such images. On every late evening news broadcast you can see souvenir hunters chipping away at what is left of the Wall. You can buy your own little piece of icon from the black market, you can even get it by mail order — now that the Wall is gone.

Mandy Sayer

THE DOWN PAYMENT

It was the tall girl at school who told Rose about the fast money. But she was older, eighteen, and slim, and Rose didn't think they'd go for her own fleshy hips and small breasts. But the tall girl laughed and said they liked a bit of fat on the bone. She gave Rose a slap on the bottom. Then she spun around and loped across the grass in her orange patent leather shoes, a black velvet cape billowing in the wind below a spray of golden hair.

After school, Rose caught the tram home to the block of flats in which she and her mother and Louie were living. She lay on her bed and stared at the ceiling. Her toy piano sat in one corner of the room, the only other piece of furniture besides her bed. Maybe one day it would suddenly have a growth spurt and shoot up into a real piano, just before they moved into a real flat of their own. Sometimes after school she'd drop into Palings Music Store, and Mad Harold, the tuner and repairman, would let her sneak down to the basement to practise on an old upright Gulbransen she was sure she would one day have enough money to buy.

As she lay on her bed, she could hear Nancy in the next room. She heard the congested wheeze and saw the picture instantly: the room in semi-darkness, cigarette ash dropping onto a frayed pillowcase, phlegm being wiped with an old cotton hanky, a pair of slippers by the bed, no longer pink or fluffy. Her health had been fine during the years they'd lived with a man who beat her. It was only after she left him for good that her lungs became infected.

It seemed that Nance was always coughing now, as if some smaller person trembled beneath her skin and was fighting to get out. Rose would tell a joke and Nancy would start laughing and if she laughed too much it would turn into loss of breath, and soon she'd be doubled over, eyes watering, a hanky to her mouth. But at least she didn't cough blood anymore. When the tests came back, the woman upstairs offered to look after Louie until Nancy got better. She brought him down every day for a visit, but always held him at a safe distance from his mother.

"Rosie!" Nancy's voice was barely audible through the concrete wall. "Rose?"

She sprang from the bed and hurried to the next room. The bright tip of Nancy's cigarette pointed directly towards her stomach.

"Time for my tablets."

Rose nodded and disappeared into the kitchen. She kept all of Nancy's eating utensils on the left side of the cabinet, and each one — every knife, fork, spoon, plate, glass, mug, and eggcup was marked with a gold star. This was Rose's idea. Every day she washed them with a mixture of chlorine and detergent, and consequently Nancy didn't have to go into hospital after all. And they would be together. And Rose would make her better.

She took a glass of water and fed her the tablets one by one. Nancy had been taking them for a month but the X-rays still revealed a shadow shaped like a crescent moon. Rose had heard of other things from a teacher at school. Herbs and poultices and things like that. But Nancy had just scoffed at the idea.

"It's only art," whined the tall girl between bites of a doughnut. They were sitting on a bench in the sun, outside the science room. The tall girl lifted one leg and pointed her toe above the roof line of the house next door. Rose followed the line of her leg until her eyes met an orange miniskirt. She must have studied ballet or something. Maybe figure skating or gymnastics.

"My mum'd have a pink fit." Rose bit into her sandwich.

"Bit of a prude, eh?"

"My mum's sick."

"So?"

"So she doesn't like being upset."

The tall girl smirked. "Chicken, are you?"

"No..." Rose's voice trailed off as she tried to think of something to say.

"Six bucks an hour," said the tall girl as she stood up and stretched. "Better than looking after those little farts and changing those shitty nappies for the old tart up the road for a dollar fifty."

Rose nibbled at her crust. Nancy earned a hundred and thirty-five dollars fifty a fortnight from her deserted wife's pension and the second week of every fortnight was always spent counting pocket change, eating pancakes with lemon juice and sugar, and tearing open old bumpers to reroll into thin cigarettes. She was saving her babysitting money to buy that secondhand piano, and towards the end of every fortnight, Nancy would appear in Rose's bedroom doorway and ask to borrow it all, just until pension day, and Rose would nod and walk to her bed, her hand stealing inside a small hole in the mattress to find the Tupperware container filled with fifty cent pieces and crumpled dollar bills. And Nancy would always pay her back every second Wednesday. And Rose always shook her head at the extra coins her mother tried to palm into her hand.

On her way to school, the tram stopped by the statue of King Edward the Seventh. Rose found herself rising from her seat and skipping onto the running board and into the street. The fog was a real pea souper, and the tram was still engulfed by it. The image of the conductor's face was framed by the back window, his staring eyes the last to disappear.

After crossing the street, she found herself alone in front of the National Gallery of Victoria. Inside, she climbed the spiral staircase and wandered into the Australian section. It was all very Victorian. Lots of wide petticoats and bustles, straw boaters, canes, and pink parasols by the sea. Nothing like what she was looking for. She peaked around a corner: the steel-grey of an overcast, outback sky. A nineteenth-century girl in a white dress and sun hat, lost among the blue gums and paspalum, almost blending into the bush, perhaps lost forever.

She tensed and swung around to find the eyes of a guard upon her. The silver buttons of his blue uniform glinted. She turned and hurried into the next room and the next, striding past a blur of desert flowers, pompadours and billy cans. Gilded frames grew wide around the untamed green, cornering figures of women in lace and garden hats.

She plunged into the next room and was almost engulfed by the open arms of a tall statue just inside the entrance. She suddenly froze, noticing the way the overhead light played off the bronze contours. Circe stood erect, staring straight ahead, arms extended like wings, down-turned palms and fingers parting as if she were about to strike the first chords of some music only she could hear. Her hips were wide and her breasts shaped like halved pomegranates, the right slightly bigger than the left. She even had an "innie" belly button, like Rose. Upon a bronze pedestal carved into intertwining limbs and open mouths, she stood like a petrified goddess or queen. Rose began to circle her, and it was then that she knew she would do it, as she glimpsed the reflection of her own eyes gazing out from the statue's rounded, glowing hip.

That night, after serving her mother the onion soup that would go untouched, after the ensuing tablets and pillow fluffing, Rose announced a library project and leaned down to kiss her on the lips, even though you weren't supposed to.

She'd already bathed and brushed her teeth and had tried to do something with her hair. She rubbed Oil of Ulan into her face and flexed her muscles in the mirror and pulled on her pair of rubber gumboots.

It took a tram and a train ride to get there. She read *A Study of Australian Art* and was up to the pioneers in Van Diemen's Land. She'd nicked a postcard of Circe from the gallery shop and used it as a bookmark when the train pulled into Glenferrie station. She walked up the hill through light rain, away from the station and an Italian-looking man she was convinced had followed her off the train and through the gates.

Mr Potapenko was old. He wore black-rimmed glasses that looked like a woman's and a maroon suit with patches on the elbows. Every time he went to say something his right eyebrow twitched. It was still twitching as he shook Rose's hand and pointed to the dressing room door.

She tried to think of an excuse: she doesn't feel well, she's only fourteen, she needs desperately to pee.

Suddenly, there were two soft knocks at the door and Mr Potapenko's even softer voice: "Miss Partridge? Rose? Whenever you're ready, dear."

She looked down at her old dress peeking out below her green duffle coat, the gumboots still glistening with water. Her fingers fumbled with the wooden toggle buttons and tensed at the rusty zipper. With coat and dress hung across the back of the chair, gumboots on the shelf, she stood trembling in her white socks, singlet and red polka dot cotton underpants that she'd nicked from Sportsgirl.

"Just a minute."

She was wrapped in Nancy's old oriental dressing gown — the embroidered butterflies and apple blossoms now frayed — as he led her to the platform draped with dark blue velvet. She stepped up and inside the circle of electric heaters pointed inwards toward her. She looked across the room. The man who had followed her off the train was sitting on a stool by the window. The woman next to him sharpened a pencil.

"We're ready, dear," Mr Potapenko prompted.

She tried to remember why she was here. The piano. Yes. When she has enough money she will catch a tram into town and make a beeline down Swanston Street with the money rolled into a cylinder bound with a rubber band inside her coat pocket. She'll stand at the Palings counter before Mad Harold, counting out the last of the dollar bills. Looking over his shoulder to make sure the manager isn't about, he'll shoo her towards the stairs. She'll walk down the spiral staircase, not thinking about all the nude drawings of herself inside folios all over Melbourne. The piano will be standing as usual in a corner within the half-light of a bare, hanging globe. She'll stack two milk crates and pull them up. Through uneasy minor chords she'll play the pale colours of her mother. Then, modulating up, she'll struggle to strike G major: gold stars, a new nightie, herbs she will buy with the remaining money, a happy key her fingers will learn to recognise, a bright note, a favourite colour, something that would be hers.

Mr Potapenko's eye twitched. Her arms slowly relaxed. The robe fell away. The heat of the electric radiators hit her skin. She stood in the tentative position her body had become, unaware of arms or legs or the poses she had repeatedly rehearsed before her bedroom mirror. The scratchy sound of pencils against paper filled the room, until Mr Potapenko abruptly called "Change" and Rose, remembering the tall girl's instructions, shifted her feet and raised one hand to her hip.

After thirty seconds he said "Change" again, and she tilted her head and leaned to one side. *Change:* her leg shot up at the back. *Change:* arms pointed up in a V. *Change:* one toe pointed to take a miniscule step.

"Okay." Mr Potapenko clapped his hands twice and everyone relaxed. Paper rustled. Chairs shifted. Rose swallowed and glanced about the room, but avoided their eyes.

He smiled and pointed to a chair standing behind her. "Have a seat, Miss Partridge. One two-hour pose, all right?"

Rose opened her mouth, wanting to say *no*, or *turn the heat down* or something, but she found herself nodding and falling into the chair. For the next couple of hours she remained frozen to the seat, thinking about Frederick McCubbins's Victorian women amongst ringbarks and campfires and wallaby tracks.

Later, however, after her break and a cup of tea, the dissonant chords of some composition she would one day finish returned to fill her last hour of purgatorial stillness.

When she had her piano she would write it out and keep it. It would outlive her and Nancy and Louie and reach someone a century away.

She wondered what the tall girl thought about as she sat in this very chair. Silk petticoats and opal rings and foreign lovers? And what did her mother think about, all those hours behind drawn curtains, in the secondhand single bed? Did she dream of the crescent moon inside her swelling, or the last flower of blood in her mouth?

When they were finished, she pulled on her robe and, at Mr Potapenko's suggestion, wandered through the crowd of wooden easels. She saw all the variations of her own image against cartridge paper: eyes closed, head resting on the back of the chair, arms spread-eagled, one leg folded against the other, a faint smile playing at the corners of her mouth, as if she'd been asleep a hundred years.

The next day, Rose was ten minutes early for her appointment. She had no trouble finding the place: red neon blinked on and off behind a plate-glass window: *St Kilda Arms*, just as one of the art students had described it. It was a kind of combination pool joint, cafe and bar. She walked in and asked for Leslie. The waiter nodded and yelled into the kitchen and presently Leslie, one of the students from the art school, came into the room, smiling.

He looked as though he could have been a surfie, his shock of blond hair bleached white with sun and salt, and a deep tan set into his face. She followed the palm trees on the back of his T-shirt up the stairs and wondered if he owned the place. He ushered her into his studio: white walls, high ceiling, venetian blinds across the windows through which the late afternoon sun filtered. Three easels were in the middle of the room. He said that another student would join them and pointed to an oriental screen behind which she could change.

Sunlight fell against her skin as she undressed. She could have stood behind the screen in the embrace of it all afternoon, but she heard an easel being dragged and the voice of the other student — a man — and her arms soon found the sleeves of the oriental robe.

They were arranging a set against one of the side walls: a group of large lace pillows, a vase of peacock feathers to the side, a Botticelli print against the wall. The other student was older, and he kept moving the vase around. Leslie was pacing the room, making sure it looked right from different angles.

"Okay, love," said the student with the accent, and though they didn't seem quite ready, Rose slipped out of the robe and stood, eyes closed, in one of the dancing positions of

Botticelli's women. She was content to dream herself backwards into frescos and cracking oils, the thick paint of fallen empires and consumptive queens.

"No, sweetheart," she heard Leslie say. "On the pillows."

She opened her eyes to find two cameras pointing at her.

"What's that?"

Leslie lowered the camera. "Technology, sweetheart." He pointed to the back wall. "We take the slides and then we project 'em, see? On the wall. Trace 'em onto the canvas. Then we colour you in. Simple."

Rose glanced dubiously at the wall.

"Nothing special about it," he went on. "Everyone's into it these days."

"Not at the college."

Leslie nodded. "That's right. Not at the college. That's cause they're from the old school, see?"

Leslie flashed a smile. Rose looked back at the wall. She heard the faint crackle of a radio in the background and a strain of violins. She sullenly lowered herself onto the pillow's white lace.

The cameras clicked away as she lay there and played dead, listening to the music.

"How about showing us your lovely face?" asked the Englishman. Rose raised her head slightly to meet the eye of his Pentax.

"Put your arms behind your head," prompted Leslie as his zoom lens slid forward.

"How about on your side?" said the English accent. "Tilt your bum towards me."

Her face was burning and she shifted slightly.

"Lovely. How 'bout taking away your hand?"

She swallowed and kept her eyes closed, each finger slowly lifting off her left breast.

"Over this way, dear."

She stole a quick glance at Leslie, who was on his knees before her, his head and camera cocked to one side. A bead of sweat hesitated at the edge of her widow's peak before rolling down her forehead.

"How 'bout a smile?"

"Give us a wink."

"Enjoy it, love. Eh?"

Through the battery of voices and winding film she tried to remember why she was here.

Tonight, when she gets home, all the lights will be out. But as she tiptoes into her bedroom she'll smell the faint odour of Nancy's cigarettes and the stench of something sharper. *Rose*? She'll pause in the darkness. Rose will find her propped up on one pillow, a puddle of undigested food on the floor beside her bed, next to the yellow bucket. She'll ease herself back onto the pillow and raise a shaking hand to her forehead. When the floor is clean and the sheet is sponged and the pillowcase is changed, she will help Nancy peel off the soiled pink nightie. With a bowl of warm water and clean flannel, Rose will bathe her as she slouches against the pillows, gently sponging her neck, rounded shoulders, loose skin the colour of eggshells, as if rubbing away at something already half-gone. Her stomach will still be rounded, crowned by the belly button that had once connected Nancy to her own mother, and into which Rose, as a child, would stick her index finger and await Nancy's coinciding *honk* that would make them both laugh and cause Rose to prod her again. She won't touch the two sagging breasts nor bother to roll her over. She'll simply rinse out the flannel and dab it across Nancy's brow, and by the time she leans down to kiss one sunken cheek her mother will be already sleeping.

Rose cupped her hands over her breasts and inhaled, pushing breath deep into her lungs, feeling it in her stomach and hips and swilling around her groin before escaping in one fantastic rush. Her palms sensed the rising and falling. She was vaguely aware of a heartbeat. Her test had come back negative, her body mysteriously evading infection. Now and then she fantasised blood into her mouth, losing four kilos, and dying one day with a throng of flowers around her bed and Nancy — tall and healthy — trying to shake her back to life.

Her eyes fluttered open to discover a zoom lens pointed at the blonde triangle below her hips, a hand adjusting the focus. The sound of her mother's steady breath melted away as her own body began to rise. She could see herself through the camera's tiny window, ascending from the pillows, breasts as small as halved pomegranates, arms parting like wings. The clicking stopped. Fading sunlight divided the room into night and day. Like a petrified woman she stood staring straight through the window. Through the frame she was taller than the tall girl, her fingers uncoiling towards the men who now looked smaller than figures in a photograph.

Moya Costello

YOU KNOW
(APHORISMS FOR THE POSTEVERYTHING AGE)

You know that you're post-forty when people called Kylie and Jason are no longer under five but over twenty;

when the Hollywood "rat pack" no longer consists of Frank Sinatra and Dean Martin etc.; not even Rob Lowe and Charlie Sheen; but people called River Phoenix — a name like the names your generation were calling themselves when they called themselves Seagull etc.;

when your teenage daughter asks for a tie-dyed T-shirt, and her birthday party will have a hippie theme and a mock peace march.

You know that it's postfeminism when you buy your first dress, your first bra, and your first tube of mascara since 1970;

when you've lived through underpants called His Pants for Her and find it impossible to predict the next fashion trend in anything, least of all underpants.

You know that it's postcapitalism when you give up trying

to find underpants that have a life span significantly longer than a bee's in high summer;

when, on a personal level, you revive the art of homecrafts like pickling and consider giving these as gifts along with pot-pourri, lavender bags, and pressed-flower bookmarks;

when you start making your own soft furnishings — curtains, cushion covers — and repairing shoes, and linen: thinning towels, torn sheets;

when, on a personal level, you revive the art of darning;

when your darning doesn't make the slightest bit of difference to the life of any item you darn.

You know that it's postfeminism when you realise you're not the first woman to ever think of doing this;

when all of your conversations with other (post)feminists are all about gardening, home decor, and house renovations;

when you feel guilty when you don't take out the garbage, which is your job now, and when you don't clean the toilet, which isn't your job any longer;

when men still stand back to let you go ahead first and you do, without any bother, while thinking, What the hell, it's your problem.

You know that you're post-forty and it's postfeminism when, on a personal level, you revive the art of skin care;

when protuberances like your breasts and bottom finally lose their valiant struggle against the force of gravity (Good one, nodules!).

You know that it's postcapitalism when nuclear warfare no longer forms part of your personal profile of angst, but skin cancer, high blood pressure, and sugar diabetes do;

when you realise you'll never drink full-cream milk, let alone from a bottle, ever again;

when, on a personal level, you revive the art of the thermos and packed lunch, which you always take with you on any excursion of any kind that's likely to be longer than one hour;

when you place an inordinate and unreasonable value on a good cup of tea, and you seriously plan political action on behalf of the tea-leaf and against the tea-bag.

And you know that it's postmodernism because you know you know.

Edward Berridge

SPEEDING

I meet this chick on the street and she says hey come here for a minute. Come over here so I can talk to you. She whispers do you want to go halvies in some speed and I sort of look left and I look right and I say how much and she says a hundred man, a hundred. I nod my head and she tells me to follow her. Well, we're not far from the Fountain and she leads me down this alley and I'm just looking at her thin butt rolling in her leggings and wondering if I'm going to get ripped off or rolled but I am unable to keep my eyes off the rise and fall of her buttocks pressed against pink elastic. I can see the band of her panties forming a V and I'm thinking to myself I'd like to fuck this chick and maybe I should ask her. Maybe the two of us should go back to her flat or my flat and get some beer and we can have a few pipes and then line the speed and fuck all afternoon with the wind gently billowing the net curtains and blowing the dust off the edge of the window box.

But she leads me up this flight of stairs next to a TV and video repair store and each step is concrete and there's a chipped black handrail and we're going past grey door after grey door until we get to the top floor and I can hear Phil

Donahue buzzing sharply from one of the apartments but we knock on another door and someone calls out who is it and the chick says it's Ruline darlin', I've got the money this time, are you going to let me in and she quickly whispers to me it's good gear mate, good gear and the door opens and a shaft of orange light shines out on the landing where we stand. There's this fat wog guy, looks like he's Lebanese or something and he's got thick greasy hair and he ain't wearing nothing but grey trackpants and brown leather sandals and he's got a ship tattooed on his chest and he says okay, you come in. So we go into this flat and I stay by the door because I feel weird going into someone's place who I don't know but this chick, she makes herself at home. She sits down on an orange lounge chair while the dude goes off into the bedroom to get the drugs. She mouths to me give me the money and I reach into my pocket and count out two twenties and two fives and she looks relieved because, of course, she don't know me from a hole in the ground and I might not have had a cent.

The wog comes back and he says one hundred and the chick gives him my money and gets a fifty-dollar note from what looks like the waist band of her panties and gives him that too and then he gets the speed out of his pocket and hands it to her. She says can we cut it here? We got to split it. But the wog says I sell hundreds and three fifties, you want to cut it you find somewhere else and I say its cool Ruline (feeling so excellent using her name) we can go back to my place to cut it. I don't live far from here. It's just across the road. She sort of looks at me sceptically but I can tell she's jittery and needing some sort of hit and she says okay.

We leave the wog's flat and as we're walking back down the stairs she tells me that she needs to take a piss and I say that's okay man, you can take a piss at my place. I've got works too. We can hit up right away and she looks at me and says I really need to get off my face, man, I'm straight as fuck, and I can sympathise because I'm pretty straight myself. We get back out on the street and I tell her that I've got some gear if she wants a couple of cones. I tell her that I was on my way to get a case when we met and if she wants to wait while I go into the bottle shop we can get fucked off our heads together. I got paid yesterday I tell her. She nods her head and so I lead her home.

She has this sweet, childlike face and long brown hair hanging down from a part in the middle. She is white and thin like all junkies but there is also this look about her like if she'd made it in the straight world she could have accomplished something with her prettiness. But I guess she never made it in the straight world and her eyes are pinched like God gave her the spirit of fear and not the sound mind and strength of power and love that the Saints said He had promised. And there is a blue circle on her left cheek like someone made a mistake with a tattoo gun trying to draw a tear and the nerves around the left-hand side of her mouth look like they are dead and the pits of her eyes are black.

When we get back to my place she goes into the bathroom and I move as much of the shit off the bed as possible. I can hear her pissing and it turns me on. I imagine it streaming out from between her swollen cunt like some scene from a Dutch porno. I want her to piss right into my mouth and then let it cascade down over my chin and over my chest and all over my body. But it's just a fleeting thought and I hear her flush and she comes out. She says let's shoot up man, I'm totally fucked. So I get out my works and a couple of fresh needles and we get it on.

I listen to her breathing deeply as she draws the speed into her vein. She closes her eyes and I can see how close she gets to God. My fingers start to curl and uncurl while I wait my turn. She goes oh fuck, oh yes and smiles and rocks gently. Then she takes out the needle and moves her arm to get the blood circulating. Oh man, she says. Full on. This is fucking shit hot gear and she hands me my belt. Do it she says. You're going to be speeding off your fucking tits right away and I can't help myself, man, my hands are shaking in anticipation. I have to steady the spoon and I hear her saying watch it man, watch it but I'm hanging for a taste. I push the needle into my arm and I'm almost peaking on that alone it feels so good and so pure. Then I get that sweet sensation around the tip like I know the speed's going in and pretty soon it's going to be rushing round my veins, pumping joy to every cell. I get that instant warmth behind my eyes and I know I'm riding something hot.

I open my eyes and she's looking at me. Fucking excellent she says. Didn't I tell you? I say yeah man, it's fucking all right and we're just smiling and feeling cool. We've got that sense of connection that only ever comes from sharing good drugs. I go to the cupboard next to my bed and get out the mull bowl and the pipe. She says I'm glad I met you darlin'. I can score for you pretty regularly. Whatever you need I can get it. Right now I know this dude who's got hash oil for sixty bucks a cap, like you'll get heaps more smoke out of it than you would for half an ounce. I swear to God. She says you must be doing all right. This ain't a bad place and you got money for drugs and grog.

I tell her about my job at the Sex-O-Rama store and I tell her again how I got paid yesterday. I tell her I'm like everybody else. I get paid and I blow most of the fucking lot in a few days and hang straight for the rest of the fortnight. I ask her if she's on smack but I can see that she is. She says she ain't addicted or nothing and that she just likes a taste on weekends and sometimes during the week when she's feeling fucked. We're starting to get that glow in anticipation of the real speed rush. I pack her a full cone and watch as she smokes. She pulls her cheeks in tight creating two light grey hollows under the dark grey half moons beneath her eyes. Her lips are drawn into a taut blue ring and a thin line of dark smoke blows gently upward from her mouth. Then she relaxes and blows the rest of the smoke out in a billowing surge. She holds the bong like a baton, looking momentarily like my sister used to look when she was about to start one of her old physical culture routines, looking a bit like some angelic majorette fallen on hard times.

She tells me that she's a dancer at the Go Go Club. She says if she wasn't on drugs she'd probably be on TV and that she'd been to some audition for *Home and Away* but argued with whoever was doing the casting. She was such a stuck-up bitch she says. I move closer to her and she shifts toward me so we're lightly pressing against each other. It feels so warm and so perfect that we're just sitting there, smiling and looking at the walls. I've never seen them look so white and I get the feeling that I'll never see them look so white again. We are both full of white light, pulsing through our bodies and getting ever whiter. Brightening to a brilliant intensity. We can feel our veins humming like warm fluorescent tubes.

I start to grind my teeth and I'm pulling my hair at the back. She's got this ring on her little finger and she keeps taking it off and putting it back on and taking it off and putting it back on and she's telling me about where she lives in Darlinghurst and how she used to stand on the corner of Forbes Street all day waiting for some action and how she got picked up by this guy once and he was wearing a nappy and he wanted her to rub his cock through the nappy until he came and fuck you know you meet some weird fucking arseholes darlin' I could tell you some fucking stories like this one guy I picked up who I swear to God had this picture of his two daughters, well he told me they were his daughters I don't fucking know for sure you never can tell and anyway right he gets me to suck his cock and all the while he just like holds up this picture of his two daughters and kisses it and shakes his head and I mean fuck how sick can you get like the kids in the picture were like eight or ten. And I say yeah man I know it I fucking know it, where I work we've got these fucking booths right with slot movies and you know the movie that's most popular, Farmyard Capers it's called, Farmyard fucking Capers and it's got this pig right, this fucking pig and this chick goes into this barn and she's got nothing on just this apron and she's carrying like a big jug, a milk jug or something and the first thing she does is milk this cow and pull this cow off but then she lies back and gets fucked by this pig, like the pig gets on top of her and you see its dick and it's like a corkscrew and it fucks her you know and that booth is like always full and the worst thing is like Saturday night you get like groups of dudes and they come in pissed and they all crowd into this booth and you can hear them shouting and making noises like pigs and killing themselves laughing and it's a funny thing, I don't know why it is, but all them booths they stink like salt and ammonia and I don't know why it is, I didn't know come smelled like salt and ammonia. Like we clean the fucking things out with bleach and Ajax but there's this real like natural ammonia that's thick in the air and you just wonder how people manage to just go into these booths and wank like that so they come over the walls. Fuck.

All the while the light within us intensifies and I look out the window at the wall of the block opposite and instead of filthy and grey it is rich jet black and polished silver. I rest my hand on my thigh and at the same time the edge of my little finger strokes her thigh and she tilts her head towards me and her hair falls on my shoulder and as she speaks her breath warms my neck and the top of my chest. Her lips are dry and she bites them until there are dark purple marks. We keep drinking and smoking and the room gets darker and darker and we press ever closer, millimetre by millimetre, adjusting to the cool of the evening. She tells me a whole lot of shit and I tell her a whole lot of shit and we laugh and we bathe in the grace and glory of God's great love. We become vessels of joy.

I ask her if she's getting cold and she says she's freezing and she laughs and pushes her chest forward and says check out my tits love, they're on high beam so I get up and I get the quilt from the bed and we press together underneath it. Her cheek touches mine and I don't pull away and then we turn toward each other and I look into her eyes and she looks into my eyes and we kiss and her mouth is warm and wet and her tongue feels so tender I want to cry out but I can't pull myself away and my left hand takes hold of her left arm and we have to shift awkwardly but we keep on kissing and her eyes are closed and she smells ever so vaguely of disinfectant and for a second I wonder why but it's not important and she is struggling to undo the top button of my jeans and now I push my left hand beneath the waistband of her leggings and I can feel the smoothness of her skin and the line of her panties and nylon lace.

We climb up onto the bed dragging the quilt along with us. She sits up to take her top off and her breasts are small and white and her nipples are light blue. There is a tattoo of a winged horse above her left thigh and on her right arm a cross within a blaze of red, yellow and orange. Her arms are bruised and peppered with needle marks. Her hair frames her face and she is so beautiful. More beautiful than anything

I have ever seen. More beautiful than grey sky through a mist of rain. More beautiful than a deserted building or nothingness that goes on forever. I could weep before her beauty but instead I hold her closely and I kiss her neck and her shoulders and her breasts and her ribs and I can feel her speeding heart between my lips and I can hear her fervoured breath and I keep kissing her while she strokes my back and pulls gently at my hair. She lays back on the white sheet and lets me kiss her vagina. There is no greater glory which I could be aware of. I cannot see I can only taste and breathe.

Then we fuck for what seems like hours, for what seems like an eternity. It is like we have died and have been granted eternal grace. Our hearts are throbbing batteries, the batteries of God, feeding beams of Heavenly white light through our veins. Hail, holy light. We rise and fall like oceans of raging fire, bathed together in boiling, spitting sweat. My cock is hard and blue with speed and she is wide and slick. From outside we can hear sirens and shouting, from the apartment next door Classic Hits. She comes pulling at my hair, scratching my right arm and drawing blood and I keep fucking her, grinding my teeth and pushing her shoulders hard into the mattress. She turns her face to the left and grunts through her teeth and then I come moaning and gasping like someone's punched me in the gut.

I say fuck man, fuck and fall on top of her and she laughs

and says I told you it was good gear darlin'. I told you you'd get a good hit and I lick her neck and she laughs again. She says I wonder what time it is, I got to meet someone at ten, so I look at the clock by the bed and it is 8.45. Her nipples are now soft and flat and a paler blue than before. She says I'd better go wipe myself and get dressed so I roll onto the bed and light a cigarette. She goes into the bathroom and I listen to her piss again. I can feel the light beginning to fade and there is a dull beating behind my eyes. I call out to her have another cone before you go and after a while she flushes and comes back and sits on the bed and puts her clothes on and I pack her a bong.

After we've had a couple of pipes she says fuck man and rubs her forehead. The greyness has returned to her face. She says I've got to fucking dance tonight and I'm going to be fucked. I'm going to have to get another hit. She says do you feel like a taste but I tell her I've got the rent to pay and I've got to go to work tomorrow too and as it is I probably won't be getting much sleep. I can feel darkness returning. I want somehow to connect with her.

But she kisses me on the forehead and says I'll see you round darlin' and she leaves me sitting on the bed. I feel the dark night all around me and everything seems dull. I think about my job and dredge up a few memories while the night struggles into early morning. I sleep fitfully and finally waken tired and cold to a filthy yellow streak of half light bleeding through the gaps between buildings. I light a cigarette and not for the first time wonder where things started to go wrong for me. But I guess there's no point in wandering over old ground. The world is before us and we choose our places of rest. Let Providence guide our paths through Eden.

BARBARA WELS

THE USUAL HISTORY OF BEER, THIGH-SLAPPING AND SCHLIMMBESSERUNGEN

The first time Ruthie ever got drunk she ended up with a shotgun at her head. She was sixteen. Her sister Erica took her to a party and she discovered that gin and tonics made you vivacious. Or so she was told. As Erica drove home, gently respectful of the curves in the road, Ruthie counted each corner on her fingers. She held back the vomit with a vision of her clean, cool bed and the relief that lying absolutely still would bring her, only relaxing with the familiar dip of their driveway. The headlights of the Volkswagen illuminated Ruthie's mother and younger brother standing in the garage, unblinking as statues of the Madonna and child in a grotto. Ruthie leaned on the car door and her high heels sank into the soft ground. After registering the image of her father beside her with his shotgun, she fell forward.

She heard her mother's voice, taut and instructive.

— Get back in the car, Ruthie. We're leaving.

Shoeless, she tipped herself into the back seat with her

brother Marcus. Even in the darkness he managed to be observant.

— What's wrong with Ruthie?

Abandoning navigational tact, Erica backed out of the driveway. They flew through streets, roundabouts, traffic lights, their mother turning now and again to look out the back window.

— Faster, can't you go any faster, Erica? *Mein Gott. Mein Gott!* He's really crazy this time. *Verrückt!*

No promise of a bed to hold her now, Ruthie threw up out the window at alternate intersections. Marcus patted her back with his cherub hands.

— Don't worry, Ruthie. He won't get us. We'll get away. The goodies always do.

Still spinning on a couch in her aunt's front room, she heard a voice.

— Men and their drinking. Pssht. And poor little Ruth. White as a ghost when she came in. Such a sensitive child!

Ruthie and Paul rent a house at the Port, where you can still buy fish and chips wrapped in newspaper and where Ingrid and Emil, and Paul's parents also, first arrived in Australia in the fifties. Passenger liners don't come to the Port much anymore, but the lovers appreciate the sight of the cargo ships as a symbol of their origins and the possibility of travel.

Besides, the rent here is cheap. He likes the graffiti in the outdoor toilet, and the flag which pops up from the letterbox to salute the arrival of mail. She translates the disrepair of the house into unrealised potential and paints the bedroom "Sublime", a pale blue. On the ceiling she constructs a map of the world, with longitude and latitude lines.

— I want you to know that I love you.

— I want you to know that I'll leave you the minute you start drinking too much.

They first met through the Junior Bavarian *Tanzgruppe.* Ruthie had plaits, a dirndl costume and old-fashioned dancing shoes with clumpy heels. Paul wore lederhosen, long white socks and an overzealously executed crewcut. The Junior Bavarian *Tanzgruppe* practised at the German Club on Tuesday nights and performed regularly at street festivals, RSL clubs and fetes. Ruthie and Paul were never partners because Ruthie was so wonderfully tall. In any case, they found each other repulsive. If one of the boys was ever unable to make a performance, Ruthie tucked her hair under a felt hat with a red feather and wore lederhosen. She partnered Erica, who was dainty. Boys were harder to get than girls, and they never lasted very long in the *Tanzgruppe* anyway. At a certain age they always lost their co-ordination.

It happened exactly like this. They noticed each other across the dance floor of a new nightclub and couldn't stop staring. They were both twenty-one. Paul noticed that Ruthie was wearing her old dancing shoes with one of those baggy, rayon 1940s dresses that girls wore. Ruthie saw how Paul still had the same haircut, except his face had grown thinner and he had an earring. He still couldn't dance. He danced as if he was surfing.

Paul is amused by Ruthie's steadfast compulsions toward solitude, monopolising the quilt and imprinting statements of herself all over the house. At jumble sales she buys clumsy hand-powered kitchen appliances. If they are broken, she revives them with glossy paints and hangs them around the kitchen window where they attract insects.

— You Germans. You Germans and your *Lebensraum*.

He can talk. He often collects these words from Ingrid, Ruthie's mother. Ingrid can be relied upon for her *Apfelstrudel* and her habit, in conversation, of translating the other person's experiences into succinct but clumsy German words which usually consist of three or more ideas pushed together.

Language fascinates Paul. He acquires dictionaries of all kinds, including dictionaries of dictionaries. His ability to recall obscure words at perfect moments charms the dancing shoes off Ruthie. He can also remember jokes, punch lines, his dreams, details of conversations he had years ago and the name of the babysitter he had when he was three.

— You're such a sponge for trivia, Paul. You *Korinthenkacker.*

This is the one obscure word Ruthie can remember, so she uses it on all possible occasions.

Only once, when Paul and Ruthie are living together, do they lapse into the old Bavarian dance routines. She comes home with the news that some of her paintings are to be featured in an exhibition. In her motorcycle boots and mini-skirt, she plays the thigh-slapping *Junge* while Paul (with a Greetings from Surfers Paradise tea towel tucked into his jeans as a dirndl apron) is whirled and spun around the kitchen as the *Mädchen.* Afterwards, Ruthie has hand-sized bruises all over her body from slapping herself.

Apart from her dysfunctional kitchen appliances, Paul's enchantment with Ruthie is clinched by her sleep-talking. Her babbles evoke tenderness, but he likes her forceful declarations the best.

— Stop the carnage!

At first Paul is convinced she must be awake. But the next morning she remembers nothing about her demand.

Propped up on his elbows, he watches his *Liebling* sleep. He has something to ask her. Ruthie wakes up to hear herself answering a question about her past. She pretends to be asleep and changes the subject. Sensing Paul's disappointment as he adjusts the quilt, she keeps her laughter for a worthy punch line.

At regular Sunday dinners, Paul drinks with Ruthie's father. Emil likes to indulge his passion for good wine or beer in company. Ingrid does not drink. Drink, says Ingrid, makes you stupid. Paul enjoys the drinking. It's a practical diversion from the political arguments which always scuttle about his feet like rodents under the dinner table. He's warmed by Emil's hospitality, and they discuss history. Ruthie's pleased her father and her lover have something in common, but she's not sure that alcohol is the common interest she had in mind. Finally she takes a glass for herself and discovers she shares this predilection for foreign beer. Sometimes they convince Emil to play *Fifty Favourite Drinking Songs*, and Ingrid half laughs and half sighs and wanders into the kitchen to bake something. The lovers stumble home on the last train to the Port with a freshly baked *Käsekuchen*, singing the songs they find so funny.

During telephone conversations, university lectures and

horror movies, Ruthie rushes off to see if her period has arrived. She returns balancing snippets of graffiti from toilet doors on the edge of her tongue to present to Paul before she forgets. *The average man is proof that women can take a joke.* It's normal for Ruthie to believe she is pregnant. She takes the Pill, but, like God, she can't quite bring herself to believe in it. At night, she lies next to Paul and imagines their child inside her, coming out of her and lying between them on the lumpy mattress in the sublime blue bedroom. They are not at the stage where they might discuss babies' names.

Ruthie has a theory that her less than ideal upbringing has made her more than an idealist. She's an avid and unashamed believer in self-help books. She isn't the sort to call her mother in the event of any crisis and Paul is grateful. But he's sometimes distressed by the titles which lie around their house for anyone to interpret. *Why Do I Think I Am Nothing Without a Man?* is one of these. He checks the paperbacks by Ruthie's side of the bed and tries to complement her current program of self-improvement. When she finishes *Fat Is a Feminist Issue* he makes a special point of never passing comment on women's bodies, either way. He writes notes for his *Liebling* on the back of supermarket dockets; poems or ideas or nonsensical sentiments. He plants these in her pockets, shoes, books or packets of favourite herbal tea.

✧ ✧ ✧

After the abortion, Paul decides to scrimp on his scholarship money and take Ruthie to Germany with him. He's researching "Language and the German World View in the Tabloid Press". Ruthie plans to visit relatives and make important discoveries about their cultural background. She's reading *The Motherland and the Displaced Psyche.*

In Cologne Frau Bäumlein, their landlady, greets them with kisses.

— *Ach ja! Meine lieben Australischen Flitterwöchner!*

— Ah, yes! My dear Australian honeymoon couple!

She totters down a corridor and opens the door of a purple room. Paul and Ruthie look at one another — marriage is not on their itinerary.

They hover in a week-long breeze of lethargy. In the mornings they get out of bed and find themselves too weary to do anything but fall back into bed and doze or make love. Thomas Mann and Heinrich Boll keep them awake some of the time. Ruthie wonders if their lassitude is the result of all the pastries they've been eating. Paul contemplates the perfect paint chart name for the offensive shade of purple which blights the walls of their room. Fräulein's Puce Nightmare? Psychedelic Edelweiss? Pudenda Fog? Eventually he settles on *Flitterwochen* Haze. Wide awake again at midnight, they drink schnapps and declare a new year. The next day they'll get up and go for a long walk to visit the German Roman Museum. But after breakfast there's the mistake of sitting on the bed to put on their shoes. The nylon floral bedspread consumes a beatific tangle of salty limbs, marzipan and Swiss chocolates. Happy New Year!

— Think of all the Deutschmark we're saving by not doing anything, says Ruthie.

But Paul finds a word for it.

— It's called *Bettschwere*. Literally: bed heaviness. It's like a state of mind so lethargic you can only sleep. That's us, *Liebling*!

The idle breeze passes. Paul works on his thesis and Ruthie talks to Frau Bäumlein, or wanders through the *Staatsgalerie*. She's glad they aren't in Italy.

— We might have spent the rest of our lives like that, for want of the right word in the wrong language.

But she twirls the hairs around Paul's nipples because it's one of the closest times they've had.

Frau Bäumlein forgives her guests for not being an actual honeymoon couple, and lets them stay on in the *Flitterwochen* suite even after the real ones arrive. Frau Bäumlein lives in pink high-heeled slippers, consumes soap operas as voraciously as her menthol cigarettes and delights in a good story. Over cream puffs in an authentic Viennese-style cafe, she tells them how she was there in 1944 when Cologne was bombed.

— Flat to the ground. *Unheimlich.* Uncanny. In dozing the wreckage of the city much was discovered about the Roman civilisation which preceded Cologne as we know it. That wonderful mosaic under the cathedral was only found after it was bombed. And most of the things in the German Römisch museum ... a gift after the rape. Strange that the destruction of what we knew, of our present, taught us so much about the past.

Paul develops a theory about Germans, that they love dogs and dislike children. He points across the cafe with expertise, as if to a famous landmark — at dachshunds and poodles sitting on cushions on chairs at tables, wagging their tails and eating from plates. Some wear pullovers, or waterproof jackets.

Frau Bäumlein snorts.

— You get paid good money these days in Germany, by the government, to have children. But nobody wants them. Only the money.

She waves cheerfully at the one child in the place.

Androgynous in its expensive clothes, its face is puckered up and its chin barely reaches the table.

In Munich, Ruthie embarks on a program to improve her German. She sneaks into movies, talks to strangers and follows her horoscope in magazines whose equivalent she'd be embarrassed to buy at home. The advertisements make her paranoid about underwear. She wonders if Paul will begin to find her undesirable in her tatty Bonds Cottontails and Berlei bras. The Germans make beautiful lingerie. Ruthie makes a private tour of department stores. She takes three bras into the changing rooms. She brings three bras out. She swaps old bras for new bras. She considers it a cultural exchange. Underpants are more of a challenge. Late one night she steals some from a washing line, and a Karl Marx T-shirt.

They fight. She flies at him, tongue contorting.

— *Korinthenkacker.* Pedant. You're always obsessed with the trivial. Relax. Enjoy your underwear fantasy.

— Breaking the law in a foreign country isn't trivial. Don't expect me to drop my research if you get deported.

Ruthie wonders why she always ends up being irritated by the things she first loves about people.

✧ ✧ ✧

It seems like a perfect moment for her to go off and visit relatives.

After a time, she meets up with Paul in Berlin. He's found a cheap room for them.

— What did you learn?

Ruthie is unzipping her backpack to reveal an elaborate art deco biscuit-cutting machine.

— Well, I don't know. My mouth was full most of the time so I didn't get to ask many questions. No, it was great. They were lovely. I think I understand more about my parents now. So much fell into place for me, being in actual people's houses. Food, drink, sex, money, work, status, collecting objects, fear of dying, dogs, children …

— The important things.

They go out for some beer and make an arrangement.

— Things will be better from now on.

After receiving the type of letter which only mothers can decipher, Ingrid writes to her daughter.

— I wish I knew how to help you, *meine Süsse.* This *Wanderlust.* I can't help wondering if by trying to improve things in this way you are perhaps only making it worse? A *Schlimmbesserung,* we would say …

✧ ✧ ✧

Returning to the Port, they take it in turns to finish the relationship. Paul paints Ruthie's toenails red, black and gold.

— We have such a history together, *Liebling*. But it's not working. And you're so unhappy.

Ruthie looks up at the ceiling, at the map of the world which is upside down from this end of the mattress. She is trying to locate Ecuador.

A few months later they are in bed, smoking dope and watching the VFL grand final. Ruthie is in the cat position. She stretches her neck and exhales.

— Paul? You know it's time I was properly alone.

The book under her pillow is *Self-Reliance Through Yoga* by Selverajan Yesudian.

In a white room, Paul leans on his elbows to watch a new girlfriend as she sleeps. He waits for her to begin talking. In a pale blue room, Ruthie continues to note unusual words of certain interest to Paul. She scrawls them on the backs of postcards, signs them *Liebling* and hopes that his lover will find them:

Koro, noun (Chinese): The hysterical fear that one's penis is shrinking.

Razbliuto, noun (Russian): The feeling a person has for someone he or she once loved but now does not.

Cavolo riscaldato, noun (Italian): Attempt to revive an old relationship.

She retrieved Selverajan Yesudian from her bookshelf for Erica, who was turning thirty. A note fell out from the chapter entitled "Special Exercises to Prevent Colds and Constipation". Typical Paul scrawl.

— Do you remember the Roman mosaic under the cathedral in Cologne? But for the bombing, it would never have been found.

Ruthie turned the docket over. Beer was so cheap when she was twenty-three.

HERB WHARTON

THE MUNTA-GUTTA

For a long time I've been going to tell a story about the Munta-gutta. It happened many years ago when all us Murris used to live in the old yumba, about a mile south of town past the cemetery. Sometimes, if we didn't catch a rabbit or shoot or snare a kangaroo or set traps, we'd be a bit short of meat. Then we'd go to our uncle, who worked at the slaughter yard. And sometimes us kids would get gingles and tripe and skirt and a bit of liver. We'd walk past the cemetery, then past the school to where the old wooden bridge spanned the big muddy waterhole of the Warrego River. Instead of walking over the bridge, we went down the steep bank and round the end of the waterhole across the sandy bottom of the creek — it was real wide, a hundred yards across. That's where the waterhole ended, just beyond the bridge. Then we walked up the bank past the big gum trees and followed the fence where a Chinaman lived, a real ancient old bloke.

He was so frail and old he looked to me a thousand years old. He used to grow the most beautiful vegetables. We'd walk past his garden into the slaughter yard where the cattle and sheep and pigs were killed to supply the town. I used to give my uncle a hand, washing away the blood or tipping things out — probably making a real mess of myself. The blood that came out of the bullocks and sheep ran through the cement drain into a trap.

That old Chinaman would come over to the slaughter yard with two buckets hanging from a pole across his shoulders, and he'd fill them with blood. That was before the days of fertilisers: the blood was the fertiliser for his garden. I can still see him with those buckets — he had a real springy little walk, and he'd jog across from his little tin humpy that stood in the midst of his vegetables, on his acre or so of ground.

Anyhow, my uncle had finished his slaughtering for the day. The butcher's truck came to pick up the carcasses and my uncle told me to stay at the yard and not go near the water. He was always telling me that — "Don't go near the river," he'd say, "the Munta-gutta lives down there." I was only about six or seven, and I didn't know what he meant. My mother always said funny things about my old uncle, that he was "one of them". If he saw you scratching around drawing images in the dirt he'd thump you and make you rub it out — he'd say it was one of the old beliefs, that you had to wipe out everything you drew.

So he was gone and it was a real hot day. I knew it was shallow at the end of the waterhole, with beautiful white sand like a beach at the edge of the brown, muddy water. I walked down past the old Chinaman's garden to the water-hole and sauntered over to the edge of the water. There was no one around. I decided to strip off. I was only wearing a pair of shorts and a shirt. I dog-paddled around in the cool water — it wasn't very deep and I couldn't have been far off the bottom.

Then my hand touched a log. I dog-paddled past it then put both my feet on it to rest them, hanging on with my hands. I was crouched down on the log with my head above water, blowing bubbles. Then I thought, if this is a log, it can't be far to the bottom. Hanging on with one hand, I tipped my head to one side and reached down with the other …

The log was thin, and bent up. And in the space between the arch of the log and the bottom, as I reached down with my hand, I felt something soft, damp and smooth. Something alive. It wasn't slimy, it was a damp, velvety sort of feeling. I traced along it with my hand and was amazed: I realised it was a bloody big thing, bigger than me. Three feet long at least. And there were two of those things, as I found out when my knuckles touched the second one, lying beside the other. The first thing I thought was — Well, this is it. This is the Munta-gutta!

I don't know how I got out of the water. I believe I sprang

from the log and turned in mid-air — maybe I ran along the top of the water to get out! But I know now that it couldn't have been more than a foot deep. Anyhow, that was the fastest I ever made it out of the water in my life. Galloping over the soft sand, I reached down to pick up my shirt and trousers and I never stopped until I got to a big old gum tree. I got behind it with my clothes in my hand. I must have been really afraid, and I remember that I was gasping for breath.

Anyhow, after a while I finally calmed down enough to think properly. I put my trousers on and had a real slow sort of peek around the tree. It really was a huge tree — about ten little kids my size could have hidden behind it. I glanced towards the water. There wasn't a ripple in it. All I could see was the deep track I made when I ran out of the waterhole, especially in the wet sand near the bank. There was my trail in the white sand all the way to the tree. I was mystified. I thought, it's got to be the Munta-gutta. But then, the way the old people talked about the Munta-gutta, I thought it was a lot bigger than the thing I had felt. I hadn't felt its head, just its satiny smooth belly.

I don't know how long I stayed there, but finally I headed up the bank back to the slaughter yard, where I was supposed to be waiting. My uncle came back about half an hour later and yarded his cattle up and was ready to go home. I carried our little sugar bag, with our gingle and tripe and a bit of skirt in it. Everyone used to carry one of those sugar bags when they walked to town to get tucker. You could roll it up under your arm then use it as your shopping bag, put all your groceries in it and chuck it over your shoulder. If it rained you could punch a little hollow in it and use it for a cape that hung over your head and shoulders.

My uncle and me were heading home, and on the way the old Chinaman sang out to us and gave us a cabbage and a couple of tomatoes. Then we went down the bank towards the water. Now my uncle was one of the best trackers in that country. Whenever anyone got lost, people would come to get him and he'd track for miles and miles out in the bush. He taught me a lot about tracking horses and cattle and other animals. He was a very smart man. He didn't need to be told anything, he could read the facts and see what had happened.

"Look, look at this," he said to me and pointed to the track. "Must've been a kid playing down here on his own. Looks like he been in the water … looks like the Muntagutta must've frightened him. I see he come out of the water and ran behind that tree there. I wonder … you never seen no kid down here, eh?"

"Nah, not me, I never seen no kid." I couldn't tell him

that I'd touched the Munta-gutta, because then I'd have got a flogging for going down to the river.

"Well, it's strange that the kid went back up the bank," my uncle said. "His tracks don't come over this way."

"I never seen no one, Uncle."

We walked home across the river bed to the yumba.

It puzzled me for a long time. I kept to myself the secret that I knew where the baby Munta-gutta slept in the shallow end of the waterhole. I wasn't going to tell anyone, not even my mates I used to play with. They'd only say I was telling lies. I kept that secret for ages.

A few years later — I suppose I might have been twelve by now — some of the old Murris from the yumba used to take us fishing for cod. We used drag-nets. When we got to the water we'd all have to be quiet, and if there was a log sticking out somewhere they'd say, "That's where he lives, over there!" They'd slide gently into the water and dog-paddle silently across the water to set the net between the log where the cods were supposed to be and the deepest part of the waterhole. That was because when you disturbed the cod it always headed for the deepest water. After they'd stretched the nets out they'd stand there silently. Sometimes the water would be over their heads, and they'd dig poles into the bottom of the creek-bed and hang on to them, just dog-paddling there quietly. Then some of them would circle around silently until they got behind the log and the nets — and at that point they'd come into the water and make a lot of noise.

Sometimes those old cods wouldn't move, and the old Murris would tell us kids to dive right down amongst the logs. The first time I ever felt a cod down there, I thought it was another Munta-gutta. This is how it happened.

We were supposed to be hunting the cods into the nets, and they told me to dive down and feel around. You couldn't see anything, it was all brown muddy water. Well, I was feeling around and suddenly my hands rested on this thing. "There's something down here," I said. Of course, I was real game with a lot of people around. I dived down again and felt the same thing, this belly part — but it was the belly of a big cod. I kept giving him a few digs and he swam into the net. And when that old cod hit the net, them fellas lifted the poles from the muddy bottom and one bloke turned his stick clockwise and another turned his anti-clockwise. The cod was ravelled in the net and the two blokes swam along and put the poles together. Then, holding the poles at each end on their shoulders, they dog-paddled out of the water onto the bank.

On the bank they unravelled the net and out flopped this big cod, about thirty or forty pound. I just stood there stroking its belly, with the same mystified feeling I'd had when I touched the baby Munta-gutta years before. After keeping that secret for so long, I thought I had solved the mystery at last. I thought: so this is the "Munta-gutta". There's no bloody Munta-gutta at all. All those years ago it was only a big Murray cod!

Not far from the place where we'd caught this cod, upriver a bit, it was all steep banks on the western side, about thirty feet down to the water. There was a cave there — in the dry time you could see the top of it. Actually there were two caves, and if the water was real low you could see the top of the second one. This was supposed to be the place where the Munta-gutta lived. Of course, the old Murris told us to stay away and never go near the place. And most of them wouldn't go there either.

Well, I stood watching the men arguing amongst themselves. We'd already caught a few yellow-bellies and a couple of catfish. Even though there was a big mob of us, it would have been enough for a feed. They were arguing about whether we should try to catch another cod, or go home. Suddenly there was a big splash in the water, up near those caves.

"That's it, boy, we gotta go," my uncle told me. He began telling all those other fellas the same. "We gotta go because that's him, that's the Munta-gutta telling us we've gotta go, we've got enough fish."

You couldn't take too many — that was our law. You only took what you could eat. We had no fridges in them days, so we probably would have wasted it. There was another big splash — it sounded like a whale flapping about.

"It's only a tree limb fallen into the water," I said.

"Don't be silly, boy. There's no tree over there big enough for that," my uncle told me.

Then we heard this drumming sound, like an emu or something. And it came from near that cave as well.

My uncle said, "That's him, come on, we gotta go!"

They picked up the cod and the nets and headed up the bank.

"That's only an emu," I said.

"Don't be silly, boy," they said. "Emus don't live in the water."

There was another big splash. Then I realised I was out on my own pondering this mystery. I thought I'd solved it when I thought of emus, but when I heard the next splash I was more confused than ever and bolted after the others. I could still hear this drumming, droning sound, just like an emu. Sometimes, in the winter time, out in the bush, you can hear an emu a great long distance away when he's drumming in the early morning and the female is laying eggs at nesting time. I thought: "Well, I still don't know about this Munta-gutta."

It wasn't far to where we had parked the old Ford truck with its flat-top back and no cabin, just a windscreen and a seat. All us Murris used to jump on the back with the nets and the fish. When we got to the truck that day, I was looking back in the direction of the caves and they were all saying that there was no argument about this thing: the Munta-gutta ruled the river, he was the one who decided whether you could take fish, and saw that you didn't take too many and deplete the stock.

According to legend, that was no ordinary cave. It was connected to every other river system to the west and the east. There was another really big waterhole, perhaps fifty miles away, and the cave was connected to it through an underground passage. Sometimes you'd be sitting down by the river and you'd see old leaves and mud come to the surface. Not because the river was running — they'd just come bubbling up. That was supposed to be the Munta-gutta cleaning out its cave, and it was a sign that a flood was on the way. The old people said that if the Munta-gutta wanted to punish people, he'd dry all the water up, all those connecting rivers, and send a drought on the land. Then the people would go without water and without fish. The Munta-gutta would go to another waterhole, and then after a while he'd send floods. They always described the Munta-gutta as something like the Loch Ness Monster.

As kids, whenever we were told not to go near the river we used to say: "Oh, that Munta-gutta, he can't catch us! We'll run out of the water onto the bank. He can't come out of the water and I'll beat him!"

But the old fella would reply: "He don't have to come out of the water, he'll send a big whirlywind, spinning and spinning around to pick you up and dump you in the river. Or he'll send a big water spout, just like that. It'll grab you and dump you right back in the water."

I used to say, "I'll fix him! I'll get my father's gun on him. I'll shoot that Munta-gutta!"

And they'd say, "You can't shoot the Munta-gutta, he's too smart for you."

I still remember those caves, though they've built a dam there now and they are permanently under water.

The old men told this story about a fella who'd done something or other to the mob that lived there, and he was going to run away. He was going to head for another waterhole. Well, one of the old men called up the Munta-gutta, to punish this fella for taking the woman. And the Munta-gutta called up a big rain to come down, a vast flood. It caught that fella as he was going over the stony crossing at the end of the waterhole, and he turned to stone himself. According to legend, he's there to this day, just below the surface of the water. One of the old men told me when I was young that if that stone fella's head appeared, you would always get a big flood.

The Munta-gutta ruled, he set the laws. You could take enough fish to eat, but you could never waste or misuse the resources of the river or you'd be punished. The waters were probably the most important thing, more so than the kangaroo. For thousands and thousands of years everything depended on the water in that part of the country. Sometimes the creeks stopped running for a year at a time. Twenty or thirty miles apart there'd be these big permanent waterholes that always filled up in the wet season, and the people moved from one waterhole to another, so that they always had water. Yes, there was always water in that country. It seems, too, that those old Murris knew about the great underground reservoirs which we call the Artesian Basin today. Water was more precious than gold or gems: everything depended on it for life. And the stories about the Munta-gutta helped to keep order and preserve the resources of the country. I think that when the white settlers came, they heard those tales and so the Munta-gutta became the white man's Bunyip. There were, in fact, creatures that could fit the description of a Bunyip that the old people described — creatures like reptiles which have now been extinct for maybe ten thousand years, but which lived on in memory.

A few years later, I reckon I finally glimpsed the Munta-gutta. It was at the other big waterhole, west of where we caught the cod that day. By this time I was seventeen or eighteen, and I was working as a stockman on the station where the legendary stone man appeared when the river reaches its lowest level … after which the biggest floods always come. Some people used to describe how they had seen that Munta-gutta struggling to get up through the netting fence there when the floods came, trying to get upstream. A few miles away, at a big bend in the river, there was another permanent waterhole.

One day I was riding around on my own looking for a stallion near the river bend. There was no sign of the missing horse, but I heard these three terrific splashes, even bigger than the splashes on that fishing day years before. I rode up to the waterhole. It wasn't very wide, probably some seventy yards across. There was a steep bank on either side, and big coolibah trees all around. And there, right in the middle of the river bend, I saw a big long head sticking out of the water, with a lump behind it like a body. And just behind it was another head at about the same height, sticking out about two feet or more, like a giant duck, except it was brown. And it had a lump behind it, too.

The first thing that came to me was the thought: "Oh, I've finally seen the Munta-gutta!" I looked again, and there was another of these things, swimming real fast towards the opposite bank. And as I sat there on my horse, gazing at this thing, I thought: "I'm gonna be the first man to see the Munta-gutta come out on the bank!" I was that excited. It got bigger and bigger as it reached the bank and began to come out of the water ... and then I saw the long, scaly legs of an emu and all the water flying off him as he took off up the bank, his neck stretched out as he bolted away. Yes, it was a bloody emu! And the other two emus came swimming out too.

So I never saw the Munta-gutta after all.

MARION HALLIGAN

HERE BE UNICORNS

When he reached out his arm I saw the tattoos.

I never could see enough of tattoos when I was a child. There was a man down the road who'd been a sailor and he had a skull on the back of his hand with a rose between its teeth, and on one bicep a pair of red lips that popped like a fish when he flexed his muscles. But I only ever got to see them when he was in the butcher's at the same time as me, and since I wasn't allowed to stare I had to steal glances at them. Like now, and there's this man with the shield on his hand and a banner winding through it, I can't make out what the writing says. I've never known anybody well enough to say Let me look at your tattoo, and pick up his hand and examine it, really look my fill.

I was rather pleased when Ed took the shop in the same block as the tattooing business. It's a rather sleazy area, but people don't mind that in the upholstering trade. Perhaps they feel they aren't paying for the address. The facades of all the shops are shabby, but handsome, too, they curve in a portly prosperous way, and are carved and grooved with flowery detailing. Ed uses the big window as a showcase for his work, I mean the doing of it, not the results; you can look in and see him fitting tapestry covers, or velvet, nailing in the gilt nails that give a smart finish. But the window in the tattoo shop is deeply curtained. Painted on it is a great whirling dragon, it looks like some kind of savage machine of war because of the way its body coils look like big round wheels. Maybe it's a sea serpent, the circles of its body hard and muscular like tractor tyres. Under its belly are pictures of people with tattoos, satisfied customers I suppose they are. I imagined furtive or colourful people slinking in and out of this shop, sort of like opium den people, but they seem to be quite ordinary; looking out of Ed's window at the passersby you can't tell which would be the tattooist's clients. Once I went past and the door was open; there was an empty room with flowered carpet and at the end a laminex coffee table and one of those nite'n'day lounges. Just inside the door was a box of toys, a milk crate with some pretty tatty looking dolls and books and blocks. The customers can't all be macho men, some must be fathers looking after little kids. Or else mothers.

Now this man stretched out his hand and moved the ashtray in front of him, and flicked his cigarette, so that the banner winding through the shield seemed to flutter, or anyway twitch. It's funny, decorating the skin like that, why would people do it? They say it hurts terribly, I heard that it's worse than the pains of childbirth, but that's hard to believe. And how could you compare? What if I asked this man? Excuse me … So many things you think of that you'd never do. He took his sweatshirt off and he had more pictures, a snake twisting around his bicep, with its mean head and spitting tongue just below his elbow, and on his shoulder an eagle with prey in its talons.

His wife was at the boiling-water machine, making mugs of coffee. She was wearing jeans that were threadbare and moccasins with fur insides that folded over the top. Her hair was perm falling out, and limp. She brought the coffee to the table and sat down with a thump. I wouldn't have spoken, just sat with my tea and sandwich, but he asked what I was in for, so I told them about Amy and the operation having to be postponed because she'd caught a chest infection.

Our Sarah's had hers today, he said.

The third, said the wife. She slumped over the coffee mug. It seemed to be weighing her down.

Mr Firth, he said. You got him?

Yes, but I haven't seen him yet.

Yeah, he's a slippery bloke to catch. We only seen him a coupla times ourselves. He's a great man, but. Really the best.

He's the one done the heart–lung transplant on that little boy the other day, said the woman, still weighed down by her coffee mug, leaning forward to take a pull from it, slurping. On the telly. In the papers too.

Your little girl — she's all right?

I didn't know whether to ask this or not, it was my first day, I wasn't sure of the rules, what to say, what not. It was before I found out how much people wanted to talk.

The man shrugged, a heavy slow twitch. The eagle flapped. Gotta wait and see. They can't tell yet.

How old is she?

Three months.

Three months is very small.

She was three weeks for the first one. What about yours?

Amy's five.

Another couple came in. This woman was fat, and limp-haired too, and her husband was just like the first man, Mick I found out he was, and his wife was Narelle; both the men quite thin, lean you might say, but not very muscular, they looked like boys, except for their faces, not that they didn't look young but they didn't look like boys. The other one, Trevor I think, had some beer, and they took it into the lounge room; the women got coffee. When I went up to bed they were sitting on the leather couch watching the television and talking. It took me a long time to go to sleep; I could feel the huge cream brick bulk of the hospital on the other side of the window and Amy there all by herself and me here and Ed back home and all the sea between us.

Amy was sitting on the end of Jack's bed when I got to

the ward. He had a guitar, I don't know whether it was a toy one or just small, and was trying to pluck out notes. Josephine was there too. Amy went a bit tearful when she saw me, nothing like what she does when I leave, though. Why don't you stay with Jack, I asked her, have a go on the guitar. But she wanted to come back to her bed with me. I got out the story book I'd brought, I mostly try to take something, one of those silver balloons they have in the foyer, or a toy or a book or a new nightie, a little painted box, a puppet, that kind of thing. Josephine came over when I was reading the story, she's three, a beautiful little girl, not fair like Amy, dark with long shining hair quite surprising on such a small person and huge brown eyes with lashes to break your heart, lying on her little golden brown cheeks when she looks down, then sweeping up. She was wearing a long striped nightie like a football shirt, and she sat on her bed with her thumb in her mouth while I read the story; it was *John Brown, Rose and the Midnight Cat.*

The thing about hospitals is that there's so much time. I've never known it hang so heavy. You want it to pass yet you're afraid of what it will bring. Amy's got a ninety-five per cent chance of surviving, said the surgeon, when we finally got to have a meeting, brief, standing in an empty office, with his eyes always sliding away from mine. Ninety-five per cent. Of course in her case it will be 100 per cent or none, won't it, he said smiling or anyway curling up his lips at the empty bookcase. This seemed horrible to me, though I didn't really know what he meant, but that five per cent seemed a lot. I mean, if you were going to shoot, say, five per cent of people in a prison, or five per cent of children at kindergarten were to be killed in a bus crash on their way to a puppet show, that would be a lot, wouldn't it, it would be a twentieth. That must mean there's a one in twenty chance of her not surviving. It doesn't sound very good to me. You wouldn't want to be depending on it. Ed sometimes puts money on a horse; he'd know what the odds mean.

So anyway the thing about hospitals is that you're terribly bored and terribly frightened. Dad always said the war was like that, but I could never imagine it, it seemed to me that one of those things would cut out the other, you couldn't be both. Here I know exactly what he means. And now the physician says there's no possibility of operating with that chest infection. We must give her every chance he says. I suddenly thought of a cash register, and the numbers popping up. One of those old metal clanking machines that ring sharp bells. Up popped the tickets saying 95, and then the 9 dropped back and there was an 8, and then a 7, and then the 5 dropped down and a 0 came up, and then the whole thing was down to just 10. I couldn't stop thinking of it, these terrible clanking numbers getting lower all the time. I get worried sick about Amy, and then this stupid old metal cash register appears and the numbers start clicking and it drives me mad. I wish I knew how to stop thinking about things.

There's a school and sometimes I take her, she won't go without me and she won't always go with me. That helps pass the time. And I always leave at nap time, that's a little routine I'm setting up, that I go away at nap time. I often take the tram into town and buy something at Myers for my tea, there aren't any shops round the hospital. And of course the little presents.

One of the women in the house has a child with her, a healthy one. When they arrived he wanted to know where Ronald McDonald was, when he was coming, when he was going to bring the hamburgers. His mother kept saying that was just the name of the house, it was called Ronald McDonald House but he didn't live here, that McDonald's just gave money for it, but he wouldn't believe her. He kept saying, when are the hamburgers coming, grizzling in that tired way children have. Mick, the tattooed man, told the mother there was a milkbar down the road, but she shook her head. You could see she was too weary for that. Tomorrow, Danny, she said, tomorrow we'll find hamburgers. Ronald McDonald will bring them, said the boy, when he comes.

It's funny to think that's the name of this place. McDonald's set it up, it's their gift to sick children, so their parents can stay close by them. Makes you think maybe you should eat their food sometimes. Ed and I could take Amy when she comes home, have a treat, say thank you Ronald McDonald in mouthfuls of Big Mac.

Danny wouldn't eat the peanut-butter sandwiches his mother made him. He was getting quite beside himself, then Narelle saved the day. She had some paddle pops in the freezer and gave him one of those. We all have our own food in the fridge and in the pantry, plus there's the staples the house supplies. He's tired, said Danny's mother. It's been a long day. She's here because of her other son who's got leukemia. They come regularly. There's a chance he'll be all right, she said, the last remission was a long one. She doesn't usually bring the little brother but her sister couldn't look after him this time.

This house is full of weariness. Everyone in it is tired. Not worn out with work, that'd be a relief. No, we're all exhausted because we can't do anything. We have no power. It's not up to us. There's nothing we can do, nothing changes. It's all decided and directed somewhere else. We can only want, and wish and hope. Buy presents and wash clothes. Not do anything.

It's funny about children. When I was pregnant I was quite

keen, I was looking forward to having this baby, I smocked little nighties and decorated a crib, went to classes and read books, Ed too, but when Amy was born and the doctor said she had something wrong with her heart nothing had prepared me for the terrible naked frantic love I felt for her. I love Ed, but there was never any danger in that, any fear. Loving Amy then was like being stalked by a wild animal that wouldn't rest until it had clawed us to death. I held her tight to my chest and ducked my head and ran, but the beast was there, I couldn't breathe for the evil stench of its breath and even though I ran and twisted and turned how ever could I outwit it?

In fact, after a bit they decided she wasn't dying, and that they could wait and see, postpone intervention as long as possible. Now she has gone into heart failure, and it is necessary to intervene. We're just waiting for the infection to go, and then Mr Firth the great surgeon will operate.

I nearly said, the great magician.

The schoolteacher has been teaching the children about music and specially wind instruments, I think it might be useful for their breathing. She's got a friend who's a professional recorder player, and she brought one in, made from a unicorn's horn. Of course, it wasn't really. It was narwhal horn, but there was quite a magic story about it. It was five hundred years old, the horn, and it was given to her by some people in Greenland, whose family passed it down through all that time. She took it to a man in Melbourne and had it made into this recorder; she said it was a delicate and terrifying business because there was a thick strong nerve through the middle that had to be drilled out. No scope for error. One slip and it was ruined. Imagine, a unicorn horn, five hundred years old, and you break it turning it into a recorder. Was he relieved when it was finished. She played it; very sweet it was, a magic piping sound, you could think of creatures coming, following, called by the sweet notes.

After the musician went Mrs Rudiger read a story about unicorns, how hunters tried to capture them but never could. They couldn't get near to them to shoot them with their arrows. What they had to do was set up a fair maiden as a trap, and the unicorn would come and lay his head in her lap, and she would put her hand on its horn, and then the hunters would come and lead the beautiful beast to the king. Amy liked this story, she liked the pictures, the lady in her rose-coloured dress and the milk-white creature like a shapely horned horse with a little jewelled collar, in a field full of flowers. And she especially liked the one where the lady shows the unicorn his reflection in a silver mirror.

At nap time I took the tram to town and bought a recorder. It comes with a book, telling you how to do it.

Amy managed several different notes. Quite small children play the recorder, and Amy is very musical.

The physician said Amy still isn't well enough. In some ways it is easier to have everything postponed but then it's not doing her any good. They're containing the heart failure at the moment but nothing's stable. I tried not to think of the cash register. All those numbers popping up and down. All so random. But I don't want it to be. I want it to be sure. Surely safe.

At night I dreamed about the unicorn. I was the maiden in the rose-coloured dress and the unicorn came up and put his head in my lap and I put my hand on his long spiralling horn like ivory, and then, well if I was a virgin which of course I'm not, not with Ed around, well I wasn't then, not with what was happening with the unicorn's horn, and I woke up all excited, I just wish Ed was here. It was a bit early to go across to the hospital so I wrote him a letter, trying to be cheerful, after all he's got the business and all the worry of that, times aren't good. At breakfast the Chinese woman couldn't find the steamer, that's what I guessed, she was hunting through the saucepan cupboard, and when I showed her where it was she was very grateful, and when she'd made their breakfast she insisted on giving me some of the oriental food she'd cooked, which I didn't really want since I'd had my toast and vegemite, but of course I accepted. I suppose they were quite nice, just little slippery doughy bundles of some sort of rawish vegetables, but I didn't really care for them, not for breakfast anyway. She has a lovely smile, the Chinese lady, but I can tell she doesn't understand a word I say.

It's funny how you've never heard of something and then when you do hear of it you keep hearing of it again, over and over, and then you wonder if it was always there and you just didn't notice. I walked the long way round to the hospital, not taking the short cut through Casualty but in the front door and through the foyer, so I could buy a paper. I like to look at the colour supplement on Saturdays. Anyway, there was an article about unicorns, well not unicorns exactly but medicines. *Cure-alls, Quacks, and Nostrums* it was called. Apparently, unicorn horn was considered good for all sorts of things, poison, epilepsy, rabies, colic, worms, fever, you name it, and so of course was very costly because it was supposed to be pretty rare too. Only rich people could afford it. If you wanted to find out if it was genuine you gave arsenic to a pair of doves and powdered unicorn horn to one of them; if that one lives and the other dies then the stuff's genuine. James I tried this with a servant and he died and the king was pretty browned off that the horn wasn't genuine. The servant too I suppose. Of course it never was genuine, unicorns being mythical beasts. It was made of narwhal horn which was in plentiful supply. The *nar* part of the word is Danish for dead bodies, that's what they feed on. I thought of the narwhal horn recorder, nourished on dead bodies. I'd rather think of unicorns and their maidens.

The liver of unicorns is good too, you grind it up with egg yolk and make ointment out of it to cure leprosy — that is, unless the patient is destined to die or God intends not to aid him. What's changed, I asked myself. This surgeon, all his skill, the best man in the southern hemisphere Mick reckons, and still there are children destined to die, whom God does not aid. I looked at Amy, sitting up in bed. We'd just washed her hair and I was brushing it dry and all the threads of it were like silk of different colours, silver and fair and shining gold and pale fawn-coloured all shimmering together, and her cheeks so rosy, I know they say dusky but there's hardly any blue at all. She looked up under her fringe and smiled, and I was thinking, if God could see that smile He couldn't not aid her. Sometimes I believe this, but not always.

The article went on to discuss psychological effects. The thing was, the false unicorn horn often did cure people, because they believed in it. Like Mick believing in the surgeon. No, it's not, not really.

Anyway, it was interesting, coming across unicorns twice running like that. I must try and get Amy a book about them.

She likes to act out the stories we read, especially princesses; ladies and unicorns would just suit her. She's been sent a huge basket of flowers, she's tickled pink. They're from the girls at work. They say in the card how much they miss me; they reckon nobody can do the money at the end of the day like me. It takes them ages, they're always home late, they want me to hurry back. It's hard to remember the busy life with too much to do, in these slow dragging days that never end and you don't know what to want of them. You used to say I wish it was Christmas or I wish there were another half a dozen hours in the day there's so much to do and at least you knew what you wanted to wish for. But here the now is so hard and yet the future might be worse. I think I wish the operation was all over, but then what if it hadn't worked? We'd be better off still waiting for it.

Little Sarah isn't doing too well. She's still in intensive care, still on the respirator. I got given a tour of intensive care today, the big bright room, it's never dark in there, never quiet night, and all the people: more adults than children. There's a nurse to every patient and then the doctors and students and assistants and all sorts of technicians. I couldn't work out which of the babies was Sarah. One of the cots had a screen round it. The instruments are fearful, all glittering metal, hard and complicated, and cords and rubber and pipes. There are little machines that measure out drugs for drips, four to a child, slowly ticking round, morphine and things like that, they're all electronic. Imagine if there was a miscalculation. The tour was so we wouldn't be frightened when we saw our child there, but I'm not sure, I think I'm having nightmares already. The soft little purplish-fleshed babies and all that machinery. They chill them for the operations and then afterwards they paralyse them so that they feel no pain. I was grateful that they aren't supposed to feel any pain. It slows them up getting better if they feel pain. They told us what they used to do this, it's called curare, they reckon it's what the South American Indians put on their darts, that they shoot out of their blowpipes, and kill people. Poison, it is, not used scientifically. That's where the unicorn horn could come in, ground up and rubbed on the place to save you from dying of it. Or would you have to swallow it? Of course they don't have unicorns in South America.

I've taught Amy a tune on the recorder. She calls it her unihorn. It's easy to play, you just follow the book. Twinkle twinkle little star. We had a concert, Amy on recorder, Jack on guitar, and Josephine singing. Thanks to Amy you could tell what the song was, Jack's not great shakes on the guitar, and Josephine's voice is still a little baby pipe. The whole thing a bit slow and quavering. They're thrilled with themselves. Every time a nurse comes in they play it again. Sister Rosemary calls them the chamber orchestra. I'm going to have to teach Amy a new tune.

Josephine's mother is knitting her a jumper. It's a pretty pattern, a kind of almond green colour with a little garden of flowers growing across the front. It'll look lovely with Josephine's dark hair. I think I might get some wool and knit one for Amy. It's very comforting looking at Josephine's mother knitting, so normal, holding the new bits up against her to make sure it will fit, that she won't grow out of it too soon. Josephine insists on standing in front of the mirror when this happens; she smooths it across her chest and beams, turning this way and that; her dark eyes sparkle. She really is a most beautiful child, that dark colouring is lovely. Her father is a very good-looking man, that's where she gets it from. She's shy, and so's Amy, but they're getting to be good friends. They're both keen on Jack, who's a bit older. He lies in bed and teases Josephine, when she looks in the mirror. Who's that funny-looking person, he says. She sticks her bottom out and walks in a comical way, and is delighted when he laughs. Only three, and so much personality.

It's a very big mirror, on a frame, with castors. The physiotherapists use them. Once when I went into the next ward I saw how. A little girl was sitting on a stool in front of it and the physiotherapist was giving her exercises and teaching her how to breathe. To straighten her shoulders and fill her lungs with air. This was only about three days after her operation — they get them to work very fast. Breathing's terribly important, they've got to get the gunge out of their lungs. Of course it's very hard, they just want to cuddle themselves, not do hard breathing. Not stress the already damaged chest. This little girl only had her panties on. That was the first time I had seen a scar. It was a bit of a shock. So long, and so crude, all cobbled up, and stained. Ugly brown with Betadine. The drainage holes caught together with rough black thread. No marks for sewing, for those surgeons. Couldn't sew a fine seam in a fit, I reckon. I thought of the fathers and the tattoos, because of course they're scars too, but works of art with arabesques and symbolic pictures and colouring-in, whereas the scars that the heart surgeons make are anything but. They try to encourage the children to be proud of them, but all I could think of was that perfect smooth skin just … well, butchered, really. Of course you wouldn't have it any other way since it saves their lives, but couldn't it be a bit neater, a bit more delicate?

When I was walking through Myers in the nap-time outing I found a unicorn in the glassware section. It's crystal, I suppose; it was rather expensive. I thought about the business which isn't doing that well, people seem to stop having things upholstered as soon as money gets tight, and me having to be careful, and then I thought, too bad, Amy has to have it, and I bought it. I was right. She took to it straightaway. She just curled her hand over it and held it tight and I could tell it was going to be a mascot for her. When I got there this morning she still had it tight in the palm of her hand, with a little red dint in her flesh where the horn had pressed in. It's a rather round and bubbly unicorn, cuddly, easy to hold; it's not slender and fragile-looking like the one in Mrs Rudiger's book, and just as well — being glass, it could break. Even the horn is sort of round, and short, a fat cone rather than a slender spike, but still it's got a point. Amy smiled at me, unfurling her fingers, a gleeful pleased smile. I said what shall we call him, and she whispered, his name is a secret.

Josephine wasn't there. It was the morning of her operation and she'd already gone down to the theatre. Theatre. Isn't that a funny word. The theatre where the surgeon performs. And what a prima donna. The surgeon doesn't want to know you. You can see why. The physician is a friend. He knows about your life, your hopes. But the surgeon stays remote. How else could he survive? He couldn't take a knife and cut through the chest, take the electric saw and cut through the bone, of a person he knew. Whose smiling eyes have looked into his. Pediatric heart surgeons kill too many children. Who would die sooner or later, of course, but sometimes the intervention speeds it up. They save a lot too, but even these can't become friends. The job has to be a matter of skill and a great performance; bravo, well done, take a bow, deafening applause. Curtain, lights up. Back to the real world. When it works.

Jack is scheduled for the afternoon. The ward won't be the same, since afterwards they'll be off to intensive care for a couple of days. It was already very quiet, since Jack had started his pre-med. He lay in bed, big-eyed, drugged, his mother, who mostly doesn't come because she has to work, sitting beside him.

He was still waiting when I left, at nap-time. A hold-up in theatre, his mother said. Then, when I came back later in the afternoon he was still there. The operation had been cancelled, Sister Rosemary said. His mother had gone and he lay still, zonked by the pre-med. Amy and I did some work on Baa Baa Black Sheep. She had to let go of the unicorn to do this. He sat on the locker and listened. The unicorn listening to the unihorn.

On my way out I asked at the desk how Josephine was. The nurse's eyes filled with tears. Josephine's parents don't have her any more, she said. As though I were a child. And then I thought, we're all children in the face of death.

That was what the hold-up was with Jack. They were still

working on Josephine, hours after her operation was supposed to finish. Until it was too late for him to go down. And too late for always for Josephine.

I used to read in books about people being heavy-hearted. Like, as he listened to the bad news, his heart grew heavy. Only it's not just hearts. It's arms and legs and heads, most especially heads. But legs too. I stood on the kerb in Gatehouse Street for a long time, afraid I wouldn't be able to cross before the traffic started again. My legs didn't want to move, and it seemed as if the weight of my head might tip me over, like some badly made toy, if I leaned over the smallest bit from vertical.

It was seven o'clock. I didn't want any dinner, but I thought I should eat so I made some coffee and some toast with vegemite. I wished Ed was here. I didn't fancy going up to my room so I sat in the lounge room. Trevor was there, and his wife, who seems to be called Heidi. I saw he had tattoos too, some lightning bolts zapping into his singlet, a planet with rings, and a sort of swirling sun. He's on the dole, Mick is too, so it's quite easy for them to stay here as long as is necessary. Trevor and Heidi come from Kyneton, and I think the others are from Tasmania; Narelle talked about growing up on an apple farm. These tattoos: is it because they're on the dole that they have them, going down to the tattooist to pass the time, the kids sitting and playing with the shabby toys while the practitioner stitches away with his needle scarring their skins with pictures? How do they choose? How decide this rather than another? What do the pictures mean? Maybe they date from an earlier time, before wives and children, when they still thought they were going to grow into tough men, virile, great muscles, wearing leather pants and roaring off on Harley Davidsons, zapping like lightning bolts, true loving for ever, not knowing they would always be meek and weedy youths and young then old men and still gentle and weedy.

And what about their wives? I'd heard of women having their nipples done — that film star Cher, for instance. And a butterfly on her bottom. Not to mention flowers in their pubic hair. And men's names on their thighs. Seems risky, that. You mean to be faithful, but …

I don't know about Heidi and Narelle. They cover up close, always sweat shirts and jeans but maybe underneath they're decorated too.

Heidi made more coffee, flapping out in her sheepskin moccasins, just like Narelle's, just as shabby. I don't know what this fashion is, the weather isn't cold. I mean the men are wearing singlets. Heidi was wearing a mauve tracksuit that made her look like a jellyfish, and her hair was still limp but she was full of beans. Their little boy Carl is doing reallywell, the operation a great success, they can go home next week.

Mick and Narelle came in and they made coffee too. She sat beside me on the couch and Mick too and put his arm round her shoulders. This time I could read the banner winding round the shield, or maybe it was a heart. *Toni love ever* it said. They all lit up cigarettes even though there's *no smoking* signs everywhere, and I decided to leave. I didn't much like the program on TV, either. Then I saw that Narelle was crying. Quiet, just tears pouring down her cheeks.

Sarah is still in intensive care, still on the respirator, they can't get her off it. She couldn't manage on her own. I'd gathered that, from conversations, and that her parents were expecting, or anyway hoping, that it'd be all right soon, that she'd stabilise and be able to breathe on her own. But it wasn't all right. It wasn't going to be.

They want to switch off the machines, said Mick.

They have to have our permission, said Narelle.

That television is a big one, a good quality set with remote control. People usually change channels a lot, sitting there zapping the buttons. Tonight there was a play on, set in an English hotel, a smart seaside place, and people dressed for dinner and talked in fluty accents. We were all sitting round the set, with these loud English voices going on, and us talking about Sarah. The play changed to something with subtitles. Mick and Narelle sat with their eyes fixed on the set, intently watching, I guessed that like me they never normally watched subtitles, so did Trevor and Heidi, watching and not registering a thing. I could see how the television was a friend, a companion, just there; they liked its safety. It just needed to be there, like they were, not needing to make sense. Take your time, the doctor said. Think it over. Talk about it. I could see that they knew they would agree, that they didn't have any choice, but they had to go through all the details first. What this doctor said, that nurse, what might have or could have happened, how she looked, what they felt. Over and over, the same detail. Trevor and Heidi listened, and repeated the ends of their words from time to time; they couldn't say much on their own behalf because their news was good. Narelle and Mick didn't have much to say either, just the same things over and over, and us listening as though it was the first time.

Trevor got beer, and Heidi made more coffee. The plaintive voices droned on. I would of thought ... if they'd have known ... he come and said ... such a good little thing ... just lying there ... so sweet ... you'd never guess ... They weren't angry, they were more puzzled. It was too hard. Mick and Narelle sat like stones, I could see how heavy they were, they could hardly move. They sat a long time between sips of their drinks, one mouthful wore them out, they had to put the mug or the glass back in their laps and wait for strength for the next go.

The doctor said they should be there when the machines are switched off. They can arrange it with him. A sort of ceremony. Narelle wanted to wait a bit longer before they decided. I went to bed. I tried to think of home, and Ed, and how good it would be to see him again. But I kept seeing Josephine and her brown eyes. Her mother knitting the jumper. Mick and Narelle standing beside a cot in intensive care with the screens up. And Amy.

When I get to the hospital the next morning the doctor's there. The friendly one, that knows us. Amy's okay, the infection's gone. They've managed to get an operation time for tomorrow. Nice and fast, says the doctor. We're lucky. Amy has the glass unicorn held tight in her hand. I hold her hand tight in mine. The cash register clicks up its numbers. Ninety-five per cent. Ninety-five per cent. Only in your case it's one hundred per cent or nothing. Josephine's. Sarah's. In everybody's case one hundred per cent or nothing. Only on some mad grand plan can the statistics make any sense. Though, and this is a cruel thought to think but I think it, they may save us. They must rule out any more disasters this week. Mustn't they? Josephine, Sarah: that's enough.

Sister Rosemary comes past. Jack's doing well, she says. Be back in the ward tomorrow, with any luck. All nice and pink, not dusky any longer. Amy and I squeeze the unicorn.

GERARD WINDSOR

A SPOILED PRIEST

On my grandmother's veranda, just inside the half-door which led to the garden and the river and the Murrurundi hills, was a shelved hallstand with books that had been in the family since my grandmother's childhood. Painted Edwardian covers done in blind, Louise Mack, *Claude Lightfoot* by Father Francis Finn. I read *Claude Lightfoot*, one of a series of boys' adventures by an American Jesuit. At the end of each book the hero signalled his intention of becoming a priest. That was straightforward. It was another book that intrigued, and mystified, me. Its title page said, "Sheehan, Rev. P.A. ... D.D., author of 'The Triumph of Failure' 'My New Curate', etc., *A Spoiled Priest & Other Stories*, with nine illustrations by M. Healy, London, T. Fisher Unwin, 1905, Unwin's Colonial Library." The book had two inscriptions. In pencil, across the top of the front free endpaper, was the owner's name "Miss Imelda Dooley, Murrundi". The misspelling confused me. On the same page, but vertically upwards along the hinge, and in ink, was the presentation inscription: "Remember me, Till darling, Dot". The owner's signature was the bolder, and the pencil much sharper and more immediately striking than the ink which had faded to a pale silver. I know now that Imelda Dooley, my grandmother, was sixteen when *A Spoiled Priest* was given her by Dorothy Fenely, her school friend at the Dominican Convent, West Maitland. By the time Imelda had a daughter, Dorothy was merely a name, someone the daughter never met. Nor did she ever hear her mother called Till.

I look at the book now, and I see that the red cloth is frayed and faded, and that the spine is skewed so that the leading edges of the boards are no longer aligned — the tell-tale signs of use. Surprising as it might be, *A Spoiled Priest* was not only what one young Australian girl might give another in the years just after Federation, but it was read as well. Perhaps Canon Sheehan was not far wrong, in his general tenor, when on page three he referred to "that shy, half-affectionate, half-reverential manner in which Irish girls are wont to speak of candidates for the priesthood". Murrurundi girls as well.

Canon Sheehan, the parish priest of Doneraile in County Cork, was a prolific and popular writer. *A Spoiled Priest* represents his one advertence to Australia. A footnote to the fifth story "Remanded" says: "This story, founded on fact (the hero-priest is buried in Doneraile), was appropriately printed in Australia at the time of certain sensational accusations publicly brought against a priest by an unhappy woman." Sheehan's good priest is falsely accused by a young female parishioner. She cannot go through with her perjury, and throws herself into a canal. Her intended victim coffins her himself and has her buried, in consecrated ground, to the sullen resentment of his other parishioners. Some days later her disinterred, decomposing body is found beside the bed of the judge who had been hearing her charge. He is "lying on the white coverlet, his head shattered into an indistinguishable mass of bone and blood, his brains blackening the white wall behind his pillow, his right hand clutching a heavy pistol".

The Coningham case in Sydney, for which Canon Sheehan had his story printed, was not lurid tragedy, nor even lurid melodrama. The Very Reverend Denis O'Haran was cited as co-respondent in divorce proceedings brought by Arthur Coningham, a former, if not especially glorious, Test cricketer. It was alleged the adultery took place in the grounds of St Mary's Cathedral. Witnesses were suborned, the posts interfered with, false information fed through spies. The case came to court in the first days of 1901. Federation was a stuffy backdrop, easily ignored as the Coningham farce got cracking. Convents throughout the country stormed heaven. At the Convent of Mercy, Murrurundi, Miss Imelda Dooley said prayers for a special intention. Denis O'Haran, certainly a vain man, was acquitted, and lies now in one of the more lavish graves in Waverley Cemetery.

It was not a Canon Sheehan style of tragedy. "Irish priests are fatalists," he had written, "they are so habituated to the drama of relentless iniquity that is always going on around them — the striking of the feeble with the mailed hand, the chaining of the captive to the victim's car, the sleek, hypocritical but unbending despotism, under which the helpless victims hopelessly writhe; the utter despair of all, as destiny for ever mockingly destroys them, — all these things make the Irish priest patient under circumstances that ordinarily drive men to madness."

Australia however had not allowed the Irish priest such an epic vision. In the new land Canon Sheehan's story had had to be reworked.

When I was a child it was the illustrations to *A Spoiled Priest* that caught my attention. Seven of them include children. But beyond that there was something odd about them. The book holds out great promise to someone leafing through these pictures. There are five plates in the first five pages, another four over the next hundred pages, and then no more for the rest of the book — half the total pagination. Why such plenitude and vigour at the beginning, such pinched meanness for the long stretch after that?

Five of the illustrations feature a priest. In "A Thorough Gentleman" three spivs, but one of them a priest, round off dinner in a hotel dining room with cigars. In "Rita, the Street Singer" the priest (another gentleman — he has lace curtains and bobble-fringed blinds) leans over the waif, and then, in the next picture, he leans over both the waif and her terminally consumptive sister.

"A Spoiled Priest", the first story in the book, has exultant illustrations. Facing the second page, small boys in a jammed barn of a classroom erupt in cheers, toss their caps and satchels in the air, knock over their ink bottles, vault across the desks. By the time they face page three, they are tidier and more orderly, waving their caps — one with even an expression of adoration, his fists clasped together under his chin in grateful supplication — as they flank a priest, a strong figure of a man of about forty, advancing straight through the picture in bowler, frock coat and cape. By the time this priest is facing page four, his hat is in his left hand, as is a cane, and his right hand is on a very small boy's curly head as he says, "And this little fellow must come too". Against page five he is again hatted and on the move, the boy in his arms, smiling. Then the pictures of him cease.

I was able to read when I took down *A Spoiled Priest* from my grandmother's shelf, but I was only about seven, and I was not impelled to go past the pictures. Most of the initial letters for the words in the captions were capitalised, and I wondered over the new, rare adjective in the final picture of the boy enfolded by the priest. "He Wrapped Him Round with the Folds of His Great Maynooth Cloak." I never came across the word in my dictionary. Yet the knowledge of its existence was a bright token of a place for me in another world.

I was both dulled and left uneasy by the title *A Spoiled Priest*. I was seven. The word priest I certainly understood. Priests were real enough. What I could not understand was how a priest could be spoiled. Children were spoiled. To be spoiled was a bad thing. Whereas priests were good.

I turned the illustrations again. One after another, what they showed was a priest blessing and making life happy for young people. The frontispiece was different. It was perhaps grotesque, certainly unnerving. A row of men sat on straight-backed chairs beside one another. Behind, in front, and beyond them, but blurred, were other men. At the end of the row, nearest the surface of the picture, was a large-featured man. The illustration was done in black pen and ink, but with a strong effect of wash. This man wore a long shapeless gown, so generous in its extent that as he sat it hung on him like classical drapery. M. Healy, the illustrator, had spread the wash of the pen, so that the material began to look like weeds, and the weeds from this central figure climbed across the seat beside him which otherwise was empty. His head was bent forward, his bony, high-bridged nose starting to sag into monstrous misshapenness, his eyes closed, his hands slack and sliding into the black and white streaks of the weeds. The caption read: "His Face Was Ashen, His Hands Were Cold and Trembling".

When, at the age of seventeen, I told my father, by letter, that I wanted to become a priest, he came to visit me, in person, at boarding school. It was late on a warm October morning, in the middle of the week; he had taken time out from a heavy schedule. I was called out of class to see him, and we sat side by side on the wooden benches in front of the First Division Building, looking down across the cricket pitch of Third Field West to the handball courts.

"You have made us all very happy," he said. "Your mother and your grandmother have prayed for this since you were a little boy."

I sort of knew this. I said nothing.

"You're sure?" he asked me.

"Yes, I'm quite sure."

"I only ask because I want you to be sure. You need to be sure."

"I know I'm sure."

"I only say this because once you're in, the worst thing that can happen to you is to come out. The most wonderful calling all right is to be a priest, but the worst thing that can happen to a man is to start out and then give it away. I've seen them. Your grandfather will tell you the same thing. Pathetic cases."

"No," I said, "I'm sure."

A Spoiled Priest appeared in the dawn of the great age of the Irish short story. George Moore's *The Untilled Field* preceded it, from the same publisher, in 1903, just two years earlier. "The clergy," says Moore, "are swallowing up the country." Yet he can be more relaxed than that. His Father MacTurnan, for example, a simple, compassionate man, grieves that the only Irish people wealthy enough to marry are the priests, while the rest of the population haemorrhages away to America. He writes to Rome asking that priestly celibacy be revoked. His bishop, tactfully, ignores the eccentricity. Instead he gives Father MacTurnan five pounds so that he can buy a pig for one of his parishioners who has no other way of winning a bride.

The classic Irish short story collection, *Dubliners*, was largely written by 1905. It opens with the words: "There was no hope for him this time: it was the third stroke." Joyce had no need to say that his subject was a priest. His priest is paralysed and mad. Yet the boy narrator believes he owes the priest much.

I did not read *A Spoiled Priest* until I was in my late twenties and my grandmother was dead. I had not got things quite right as a child. Perhaps M. Healy, the illustrator, was to blame. A character, Rita, for example, was depicted as a child of five, but the text told me she was "any age between eight and fourteen". And the mature, broad-shouldered, tortured priest of the frontispiece was not a priest at all. He was a youth, a seminarian, still in his early twenties. On the first page the title story is asterisked, and the footnote is as long as the body of the text itself. In a most delicately toned statement Canon Sheehan explains his title: "This is the term used in some parts of the country to express the failure of a student who has just put his foot within the precincts of the sanctuary, and been rejected. Up to quite a recent period such an ill-fated youth was regarded by the peasantry with a certain amount of scorn, not unmingled with superstition. Happily, larger ideas are being developed even on this subject;

and not many now believe that no good fortune can ever be the lot of him who has made the gravest initial mistake of his life."

When I was older I noticed that my grandmother also read John Galsworthy, Frances Parkinson Keyes, M. Barnard Eldershaw, Kate O'Brien.

She never missed writing to me at Easter, blue-black ink in a confident hand. She always ended her letters with the wish: "May the Risen Lord bring you all the joy of the Resurrection morn."

The first time that I brought a girl home to meet her after I left the Society of Jesus, my grandmother was not only courteous, but even welcoming. Cushioned in her invalid's armchair, waited on by my mother, she detailed how a little glass of port wine was very medicinal.

"Is it your preferred drink?" asked the girl.

"At luncheon," said my grandmother. "It goes very nicely with a little broth. But for my dinner I always take a drop of stout."

The girl wrinkled her nose in a friendly fashion.

My grandmother let fly a small, elderly laugh. "It's most nutritious. Ensures a little flesh."

The girl was slim.

Later my grandmother said to me: "And very nice too. Of course you don't have to marry the first one you fall for."

GILLIAN MEARS

OUR POSITION ON THE MAP

My first memory of the city is my Florentine dress. I am not looking out the window underneath the arrondissement where I have been separated from my family but, if I let myself, all I can see is darkness. I look down. I am watching the flowers in my lap. The brakes are screaming in my ears and there is a mosquito on the métro. When I am eight years old and first lost in Paris I do not like the experience. I look down at the sprigs of patterned flowers on my dress. The policeman I am delivered to says in English that he knows I am Australian by the gold kangaroo badge pinned to one side of my dress. I won't talk. I do not like his moustache. I don't like the toilet I have to use. In the way of my mother in French toilets, I try to crouch over the seat. The policeman doesn't realise what has happened and takes me back on his knee. Now I am even more upset. I cry so much that by the time I am reunited with my family, the collar of the dress is as saturated as my underpants. The policeman makes a joke. She doesn't like French men, he says. Everyone, even my sisters, laughs. My mother gathers up my salty smelling body and isn't angry. My father tries to explain how I was left on the métro when the rest of the family got off at St Ambroise.

"St Ambroise, Richard Lenoir," says my eldest sister who is learning off by heart the names of the métro stations.

There are lilies of the valley in the posies of flowers on the Florentine dress. I still have the dress hanging in the wardrobe at the farmhouse, next to my father's English lace christening robe. The dress and the robe are waiting for the child I never have.

I try to repair the collar of the old dress but in twenty-two years of waiting, the cloth has become too fragile. The collar rips more in my fingers so that the child would look too frail. Such a collar would give the impression of torn wings or old flowers. Faint smudges of dirt are on the inside seams as if the last time I wore the dress my mother hung it up quickly, without a wash, in the expectation that I would soon be wearing it again.

My second memory of Paris is also of being lost. My husband is driving. I am navigating. We're meant to be meeting my friend Paul and his friend Jean-Paul at four o'clock in the afternoon. I have yet to meet Pierrette but she too is in the city. The sun is strong through the window and many terse moments have already filled the small red rent-a-car. "Where are we?" my husband is yelling.

I am saying I'm afraid I don't know. I'm explaining that I've temporarily lost our position on the map.

"Find the Eiffel Tower, we're about to drive past the Eiffel Tower."

"I can't find the Eiffel Tower."

"What do you mean, you can't find the frigging Eiffel Tower?"

"It's not on the map. Don't swear at me." I look out the window feeling the strangeness of sitting on the wrong side of the car.

"Have you found it?" My husband sounds as though he might cry. There it is after all. The Eiffel Tower has been under my left thumb. A tear falls from my own eye and lands on the tiny depiction of the monument. When I look back the traffic is surging after us. There is barely a moment to see the real Eiffel Tower, its arches uplifted against a blue sky.

"I'm sorry I yelled," says my husband.

I shrug my shoulders and snap on the radio. I am twenty-two years old. Bellini's "Casta Diva" from his opera *Norma* begins to break my heart. I cry a lot when I am a young wife in a way I can't imagine crying now. As a young wife I cry at the hint of any criticism or simply on evenings in Europe when looking up into the full moon makes me bow my head to feelings of sadness. The feelings are to do with no longer wanting to be married.

"When we were in Paris as children," I say to my husband, whose name sounds more exotic in the French version of it, "we went up by the steps not the lift, to save money."

"Bir Hakeim bridge. Pont de Bir Hakeim!!" My husband's voice begins to rise again. "Which way do we turn?"

I look down at the map. I remember how as a child I always failed map reading in the IQ tests. I am twenty-two years old and haven't yet been kissed by a woman. Somehow I direct my husband to the car park under the ground that Paul's instructions have specified. We are in the first arrondissement. My knees are weak with relief to be out of the car. I wish I was the wildly beautiful woman pranging her Citroën as she attempts to park in the space for a motorbike. I look down a wide avenue and see at its end the facade of the Opera House, glittering in the late light. We are only forty minutes late.

My husband and I are travelling around with too much luggage. We have identical brown backpacks and identical green Gore-Tex jackets. Although I always try to make sure I'm not wearing my Gore-Tex at the same time as my husband, he often decides upon seeing me in mine, that he too should wear his. On the late afternoon in Paris that I meet Pierrette, such a collision occurs. Matching marriage wear, says Paul, following introductions. He raises an eyebrow and I realise that we are an embarrassment.

Sitting at Pierrette's, Jean-Paul's hand is never far from Paul's thigh. My husband feels so uncomfortable at an open display of homosexual affection that he insists on going back to the car to fetch all our bags. We listen to his footsteps going down the long steep stairs and have finished a bottle of wine before he comes back. I'm not used to drinking but in this hour begin to turn into the drinker I will one day become. Is my husband a herd of elephants, Pierrette asks, at the sound of him on the stairs. I feel ashamed of and sad for my husband. I feel sad that I offer not one protective word in his defence. Then Pierrette, who has made me feel helpless, says something consoling. She is immediately knowable. I feel I have always been sitting drinking wine on the edge of her low bed. Opposite the bed at the other end of the room is a huge mirror where she flirts with us all, even with my husband, so that he loves her too. As the light leaves her apartment and we all become drunker, I want to tell her that she is like stained glass at night, glittery and dark. Near the bookcase she pulls up her skirt to show me not only that she wears no underpants but also how one buttock always tans a deeper brown than the other on her visits to the South.

On the third evening she tells me in front of my husband that when I am rich and famous she will pretend she seduced me in her bathroom. On the seventh morning of staying at

Pierrette's, when I have tiptoed from the spare room where my husband still sleeps, down the corridor into Pierrette's to have my early shower, she steps through the shower curtain also, to assist she says, with the temperamental shower. I am wet before the water has begun to spurt. Pierrette adjusts the swivel. I can feel a prickle in the finger that is moving on my skin. She says she must have picked it up when she was weeding her mother's garden on the eastern edge of Paris but the finger does not stop its journey. From Pierrette's shower and over her shoulder, I see the lights on the tip of the Eiffel Tower go out. Five o'clock says the BBC World News reader from the radio-alarm clock next to Pierrette's bed.

Because I am alone the third time in Paris, I don't get lost until my father arrives. Even coming home so drunk at dawn from La Privilège that I pick a posy of roses from the Hôtel de Ville flower beds without noticing until the last moment the policeman who is watching me, I don't pass out or lose my way. I write postcards, not mentioning the drinking but making much over my sudden ability to remember streets and directions from when I was here as a wife. "You are very different!" say Jean-Paul and Paul, offering me cherries in a glass of brandy. It is years since I have worn a dress but Jean-Paul who is the size of a child has dressed up in crimson stockings underneath a small green skirt. He lifts his lips like an old dog flaring her teeth at me and passes me Pierrette's new number. He splits the cherry pips between his teeth and says that of course he will lend my father a coat if he arrives in Paris from Algiers without one.

"My love, if you don't mind me saying, you look like a penguin," says my father, not mincing his words about my outfit when I meet him at Gare de Lyon. He looks old and worn but also gleeful. I can't remember him like this since well before my mother's death. His good mood is not about seeing me or Paris again but because he has escaped the amorous advances of an old flame. He is a fortnight early. "Thank goodness I had the excuse of having to see you in Paris." He takes off his battered Akubra and hits my shoulder playfully. On the TGV he says he couldn't work out how to use the coffee and filter system so he drank the hot water, and put the coffee in his bag where it has spilt all through his socks. It is clear now, he says, that he will marry a lovely lady with blue eyes who is waiting for him in Australia, rather than dally around any further with transatlantic romances. All he must do is wait in Paris with me until he can change his flight home.

I do not know what to do with my father in Paris. I am not answering my telephone and he can't understand why. At first he answers my phone eagerly. But it is never the blue-eyed Australian woman and he gets sick of taking messages and saying that I am at the library. As the days go by and he can't get an earlier flight home without paying first class, he becomes more and more subdued. He too stops answering the telephone. "Honestly," he says but sits at the table in the middle of the room, letting the phone ring out. Only my k.d. lang tapes and wine from the Franprix in the evening encourage his mood to lighten. He endlessly re-winds a tape back to his favourite. *Don't let the stars get in your eyes, don't let the moon steal your heart*, he sings, looking out to the fairytale shape of the Bibliothèque Forney and wondering whether he could paint its roofline. I can never see the stars in Paris but sometimes I have seen the full moon shooting unexpectedly over the top of a wall. He always pours himself a glass of wine first, downs it and then pours another for himself and one for me. When I mention this he looks so miserable I wish I hadn't bothered to say anything. I wish I had given up drinking as I had promised myself I would six months ago.

Circles of light from the Bateaux Mouches on the river throw colours onto the wall above the car park. My father stares at my homemade calendar as if he can erase the days. "She told me her heart was bubblegum," says my small handwriting in a circle around a row of tiny hearts at the top of the calendar. I sculpted the hearts from real bubblegum after seeing the Jim Dine paintings at the Pompidou and after buying a small sackful of bubblegum instead of jubes from the confiserie on rue Sainte-Croix de la Bretonnerie. My father never asks me the meaning of my calendar. He chews bubblegum moodily and blows pathetic pink bubbles which get stuck on his lips.

In the mornings my father says, "Time for an Oxygen exchange," and stumbles out of the storeroom where I make my visitors sleep. Everything mildly irritates him; the weather, the temperature inside, his own unfinished paintings, British Airways and Mastercard Australia. He brings his old habit of diluting things into the studio — water into shampoo and juice — and I begin to feel that somehow he is even watering down Paris.

He goes out to paint but he can't bear the tourists who come to peer over his shoulder. He sketches Notre Dame in a way that makes the flying buttresses look as though they're coming unhinged. He makes a list of what he would like to see in Paris and from then on only takes out his watercolours to cross off each item. I take him to see my favourites at the Pompidou. In Jean-Paul's black down-filled coat he looks like a gloomy gnome. I glance away from my father through the glass walls to the place where I told my husband I could not stay married. He was crouched down, taking pictures of the rooflines in the direction of Sacré-

Coeur. It was the day that Pierrette had kissed me under the shower. I didn't tell my husband about *the kiss* but I told him we were doomed. We could see the head of the fat man and the heads of the huge crowd that had begun to gather. I didn't ever tell my husband about *the kiss* but whenever I hear that expression and standing in front of the Rodin statue of that name with my father at the Rodin Museum, it is of Pierrette that I immediately think.

Every few days I walk with my father to the front of the Pompidou in the hope of showing him the fat man. I make my father laugh, telling him how the fat man singled out my husband years before. The fat man who never wore a shirt and who reminded me of Obelisk from the Asterix books, made my husband lift up his jumper and then his shirt, to show the crowd the size of his own belly. The crowd roared with laughter. I tell the story as a comedy, walking my father past the props the fat man always leaves in the same place, ready for his next show. I remember how hard it was for my husband to keep in his tears as the fat man pranced around, making lewd remarks in other languages about the size of my husband's telescopic camera lens. I show my father broken bottles on the paving stones, such as the ones the fat man lay his belly on while my husband was made to stomp on top of the fat man's back. I don't mention to my father that up on the third floor of the Pompidou, near some of the open air sculptures, I told my husband that I sensed I preferred women to men. For all this not telling, I feel shabby and depressed. k.d. lang is in *Salmonberries* at the cinema across from where the fat man never is and although I saw it in London I see it again with my father. He is more excited about the soundtrack than about the stained glass in La Chapelle. It doesn't matter that I tell my father that the French do not like k.d. lang; that at her concert in Paris, the Elysée Montmartre was full of women from America, England and Australia; he will not be deterred from spending a fruitless hour searching in one of the record shops underneath Les Halles for the CD.

The fat man is still never there. Paul and Jean-Paul, who have taken a sympathetic approach to my father's misery, suggest an outing instead, a walk down the Canal St-Martin into Paris. This is something they have long wanted to do and we get off the train at La Villette in high spirits. Even my father is keen, enthusing every bridge or two about the prospect of a canal holiday.

I am carrying a Galeries Lafayette bag with a picnic which, because of the increasing wind, we eat as we walk. It is quite boring walking along the Canal St-Martin with my father. Paul and Jean-Paul have breezed ahead and none of the graffiti is worth a photo. Every now and then my father stops to line his hand up with the sun, to make sure we are travelling in the right direction.

"How exactly did I get left behind on the métro when I was eight?"

"Daydreaming. I think you were always rather dreamy."

Paul, Jean-Paul, my father and I walk so far in the wrong direction that we can see speckled cows with calves on a hill up ahead. After so long in a city I feel like running towards them.

"Have you told your father of the plan?" whispers Paul, making small noises like a calf or baby sucking.

I shake my head. "Don't say anything. He'd only feel worried."

"But why! You know we take the test every two months. We're as safe as houses."

"I'd walk through the snow barefoot," hums my father back in Paris and happiest it seems in the postcard and poster shop at the bottom of the Pompidou Centre, hovering over Monet prints or in front of one of the hot crepe vans. For Obelisk, we are always too early or a little too late. What do you think of the Nikki de St Phalle fountain? I ask my father. The spinning lips remind me always of Pierrette. Paul and Jean-Paul say that she is far from well and that she no longer lives in her foxhole over Avenue de l'Opera. She would love to see me they say, but I never do go to see Pierrette.

Somewhere in the city she'd be pouring a drink. One day she'll fall into a sugar coma and die a diabetic's death and no one will ever write to me. The French, says Jean-Paul with a dramatic sigh, have forgotten how to write letters. I would've liked to love Pierrette in the intense devotional way my father loved my mother, but she was wanting only to play. My father says that every time he has gone past the salmon restaurant's windows, he has imagined sitting at one of the small turquoise square tables in the sun, eating pink salmon opposite my mother. He says he has imagined this so strongly it is like a true memory.

On dark rue de Rivoli on the day of his departure, my father nearly overtopples on his old knees. Jean-Paul and I catch him by his elbows and put him into the back seat of the taxi. My father moves over, misunderstanding, even though I have told him that I will save my money and not come out to Charles de Gaulle. When he realises we are saying goodbye my father begins to cry. I feel sad, as if he will be dead before I see him again. Back at my room silver hairs are all over the mirror in the bathroom. Jean-Paul phones Paul, who, as in October, November and December, comes round drenched in the perfume he is sure will assist conception.

They are both wearing white jeans. Jean-Paul has a crimson and gold cravat whereas Paul's is blue. Paul takes

Jean-Paul into the storeroom and their noises sound like the pigeons cooing on the railings outside. Jean-Paul comes out with a glass covered with a large white handkerchief. He gives it to me with a flourish. I go into the storeroom and lie down with the syringe Paul has warmed in water. I think of Pierrette first inside me, the fine prickle in her finger. *How could I leave him*, I remember my husband writing to me in a letter, *before we have had any Passion Fruit? Didn't I remember, I was going to have four before I was thirty?*

Jean-Paul and Paul are making champagne kirs. I can hear their elation. They are certain this will be the day. "If only your father could know, flying over the English Channel, that he has become a grandfather!" bursts out Paul, making me suspect that this time it would be Paul who would be the blood father. Four sections of chestnut police horses go clattering up the road making us all go to the window to watch. They are very showy against the restless green of the Seine but my eye is caught by a faded nun, immediately below, carrying a saucepan. She looks up at me and, seeming to shake her head, hurries on. But it isn't until I'm surrounded by French officials at the airport, demanding three thousand francs for excess luggage that I know for sure I'm not pregnant. A man in a grey suit tells me to go to stand in the corner and think about not travelling. I cannot fly he says unless I pay the excess. I think about not being pregnant and not leaving Paris. I hand the man my Visa card. I watch my suitcase full of books about pregnancy and soft Barbar the elephants from the men who were to have been the faraway fathers, disappear behind the counter. I am not wearing clothes dark enough to disguise my blood. I am thirty-three years old. I think of Vincenzo Bellini. Vincenzo Bellini died when he was thirty-three and the second performance of his opera *I Puritani* was coincidental with the eve of his funeral. During the whole performance, the singers, audience and members of the orchestra sobbed with grief. It is on the plane taking me away from Paris that I first think I will stop trying to get pregnant. I think about writing to Jean-Paul and Paul. I always imagined Bellini's *Puritani* would've been performed under the dome of the Opera House where Chagall would later paint his whimsical interpretations but all the weeping took place in the Théâtre des Italiens. I find a postcard. My pen feels like the breath of the man I once saw in the Eglise St-Roch, blowing out the spirit candles with sharp little puffs.

CASSANDRA PYBUS

TILL APPLES GROW ON AN ORANGE TREE

I saw Chloe the other day, through the window of one of those ubiquitous cafes which jostle each other along the length of Glebe Point Road.

I looked up from the *London Review of Books* and there she was.

Even at a distance there is really no mistaking Chloe. I catch sight of her tangled dark hair or the line of her cheekbone and my heart is in my mouth.

These sightings have become rare.

It has been years and years since I last saw her, standing on the upper deck of a ferry as it drew away from the Quay. On that occasion I opened my mouth to call, before checking myself and turning away in hot-cheeked confusion. This time, sensibly, I forced my eyes back to the newspaper and waited for the thrumming in my head to subside.

It was especially disconcerting to see Chloe in the Glebe. I scarcely ever go there, so much has its character changed in the thirty years since I set up house with Duncan. It reeks of sophistication and money now. No more peeling facades and dank little shops; even the corner pubs look inviting.

Flophouses with boarded-up windows and rheumy-eyed old men hanging soiled long johns over the wrought-iron balconies have been banished. The scant comfort of charity is no longer needed in the smug and elegant prosperity of the new Glebe.

Simon Brooke has been forgotten, by and large.

I have always wanted to write about Chloe, the friend of my youth who died violently by her own hand in the year we both turned twenty-one. My entire adult life has been lived with her absence and yet she haunts me still. Long before I even dreamt of being a writer I tried to write a short story. It didn't work. What happened to Chloe and Duncan and me is the stuff of classic tragedy, but it isn't fiction.

Seeing her again like that, unbidden and unexpected, has made me want to try again to tell this story.

Where do I begin?

I could start where her life ended, a place so remote from the Sydney of our shared dreams that I had never expected to see it.

A few years ago I went there, by sheer chance.

Oh, I don't deny that for many years I had fantasies about confronting Duncan if I ever found myself in England, yet by this time he had become no more than a faint, disquieting memory.

I was in England to research a book. My visit to Cambridge University was badly timed; a festival was in progress and no accommodation was available in the town. At the information centre I queued for Bed and Breakfasts in the local villages, scanning the options on the handouts as the line inched closer to the desk. There it was: the Manor, Swaffen Prior. You don't forget a place with a name like that. Enveloped in a sudden hot flush I reached the desk clutching this piece of paper.

Ah yes, Duncan Mitchell-Smythe's beautiful home.

The centre manager dialled the number and handed me the phone. Rooted to the spot, speechless, I listened to the phone ring out.

The Manor was on the market, she said. Very briskly, hardly noticing my muteness, she found me somewhere in the adjoining village.

Next morning, trembling with anxiety, I drove to see the Manor in Swaffen Prior.

A lifetime ago, when I lived in the Glebe, I heard so much about this house. Duncan's mother had sent a photo spread of it published in *Country Life*. Built in the fifteenth century, it was one of the oldest houses in that part of England. Duncan was crazy about the house, desperate that it should come to him and not his older brother. I remember being shocked by this naked concern with inheritance. My family may have been irredeemably bourgeois – as he continually reminded me — but it seemed to me that the aristocracy could be graspingly vulgar. That he had inherited was apparent: the B&B brochure listed him and his wife as the proprietors.

Now he was about to sell his pride and joy. A real estate notice was driven into the lawn.

Who could blame him? However ancient and lovely, it was a house with terrible memories. Chloe had chosen both her place and her weapon with an eye for their symbolic value.

Not an innocent act.

I should be able to describe the house, to give a feeling for the place where Chloe had snuffed out her possibilities in one brutal moment. But I can't. Apart from my surprise at how small it was — I had been expecting the grandeur of a later period — I do not recall a single detail of the architecture or of the setting. Having got there, I was immobilised by shock and a whole raft of emotions that I cannot even put a name to. Unable to get out of my car or to drive away I just sat outside the house and looked and looked for hours.

Somebody was home all right; there was a black Porsche in the garage. No one came out to disturb my reverie.

✧ ✧ ✧

Chloe and I were at school together in 1963, although to say we were not at school together would be more precise, since we were chronic truants. At North Sydney Girls High School she and I were the excluded ones, both unwelcome among the giggling conspiracies of the fifth-year common room. We kept our own company, roaming the harbour parks while the other girls — how we despised them — strove to please their stern teachers and excel in their exams, as North Sydney girls were meant to do. At Bradleys Head we would perch among the branches of a big Moreton Bay fig and sing old English folk songs in two-part harmony.

I know my love by his way of walking
And I know my love by his way of talking
And I know my love by his suit of blue
And if my love leaves me what will I do.
Still she cries: I love you the best,
A troubled mind sure can know no rest.
Still she cries: bonny boys are few,
And if my love leaves me what will I do.

The nature of love was a subject of endless speculation.

We'd just discovered *By Grand Central Station I Sat Down and Wept*, and Elizabeth Smart had joined Emily Brontë as an emotional mentor, although we still reserved a soft spot for Seymour Glass from "A Perfect Day for Bananafish".

From this far distance I am utterly bemused that we could have been so taken with J.D. Salinger's Glass ménage, or that we had pooled our pocket money to buy a hardback copy of *Franny and Zooey* when it came out. I have it still, with our names neatly written on the fly leaf. Silly book. Tedious people.

When it rained or when the air was thick with humidity, Chloe and I would sprawl on the floor of my parents' harbourside apartment debating whether Bob Dylan was a true ethnomusicologist or if John Kennedy had planned the Bay of Pigs.

We practised kissing on each other, acquiring an oral deftness which earned us quite a reputation at the local sailing club. It was not for these robust youths that we were in training; we had our sights on the bohemian hinterland we knew lay beyond the clean blue lines of the harbour, if only we could find a way to enter it.

Secretly we joined the Eureka Youth League to which we had been introduced by a girl from our school whose parents were prominent in the Communist Party. Innocent as we were of politics, it was the folk singing that attracted us to the Communist fringe, specifically a young man named Kevin who sang like Woody Guthrie. He was the boyfriend of our acquaintance from school. We couldn't see what he saw in her; for all her notorious parents and unorthodox social life, in school uniform she was a model of middle-class conformity. Not like us. No one was like us in the Eureka Youth League. They were too stolid and earnest, we thought; too full of slogans.

At the Trial Leaving Certificate I failed miserably and Chloe didn't do much better. Parents were summoned. Chloe's mother and stepfather were indignant, identifying me as the bad influence. My parents each took a half day from work to endure a prim dressing-down from the headmistress. North Sydney did not allow for failures; if my work and attitude did not improve I would have to leave. I'd been at North Sydney for less than a year, my parents fervently hoping my expulsion from my previous school was an episode they could forget. They were deeply ashamed.

I was expelled soon after for my performance at the school concert of a Lenny Bruce monologue. I had simply memorised the routine from a banned record in my parents' collection, imported clandestinely from the USA. I had not the faintest notion what necrophilia meant.

Chloe was thrown out for truancy about a fortnight later.

My furious father said I'd take the matriculation exams even if he had to nail me to the floor. He need not have ranted so. Now that the exams were no longer a matter of sitting in classrooms and wearing uniforms, studying had a very different complexion. As private students we could elect which subjects to take. No more of the hated German. We chose the lowest level of Maths and Biology. At Sydney University's Fisher Library copies of the last five years' exam questions in History (Ancient and Modern), English and Art allowed us to identify five common questions in each subject, on which we constructed essays that we then learnt by heart. Our parents were astounded by our diligence, failing to grasp that we had located the scent of bohemia on the Sydney University campus: folk concerts in the Manning lecture theatre and interesting-looking men in the Refectory.

Neither of us did well in our exams. I managed to scrape into a place at a teachers' college and Chloe had to repeat.

By then I had a boyfriend: a six-foot-two midshipman of nineteen from the RAN, with tight curly hair and a broad smile. I had met him at Speakers Corner in the Domain one empty Sunday when Chloe was visiting her half-brother. He offered to buy me an ice-cream. Not exactly a worldly bohemian affair, I ruefully conceded, but we got along so very well and, having moved beyond kissing into the mysteries of sex, I found I liked it very much.

Chloe was not impressed, although she would sometimes come with us when we caught the bus to Bilgola beach for a day of sun and surf — not that she ever went in the water or allowed the sun on her pale face — and she accepted

Michael's invitations to naval cocktail parties. His fellow officers told him they thought she was weird.

Chloe and I discussed Michael at length. We agreed that while he was very nice, he wasn't the kind of man we had in mind: too ordinary.

Six months later he was posted to Dartmouth in England for two years or more. A photograph of his farewell at the airport shows his sad-eyed mother holding his cabin bag, me clinging possessively to his arm and Chloe a little to one side, looking wistful with a large bunch of flowers.

When he married in England Chloe and I sent a telegram with a quote taken from the latest book of J. D. Salinger:

RAISE HIGH THE ROOF BEAM CARPENTERS STOP LIKE ARES COMES THE BRIDEGROOM STOP TALLER FAR THAN A TALL MAN

Conjuring up those lines I can see her dark head and my fair one conspiring over the wording of address on the telegram form in the Neutral Bay Post Office. Our Darling Michael, we agreed would do the trick, signed by us both.

It had not taken long to discover bohemia was the front bar of the Newcastle Hotel. From the moment Chloe and I pushed our way into the noisy, tobacco-saturated, overheated crush we knew that Neutral Bay could never claim us again.

Looking back, it seems laughable that the front bar of Jim Buckley's pub could have held such allure for two such sassy girls; that we could have dressed up with so much excitement every Friday evening to hang off the conversation of ageing males who talked about horseracing and other matters of utter banality. I exaggerate. Some men did talk of politics, but not the kind we could recognise; they talked with great seriousness about the ideas of John Anderson, which we affected to understand even though they bored us rigid. Other men, not quite so old, talked about films. American films. That was worth our attention. *Wild Strawberries* went out the door. We became students of the films of Jerry Lewis.

Not all the men I met in the Newcastle were old.

Duncan came to the pub with one of the Anderson disciples. He was only twenty-three. Tall and slender with skin that tanned to honey and a thatch of dark-blond hair above clear blue eyes, he was wonderfully handsome. At least that is how I remember him. I have no photos of Duncan.

I'd never met his like before; an English aristocrat of sorts, an Honourable. He had a job as a postman, of all things. I don't believe they quite knew what to do with him at the GPO. Lord Dungfungus Macgregor was the nickname they gave him, as well as providing him with the world's most attractive postal run: twice a day he would saunter from the Art Gallery through the Botanical Gardens to the State Library, stopping to read and sunbake on the various park benches overlooking the harbour.

Rather than infuriate, Duncan's languid haughtiness encouraged indulgence from everyone: employers, shop-keepers, bus conductors, pawnbrokers.

Me? I was in love with him. Light-headed. Absorbed. Beguiled.

Almost from the first moment we met in the crush of the front bar, no one else existed in the hothouse enclave we created about ourselves.

It was Duncan who showed me the dilapidated grandeur of the Glebe, his aristocratic eye seeing the original Victorian elegance where I saw only poverty and squalor. We found a large ground-floor flat near Jubilee Park, in an old house in Allen Street, and we moved in to whitewash the walls and paint the floorboards and brighten the gloom with bold posters of Roy Lichtenstein.

POW! WOW! BAM! We two were the universe.

Oh, the giddy, erotic intoxication of love at nineteen: dreamy afternoons with every nerve end tuned to the sound of his key in the lock; sexual games with a coercive edge I had not yet learnt to name; a sure sense that my life would radiate with bliss for ever.

Chloe hovered on the edge of my firmament trying to shake off the terrible ordinariness of life in Neutral Bay where she was still marooned. Had I cared enough, or been less self-satisfied, I would have seen desperation in her increasingly loopy behaviour, but at nineteen I didn't have a name for that either.

She drank too much, with too much abandon. She was forever falling into bed with some dishevelled lout picked up at a folk club or a party and she seemed to actually court men's disrespect; to relish their gross put-downs. I couldn't see what she was playing at in her dreary black dresses and her affectations of being a witch. What had been vague melancholy was turning into self-abuse and fatalism which I thought neither interesting nor avant garde.

I had tried to keep her away from Duncan. He had a poor opinion of Australian women and I knew he'd be displeased with Chloe's occult babble or her obsession with the moon.

I was wrong about that. He liked Chloe as it turned out.

She had an unusually fine mind, he said. She looked as though she had just stepped out of a painting by Burne-Jones. The Pre-Raphaelites were his particular passion.

So I let her attach herself to us. Our fey shadow.

There was a tiny spare room where she would stay some

nights to get away from her parents. No more than a walk-in cupboard, really, that she made into her own, with a Rousseau print on the wall and *The White Goddess* perpetually open face-down among the seed pods and feathers on the table beside the narrow camp bed. I was happy to have her company because Duncan didn't talk to me much and she could help me prepare the elaborate dinner parties he liked to give.

We retained our intimacy, chatting over the preparation of nasi goreng.

You let him do that?

There were secrets now, hidden places.

In our flat in Allen Street, Duncan and I could hear our neighbours through the ceiling, though we never once spoke to them; old-time residents of the Glebe, they might just as well have been from Mars. We were not the only *déclassé* residents in the neighbourhood: some university lecturers and young professionals were moving in. The inner city, even places as tatty as the Glebe, was looking increasingly attractive. Duncan considered this a bad sign, especially when the elegant old hulks were torn down by property developers.

Our favourite place was where our street ended, a dog leg of a laneway off Jubilee Park. On one side of the lane was a shabby Chinese joss house where there were always fresh joss sticks burning, although we never saw a Chinese visitor. Opposite was a once grand Victorian mansion, completely derelict. It was easy to scale the fence into the overgrown garden and what was left of the house was wide open. Duncan had taken a fancy to that ruined old house with its black and white tiled floors and ornate pressed ceilings. He liked to fantasise that we would buy it and restore its original grace. He was utterly dismayed when some shonkie developer knocked it down to jerry-build a block of brick units, and he continued to poke around in the half-finished substitute exclaiming at the poor workmanship, the lousy wiring, the *petit bourgeois* vulgarity of it.

He was very attached to that phrase: *petit bourgeois*.

I do not know if Duncan was poking around in those half-built units on Saturday 18 May 1968 because I was at Fisher Library finishing an essay on W. B. Yeats. Something about swans. I had done with teaching primary school — a *petit bourgeois* occupation if there ever was one — and was now doing an Arts degree. I fancied becoming an academic.

It was a miserable day. I recall that as I walked home along Glebe Point Road the rain began to fall in huge, heavy drops which soon became a total deluge. Drenched, I burst through our front door to an empty chill.

He had left me.

There was a brief note from Chloe, affectionate and penitent.

I screamed and wailed till the neighbours pounded on the ceiling. I tore at my hair and face. I opened the windows and let the rain beat on the furniture. I smashed the records she had given me and tore up her poetry. Nothing could quell the terrible sobs which tore out of me till my chest ached. I found all the photographs of Duncan and of Chloe and burnt them with my cigarette lighter. One by one. Watching those images of our youthful pleasures curl, blacken and dissolve, I felt as if my life had ended, there and then.

During the night my orgy of self-pity was interrupted by the man from upstairs who had come down to demand I be quiet. What must he have thought when I opened the door, mucus streaming from my nose, bleeding scratches on my face? He didn't give a hoot when I screamed at him that my husband had left me.

Some husband. His voice was loaded with disgust.

Embarrassed, finally, I closed the windows and turned on the radio. On the news broadcast I heard that three-year-old Simon Brooke, the son of a university lecturer who lived near Jubilee Park, had been missing since lunchtime. Search parties were looking for him in the rain. Frogmen were dragging the bay.

Life seemed no less cruel on Sunday morning when I opened my eyes to the awful realisation that I'd been duped and abandoned. This was a scenario I had never entertained; until the previous afternoon such pain was beyond my comprehension.

Outside my misery the universe had also changed its colours irrevocably.

Early that morning Simon Brooke had been found, murdered. He had been sexually assaulted and horribly mutilated with a razor.

When I ventured out of doors there was yet another shock around the corner where the police had erected barricades. The child's body had been found in the overgrown garden at the back of those half-finished units that Duncan and I knew so well.

Monday morning the police came around to see me. Just routine, they were talking to everyone in the street.

Had I seen anything? Could I shed any light?

I was in no good shape to be talking to them, red-eyed and dishevelled. I had nothing to tell them.

What about your ... um, boyfriend?

I said Duncan had left on Saturday. No, I didn't expect him back because he'd taken all his clothes and personal effects.

No mention of Chloe. I saw no reason to expose my

humiliation and distress to the police. It was just a routine check. They betrayed no special interest.

Two days later they were back again, more insistent this time and with a great deal more knowledge about me and my … um boyfriend. They were very interested in Duncan. I couldn't for my life see why.

No, I had no photographs. I'd burnt them. On Saturday night.

Their interest became clear to me when I saw the newspaper next morning and read in numb horror that the police suspect was a young man in his early twenties, described as being well groomed with blond hair.

They thought Duncan had done this horrendous thing.

Of course. People would have seen him making his quality checks of the building at the murder site. Then there was my performance on the evening of the murder. The neighbours would have told all about that.

Put two and two together. *Some husband.*

Next time the police called I understood what they were asking me.

These many years later I can recognise this time as my brutal rite of passage from innocence into knowledge; a soul-searing experience that changed my understanding of the world forever.

My trusting, bliss-filled love affair was shattered and now

I had to contemplate the possibility that the man with whom I had explored the dizzying reaches of sexual pleasure could be capable of raping a three-year-old child, systematically mutilating him with a razor-blade and stuffing wads of newspaper down his throat to stifle his screams.

A week before I had not known such things were possible. Now the unspeakable had come right up to me; had climbed into bed with me.

Did the monstrous lie in the deep recesses of sexuality in any one of us?

Was this our original sin?

It couldn't possibly have been Duncan. He was with Chloe. I was not able to bring myself to say that.

No, I did not know his whereabouts. Yes, I knew how I could contact him.

I rang a friend and told him that the Glebe police needed to interview Duncan urgently.

The police never called on me again.

No one has ever been charged with the murder of Simon Brooke even though quite a few people have happily confessed to that terrible crime.

I stayed on alone in the flat in Allen Street. I could afford it.

In those days Commonwealth scholarships were very generous, if you could get one, and as a self-supporting person of twenty-one I had the most generous of them all. I'd won that scholarship after doing brilliantly in my first-year part-time subjects and I needed to hang on to it. University was my lifeline; the only thing that kept me from terminal despair. Every day I trudged off to my lectures in a fug of unhappiness, enduring the disdainful looks of my immediate neighbours.

Late at night I roused their fury by playing, over and over, maudlin recordings of Judy Garland and Billie Holiday or the melancholy folk songs of Glen Tomasetti:

There's a bird that sits on yonder tree
They say he's blind and cannot see.
Well I wish it had been the same with me
Since before I met with his company.
I wish I wish but all in vain
I wish I were a maid again.
But a maid again I never can be
Till apples grow on an orange tree.

The loneliness was dreadful. I rarely went out at night.

Chloe had tried several times to make contact with me but I wouldn't have it. I determined never to speak to her again. Among our mutual friends and acquaintances she was ostracised and isolated. There was a grim satisfaction in the long miserable nights that she would have no one except for Duncan and I believed she would find cold comfort there.

She'd never live up to his exacting standards.

It was Richard, her half-brother, who told me that Duncan and Chloe had left for England. Chloe had seemed withdrawn and listless at the airport, he reported.

A small triumph helped to dull the keen edge of my loss.

Nevertheless it was the loss I was feeling late one night when Richard banged on the front door, drunk and raving.

A message from that highborn ponce you used to live with, he announced, sweeping his arm low to the ground in an unsteady flourish.

I would not let him past the door. It was nearly midnight.

He was persistent. Lord Dungfungus, that eminent personage, wishes me to convey to you information about his beloved.

I cut him short with my surmise that they were going to be married.

Wrong. Wrong. Wrong. Richard seemed almost hysterical. She is not marrying anyone. She blew her head off with Dungfungus's shotgun. She is with us no more.

The man upstairs had put his head over the stair railing and was shouting something at me. I pulled Richard inside and made him sit down. He was sobbing so hard I could not make head nor tail of what he was saying. When his sobs gave way to giggles and bad puns I turfed him out confident that it was no more than a bad speed rave.

Just before dawn I woke to the sure knowledge that his anguish was real.

My first call to the *Sydney Morning Herald* was negative and might have reassured had not my panic begun to escalate uncontrollably in the eerie pre-dawn light. Two panes of glass were missing from the phone box and the air was bitter. I tried and tried the *Daily Telegraph* before finally contacting a weary sub-editor who mumbled something about a suicide report and left me hanging for five minutes while he checked it out.

I clung onto the phone, stamping my feet repeatedly while I sucked air in between my clenched teeth.

Finally he returned. Chloe Eugenia Brampton? Aged twenty-one?

The inquest was to be held the next day.

The coroner found it was suicide with no suspicious circumstances.

On the day of the event the deceased had left the cottage where she was living in Cambridgeshire and had walked several miles into the village of Swaffen Prior, where she had posted a letter to Australia. She had then gone to the Manor where her fiancé, the Hon. Duncan Mitchell-Smythe, was living, but from which he was absent at the time. She had removed a hunting gun from the gun cabinet and fitted it with ammunition she had purchased the previous day. Returning to the front steps of the house she had managed to put the gun to her head and pull the trigger, causing decapitation. Death was instantaneous. The body was found by her fiancé on his return from London. The deceased was said to have been in a depressed state for some weeks.

In my hard, dry-eyed grief I might have been persuaded that Duncan had killed her. I had some knowledge of the dark edges of his passions.

Her letter made me see that was not how it was.

I felt an electric tremor run through my body when I pulled Chloe's familiar handwriting from my letterbox, ten days after her death. She told me that she loved me, that she had always loved me, that she had gone with Duncan because he was something of mine that she could possess. Instead she found him arid and cold while I was totally lost to her. She hated England and hated his stupid, haughty family. I remember she used the metaphor of cabbages and said her life had been reduced to tending the cabbage plot. Marrying Duncan was repugnant and she saw nothing but emptiness and anguish ahead. She didn't say that she would kill herself, although the letter concluded with a rather mundane paragraph about those of her things, including her poems, she wanted me to have.

Mercifully these things never turned up.

I couldn't understand it. I could not understand any of it. Not then; not now. Not what she told me nor the appalling thing she had done.

It had been a joke about us at school: les be friends, the other girls would chorus. A common refrain in an all girls' school. Not just about Chloe and me. It didn't mean anything.

Chloe wasn't a lesbian. Was she?

In the early days of Women's Liberation I anguished obsessively about this in consciousness-raising groups, castigating myself for her death, for not having privileged my relationship with Chloe above an affair with a man who would inevitably use me and betray me. Chloe's duplicitous behaviour was rationalised as social conditioning which had forced her into denial of her true feelings.

My true feelings also?

Inevitably, this process of recrimination and confession led to an examination of my own false consciousness. It did no good and I gave it up after a while.

The simple truth was that I had loved Duncan with a passion which had nothing to do with the expectations of the patriarchal society; which I could no more have contrived than the ocean can orchestrate the tides.

The ideology of sisterhood can not make the earth spin on a different axis.

I fail to see how it could have been any other way. That is the tragedy; the terrible, pointless waste.

Still she cries: I love you the best
A troubled mind sure can know no rest.

I kept Chloe's letter and the newspaper cuttings for five years, then I burned them, as I once had her photographs, not out of rejection but for fear of their morbid exudation.

It was essential to let go.

I had written Duncan a letter of savage accusation, entirely blind to the possibility that he would also be suffering the loss of the woman he had chosen in preference to me. He was no more to blame than I was. How terrible it must have been for him to have found his prospective bride on his doorstep, her head a bloody pulp. How calculatingly cruel she had been to despatch herself in that way: to use the symbol of his aristocratic maleness as the instrument of her disfigurement and death; to defile the ancestral house he had so long coveted.

Because he was a disappointment to her: too ordinary.

I had been sitting outside the Manor in Swaffen Prior for

some hours when I became aware of a twitch in the curtain of the upstairs front window. Surveillance. What did they think I was doing? A prospective buyer, perhaps.

I wanted so much to go to the front door, to walk up those steps.

What could I say to him?

Hello, you remember me. I've come to forgive you for driving iron into my soul.

His wife might answer the door.

You don't know me. I'm an old flame of your husband and I just dropped in to discuss a mutual friend who killed herself, right here where I am standing.

Ridiculous.

Eventually a child came by and asked me what I was doing. I made some inadequate response and drove away.

An opportunity lost.

There will never be another.

ACKNOWLEDGMENTS

All the collections from which the stories in this anthology were chosen were published by the University of Queensland Press.

Venero Armanno, "Now That the Wall is Gone" from *Jumping at the Moon* (1992); Thea Astley, "Cubby" from *Collected Stories* (1997); Murray Bail, "Portrait of Electricity" from *Contemporary Portraits* (1975), reprinted as *The Drover's Wife and other stories* (1980); Edward Berridge, "Speeding" from *The Lives of the Saints* (1995); Lily Brett, "What God Wants" from *What God Wants* (1991); David Campbell, "I Wouldn't Miss Christmas" from *Flame and Shadow* (1976), also published as *Evening Under Lamplight* (1959, 1976); Peter Carey, "Conversations with Unicorns" from *The Fat Man in History* (1974); Matthew Condon, "Mud and Ivory Elephants" from *The Motorcycle Cafe* (1988); Moya Costello, "You Know (Aphorisms for the Posteverything Age)" from *Small Ecstasies* (1994); Liam Davison, "The Shipwreck Party" from *The Shipwreck Party* (1989); Nick Earls, "Plaza" from *Passion* (1992); Suzanne Edgar, "Violet and Rose" from *Counting Backwards* (1991); Marian Eldridge, "The Woman at the Window" from *The Woman at the Window* (1989); John

Emery, "Pine Gap" from *Summer Ends Now* (1980); Beverley Farmer, "Black Genoa" from *A Body of Water* (1990); Kate Grenville, "Refractions" from *Bearded Ladies* (1984); Marion Halligan, "Here Be Unicorns" from *Collected Stories* (1997); Barbara Hanrahan, "Sleeping Beauties" from *Iris in Her Garden* (1991); Janette Turner Hospital, "Morgan, Morgan" from *Dislocations* (1987); Nicholas Jose, "Beer and Wine" from *The Possession of Amber* (1980); Victor Kelleher, "The Road" from *Africa and After* (1983), reprinted as *The Traveller: Stories of Two Continents* (1987); Gerard Lee, "Pieces for a Glass Piano" from *Pieces for a Glass Piano* (1978); Angelo Loukakis, "Dancing" from *For the Patriarch* (1981); Olga Masters, "A Young Man's Fancy" from *The Home Girls* (1982); Gillian Mears, "Our Position on the Map" from *Collected Stories* (1997); Cassandra Pybus, "Till Apples Grow on an Orange Tree" from *Till Apples Grow on an Orange Tree* (1998); Mandy Sayer, "The Down Payment" from *Blind Luck* (1993); Rosie Scott, "Senseless Violets" from *Queen of Love* (1993); Trevor Shearston, "Cowries" from *Something in the Blood* (1979); Peter Skrzynecki, "The Biggest Bonfire of All" from *The Wild Dogs* (1987); Barbara Wels, "The Usual History of Beer, Thigh-Slapping and Schlimmbesserungen" from *The Lifestyles of Previous Tenants* (1995); Herb Wharton, "The Munta-gutta" from *Where Ya' Been, Mate?* (1996); Michael Wilding, "Joe's Absence" from *Aspects of the Dying*

Process (1972); and Gerard Windsor, "A Spoiled Priest"
Heaven Where the Bachelors Sit (1996).

NOTES ON THE AUTHORS

VENERO ARMANNO is the author of one book of short stories, *Jumping at the Moon* (UQP 1992), which was equal runner-up in the Steele Rudd Award in 1993, and four critically acclaimed novels, *The Lonely Hunter, Romeo of the Underworld, My Beautiful Friend* and *Strange Rain*. His screenplay of *Strange Rain* is planned to be in production during 1999, and his latest novel, *Firehead*, will be released in 1999. Armanno is a Brisbane writer who spends as much time as he can travelling and living overseas, and several of his books will soon be published internationally in various translations. He is also a book and film reviewer and the writing coordinator for the Queensland Theatre Company. He is an occasional writer-in-residence at schools and has published two books for younger readers.

THEA ASTLEY was born in Brisbane and now lives on the New South Wales south coast. Since 1958 she has published fifteen books. Her first collection of short stories, *Hunting the Wild Pineapple*, won the Townsville Literary Foundation Award in 1979, and *It's Raining in Mango* won the Steele Rudd Award and the 1988 FAW ANA Literature Award. She has won the Miles Franklin Award three times, for *The Well Dressed Explorer, The Slow Natives* and *The Acolyte. A Kindness Cup* won the *Age* Book of the Year Award, *Beachmasters* won the Australian Literary Society Gold Medal in 1987, and *Reaching Tin*

River won the New South Wales Award for fiction. Her most recent novels are *Vanishing Points, Coda* and *The Multiple Effects of Rainshadow*, which won the *Age* Book of the Year in 1997. *Collected Stories* was published by UQP in 1997.

MURRAY BAIL was born in Adelaide in 1941, and now lives in Sydney. His short stories have been published in a number of anthologies in Australia and Britain, and in the *New Yorker*. They were published in 1975 by UQP in a collection entitled *Contemporary Portraits*; the title was changed to *The Drover's Wife and other stories* for the 1980 and subsequent editions. His first novel *Homesickness* won both the 1980 National Book Council Award and the *Age* Book of the Year Award, and his next novel *Holden's Performance* won the Vance Palmer Prize for Fiction. His latest novel *Eucalyptus* was published in 1998 to critical acclaim.

EDWARD BERRIDGE lives in Sydney. Since the publication of his first collection of short stories, *The Lives of the Saints* (UQP 1995), he has been in demand as a commentator on popular culture on radio, TV and at literary festivals. He is currently writing a semi-fictional journal of pregnancy for "het" millennial couples.

LILY BRETT is the author of six volumes of poetry, three books of fiction and one book of essays. Her short story collections are *Things Could Be Worse* (UQP 1992) and *What God Wants* (UQP 1991). Her novel *Just Like That* won the New South Wales Premier's Award, and her *Collected Stories* will be published by UQP in 1999. She lives in New York and is married to the painter David Rankin.

DAVID CAMPBELL was born in 1915 on a sheep station near Adelong, New South Wales. He was educated in Australia and then at Cambridge, where he graduated in Arts. During World War II he was a pilot in the RAAF and was awarded the DFC and bar. He then lived on various properties near Canberra, farming and writing poetry, until his death in 1979. David Campbell is regarded as one of Australia's finest lyric poets and received numerous awards for his work, including the second Patrick White Award in 1975, the Henry Lawson Australian Arts Award in 1970, plus the New South Wales Premier's Award and the Fellowship of Australian Writers' Christopher Brennan Award in 1980. His short stories were published as *Evening Under Lamplight* in 1959 and 1987, and as *Flame and Shadow* in 1976.

PETER CAREY was born in Bacchus Marsh, Victoria in 1943, and presently lives in New York with his wife Alison Summers and their two sons. He is the author of six novels, *Bliss, Illywhacker, Oscar and Lucinda, The Tax Inspector, The Unusual Life of Tristan Smith* and *Jack Maggs*, which between them have won every major literary award in Australia, as well as the Booker Prize in the UK in 1988 for *Oscar and Lucinda* and the Commonwealth Writers Prize for *Jack Maggs* in 1998. *Jack Maggs* gave Carey his third Miles Franklin Award in 1998. *The Big Bazoohley* (for children) won a Children's Book Council Honour Award in 1995. Carey's first bestselling book, *The Fat Man in History*, was followed by another story collection, *War Crimes*, which won the New South Wales Premier's Award in 1980. In 1994 the two collections were combined with three other stories in *Collected Stories*.

MATTHEW CONDON was born in Brisbane in 1962. He has written several works of fiction including *The Motorcycle Cafe* (UQP 1988), *Usher* (UQP 1991) and *The Ancient Guild of Tycoons* (UQP 1994). All were shortlisted for major national awards. His collections of short fiction — *A Night at the Pink Poodle* (Random 1995) and *The Lulu Magnet* (Random 1996) — both won the Steele Rudd Award. His latest novel is *The Pillow Fight*. He currently lives in Sydney.

MOYA COSTELLO is a writer, teacher, editor and occasional broadcaster. She has had short fiction published in various magazines and in anthologies, including *Frictions* (Sybylla Press 1982), *Transgressions* (Penguin 1986), and the *Macmillan Anthology of Australian Literature* (1990). Her work has also been broadcast on radio, in particular on ABC Radio's "Science Show", and a number of her scripts have been produced for television. A collection of prose, *Kites in Jakarta*, was published by Sea Cruise Books in 1985, and *Small Ecstasies* was published by UQP in 1994. She grew up in Sydney and currently lives in Adelaide.

LIAM DAVISON was born in Melbourne in 1957. He has published three novels: *The Velodrome*, shortlisted for the Vogel/*Australian* Award in 1987, *Soundings* (UQP 1993) and *The White Woman* (UQP 1994), and a collection of short stories, *The Shipwreck Party* (UQP 1989). He was awarded the National Book Council's Banjo Award for Fiction in 1993 for *Soundings* and was the recipient of the Marten Bequest Travelling Scholarship for Prose. He has received numerous awards for his short fiction. His work is published in France by *Editions Actes Sud*.

NICK EARLS is the author of the award-winning young-adult novel *After January* and the bestselling adult novels *Zigzag Street* and *Bachelor Kisses*. His work is published in other English-language markets and in translation. *Passion*, a collection of short stories published by UQP in 1992, was Nick Earls' first book. Since then, he has contributed short stories to more than a dozen anthologies. The short story "Plaza" was written in 1990, and probably owes at least something to his enthusiasm for Peter Carey's *The Fat Man in History* and the motion picture *Brazil*. His present vision of the future is somewhat less apocalyptic.

SUZANNE EDGAR worked as an editor on the *Australian Dictionary of Biography* but has recently begun to write full time. She has published fiction, features and poetry, and her short stories have appeared in several anthologies. She belongs to Seven Writers whose *Canberra Tales* (Penguin 1988) was re-issued as *The Division of Love* in 1996. Her collection, *Counting Backwards* (UQP 1991), was shortlisted for the Steele Rudd Award in 1992.

MARIAN ELDRIDGE (1936–1997) was the author of three collections of short stories, *Walking the Dog* (UQP 1984), *Woman at the Window*

(UQP 1989), and *The Wild Sweet Flowers: Alvie Skerrit Stories* (UQP 1994), and the novel *Springfield* (UQP 1992). She was awarded an Australia Council Literature Board grant in 1992, and the 1992 ACT Arts Bureau Literary Fellowship to complete *The Wild Sweet Flowers*, which in 1994 won the International Year of the Family Award in the New South Wales State Literary Awards. In the last months of her life Marian recommenced writing poetry, and her poems were published in *The Canberra Times* and *Voices*, and in the *Senate Hansard* of 19 June 1997. Marian Eldridge's articles and book reviews as well as her short stories have been published in literary journals, anthologies and newspapers in Australia and overseas.

JOHN EMERY is a full-time writer. He has published four works of fiction: *Summer Ends Now, Freedom, The Sky People* and *Savage Triangle*. He has worked in television and for newspapers, and has had three original movie-scripts produced. He lives in Adelaide and is committed to writing and producing his own movies. Currently in development are: *Paradise Lost/Paradise Found* (what happened after the mutiny on the *Bounty*); *Windradyne, The Last Warrior* (the Aboriginal wars of 1824); and *Ill-Starred Captains* (the voyages of Flinders and Baudin).

BEVERLEY FARMER was born in Melbourne in 1941. After graduating from the University of Melbourne she worked in the restaurant trade and taught English and French in secondary schools. In 1965 she married a Greek migrant and they went to live, for three years, under the Junta in his parents' village on the Macedonian plain north of Thessaloniki. While there she wrote her first book, *Alone* (1980). Several of the stories in the collections *Milk* (1983) and *Home Time* (1985) draw on the experience of Greece, as does her novel *The House in the Light* (UQP 1995). She lives on the Victorian coast, the setting for *A Body of Water* (UQP 1990) and *The Seal Woman* (UQP 1992). Her latest book is *Collected Stories* (UQP 1996) and her latest passion, black-and-white photography. She has an adult son.

KATE GRENVILLE was born in Sydney in 1950 and holds degrees from the Universities of Sydney and Colorado. She has taught Creative Writing in Colorado and has worked as a film editor, journalist, typist, teacher and sub-titler for SBS. Her first novel *Lilian's Story* won the Vogel/*Australian* Award in 1985 and the Talking Book of the Year Award in 1986. A major film based on the novel was released nationally in 1996. She has also published one collection of short stories, *Bearded Ladies*, and the novels *Dreamhouse* and *Joan Makes History* (all with UQP). Her most recent novel *Dark Places* was released in 1994, and won the Victorian Premier's Prize in 1995. Her novels have been published to wide acclaim in the US and the UK. Kate Grenville is also the author of two non-fiction books, *The Writing Book* and *Making Stories*, written with Sue Woolfe.

MARION HALLIGAN was born in Newcastle and now lives in Canberra. She has published four collections of short stories, *The Living Hothouse*, which won the Steele Rudd Award for the best collection of stories in 1989 and the Braille Book of the Year, *The Hanged Man in the Garden*, *The Worry Box* and *Collected Stories* (UQP

1997), which included a number of stories previously uncollected. More than sixty of her short stories have been published in journals and magazines, and her work has been widely anthologised. She is also the author of five novels, *Self-Possession, Spidercup, Lovers' Knots, Wishbone* and *The Golden Dress*, which have been nominated for most of the major literary prizes. *Lovers' Knots* won the *Age* Book of the Year Award, the ACT Book of the Year Award, the 3M Talking Book of the Year Award and the Nita B. Kibble Literary Award. Marion Halligan has also written three nonfiction books, *Eat My Words, Cockles of the Heart* and *Those Women Who Go to Hotels* (with Lucy Frost), and she won the Geraldine Pascal Prize for critical writing. She was chair of the Literature Board of the Australia Council from 1992–95.

BARBARA HANRAHAN, artist and novelist, was fifty-two years of age when she died in 1991. For many years she divided her time between London and Adelaide, where much of her writing is set. Her art is held in the Australian National Gallery as well as most state galleries. Her first book, *The Scent of Eucalyptus*, was published in 1973 and her last book, *Michael and Me and the Sun*, was published in 1992. She is the author of fifteen books, including two collections of stories, *Dream People* and *Iris in Her Garden,* and the novels *The Albatross Muff* (1977), *Where the Queens all Strayed* (1978), *The Peach Groves* (1979), *The Frangipani Gardens* (1980), *Annie Magdalene* (1985), *Flawless Jade* (1989) and *Good Night, Mr Moon* (1992). *The Diaries of Barbara Hanrahan 1960–1991*, edited by Elaine Lindsay, and *Woman and*

Herself: A Critical Study of the Works of Barbara Hanrahan by Annette M. Stewart, were both published in 1998.

JANETTE TURNER HOSPITAL was born in Melbourne in 1942. When she was seven her family moved to Brisbane, where she grew up and attended university. In the 1960s she taught in Queensland high schools then moved to the United States. Since then she has lectured in universities in Australia, Canada, USA, England and Europe. She is the author of six internationally acclaimed novels: *The Ivory Swing* (1982, UQP 1991), winner of Canada's Seal Award, *The Tiger in the Tiger Pit* (1984, UQP 1990), *Borderline* (1985), *Charades* (1988), *The Last Magician* (1992) and *Oyster* (1996). Her short story collection *Dislocations* (UQP 1987) won the FAW Australian Natives Association Award in 1988. *Isobars*, published in 1990, was shortlisted for Canada's Trillium Award, and one of the stories from the collection was included in the UK's Annual Best Short Stories for 1990. *Collected Stories* (UQP 1995) brings together all her short stories in one volume and includes a number previously unpublished. In 1995 Griffith University awarded Janette Turner Hospital an honorary doctorate for services to Australian literature.

NICHOLAS JOSE has published two collections of stories, a book of essays mostly about China, and five novels. "Beer and Wine" was published in his first book, *The Possession of Amber* (UQP 1980), and he says: "Of all the stories in that book, and of all my published work, it is the earliest written piece, dating back to not long after 1971 when the story is set (as indicated by the Bread song "It Don't Matter to Me") and when I was nineteen. Its focus on the possibilities contained within an ambivalent moment anticipates much of my later writing." At present Nicholas Jose lives in Sydney, and his novels include *Paper Nautilus* (1978), *The Rose Crossing* (1994) and *The Custodians* (1997).

VICTOR KELLEHER was born in London, left England at fifteen, and spent the next twenty years in various parts of Africa. In 1976 he settled in Australia. Formerly an Associate Professor of English at the University of New England, he now lives in Sydney with his family and earns his living as a writer, dividing his time between adult and young adult fiction. To date he has nearly thirty titles to his credit. He has won many literary prizes (e.g. the Children's Book of the Year Award, the Australian Science Fiction Achievement Award, numerous children's choice awards, etc.) and has been shortlisted for many more, including the "Banjo", the Premiers' Awards, and the Carnegie Medal in Britain. His most recent books are *Storyman* (for adults), and *Slow Burn*, a crossover novel intended for old and young alike.

GERARD LEE has travelled widely in Australia, Indonesia and Europe. He is the author of two novels *True Love and How to Get It* and *Troppo Man*, and two collections of stories, *Pieces for a Glass Piano* and *Eating Dog*. He co-wrote the award-winning film *Sweetie* with Jane Campion, and wrote and directed *All Men Are Liars*. After completing a BA at the University of Queensland, Lee attended the

Australian Film and Television School. He has also worked as a journalist, and is currently working on several new film projects.

ANGELO LOUKAKIS has had five books published, three of fiction and two non-fiction. He has also written for television and had a number of his plays produced. His short stories have been published widely in literary magazines and anthologies, and he has contributed articles and journalism to a number of Australian magazines and newspapers. He has been a member of the Literature Board of the Australia Council, was founding chair of the NSW Writers Centre, and is presently a member of the Literature and History Committee of the NSW Arts Advisory Panel. He has served as a judge of a range of literary awards, and currently occupies the position of head publisher at HarperCollins Publishers, where he oversees a large and diverse Australian publishing program.

OLGA MASTERS was born in Pambula in New South Wales in 1919. With a family of seven children and part-time work in journalism, she had little opportunity to develop her interest in writing fiction until she was in her fifties. In the 1970s she wrote a successful radio play and a stage play, and between 1977 and 1981 won prizes for her short stories. *The Home Girls*, her first book, won a National Book Council Award in 1983 and her first novel, *Loving Daughters*, was highly commended for the same award. Her third and fourth books, *A Long Time Dying* and *Amy's Children*, also received critical acclaim. After her death in 1986, a collection of stories was published entitled

The Rose Fancier. A collection of Olga Masters' journalism, *Reporting Home*, edited by Deirdre Coleman was published in 1990, and a biography by Julie Lewis in 1991. In 1996 her stories were published together as *Collected Stories*.

GILLIAN MEARS lives and writes near Grafton in northern New South Wales. She has published three collections of short stories: *Ride a Cock Horse*, which won the Commonwealth Writers Regional First Book Prize in 1989, *Fineflour*, published to critical acclaim in 1990, and *Collected Stories* (1997). Her first novel *The Mint Lawn* was awarded the Vogel/*Australian* prize in 1990, and *The Grass Sister* was awarded the Commownealth Writers Regional Best Book Prize in 1996. Her forthcoming novel is called *Remnant*, and in 1997 she published *Paradise is a Place*, a photo essay in collaboration with Sydney photographer Sandy Edwards.

CASSANDRA PYBUS lives at Lower Snug in southern Tasmania and is the author of *Community of Thieves* (1991); *Gross Moral Turpitude: The Orr Case Reconsidered* (1993), which won the Colin Roderick Award for the Best Australian Book in 1993, and was later published in a revised and extended edition titled *Seduction and Consent*; *White Rajah: A Dynastic Intrigue* (UQP 1996) and *Till Apples Grow on an Orange Tree* (UQP 1998), a candid journey through personal memory and history. Between 1989 and 1994 she was the editor of *Island* magazine as well as contributing editor (with Richard Flanagan) of *The Rest of the World is Watching: Tasmania and the Greens* (1990) and editor of *Columbus' Blindness and Other Essays* (UQP 1994). Cassandra Pybus is the founding editor of *Australian Humanities Review*, an electronic journal published on the world wide web. Her political biography of James McAuley will be published in 1999.

MANDY SAYER won the Vogel / *Australian* Award with her first book, *Mood Indigo*, in 1989. Her second work of fiction, *Blind Luck* (UQP 1993), is a collection of linked stories that form a novel. It was followed by *The Cross* which was a finalist for the Ned Kelly Award for Best First Crime Novel, was shortlisted for the Kibble Award, and was nominated for the 1997 International IMPAC Dublin Literary Award. *Dreamtime Alice*, published in 1998, draws on her experiences touring the US as a street performer with her jazz drummer father. Mandy Sayer has an MA in Creative Writing and English from Indiana University, and was named one of the ten Best Young Australian Novelists by the *Sydney Morning Herald*.

ROSIE SCOTT has published five novels, *Glory Days, Nights with Grace, Feral City, Lives on Fire* and *Movie Dreams*, a collection of poetry, *Flesh and Blood*, and one of short stories, *Queen of Love*. Her novels were shortlisted for the National Book Council Banjo Award, the New South Wales Christina Stead Premier's Award, and the New Zealand National Book Award. Her play won the National *Sunday Times* Playwright Award and was the basis for the international award-winning film *Redheads*. Her essays and short stories have been published in numerous anthologies and magazines, and her novels have been published in the UK, USA and Germany. She lives in Sydney.

TREVOR SHEARSTON was born in Sydney in 1946, and spent seven years teaching in Papua New Guinea. He has published a collection of stories, *Something in the Blood* (UQP 1979), and three novels, *Sticks That Kill* (UQP 1983), *White Lies* (UQP 1986), and *Concertinas*. He currently lives in Katoomba.

PETER SKRZYNECKI has published thirteen books and won several literary prizes, including the Grace Leven Poetry Prize and the Henry Lawson Short Story Award. His seventh and most recent book of poetry is *Easter Sunday* (1993) and other titles include *Immigrant Chronicle* (1975), set for the New South Wales Higher School Certificate, and *Night Swim* (1989). He has published two collections of short stories, *The Wild Dogs* and *Rock'n'Roll Heroes*, and two novels, the most recent being *The Cry of the Goldfinch* (1996). He has also edited two anthologies of contemporary Australian writing, *Joseph's Coat: Anthology of Multicultural Writing in Australia* (1985) and *Influence: Australian Voices* (1997). He teaches at the University of Western Sydney, Macarthur.

BARBARA WELS is a Melbourne writer. Her work to date includes *Finwood & Lisa* for young adults (UQP 1993) and *The Lifestyles of Previous Tenants* (UQP 1995). She was the recipient of the Marten Bequest Travelling Scholarship in 1996. Her short fiction has been published in various anthologies including *Smashed* (Random House 1997), *Blur* (Random House 1996) and *Who Do You Think You Are?* (Women's Redress Press 1992).

HERB WHARTON was born in Cunnamulla, Queensland, and began his working life in his teenage years as a drover. His maternal grandmother was of the Kooma people; his grandfathers were Irish and English. His first book, *Unbranded* (UQP 1992), is a novel based on his experiences of people and events during his long years on the stock routes of inland Australia. His second book, *Cattle Camp*, is a collection of stories told by Murri stockmen and women, and *Where Ya' Been, Mate?* is comprised of his own stories and yarns from childhood, the bush and the literary life. Herb Wharton has served as a writer-in-residence and conducted workshops all over Australia. During the last three years he has toured extensively as an Australian writer throughout Europe, he participated in the Edinburgh Festival, and in 1998 was writer-in-residence at the Australia Council's Paris studio.

MICHAEL WILDING was born in 1942, and holds a personal chair at the University of Sydney. His novels include *Living Together* (UQP 1974), *The Short Story Embassy*, *Scenic Drive*, *Pacific Highway*, *The Paraguayan Experiment*, and *Wildest Dreams* (UQP 1998). His stories have appeared in *The New Yorker, Harpers*, and *London Magazine*, and have been collected in *Aspects of the Dying Process* (UQP 1972), *The West Midland Underground* (UQP 1974), *The Phallic Forest*, *Reading the*

Signs, Under Saturn, This Is For You and the selections *The Man of Slow Feeling, Great Climate* (London: Faber 1980), *Her Most Bizarre Sexual Experience* (New York: W.W. Norton 1991), *Book of the Reading* and *Somewhere New*. He has written a number of critical studies and has edited *Marcus Clarke* (UQP 1976), *The Tabloid Story Pocket Book* (1978) and *The Oxford Book of Australian Short Stories* (1994).

GERARD WINDSOR was born in Sydney in 1944. He spent seven years as a Jesuit, but left before ordination. He later obtained degrees from the Australian National University and Sydney University. He has published five books since 1982. The most recent have been autobiographical meditations, partly in short story, partly in essay form. *Family Lore* (1990) told stories of traditions running between four generations of males in his family. *Heaven Where the Bachelors Sit* (UQP 1996) is an account of his Jesuit years and something of a farewell to the Catholic culture that was so pervasive for so long in Australian society. He is currently working on an account of his long-time affair with Ireland. His reviews and literary commentary have been published widely.